Praise for the novels o

"A beautiful story of love and redemption about a woman struggling to find her voice and her way amidst the turmoil of World War II."
—Kristin Hannah, #1 *New York Times* bestselling author of *The Nightingale*

"*The Orphan's Tale* is a compelling and beautifully told story about the power of female friendship, with all its complications." —*PopSugar*

"When it comes to bringing an era to life, this author has no peer."
—Susan Wiggs, #1 *New York Times* bestselling author

"Heartfelt, stirring… Definitely one for my keeper shelf."
—Karen White, *New York Times* bestselling author

"A warm and heartfelt story of emotional survival."
—Diane Chamberlain, *USA TODAY* bestselling author

"The kind of book that absorbs you from the beginning and doesn't let go."
—Beatriz Williams, *New York Times* bestselling author

"Atmospheric, tender, and as realistic as any Holocaust survivor testimony, *The Winter Guest* is a must-read."
—Jenna Blum, *New York Times* bestselling author

"A gripping story about the power of friendship to save and redeem even in the darkest of circumstances. This is a book not to be missed."
—Melanie Benjamin, *New York Times* bestselling author of *The Aviator's Wife*

"Jenoff expertly performs a pirouetting tale worthy of a standing ovation….*The Orphan's Tale* proves that the human spirit defies hate, fear, and gravity with a triumphant ta-da!"
—Sarah McCoy, *New York Times* bestselling author of *The Mapmaker's Children*

"Riveting…. With deftness and emotion, Jenoff sets in motion a compelling story of friendship and courage."
—Charles Belfoure, author of *The Paris Architect* and *House of Thieves*

THE ORPHAN'S TALE

PAM JENOFF

PARK
ROW
BOOKS

PARK
ROW
BOOKS

Recycling programs
for this product may
not exist in your area.

ISBN-13: 978-0-7783-6899-1

The Orphan's Tale

For questions and comments about the quality of this book, please contact us at
CustomerService@Harlequin.com.

ParkRowBooks.com
BookClubbish.com

Printed in U.S.A.

For my family.

THE ORPHAN'S TALE

Prologue

Paris

They will be looking for me by now.

I pause on the granite steps of the museum, reaching for the railing to steady myself. Pain, sharper than ever, creaks through my left hip, not perfectly healed from last year's break. Across the Avenue Winston Churchill, behind the glass dome of the Grand Palais, the March sky is rosy at dusk.

I peer around the edge of the arched entranceway of the Petit Palais. From the massive stone columns hangs a red banner two stories high: *Deux Cents ans de Magie du Cirque*— Two Hundred Years of Circus Magic. It is festooned with elephants, a tiger and a clown, their colors so much brighter in my memories.

I should have told someone I was going. They would have only tried to stop me, though. My escape, months in the planning since I'd read about the upcoming exhibit in the *Times*, had been well orchestrated: I had bribed an aide at the nursing home to take the photo I needed to mail to the passport office, paid for the plane ticket in cash. I'd almost been caught when the taxicab I'd called pulled up in front of the home in the predawn darkness and honked loudly. But the guard at the desk remained asleep.

Summoning my strength now, I begin to climb again, taking each painful step one by one. Inside the lobby, the opening gala is already in full swing, clusters of men in tuxedos and women in evening gowns mingling beneath the elaborately painted dome ceiling. Conversations in French bubble around me like a long-forgotten perfume I am desperate to inhale. Familiar words trickle back, first in a stream then a river, though I've scarcely heard them in half a century.

I do not stop at the reception desk to check in; they are not expecting me. Instead, dodging the butlered hors d'oeuvres and champagne, I make my way along the mosaic floors, past walls of murals to the circus exhibit, its entrance marked by a smaller version of the banner outside. There are photos blown up and hung from the ceiling by wire too fine to see, images of a sword swallower and dancing horses and still more clowns. From the labels below each picture, the names come back to me like a song: Lorch, D'Augny, Neuhoff—great European circus dynasties felled by war and time. At the last of these names, my eyes begin to burn.

Beyond the photos hangs a tall, worn placard of a woman suspended from silk ropes by her arms, one leg extended behind her in a midair arabesque. Her youthful face and body are barely recognizable to me. In my mind, the song of the carousel begins to play tinny and faint like a music box. I feel the searing heat of the lights, so hot it could almost peel off my skin. A flying trapeze hangs above the exhibit, fixed as if in midflight. Even now, my almost ninety-year-old legs ache with yearning to climb up there.

But there is no time for memories. Getting here took longer than I thought, like everything else these days, and there isn't a minute to spare. Pushing down the lump in my throat,

I press forward, past the costumes and headdresses, artifacts of a lost civilization. Finally, I reach the railcar. Some of the side panels have been removed to reveal the close, tiny berths inside. I am struck by the compact size, less than half my shared room at the nursing home. It had seemed so much larger in my mind. Had we really lived in there for months on end? I reach out my hand to touch the rotting wood. Though I had known the railcar was the same the minute I had seen it in the paper, some piece of my heart had been too afraid to believe it until now.

Voices grow louder behind me. I glance quickly over my shoulder. The reception is breaking up and the attendees drawing closer to the exhibit. In a few more minutes, it will be too late.

I look back once more, then crouch to slip beneath the roped stanchion. Hide, a voice seems to say, the long-buried instinct rising up in me once more. Instead, I run my hand under the bottom of the railcar. The compartment is there, exactly as I remembered. The door still sticks, but if I press on it just so... It snaps open and I imagine the rush of excitement of a young girl looking for a scribbled invitation to a secret rendezvous.

But as I reach inside, my fingers close around cold, dark space. The compartment is empty and the dream I had that it might hold the answers evaporates like cool mist.

1

Noa

Germany, 1944

The sound comes low like the buzzing of the bees that once chased Papa across the farm and caused him to spend a week swathed in bandages.

I set down the brush I'd been using to scrub the floor, once-elegant marble now cracked beneath boot heels and set with fine lines of mud and ash that will never lift. Listening for the direction of the sound, I cross the station beneath the sign announcing in bold black: Bahnhof Bensheim. A big name for nothing more than a waiting room with two toilets, a ticket window and a wurst stand that operates when there is meat to be had and the weather is not awful. I bend to pick up a coin at the base of one of the benches, pocket it. It amazes me the things that people forget or leave behind.

Outside, my breath rises in puffs in the February night air. The sky is a collage of ivory and gray, more snow threatening. The station sits low in a valley, surrounded by lush hills of pine trees on three sides, their pointed green tips poking out above snow-covered branches. The air has a slightly burnt smell. Before the war, Bensheim had been just another tiny stop that most travelers passed through without noticing. But the Germans make use of everything it seems, and the location is good for parking trains and switching out engines during the night.

I've been here almost four months. It hadn't been so bad in the autumn and I was happy to find shelter after I'd been sent packing with two days' worth of food, three if I stretched it. The girls' home where I lived after my parents found out I was expecting and kicked me out had been located far from anywhere in the name of discretion and they could have dropped me off in Mainz, or at least the nearest town. They simply opened the door, though, dismissing me on foot. I'd headed to the train station before realizing that I had nowhere to go. More than once during my months away, I had thought of returning home, begging forgiveness. It was not that I was too proud. I would have gotten down on my knees if I thought it would do any good. But I knew from the fury in my father's eyes the day he forced me out that his heart was closed. I could not stand rejection twice.

In a moment of luck, though, the station had needed a cleaner. I peer around the back of the building now toward the tiny closet where I sleep on a mattress on the floor. The maternity dress is the same one I wore the day I left the home, except that the full front now hangs limply. It will not always be this way, of course. I will find a real job— one that pays in more than not-quite-moldy bread—and a proper home.

I see myself in the train station window. I have the kind of looks that just fit in, dishwater hair that whitens with the summer sun, pale blue eyes. Once my plainness bothered me; here it is a benefit. The two other station workers, the ticket girl and the man at the kiosk, come and then go home each night, hardly speaking to me. The travelers pass through the station with the daily edition of *Der Stürmer* tucked under their arms, grinding cigarettes into the floor, not caring who I am or where I came from. Though lonely, I need it that way. I cannot answer questions about the past.

No, they do not notice me. I see them, though, the soldiers on leave and the mothers and wives who come each day to scan the platform hopefully for a son or husband before leaving alone. You can always tell the ones who are trying to flee. They try to look normal, as if just going on vacation. But their clothes are too tight from the layers padded underneath and bags so full they threaten to burst at any second. They do not make eye contact, but hustle their children along with pale, strained faces.

The buzzing noise grows louder and more high-pitched. It is coming from the train I'd heard screech in earlier, now parked on the far track. I start toward it, past the nearly empty coal bins, most of their stores long taken for troops fighting in the east. Perhaps someone has left on an engine or other machinery. I do not want to be blamed, and risk losing my job. Despite the grimness of my situation, I know it could be worse—and that I am lucky to be here.

Lucky. I'd heard it first from an elderly German woman who shared some herring with me on the bus to Den Hague after leaving my parents. "You are the Aryan ideal," she told me between fishy lip smacks, as we wound through detours and cratered roads.

I thought she was joking; I had plain blond hair and a little stump of a nose. My body was sturdy—athletic, until it had begun to soften out and grow curvy. Other than when the German had whispered soft words into my ear at night, I had always considered myself unremarkable. But now I'd been told I was just right. I found myself confiding in the woman about my pregnancy and how I had been thrown out. She told me to go to Wiesbaden, and scribbled a note saying I was carrying a child of the Reich. I took it and went. It did not occur to me whether it was dangerous to go to Germany or that I should refuse. Somebody wanted children like mine. My parents would have sooner died than accepted help from the Germans. But the woman said they would give me shelter; how bad could they be? I had nowhere else to go.

I was lucky, they said again when I reached the girls' home. Though Dutch, I was considered of Aryan race and my child—otherwise shamed as an *uneheliches Kind*, conceived out of wedlock—might just be accepted into the Lebensborn program and raised by a good German family. I'd spent nearly six months there, reading and helping with the housework until my stomach became too bulky. The facility, if not grand, was modern and clean, designed to deliver babies in good health to the Reich. I'd gotten to know a sturdy girl called Eva who was a few months further along than me, but one night she awoke in blood and they took her to the hospital and I did not see her again. After that, I kept to myself. None of us would be there for long.

My time came on a cold October morning when I stood up from the breakfast table at the girls' home and my water broke. The next eighteen hours were a blur of awful pain, punctuated by words of command, without encouragement or a soothing touch. At last, the baby had emerged with a wail and my entire body shuddered with emptiness, a machine shutting down. A strange look crossed the nurse's face.

"What is it?" I demanded. I was not supposed to see the child. But I struggled against pain to sit upright. "What's wrong?"

"Everything is fine," the doctor assured. "The child is healthy." His voice was perturbed, though, face stormy through thick glasses above the draped cream sheet. I leaned forward and a set of piercing coal eyes met mine.

Those eyes that were not Aryan.

I understood then the doctor's distress. The child looked nothing like the perfect race. Some hidden gene, on my side or the German's, had given him dark eyes and olive skin. He would not be accepted into the Lebensborn program.

My baby cried out, shrill and high-pitched, as though he had heard his fate and was protesting. I had reached for him through the pain. "I want to hold him."

The doctor and the nurse, who had been recording details about the child on some sort of form, exchanged uneasy looks. "We don't, that is, the Lebensborn program does not allow that."

I struggled to sit up. "Then I'll take him and leave." It had been a bluff; I had nowhere to go. I had signed papers giving up my rights when I arrived in exchange for letting me stay, there were hospital guards… I could barely even walk. "Please let me have him for a second."

"Nein." The nurse shook her head emphatically, slipping from the room as I continued to plead.

Once she was out of sight, something in my voice forced the doctor to relent. "Just for a moment," he said, reluctantly handing me the child. I stared at the red face, inhaled the delicious scent of his head that was pointed from so many hours of struggling to be born and I focused on his eyes. Those beautiful eyes. How could something so perfect not be their ideal?

He was mine, though. A wave of love crested and broke over me. I had not wanted this child, but in that moment, all the regret washed away, replaced by longing. Panic and relief swept me under. They would not want him now. I'd have to take him home because there was no other choice. I would keep him, find a way... Then the nurse returned and ripped him from my arms. "No, wait," I protested. As I struggled to reach for my baby, something sharp pierced my arm. My head swam. Hands pressed me back on the bed. I faded, still seeing those dark eyes.

I awoke alone in that cold, sterile delivery room, without my child, or a husband or mother or even a nurse, an empty vessel that no one wanted anymore. They said afterward that he went to a good home. I had no way of knowing if they were telling the truth.

I swallow against the dryness of my throat, forcing the memory away. Then I step from the station into the biting cold air, relieved that the *Schutzpolizei des Reiches*, the leering state police who patrol the station, are nowhere to be seen. Most likely they are fighting the cold in their truck with a flask. I scan the train, trying to pinpoint the buzzing sound. It comes from the last boxcar, adjacent to the caboose—not from the engine. No, the noise comes from something inside the train. Something alive.

I stop. I have made it a point to never go near the trains, to look away when they pass by—because they are carrying Jews.

I was still living at home in our village the first time I had seen the sorry roundup of men, women and children in the market square. I had run to my father, crying. He was a patriot and stood up for everything else—why not this? "It's awful," he conceded through his graying beard, stained yellow from pipe smoke. He had wiped my tear-stained cheeks and given me some vague explanation about how there were ways to handle things. But those ways had not stopped my classmate Steffi Klein from being marched to the train station with her younger brother and parents in the same dress she'd worn to my birthday a month earlier.

The sound continues to grow, almost a keening now, like a wounded animal in the brush. I scan the empty platform and peer around the edge of the station. Can the police hear the noise, too? I stand uncertainly at the platform's edge, peering down the barren railway tracks that separate me from the boxcar. I should just walk away. Keep your eyes down, that has been the lesson of the years of war. No good ever came from noticing the business of others. If I am caught nosing into parts of the station where I do not belong, I will be let go from my job, left without a place to live, or perhaps even arrested. But I have never been any good at not looking. Too curious, my mother said when I was little. I have always needed to know. I step forward, unable to ignore the sound that, as I draw closer now, sounds like cries.

Or the tiny foot that is visible through the open door of the railcar.

I pull back the door. "Oh!" My voice echoes dangerously through the darkness, inviting detection. There are babies, tiny bodies too many to count, lying on the hay-covered floor of the railcar, packed close and atop one another. Most do not move and I can't tell whether they are dead or sleeping. From amid the stillness, piteous cries mix with gasps and moans like the bleating of lambs.

I grasp the side of the railcar, struggling to breathe over the wall of urine and feces and vomit that assaults me. Since coming here, I have dulled myself to the images, like a bad dream or a film that couldn't possibly be real. This is different, though. So many infants, all alone, ripped from the arms of their mothers. My lower stomach begins to burn.

I stand helplessly in front of the boxcar, frozen in shock. Where had these babies come from? They must have just arrived, for surely they could not last long in the icy temperatures.

I have seen the trains going east for months, people where the cattle and sacks of grain should have been. Despite the awfulness of the transport, I had told myself they were going somewhere like a camp or a village, just being kept in one place. The notion was fuzzy in my mind, but I imagined somewhere maybe with cabins or tents like the seaside campsite south of our village in Holland for those who couldn't afford a real holiday or preferred something more rustic. Resettlement. In these dead and dying babies, though, I see the wholeness of the lie.

I glance over my shoulder. The trains of people are always guarded. But here there is no one—because there is simply no chance of the infants getting away.

Closest to me lies a baby with gray skin, its lips blue. I try to brush the thin layer of frost from its eyelashes but the child is already stiff and gone. I yank my hand back, scanning the others. Most of the infants are naked or just wrapped in a blanket or cloth, stripped of anything that would have protected them from the harsh cold. But in the center of the car, two perfect pale pink booties stick stiffly up in the air, attached to a baby who is otherwise naked. Someone had cared enough to knit those, stitch by stitch. A sob escapes through my lips.

A head peeks out among the others. Straw and feces cover its heart-shaped face. The child does not look pained or distressed, but wears a puzzled expression, as if to say "Now what am I doing here?" There is something familiar about it: coal-dark eyes, piercing through me, just as they had the day I had given birth. My heart swells.

The baby's face crumples suddenly and it squalls. My hands shoot out, and I strain to reach it over the others before anyone else hears. My grasp falls short of the infant, who wails louder. I try to climb into the car, but the children are packed so tightly, I can't manage for fear of stepping on one. Desperately, I strain my arms once more, just reaching. I pick up the crying child, needing to silence it. Its skin is icy as I pluck it from the car, naked save for a soiled cloth diaper.

The baby in my arms now, only the second I'd ever held, seems to calm in the crook of my elbow. Could this possibly be my child, brought back to me by fate or chance? The child's eyes close and its head bows forward. Whether it is sleeping or dying, I cannot say. Clutching it, I start away from the train. Then I turn back: if any of those other children are still alive, I am their only chance. I should take more.

But the baby I am holding cries again, the shrill sound cutting through the silence. I cover its mouth and run back into the station.

I walk toward the closet where I sleep. Stopping at the door, I look around desperately. I have nothing. Instead I walk into the women's toilet, the usually dank smell hardly noticeable after the boxcar. At the sink, I wipe the filth from the infant's face with one of the rags I use for cleaning. The baby is warmer now, but two of its toes are blue and I wonder if it might lose them. Where did it come from?

I open the filthy diaper. The child is a boy like my own had been. Closer now I can see that his tiny penis looks different from the German's, or that of the boy at school who had shown me his when I was seven. Circumcised. Steffi had told me the word once, explaining what they had done to her little brother. The child is Jewish. Not mine.

I step back as the reality I had known all along sinks in: I cannot keep a Jewish baby, or a baby at all, by myself and cleaning the station twelve hours a day. What had I been thinking?

The baby begins to roll sideways from the ledge by the sink where I had left him. I leap forward, catching him before he falls to the hard tile floor. I am unfamiliar with infants and I hold him at arm's length now, like a dangerous animal. But he moves closer, nuzzling against my neck. I clumsily make a diaper out of the other rag, then carry the child from the toilet and out of the station, heading back toward the railcar. I have to put him back on the train, as if none of this ever happened.

At the edge of the platform, I freeze. One of the guards is now walking along the tracks, blocking my way back to the train. I search desperately in all directions. Close to the side of the station sits a milk delivery truck, the rear stacked high with large cans. Impulsively I start toward it. I slide the baby into one of the empty jugs, trying not to think about how icy the metal must be against his bare skin. He does not make a sound but just stares at me helplessly.

I duck behind a bench as the truck door slams. In a second, it will leave, taking the infant with it.

And no one will know what I have done.

2

Astrid

Germany, 1942—fourteen months earlier

I stand at the edge of the withered grounds that had once
been our winter quarters. Though there has been no fighting here, the valley looks like a battlefield, broken wagons
and scrap metal scattered everywhere. A cold wind blows
through the hollow window frames of the deserted cabins,
sending tattered fabric curtains wafting upward before they
fall deflated. Most of the windows are shattered and I try
not to wonder if that had happened with time, or if someone had smashed them in a struggle or rage. The creaking
doors are open, properties fallen into disrepair as they surely
never would have if Mama had been here to care for them.
There is a hint of smoke on the air as though someone has
been burning brush recently. In the distance, a crow cries
out in protest.

Drawing my coat closer around me, I walk away from
the wreckage and start up toward the villa that once was my
home. The grounds are exactly as they had been when I was
a girl, the hill rising before the front door in that way that

sent the water rushing haphazardly into the foyer when the spring rains came. But the garden where my mother tended hydrangeas so lovingly each spring is withered and crushed to dirt. I see my brothers wrestling in the front yard before being cowed into practice, scolded for wasting their energy and risking an injury that would jeopardize the show. As children we loved to sleep under the open sky in the yard in summer, fingers intertwined, the sky a canopy of stars above us.

I stop. A large red flag with a black swastika hangs above the door. Someone, a high-ranking SS officer no doubt, has moved into the home that once was ours. I clench my fists, sickened to think of them using our linens and dishes, soiling Mama's beautiful sofa and rugs with their boots. Then I look away. It is not the material things for which I mourn.

I search the windows of the villa, looking in vain for a familiar face. I had known that my family was no longer here ever since my last letter returned undeliverable. I had come anyway, though, some part of me imagining life unchanged, or at least hoping for a clue as to where they had gone. But wind blows through the desolate grounds. There is nothing left anymore.

I should not be here either, I realize. Anxiety quickly replaces my sadness. I cannot afford to loiter and risk being spotted by whoever lives here now, or face questions about who I am and why I have come. My eyes travel across the hill toward the adjacent estate where the Circus Neuhoff has their winter quarters. Their hulking slate villa stands opposite ours, two sentries guarding the Rheinhessen valley between.

Earlier as the train neared Darmstadt, I saw a poster advertising the Circus Neuhoff. At first, my usual distaste at the name rose. Klemt and Neuhoff were rival circuses and we had competed for years, trying to outdo one another. But the circus, though dysfunctional, was still a family. Our two circuses had grown up alongside one another like siblings in separate bedrooms. We had been rivals on the road. In the off-season, though, we children went to school and played together, sledding down the hill and occasionally sharing meals. Once when Herr Neuhoff had been felled by a bad back and could not serve as ringmaster, we sent my brother Jules to help their show.

I have not seen Herr Neuhoff in years, though. And he is Gentile, so everything has changed. His circus flourishes while ours is gone. No, I cannot expect help from Herr Neuhoff, but perhaps he knows what became of my family.

When I reach the Neuhoff estate, a maidservant I do not recognize opens the door. *"Guten Abend,"* I say. *"Ist Herr Neuhoff hier?"* I am suddenly shy, embarrassed to arrive unannounced on their doorstep like some sort of beggar. "I'm Ingrid Klemt." I use my maiden name. The woman's face reveals that she already knows who I am, though from the circus or from somewhere else, I cannot tell. My departure years earlier had been remarkable, whispered about for miles around.

One did not leave to marry a German officer as I had—especially if one was Jewish.

Erich had first come to the circus in the spring of 1934. I noticed him from behind the curtains—it is a myth that we cannot see the audience beyond the lights—not only because of his uniform but because he sat alone, without a wife or children. I was not some young girl, easily wooed, but nearly twenty-nine. Busy with the circus and constantly on the road, I had assumed that marriage had passed me by. Erich was impossibly handsome, though, with a strong jaw marred only by a cleft chin, and square features softened by the bluest of eyes. He came a second night and pink roses appeared before my dressing room door. We courted that spring, and he made the long trip down from Berlin every weekend to the cities where we performed to spend time with me between shows and on Sundays.

We should have known even then that our relationship was doomed. Though Hitler had just come to power a year earlier, the Reich had already made clear its hatred for the Jews. But there was passion and intensity in Erich's eyes that made everything around us cease to exist. When he proposed, I didn't think twice. We did not see the problems that loomed large, making our future together impossible—we simply looked the other way.

My father had not fought me on leaving with Erich. I expected him to rebuke me for marrying a non-Jew, but he only smiled sadly when I told him. "I always thought you would have taken over the show for me," he'd said, his sad chocolate eyes a mirror of my own behind his spectacles. I was surprised. I had three older brothers, four if you counted Isadore, who had been killed at Verdun; there was no reason to think that Papa might have considered me. "Especially with Jules taking his own branch of the show to Nice. And the twins..." Papa had shaken his head ruefully. Mathias and Markus were strong and graceful, performing acrobatic marvels that made the audience gasp. Their skills were purely physical, though. "It was you, *liebchen*, with the head for business and the flair of showmanship. But I'm not going to keep you like a caged animal."

I'd never known he saw me that way. Only now I was leaving him. I could have changed my mind and stayed. But Erich and the life I thought I always wanted beckoned. So I left for Berlin, taking Papa's blessing with me.

Perhaps if I hadn't, my family might still be here.

The maid ushers me to a sitting room that, though still grand, shows signs of wear. The rugs are a bit frayed and there are some spaces in the silver cabinet that are empty, as though the bigger pieces had been taken or sold. Stale cigar smoke mixes with the scent of lemon polish. I peer out the window, straining to see my family's estate through the fog that has settled above the valley. I wonder who lives in our villa now and what they see when they look down at the barren deserted winter quarters.

After our wedding, a small ceremony with a justice of the peace, I moved into Erich's spacious apartment overlooking the Tiergarten. I spent my days strolling the shops along Bergmannstrasse, buying richly colored paintings and rugs and embroidered satin pillows, little things that would make his once-sparse quarters our home. Our biggest dilemma was which café to frequent for Sunday brunch.

I'd been in Berlin for almost five years when the war broke out. Erich received a promotion to something I didn't understand having to do with munitions and his days became longer. He would come home either dark and moody, or heady with excitement about things he could not share with me. "It will all be so different when the Reich is victorious, trust me." But I didn't want different. I liked our life just as it had been. What was so wrong with the old ways?

Things had not gone back to the way they had been, though. Instead they worsened rapidly. They said awful things about Jews on the radio and in the newspapers. Jewish shop windows were broken and doors painted. "My family..." I'd fretted to Erich over brunch in our Berlin apartment after I'd seen the windows of a Jewish butcher shop on Oranienburger Strasse shattered. I was the wife of a German officer. I was safe. But what about my family back home?

"Nothing will hurt them, Inna," he soothed, rubbing my shoulders.

"If it's happening here," I pressed, "then Darmstadt can be no better."

He wrapped his arms around me. "Shh. There have just been a few acts of vandalism in the city, a showing. Look around you. Everything is fine." The apartment was scented with the smell of rich coffee. A pitcher of fresh orange juice sat on the table. Surely it could not be so much worse elsewhere. I rested my head on the broad shelf of Erich's shoulder, inhaling the familiar warmth of his neck. "The Klemt family circus is internationally known," he reassured. He was right. Our family circus had been generations in the making, born from the old horse shows in Prussia—my great-great-grandfather, they said, had left the Lipizzaner Stallions in Vienna to start our first circus. And the next generation had followed and the one after that, the very oddest sort of family business.

Erich continued, "That's why I stopped to see the show on my way back from Munich that day. And then I saw you..." He pulled me onto his lap.

I raised my hand, cutting him off. Normally I loved his retelling of how we met, but I was too worried to listen. "I should go check on them."

"How will you find them on tour?" he asked, a note of impatience creeping into his voice. It was true; midsummer, they could be almost anywhere in Germany or France. "And what would you do to help them? No, they would want you to stay here. Safe. With me." He nuzzled me playfully.

He was right of course, I had told myself, lulled by his lips upon my neck. But still the worry nagged. Then one day the letter came. "Dearest Ingrid, we have disbanded the circus..." Papa's tone was matter-of-fact, no plea for help, though I could only imagine his anguish at taking apart the family business that had flourished for more than a century.

It did not say what they would do next or if they would leave, and I wondered if that was by design.

I wrote immediately, begging him to tell me what their plans were, if they needed money. I would have brought the whole family to Berlin and fit them into our apartment. But that would only have meant drawing them closer to the danger. In any event, the point was moot: my letter came back unopened. That had been six months earlier and there had been no word. Where had they gone?

"Ingrid!" Herr Neuhoff booms as he enters the sitting room. If he is surprised to see me, he gives no indication. Herr Neuhoff is not as old as my father and in my childhood memories, he had been dashing and handsome, if portly, with dark hair and a mustache. But he is shorter than I remembered, with a full stomach and just a gray fringe of hair. I rise and start toward him. Then, seeing the small swastika pin on his lapel, I stop. Coming here had been a mistake. "For appearances," he says hastily.

"Yes, of course." But I am not sure whether to believe him. I should just go. His face appears genuinely glad to see me, though. I decide to take a chance.

He gestures to a chair overlaid with lace and I sit, perching uneasily. "Cognac?" he offers.

I falter. "That would be lovely." He rings a bell and the same woman who answered the door brings in a tray—one house servant where there used to be many. The Circus Neuhoff has not been left untouched by the war. I feign a sip from the glass she offers me. I do not want to be rude, but I need to keep my head about me to figure out where I am going from here. There is no resting place for me in Darmstadt anymore.

"You've just come from Berlin?" His tone is polite, one step short of asking what I am doing here.

"Yes. Papa wrote that he disbanded the circus." Herr Neuhoff's brow creases with his unspoken question: the circus broke up months ago. Why have I come now? "More recently I lost contact and my letters came back unanswered," I add. "Have you heard from them?"

"I'm afraid nothing," he replies. "There were only a few of them left at the end, all of the workers had gone." Because it was illegal to work for the Jews. My father had treated his performers and even the manual laborers like family, caring for them when they were sick, inviting them to family celebrations, such as my brothers' bar mitzvahs. He'd given generously to the town, too, doing charity shows for the hospital and donating to the political officials to curry favor. Trying so very hard to make us one of them. We had nearly forgotten that we weren't.

Herr Neuhoff continues, "I went looking for them you know, after. But the house was empty. They were gone, though whether they went on their own or something had happened, I couldn't say." He walks to the mahogany desk in the corner and opens a drawer. "I do have this." He reveals a Kiddush cup and I rise, fighting the urge to cry out at the familiar Hebrew letters. "This was yours, no?"

I nod, taking it from him. How had he gotten it? There had been a menorah, as well, and other things. The Germans must have taken those. I run my finger along the edge of the cup. On the road my family would have gathered in our railcar just to light the candles and share a bit of whatever wine and bread could be found, a few minutes of just us. I see shoulders pressed close to fit around the tiny table, my brothers' faces illuminated by candlelight. We were not so very religious—we had to perform on Saturdays and had not managed to keep kosher on the road. But we clung fast to the little things, a moment's observance each week. No matter how happy I had been with Erich, some part of my heart always drifted from the gay Berlin cafés back to the quiet Sabbaths.

I sink down once more. "I should never have left."

"The Germans still would have put your father out of business," he points out. If I had been here, though, perhaps the Germans would not have forced my family from their home or arrested them, or done whatever had caused them to not be here any longer. My connection to Erich, which I had held up like such a shield, had in the end proved worthless.

Herr Neuhoff coughs once, then again, his face reddening. I wonder if he is ill.

"I'm sorry I can't be of more help," he says when he has recovered. "You'll go back to Berlin now?"

I shift awkwardly. "I'm afraid not."

It has been three days since Erich returned unexpectedly early from work to our apartment. I threw myself into his arms. "I'm so glad to see you," I exclaimed. "Dinner isn't quite ready yet, but we could have a drink." He spent so many nights at official dinners or buried in his study with papers. It seemed like forever since we'd shared a quiet evening together.

He did not put his arms around me but remained stiff. "Ingrid," he said, using my full name and not the pet name he'd given me, "we need to divorce."

"Divorce?" I wasn't sure I had ever said the word before. Divorce was something that happened in a movie or a book about rich people. I didn't know anyone who had ever done it—in my world you married until you died. "Is there another woman?" I croaked, barely able to manage the words. Of course there was not. The passion between us had been unbreakable—until now.

Surprise and pain flashed over his face at the very idea.

"No!" And in that one word I knew exactly the depths of his love and that this awful thing was hurting him. So why would he even say it? "The Reich has ordered all officers with Jewish wives to divorce," he explained. How many, I wondered, could there possibly be? He pulled out some documents and handed them to me with smooth strong hands. The papers carried a hint of his cologne. There was not even a spot for me to sign, my agreement or disagreement irrelevant—it was a fait accompli. "It has been ordered by the Führer," he adds. His voice was dispassionate, as though describing the day-to-day matters that went on in his department. "There is no choice."

"We'll run," I said, forcing the quaver from my voice. "I can be packed in half an hour." Improbably I lifted the roast from the table, as though that was the first thing I would take. "Bring the brown suitcase." But Erich stood stiffly, feet planted. "What is it?"

"My job," he replied. "People would know I was gone." He would not go with me. The roast dropped from my hands, plate shattering, the smell of warm meat and gravy wafting sickeningly upward. It was preferable to the rest of the immaculate table, a caricature of the perfect life I thought we'd had. The brown liquid splattered upward against my stockings, staining them.

I jutted my chin defiantly. "Then I shall keep the apartment."

But he shook his head, reaching into his billfold and emptying the contents into my hands. "You need to go. Now." Go where? My family was all gone; I did not have papers out of Germany. Still I found my suitcase and packed mechanically, as if going on holiday. I had no idea what to take.

Two hours later when I was packed and ready to go, Erich stood before me in his uniform, so very much like the man I had spied in the audience beyond the lights the day we met. He waited awkwardly as I started for the door, as if seeing out a guest.

I stood in front of him for several seconds, staring up beseechingly, willing his eyes to meet mine. "How can you do this?" I asked. He did not answer. This is not happening, a voice inside me seemed to say. In other circumstances, I would have refused to go. But I had been caught off guard, the wind knocked out of me by an unexpected punch. I was simply too stunned to fight. "Here." I pulled off my wedding band and held it out. "This isn't mine anymore."

Looking down at the ring, his whole face seemed to fall, as if realizing for the first time the finality of what he was doing. I wondered in that moment if he would tear up the papers that decreed our marriage over and say we would face the future together, whatever the odds. He swiped at his eyes.

When his hand moved away the hardness of the "new Erich," as I called him in the recent months when it had all seemed to change, reappeared. He pushed the ring away and it clattered to the floor. I hurried to pick it up, cheeks stinging from the roughness of his once-gentle touch. "You keep it," he said. "You can sell it if you need money." As if the one thing that bound us together meant so little to me. He fled the apartment without looking back and in that moment the years we shared seemed to evaporate and disappear.

Of course I do not know Herr Neuhoff well enough to tell him any of this. "I've left Berlin for good," I say, firmly enough to foreclose further discussion. I run my finger over my wedding band, which I had put on once more as I'd left Berlin so as to attract less attention while traveling.

"So where will you go?" Herr Neuhoff asks. I do not answer. "You should leave Germany," he adds gently. Leaving. It was the thing that no one talked about anymore, the door that had closed. I'd heard Mama suggest it once years earlier, before things had gotten bad. Then the idea had seemed laughable—we were Germans and our circus had been here for centuries. In hindsight it was the only option, but none of us had been wise enough to take it because no one knew how bad things would become. And now that chance was gone. "Or you could join us," Herr Neuhoff adds.

"Join you?" The surprise in my voice borders on rude.

He nods. "Our circus. I am missing an aerialist since Angelina broke her hip." I stare at him, disbelieving. Though the seasonal workers and even performers might transfer between circuses, one circus family working for another is unheard of— I can no more imagine myself part of the Circus Neuhoff than a leopard changing its spots. The suggestion makes sense, though—and the way he phrases it does not sound as if he is offering me charity, but rather that I would be filling a need.

Still, my spine stiffens. "I couldn't possibly." To stay here would mean being beholden to Herr Neuhoff, another man. After Erich, I will never do that again.

"Really, you'd be doing me a huge service." His voice is sincere. I am more than just a spare performer. Having a Klemt join his circus, well, that would be something, at least to the older folks who remembered our act at its heyday. With my name and reputation as an aerialist, I am like a collectible, an item to be had.

"I'm a Jew," I say. "To employ me now would be a crime. Why would he take on such danger?

"I'm aware." His mustache twitches with amusement. "You are *Zirkus Volk*," he adds quietly. That transcends all else.

Still my doubts linger. "You have SS living next door now, don't you? It will be so dangerous."

He waves his hand, as if this is of no consequence. "We'll change your name." But my name is what he wants—the very thing that makes me most valuable to him. "Astrid," he pronounces.

"Astrid," I repeat, trying it on for size. Close to Ingrid, but not the same. And it sounds Scandinavian, vaguely exotic— perfect for the circus. "Astrid Sorrell."

His eyebrows rise. "Wasn't that your husband's surname?"

For a second, I falter, surprised that he had known. Then I nod. Erich had taken everything from me but that. He would never know.

"Plus, I could use your good sense about the business," he adds. "It's only me and Emmet." Herr Neuhoff had been dealt a cruel blow. In the circus, large families are the norm; ours had four brothers, each more handsome and talented than the next. But Herr Neuhoff's wife had died birthing Emmet and he had not remarried, leaving him alone with just one shiftless heir who had neither the talent to perform nor the head to run the business. Instead, Emmet spent his time gambling in the cities on tour and ogling the dancing girls. I shudder to think what might become of this circus when his father is gone.

"So you'll stay?" Herr Neuhoff asks. I consider the question. Our two families had not always gotten along. My coming here today had been a change. We were rivals, more so than allies—until now.

I want to say no, to get on a train and keep searching for my family. I've had enough of depending on others. But Herr Neuhoff's eyes are soft; he takes no joy in the misfortune that has befallen my family and is only trying to help. I can already hear the music of the orchestra, and the ache to perform, buried so deep I'd almost forgotten, rises sharply within me. A second chance.

"All right then," I say finally. I cannot refuse him—and I have nowhere else to go. "We'll try it. Perhaps on the road, we might hear word of where my family has gone." He presses his lips together, not wanting to give me false hope. "You can stay at the house," he offers. He does not expect me to live in the women's lodge like a common performer. "It would be good to have the company."

But I cannot stay up here and hope to have the girls accept me as one of them. "That's very kind, but I should stay with the others." As a child, I had always felt more comfortable down in the cabins with the performers. I had yearned to sleep in the women's quarters, which, despite the too many bodies, smells and noises, had a kind of solidarity.

He nods, acquiescing to the truth in my words. "We'll pay you thirty a week." In our circus, money had not been discussed. Wages were paid fairly, with increases over the years. He pulls a paper from the desk drawer and scribbles on it. "Your contract," he explains. I look at him, confused. With us there had been no contracts—people made verbal agreements and kept them over decades of working together. He continues, "It just says that if you want to leave before the season is over, you will pay us back." I feel owned in a way I never have before and I hate it.

"Come, I'll help you get settled." He leads me out of the house and down the hill in the direction of the cabins. I keep my eyes straight forward, not looking back in the direction of my former home. We near an old gymnasium and my throat tightens. Once my family had practiced here. "They weren't using it anymore," he offers, his voice apologetic. But it had been ours. In that moment, I regret the bargain I have made. Working for another circus family feels like treason.

Herr Neuhoff continues on, but I stop in front of the gymnasium door. "I should practice," I say.

"There's no need to start today. Surely you will want to get settled."

"I should practice," I repeat. If I don't start now, I never will.

He nods. "Very well. I'll leave you to it." As he starts away, I look up from the base of the hill across the valley toward my family home. How can I stay here, so unbearably close to the shadows of the past? I see my brothers' faces. I will perform where they cannot.

The door to the gymnasium creaks as I pull it open. I set down my valise, twisting my wedding band around my finger. There are a few other performers scattered through the practice hall. Some faces are vaguely familiar, as if from another lifetime; others I do not know at all. At the back of the practice hall by the piano, there is a tall man with a long somber face. Our eyes meet and though I do not recognize him from my circus years, it seems we have met somewhere before. He holds my gaze for several seconds before finally turning away.

I inhale the familiar smell of hay and manure and cigarette smoke and perfume, not so very different. The thick rosin coats the insides of my nostrils and it is as if I had never left.

I take off the wedding band and put it in my pocket, then go to change for rehearsal.

3

Noa

Of course I did not leave him.

I started away from the child, imagining my life just as it had been a few short minutes earlier. The milk truck would go and I could return to my work and pretend none of it ever happened. Then I stopped again. I couldn't abandon a helpless infant and leave him alone there to die, just as surely as he would have on the train. Quickly I raced to the sour-smelling milk can and pulled him out. A moment later, the engine roared and the truck lurched forward. I clutched the child tighter and he nestled against me forgivingly. His warmth filled my arms. In that second, everything was all right.

The policeman near the train yelled something I couldn't make out. A second guard appeared on the station platform, holding a snarling Alsatian on a leash. In my panic, I jumped, and the child nearly slipped from my arms. Tightening my hold on him, I ducked around the corner as they raced past me to the train. They couldn't have possibly noticed one baby missing amid so many. They were pointing, though, from the boxcar door I left open in my haste to my telltale footprints in the snow.

I ran desperately into the station toward the closet where I slept. At the back of the closet there was a rickety ladder leading to the attic. As I reached for it, my foot tangled around a threadbare blanket on the floor. Shaking it off, I started to climb the ladder. But I had only one arm to hold on and I slipped from the second rung, nearly dropping the baby, whose wail rang out, threatening to expose us.

Recovering, I started upward again. The voices grew louder, broken by a sharp bark. I reached the attic, a space with a low ceiling smelling of dead rodents and mold. I hurried through the tangle of empty boxes toward the lone window. My nails ripped as I pried it open. A blast of icy air smacked my face. I leaned forward and put my head through the window, but it was too small. I could not make it past my shoulders.

Below I heard the guards, inside the building now. I pushed the baby quickly through the window and placed him on the sloping, snow-covered roof that overhung the station platform. I steadied him there, praying he did not roll downward or cry out from the iciness against his skin.

I closed the window and hurried down the attic steps, grabbing my broom. As I walked out of the closet, I nearly slammed into one of the guards.

"*Guten abend…*" I stammered, forcing myself to meet his eyes. He did not respond, but stared at me piercingly.

"*Entschuldigen Sie, bitte.*" Excusing myself, I walked around the guard, feeling his eyes on me, bracing for his command to stop. I slipped outside and pretended to sweep the coal-tinged snow from the platform until I was sure he wasn't watching me. Then I raced around the side of the station, staying close to the shadow of the building. I looked up at the low roof, searching for a foothold to reach it. Finding none, I climbed the drainpipe, iciness soaking through my torn tights. As I neared the top, my arms burned. I reached up, praying that the infant was still there. But my fingers closed around emptiness.

My stomach dropped. Had the Germans found the baby? I stretched again, arms straining farther and finding a bit of cloth. I pulled on it, trying to draw the child toward me. But he rolled past my fingertips. I reached for him frantically, grabbing the edge of the cloth diaper just before he fell.

I drew him close to me and scampered down, nearly slipping myself as I struggled to hold on with one hand. At last I reached the ground and tucked the baby securely in my coat. But the Germans were just around the corner, their voices close and angry. Not daring to linger another second, I ran, footsteps breaking the smoothness of snow.

Hours have passed since I fled the station. I don't know how many, only that it is deepest night and snowing again, the sky a muted gray. Or it would have been, if I could look up. The storm has grown heavier, though, sharp bits of ice cutting at my eyes and forcing me to tuck my chin once more. I'd gone in the direction away from the hills and toward the shelter of the woods, but the ground that appeared flat in the distance rolls and dips, straining my legs. I cling instead to a smoother path that runs too close to the edge of the forest. I glance nervously at the narrow road that runs parallel to the trees. So far it has thankfully remained deserted.

In the endless blanket of white I imagine our tiny farm, close to the Dutch coast, the air thick with salt and chilled by the North Sea, where I lived with only my parents. Though we had been spared from the air raids that had brought Rotterdam to rubble, occupation had come down hard. The Germans had focused on defending the coastal towns, mining the beaches so we could no longer walk them and billeting soldiers everywhere—which is how I met the one who fathered my child.

He hadn't forced me. If he had, or if I had pretended it, my parents might have been more forgiving. He had not even tried during the fortnight he stayed at our farm, though I could tell from the long looks across the table that he wanted to. His tall, broad-shouldered presence had been too large in the close cottage space, a piece of furniture that did not fit. We all breathed a sigh of relief once he had been moved to new quarters. But he returned, bringing a half-dozen fresh eggs like we hadn't seen since before the war, and later chocolate to thank us. I was weary—the war had been raging since I was twelve, taking all of the dances and normal things I might have known as a teenager with it. For the first time with the soldier, not much more than a boy himself, it seemed like I stood out.

So when he came to me in the night, slipping through the back door and into my cold, narrow bed, I'd felt chosen, and excited by his touch—a man so much more certain than the fumbling boys I'd known at school. I didn't see the uniform, with the same insignia that the SS marching Steffi Klein away had worn. He was just a soldier who had been conscripted into the army. Not one of them. My memories of our one night together are hazy, like a half-forgotten dream of desire and then pain that caused me to cover my own mouth so my parents wouldn't hear my cry. It was over just as quickly, leaving me with a longing not quite fulfilled and a sense that there should have been more to it.

Then he was gone. The German did not come around again and two days later I learned that his unit had moved on. I knew then I had made a mistake. It wasn't until about a month later that I realized how serious my mistake had been.

The end came without warning on a spring day warmer than most. Morning sun bathed our seaside village of Scheveningen and gulls called to one another above the inlet. Lying in my bed, it had almost been possible to forget about the war for a few minutes.

Then my bedroom door swung open and the knowledge of the truth raged in my father's bulging eyes. "Out!"

I stared at him in disbelief. How could he possibly have known? I had told no one. I had not expected to be able to keep it a secret forever, but surely for another month or so, long enough to figure out what to do. Mama, who had walked in while I was dressing a few days earlier, must have seen the slight curve of my stomach. The rest, the timing of when the German had been with us, would not have been so very hard to figure out.

Papa was proud and staunchly Dutch, with a limp from the Great War to prove it. My affair with the German was the greatest betrayal. Surely, though, he did not mean for me, his only daughter and just sixteen, to leave. But the same man who had once laced my boots and carried me on his shoulders now unrelentingly held the door open for me to walk through a final time.

I braced for him to strike me or berate me further, but he simply pointed to the door. "Go." His eyes did not meet mine.

"No!" Mama cried as I went. There was no strength behind her voice, though. As she ran after me, my heart lifted. Perhaps just this once she would stand up to him and fight for me. Instead she just pressed the money she had tucked away into my palm. I waited for her to embrace me.

She did not.

A horn whistles long and low in the distance. I duck behind a tree as a train appears from the same direction we'd come, snaking a path through the field of white. Though I can't be sure, from a far distance there is a train car that looks exactly like the one from which I pulled the baby. Headed east, like the other trains of Jews. Babies taken, as my own had been, but from families with two parents who loved, wanted them. Stifling a cry, I step from the trees, wanting to run after it and take other children as I had this one. But the baby's body sinks warm and heavy in my arms, the lone life I have saved.

Saved—at least for now. Behind the receding train, the sky is lightening to gray in the east. It will be dawn soon and we are still too close to the station. The police could come at any moment. Snow falls heavy, soaking my thin coat and reaching the child beneath it. We must keep going. I push deeper into the woods, out of sight. The air is still with that silence that only snow can bring. My feet are icy bricks now, legs weary. I am weak from the little I've eaten in my months at the station and my mouth is dry with thirst. There is nothing beyond the trees but endless white. I try to remember from my journey to the girls' home months earlier how far it is to the next village. But even if we make it there, no one will risk his own life to shelter us.

I switch the baby to my other hip, brushing the snow from his forehead. How long has it been since he last ate? He has not moved or cried since we left the station and I wonder if he is still breathing. Hurriedly I pull aside into a thick cluster of trees and unwrap him a bit more, keeping him close for warmth. His eyes are closed and he is sleeping—or so I hope. His lips are cracked and bleeding from dehydration, but his chest rises and falls evenly. His bare feet are like tiny bricks of ice.

I scan the forest desperately, remembering the other babies on the train, most already gone. I should have taken some of their clothes for the child. I am repulsed at the thought. I unbutton my coat and blouse, grimacing at the blast of ice and snow against my skin. I hold the baby to my breast, willing some of the thin gray liquid that I'd squeezed out to relieve my discomfort nearly four months earlier to appear in tiny dots. But my movements are clumsy—no one had taught me how to nurse, and the child is too weak to latch on. My breasts ache with longing but nothing comes. My milk is gone, dried up. After I'd given birth, the nurse had told me there were women who would pay for my milk. I'd shaken my head, unwilling no matter how much I needed the money to have that taken from me, too. With my child gone, I was desperate to be done with the whole thing as quickly as possible.

My child. Part of me wishes I had not held my baby that once, that my arms had not memorized the shape of his body and head. Maybe then my arms would not ache every second. Once I had considered what I would have called him. But as names appeared in my mind, a knife of pain shot through me and I had clamped down on the thought. I wonder what he is called now, praying he had reached people who cared enough to give him a really good, strong name.

Pushing thoughts of my own child aside, I study the baby in my arms. His face is squared off a bit around the full cheeks and perfectly pointed at the chin. The shape is distinct and I just know there is a whole family out there—please let them still be out there—with faces exactly that same shape.

Something crackles behind me in the distance beyond the trees. I turn back, squinting to see through the falling snow, but the way we've come is obscured by the tangle of branches and brush. My heartbeat quickens. It might be a car engine.

Though we are well-hidden by the trees now, there is a road not far from the edge of the woods. If the police followed us, my footprints in the snow would easily lead them here. I hold my breath, feeling like a hunted animal as I strain to listen through the stillness for voices or other sounds. Nothing—at least for now.

Closing my coat, I press forward through the trees. I hold the baby clumsily in one arm, using the other to clear a low branch in front of us. Snow shakes from it and falls down the collar of my coat, icy and wet. My feet, soaked through the patchy secondhand boots, begin to ache.

The baby grows heavier with every step. I slow, breathing heavily, then reach down for a handful of snow to ease the dryness of my mouth, the coldness burning through the holes in my glove. I straighten, nearly dropping the child. Is he thirsty? I wonder if giving him a bit of snow will help or make things worse. Holding him at arm's length, I am suddenly helpless. There is so much I do not know. Other than those fleeting seconds after I had given birth, I have never held a child, much less cared for one. I want to set him down. Empty-handed I might make it to the next village. He would have died in that train car anyway. Would this be so much worse?

The baby's hand, no bigger than a walnut, shoots up, grasping for my finger and holding tight. What does he think when he looks up and sees a face different from the one that he had known since birth? He is almost the exact same age that my own child would be. I imagine a mother whose scars still ache like mine. Looking at this child, my heart breaks open. He once had a name. How could a child too young to know his own name ever hope to find his parents? I will him to breathe, to keep going until we can find shelter.

I cradle his head gently before covering it once more.

Then redoubling my efforts, I press on. But the wind grows stronger now, whipping the snow-clad branches at me and making it hard to breathe. Stopping a second time had been a mistake. There is no shelter other than the train station for many kilometers. If we stay here, we will die, just as surely as the child would have on that train.

"I can't do this!" I cry aloud, forgetting in my desperation that I must not be heard.

The wind howls louder in response.

I try to move forward again. My toes are numb now, legs leaden. Each step into the sharp wind grows harder. The snow turns to icy sleet, forming a layer on us. The world around us has turned strangely gray at the edges. The child's eyes are closed, and he is resigned to the fate that has always been his. I take a step forward and stumble and stand again.

"I'm sorry," I say, unable to hold him any longer. Then I fall forward and everything goes black.

4

Astrid

The squeak of a doorknob turning, hands pressing against hard wood. At first, they seem part of a dream I cannot quite make out.

The sounds come again, though, louder this time, followed by the scraping of the door opening. I struggle to sit. Sharp terror shoots through me. Inspections have come without warning in the fifteen months since my return, Gestapo or the local police who do their bidding. They have not noticed me yet, nor asked for the *ausweis* Herr Neuhoff had gotten for me, the identification card I fear will not be good enough. My reputation as a performer is a blessing and a curse in Darmstadt, giving me the means to survive, but at the same time making my false identity a thin veneer, nearly impossible to maintain. So when the inspectors come I disappear into the bottom of one of the tarp-covered wagons, or if there is no time, into the woods. But here in Peter's cabin, with its lone door and no cellar, I am trapped.

A deep male voice cuts through the darkness. "It's only me." Peter's hands, which I feel so often in the night these past months, stirring me from dreams of the past I do not want to leave, rub my back gently. "Someone has been found in the forest."

I roll over. "Who found them, you?" I ask. Peter hardly sleeps, but walks at night, prowling the countryside like a restless coyote even in deepest winter. I reach up to touch his stubbled cheek, noting with concern the circles that ring his eyes more darkly now.

"I was down by the stream," he replies. "I thought it was a wounded animal." Peter's vowels are over-rounded, *v*'s nearly *w*'s, his Russian accent undiluted by time as though he had left Leningrad weeks and not years ago.

"So naturally, you went closer," I say, my voice chiding. I would have gone the other way.

"Yes." He helps me to my feet. "They weren't conscious so I carried them back here." His breath holds a hint of liquor, drunk too recently to have gone sour.

"They?" I repeat, the word now a question.

"A woman." A bit of jealousy passes through me as I imagine him holding someone else. "There was also a child." He pulls a hand-rolled cigarette from his pocket.

A woman and child, alone in the woods at night. This is queer, even for the circus. No good can come from strange happenings—or strangers.

I dress hurriedly and pull on my coat. Below the lapel I can feel the rough outline of torn threads where the yellow star had once been sewn. I follow Peter out into the frigid darkness, tucking my chin low against the biting wind. His cottage is one of a half dozen scattered across the gently sloping valley, private quarters saved for the most senior and skilled of performers. Though my official residence is in the lodge, a long building set apart where most of the other girls sleep, staying with Peter had quickly become the norm. I slip back and forth at night and before dawn with only the slightest pretense.

When I came back to Darmstadt, I had meant to stay only long enough for Herr Neuhoff to find a replacement aerialist and for me to figure out where I was going. But the arrangement worked, and as I prepared to join the circus on the road that first year, my visions of leaving waned. And I met Peter, who had joined the Circus Neuhoff during the years that I was gone. He is a clown, though not the type of buffoon whom noncircus folk normally associate with the title. His performances are original and elaborate and they combine comedy, satire and irony with an artistry that even I have never seen before.

I had not expected to be with anyone again, much less fall in love. Peter is a decade older, and different from the rest of the performers. He had been born to the Russian aristocracy when there was one; some said he was the cousin of Czar Nicholas. In another life we never would have met. The circus is a great equalizer, though; no matter class or race or background, we are all the same here, judged on our talent. Peter fought in the Great War. He had not sustained injuries, at least none that were visible, but there is a kind of melancholy that suggested he has never recovered. His sadness resonated with me and we were drawn to one another.

I start toward the women's lodge. Peter shakes his head and guides me in a different direction. "Up there." The light of his cigarette gleams like a torch as he inhales.

The newcomers are at Herr Neuhoff's villa—also rather unusual. "They can't stay," I whisper, though there is no one else around to hear.

"Of course not," Peter replies. "Just temporary shelter so they wouldn't die from the storm." His shadow looms over me. It is not only Peter's sorrow that makes his greatness as a clown so improbable. He told me once that the first time he had tried to join a circus, they sent him away, saying he was too tall to be a clown. So he'd apprenticed at a theater in Kiev, developed an ironic persona that suited his craggy features and long-legged style and then gone from circus to circus, building fame around his act. Peter's antics, which often feature a humorous disregard for authority, are known far and wide. Through the war years, his routines had grown more caustic and his hatred of war and fascism less veiled. As his reputation for daring irreverence grew, so did the crowds.

He opens the door to the villa, where I've been only for the holiday party Herr Neuhoff throws for the entire circus each December and a handful of other times since my return. We slip inside without knocking. From the top of the staircase, Herr Neuhoff gestures that we should join him. In one of the guest rooms, a girl with long blond hair sleeps in a mahogany four-poster bed. Her pale skin is almost translucent against the rich burgundy sheets.

On the low table beside her, a baby lies in a makeshift bassinet, fashioned from a large woven basket. Moses on the Nile, watching us with dark, interested eyes. The child cannot be more than a few months old, I guess, though I have no experience with such things. It has long lashes and round cheeks that one seldom sees for all of the deprivation these days. Beautiful—but aren't they all at that age?

Herr Neuhoff nods toward the child. "Before she passed out, she said he is her brother."

A boy. "But where did they come from?" I ask. Herr Neuhoff simply shrugs.

The girl sleeps soundly. With a clear conscience, my mother might have said. She has thick, blond plaits, like a lass out of a Hans Christian Andersen tale. She could have been one of the Bund Deutscher Mädel, the League of German Girls, striding along Alexanderplatz with arms linked, singing vile songs about the Fatherland and killing Jews. Peter had described her as a woman but she could not be more than seventeen. I feel so very old and tired by comparison.

The girl stirs. Her arms shoot straight out, searching for the baby in a gesture I know all too well from my own dreams. Then sensing emptiness, she begins to flail.

Watching her desperation, the words run through my head: *there is no way that is her brother.*

Herr Neuhoff lifts the child and places it in the young woman's arms and instantly she calms. *"Waar ben ik?"* Dutch. She blinks, then repeats the question in German: *Where am I?* Her voice is thin, wavering.

"Darmstadt," Herr Neuhoff replies. No recognition registers on her face. She is not from these parts. "You are with the Circus Neuhoff."

She blinks. "A circus." Though to us it seems quite normal—indeed for more than half of my life it was all I had known—to her it must sound like something from a fantasy tale. A freak show. I stiffen, instantly reverting to the defensive girl facing down stares on the schoolyard. Throw her back out into the snow if we aren't good enough.

"How old are you, child?" Herr Neuhoff asks gently.

"I'll be seventeen next month. I fled my father's house," she offers, her German smoother now. "I'm Noa Weil and this is my brother." Her words come too quickly, answering questions that no one has asked.

"What's his name?" I ask.

A moment's hesitation. "Theo. We're from the Dutch coast," she says with another pause. "Things were very bad. My father drank and beat us. Mother died in childbirth. So I took my brother and we left." What is she doing here, hundreds of miles from home? No one would flee Holland for Germany now. Her story does not make sense. I wait for Herr Neuhoff to ask if she has papers.

The girl studies the child's face with darting eyes. "Is he all right?"

"Yes, he ate well before falling asleep," Herr Neuhoff reassures.

The girl's brow wrinkles. "Ate?"

"Drank, I should say," Herr Neuhoff corrects. "Some formula our cook made from sugar and honey." Surely the girl would know that if she had been caring for the child.

I step back toward Peter, who reclines in a chair by the door. "She's lying," I say in a low voice. The fool girl had probably gotten pregnant. One does not speak of such things, though.

Peter shrugs with detachment. "She must have her reasons for running. We all do."

"You are welcome to stay," Herr Neuhoff says. I stare at him dumbfounded: What can he be thinking? He continues, "You'll have to work, of course, when you're well enough."

"Of course." The girl sits up, spine stiffening, at the suggestion that she might expect charity. "I can clean and cook." I scoff at her naïveté, imagining her in the cookhouse making pancakes and peeling potatoes by the hundreds.

Herr Neuhoff waves his hand. "Cooks and cleaners we have. No, with your looks that would be a waste. I want you to perform." Peter shoots me a puzzled look. New performers are recruited from across Europe and beyond; the spots are competitive and hard fought, possible only with a lifetime of training. One does not simply find talent on the street—or in the forest. Herr Neuhoff knows that. He turns to me. "You need a new aerialist, yes?" Over his shoulder, the girl's eyes widen.

I hesitate. Once the act might have had a dozen or more

aerialists, throwing parallel passes and somersaulting past one another in midair. But we have only three now and since my return I'd been largely reduced to the *corde lisse* and Spanish web. "Of course, but she has never performed. I can't simply teach her the flying trapeze. Perhaps she could ride a horse or sell programs." There are dozens of easier jobs she can do. What is making Herr Neuhoff think that she can perform? Usually I can scout talent a mile away. Here I see nothing. He is trying to make a duck into a swan and such a plan would only be met with failure.

"We don't have time to find another aerialist before we go on the road," Herr Neuhoff replies. "She has the right look. We have almost six weeks until we leave for tour." He does not meet my eyes as he says this. Six weeks is a blink of an eye compared with the lifetime of training the rest of us have endured. He is asking me to perform the impossible and he knows it.

"She's too thick to be an aerialist," I say, appraising her body critically. Even beneath the duvet, it is plump around the hips and thighs. She is weak, soft in the middle with an innocence that suggests she has never known hard work. She would not have survived the night in the snow if Peter had not found her. And she will not last the week here.

Hearing a shuffling sound, I turn. Herr Neuhoff's son, Emmet, watches from the doorway, his doughy mouth curled as he takes in our disagreement. He had always been an odd child, playing mean-spirited pranks and getting in trouble. "Wouldn't want to be upstaged, would you?" he sneers at me.

I look away, ignoring him. The girl is prettier than me, I have to admit, cataloging her looks relative to my own in that way all women do. Good looks will not carry her here, though. In the circus what matters is the talent and experience—of which she has none.

"She can't stay," Peter says from his chair, the forcefulness of his voice causing me to jump. Herr Neuhoff is a kind man, but it is his circus and even the star performers such as Peter do not dare to disagree with him openly. "I mean, when she's well enough she'll have to go," he clarifies.

"Where?" Herr Neuhoff demands.

"I don't know," Peter admits. "But how can she stay? A girl with a baby, people will ask questions." He is thinking of me, the additional scrutiny and danger their arrival might bring. Though my identity and past are quietly known among the circus folk, we've been able to maintain the pretense with outsiders—at least until now. "We can't risk the attention."

"It won't be a problem if she is part of our act," Herr Neuhoff counters. "Performers join circuses all of the time."

They used to, I correct in my head. New performers had joined the circus many times over the years—once we had Serbian animal trainers, a juggler from China. Everything had grown leaner in recent years, though. These days there simply isn't the money to bring on more acts.

"A cousin from one of the other circuses," Herr Neuhoff suggests, his plan unfurling. Our own performers would know differently, but the story might satisfy the seasonal workers. "If she's all ready to perform, then no one will notice," he adds. It is true that the audience would not pay any attention; they come faithfully each year, but they do not see the people behind the performances.

"That's very kind of you to offer me a place," the girl interjects. She struggles to rise from the bed without letting go of the baby, but the very effort seems to wind her and she leans back once more. "But we wouldn't want to be a burden. As soon as we've rested and the weather breaks, we'll be on our way." I can see the panic in her eyes. They have nowhere to go.

Vindicated, I turn to Herr Neuhoff. "You see, she can't do it."

"I didn't say that." The girl straightens again, lifting her chin. "I'm a hard worker and I'm sure that with enough training I can." Suddenly she seems eager to prove herself where a minute earlier she had not even wanted to try, a kind of defiance I recognize from myself. I wonder if she even knows what she is getting herself into.

"But we can't possibly have her ready," I repeat, searching for another argument to persuade him that this will not work.

"You can do this, Astrid." There is a new forcefulness to Herr Neuhoff's words. He stops a step short of ordering, instead willing me to agree. "You found shelter here. You need to do this." His eyes burn into me. So this is how my debt is to be repaid. The whole circus had risked themselves to hide me, now I am to do the same for this stranger. His face softens. "Two innocents. If we do not help them, they will surely die. I won't have that on my hands." He could no sooner turn her and the baby away than he could have me.

My eyes meet Peter's and he opens his mouth to protest once more that we would be risking everything. But then he closes it, knowing as I do that arguing further will do no good.

"Fine," I say at last. There are limits to what Herr Neuhoff can ask of me, though. "Six weeks," I say. "I will try to have her ready by the time we go on the road. And if not, then she must leave." It is the most I have ever stood up to him and for a second it is as if we are equals once more. But those are bygone days. I meet his stare, willing myself not to blink.

"Agreed," he relents, surprising me.

"We start tomorrow at dawn," I pronounce. Six weeks or six years it does not matter—she will still not be able to do it. The girl watches me closely and I wait for her to protest. She remains silent, though, a hint of gratitude in her wide, fearful eyes.

"But she was nearly frozen," Herr Neuhoff protests. "She's exhausted. She needs time to recover."

"Tomorrow," I insist. She will fail and we will be done with her.

5

Noa

She comes for me before dawn.

I am already awake, wearing a dressing gown that is not my own. Moments earlier, I bolted upright, shaken. I'd dreamed that I had gone back to the railcar at the station a second time, not just to save more babies but because I somehow knew that my own child was among them. But when I pulled open the door to the train car it was empty. I reached into the pitch-blackness and shrieked as my arms closed around nothing.

I'd awoken from the dream, hoping I had not screamed aloud and startled others in the strange house. I fought to close my eyes again. I had to go back and save my child. But the image was gone.

As my trembling ebbed, I reached for the baby, who slept peacefully in the basket they had made into a bassinet by my bedside. I pulled him to me, his warmth soothing. I adjusted my eyes to the still room, partly lit by the moonlight that filtered in through curtains held back by braided ropes. A low fire burned in the corner. The fine furnishings were

grander than any I'd ever seen. I recalled the odd faces assembled when I'd awoken the previous day, the round circus
owner and the woman who looked at me with such distaste
and the long-faced man who had sat in the chair watching,
like the cast of characters from a story my mother read to
me as a child. The circus, they said—it is hard to believe
that such a world still exists even during the war. I might
have been less surprised to find myself on the moon. I had
been to the circus only once when I was three and I cried at
the glaring lights and loud noises until my father had taken
me out of the tent. And now here I am. It is strange, but no
stranger than finding a boxcar full of infants, or any of the
things that have happened to me since leaving home.

I gaze down at the baby, freshly bathed and nestled in
my arms. Theo, I'd called him without thinking when they
asked. I don't know where the name had come from. He
sleeps in the crook of my elbow and I hold still so as not to
disturb him. His face is peaceful, cheeks now rosy. Where
had he slept before being put in the train? I imagine a warm
crib, hands that patted his back to soothe him. I pray that
my own child is sleeping somewhere just as safe.

The previous evening they had spoken about me as though
I was not there. "She's got a circus look about her, don't you
think?" the circus owner had said when my eyes were closed
and they thought I wasn't listening. They were sizing me up
like a horse they were about to buy. I wanted to stand and
say thank-you-but-no-thank-you, to pick up the baby and
walk into the night. But the fierce winds still howled and
through the window the hills were an unbroken sea of white.
If I started out with Theo again, we would not make it to
another shelter. So I let them talk about me. This isn't our
place, though. We will stay long enough to save some money
and then leave. Where we will go exactly, I don't know.

"You'll be paid ten marks a week," the circus owner had said. The price seemed shrewd, but not so low that he was taking advantage. Should I have asked for more? Perhaps it was a generous sum for one who had never performed. I know so little about money, and I am hardly in a position to bargain.

After the circus people had finished talking about me, they had left the room and I'd fallen asleep. I'd awoken once and found my way to the water closet in the darkness. A few times something rumbled in the distance, seeming to echo off the hills. Air raids perhaps, like the ones I'd heard so many times at the rail station. But they were not close enough to cause alarm.

No one had come to the room again—until now. Hearing footsteps in the hall, I slide from the bed carefully so as not to wake Theo, wanting to open the door before anyone knocks. The woman they had called Astrid, the one who had watched me so disdainfully the previous night, stands before me now in the semidarkness, the moonlight behind giving her a strange glow. Her jet-black hair is bobbed short and curled at the ends, framing her face. She wears no jewelry except for a pair of gold earrings with a small crimson gem in each. She is beautiful in an exotic way with too-large features that fit together perfectly. She does not smile.

"You've slept long enough," she declares without greeting or introduction. "Time to get up and start working." She throws a leotard in my direction, faded and mended at the toe. "You'll need to wear this." I have no idea where my own clothes, soaked and tattered, have gone. I wait for her to leave so I can change, but she simply half turns away. "We haven't a day to lose. I will train you—or attempt to, anyway. I don't think you can manage it, but if you do, you may travel with us."

"Train to do what, exactly?" I ask, wishing I had thought to ask the previous evening before saying I could do it.

"Learn the flying trapeze," she answers.

I had heard them discuss this the previous evening. They used the word "aerialist," I recall now. Through the fog of my exhaustion, I had not contemplated what it really meant. Now the outrageousness of the proposal crashes down upon me: they want me to climb to the ceiling and risk my life swinging like a monkey. I'm not captive here. I don't have to do this. "That's very kind of you, but I hardly think…" I don't want to offend her. "I can't possibly do that. I can clean, or perhaps cook," I offer, as I had the night before.

"Herr Neuhoff owns the circus," she informs me. "This is what he wants." Her diction is polished, as if she is not from around here. "Of course if you can't manage it…you have maybe a rich uncle waiting to take you in?" Though her tone is mocking, she has a point. I cannot go back to the station where surely the baby and I have both been noticed missing by now. On my own I might have kept running. But the bitter cold had nearly killed us once. We would not make it a second time.

I bite my lip. "I'll try. Two weeks." Two weeks will give me time to get stronger and find somewhere for Theo and me to go. We will not, of course, stay with the circus.

"We were going to give you six." She shrugs, not seeming to care. "Let's go." I change into the leotard as modestly as I can beneath the gown.

"Wait." I hesitate, looking at Theo, who still sleeps on the bed.

"Your *brother*," she says, emphasizing the second word. "Theo, isn't it?"

"Yes."

She hesitates for a beat, watching me. Then she picks him

up. I fight the urge to protest, the notion of anyone else holding him unbearable. She places him into the makeshift bassinet. "I've asked the housemaid, Greta, to come up and watch him."

"He's colicky," I say.

"Greta has raised eight of her own. She'll manage."

Still I hesitate. It is more than just Theo's care that concerns me: if the maid changes his diaper, she will learn that he is a Jew. I take in his clean outfit and realize it's too late. Someone already knows the truth about his identity.

I follow Astrid down the stairs of the darkened house, the air musty and burnt. Then I put on my still-damp boots, which stand by the front door. She hands me my coat, and I notice that she does not wear one. Her figure is flawless, lean legs that belie her strength and a perfectly flat waist like I'd had before the baby. She is shorter than I thought the previous day. But her body is like a statue, elegant lines seemingly carved from granite.

Outside, we pad silently across the open field, our footsteps crackling against the ice. The air is dry and milder, though; had it been like this a day ago, I might have made it farther into the woods without collapsing. Moonlight shines down brightly. The night sky is filled with stars and for a second it seems that each is for one of the infants on the train. Somewhere, if they are still alive, Theo's parents are wondering where their child has gone, hearts crying out in anguish, just as my own does. I look at the sky and send up a silent prayer, wishing they might know their son is alive.

Astrid unlocks the door to a large building. She flicks a switch and lights splutter on overhead. Inside, it is a run-down gymnasium that smells of sweat, old tumbling mats rotting in the corner. It is dingy and worn, worlds away from the glamour and sparkle I'd always associated with the circus.

"Take off your coat," she instructs, stepping closer. Her bare arm brushes mine. My own pale skin is marred a thousand times with moles and scars, but Astrid's is a smooth, unbroken canvas of olive, like a lake on a day without wind. She produces beige tape that she wraps around my wrists slowly and methodically, then kneels and covers my legs with chalk, taking care not to miss a single spot. Her nails are perfectly polished, but her hands are lined and coarse, unable to hide the years the way her face and body can. She must be close to forty.

Finally she pats a thick powder onto my hands. "Rosin. You must keep your hands dry always. Otherwise, you will slip. Do not assume the net will save you. If you hit too hard it will drop to the floor or you'll be thrown off. You must land in the center of the net, not by the edge." There is no warmth in her voice as she rattles off instructions, practiced over time, that will help to keep me from falling, or killing myself if I do. My mind reels: Does she actually think I can manage this?

She gestures that I should follow her to a ladder that stands close to one of the walls, bolted perfectly upright. "The act will have to be simplified of course," she says, as if reminding me that I can never possibly be good enough. "It takes a lifetime of training to truly become an aerialist. There are ways to compensate so that the audience will not notice. Of course, there is no room for conjuring in the circus. The audience has to trust that all of our feats are real."

She begins to climb the ladder with the ease of a cat, then looks down expectantly to where I stand, not moving. I scan the length of the ladder to the high ceiling. The top must be at least forty feet from the ground, with nothing below but a tired-looking net just a meter or so off the hard floor. I have never been afraid of heights, but I've had no cause:

our house in the village was a single story and there were no mountains for hundreds of kilometers. I've never imagined anything like this.

"There has to be something else," I say, a note of pleading creeping into my voice.

"Herr Neuhoff wants you to learn the aerial act," she replies firmly. "The trapeze is actually easier than many of the other acts." I can't imagine anything more difficult. She continues, "I can guide you, put you where you need to be. Or not." She looks at me evenly. "Perhaps we should go tell Herr Neuhoff that this isn't going to work out."

And have him cast you out into the cold, seems her unspoken conclusion. I'm not sure the kind-faced circus owner would actually do that, but I don't want to find out. More important, I'm not going to give Astrid the satisfaction of being right.

Reluctantly, I begin climbing rung by rung, trying not to tremble. I tighten my grip, wondering when the bolts had last been checked and whether it is sturdy enough for both of us. We reach a tiny ledge, scarcely big enough for two people. I wait for Astrid to help me onto it. When she does not, I carefully squeeze myself on, standing too close beside her. She unlatches a trapeze bar from its catch.

Astrid leaps from the platform, sending it rocking so that I grasp for something to hold on to to keep myself from falling. I marvel at how she swings easily through the air, somersaulting around the bar, twirling with just one hand. Then she opens her body like a diving gull, hanging upside down beneath the bar. She rights herself and returns, aiming for the platform and landing neatly in the tiny space beside me. "Like that," she says, as though it were easy.

I am too stunned to speak. She hands the bar to me. It is

thick and unfamiliar in my hand. "Here." She adjusts my grip impatiently.

I look from her to my hands, then back again. "I can't possibly. I'm not ready."

"Just hang on and swing," she urges. I stand frozen. There have been moments when I have acknowledged death—during childbirth when life seemed to rush from my body, when I saw the babies on the train, and as I struggled through the snow with Theo just days earlier. But it lies before me more real than ever now in the abyss between the platform and the ground.

An image of my mother pops improbably into my mind. In the months since I had been gone, I'd struggled to push away thoughts of home: the patchwork quilt on my bed tucked in the alcove, the corner nook by the stove where we used to sit and read. I have not allowed myself to think of such things, knowing that if I allowed even a trickle of memories I would be drowned in a flood I could not stop. But homesickness washes over me now. I do not want to be here on this tiny platform about to leap to my death. I want my mother. I want to be home.

"Are there other aerialists?" I ask, stalling for time.

Astrid hesitates. "Two others, and one of them will help us when we get further along. But they will primarily be working on the cradle swing, or the Spanish web, which is my other act. They will not be working with us." I am surprised. I imagine that the flying trapeze is the centerpiece of the show, the goal for any aerialist. Perhaps they do not want to work with me either.

"Come now," she says, before I can ask further. "You can sit on the swing, if you aren't ready. Pretend you are on a playground." Her tone is condescending. She takes the bar and draws it close to me. "Balance just below your backside," she instructs. I sit on it, trying to get comfortable. "Like that. Good." She lets go. I swing out from the platform, grasping the wires on either side so tightly that they cut into my hands. There is a kind of natural flow to it, like getting your feet under you on a boat. "Now lean back." Surely she is joking. But her voice is serious, her face unsmiling. I lean back too fast and upset my balance, nearly slipping from the seat. As I swing back closer to the platform, she reaches out and grabs the ropes above the bar, pulling me onto the board and helping me off.

She sits on the bar and swings out, then lets go. I gasp as she starts to fall. But she catches herself by her knees and swings upside down. Her dark hair fans out beneath her, and her inverted eyebrows arch toward the ground. She rights herself and climbs back onto the platform. "Hock hang," she informs me.

"How did you come to be with the circus?" I ask.

"I was born into a circus family nearby," she replies. "Not this one." She hands me the bar. "Your turn, for real this time." She puts the bar in my hand, adjusting my grip. "Jump and swing by your arms."

I stand motionless, legs locked. "Of course if you can't do it, I can just tell Herr Neuhoff that you quit," she taunts once more.

"No, no," I reply quickly. "Give me a second."

"This time you will swing by your arms. Hold the bar down here." She indicates a spot just below my hips. "Then raise it above your head when you jump off to get height."

It is now or never. I take a deep breath, then leap. My feet flail and I flop helplessly like a fish on a line, the furthest thing from Astrid's own graceful movement. But I am doing it.

"Use your legs to take you higher," Astrid calls, urging

me onward. "It's called the kick out. Like on a swing when you were a child." I shoot my legs out. "Keep your ankles together." It is working, I think. "No, no!" Astrid's voice rises even louder, her dissatisfaction echoing across the practice hall. "Keep your body in a line when you return. First in the neutral position. Head straight." Her instructions are rapid-fire and endless and I struggle to keep them all in my head at once. "Now kick your legs back. That is called the sweep."

I gain momentum, swinging back and forth until the air whooshes past my ears and Astrid's voice seems to fade. The ground slips and slides beneath me. This is not so bad. I had done gymnastics for years and those muscles bounce back now. Not the flips and twists that Astrid had done, but I am managing.

Then my arms begin to ache. I cannot hold on much longer. "Help!" I cry. I had not thought about how to get back.

"You have to do it yourself," she calls in return. "Use your legs to swing higher." It is quite impossible. My arms are burning now. I kick my legs forward to increase my momentum. I near the board this time, but it is not enough. I am going to fall, injure myself, maybe even die, and for what? With one last desperate kick, I send myself higher.

Astrid catches the ropes as I near the board, pulling me in and helping me to my feet.

"That was close," I pant, legs trembling.

"Again," she says coolly, and I stare at her in disbelief. I can't imagine getting up there once more after nearly falling, much less right away. But to earn my keep, and Theo's, I have no other choice. I start to grab the bar once more. "Wait," she calls. I turn back hopefully. Has she changed her mind?

"Those." She is pointing to my breasts. I look down self-consciously. They had grown fuller since I'd given birth, even though the milk had since dried up and gone away.

"They're too big for when you are in the air." She climbs down the ladder and returns with a roll of thick gauze. "Take down your top," she instructs. I look down at the practice hall below to make sure no one else is there. Then I lower the leotard, trying not to blush as she binds me so tightly it is hard to breathe. She doesn't seem to notice my embarrassment. "You're soft here," she says, patting my stomach, an intimate gesture that makes me pull back. "That will change with training."

Other performers have begun to trickle into the practice hall, stretching and juggling in opposite corners. "What happened to the last girl, the one who swung with you before me?"

"Don't ask," she replies as she steps back to study her work. "For the show, we'll find a corset." So she thinks I might be able to do it after all. I exhale quietly.

"Again." I take the bar and jump once more, this time with a bit less hesitation. "Dance, use your muscles, take charge, take flight," she pushes, never satisfied. We work all morning on that same swinging motion, kick out, neutral, sweep. I strive hard to point my toes and make my body exactly like hers. I attempt to mimic her patterns, but my motions are clumsy and unfamiliar, a joke in comparison with hers. I improve, I think. But no praise comes. I keep trying, evermore eager to please her.

"That was not awful," Astrid concedes at last. She sounds almost disappointed that I am not a total failure. "You studied dance?"

"Gymnastics." More than studied, actually. I practiced six days a week, more when I could. I had been a natural and I might have gone to the national team if Papa had not declared it a worthless endeavor. Though it has been more than a year after I had last trained and my stomach is weak from childbirth, the muscles in my arms and legs are still strong and quick.

"It's just like gymnastics," Astrid says. "Only your feet never touch the ground." A faint smile appears on her face for the first time. Then it fades just as quickly. "Again."

Nearly an hour passes and we are still working. "Water," I pant.

Astrid looks at me in surprise, a pet she has forgotten to feed. "We can break for a quick lunch. And then after, we will begin again."

We climb down. I swallow a capful of tepid water Astrid offers from a thermos. She drops to one of the mats and pulls bread and cheese from a small pail. "Not too much food," she cautions. "We only have time for a short break and you don't want to cramp."

I take a bite of the bread she has offered me, taking in the now-bustling practice hall. My eyes stop on a heavyset man of about twenty in the doorway. I recall seeing him the previous night. Then, as now, he slouches idly, watching.

"Keep an eye out for that one," Astrid says in a low voice. "Herr Neuhoff's son, Emmet." I wait for her to elaborate, but she does not. Emmet has his father's paunchy build, and he does not wear it well. He is stoop-shouldered, pants gapping a bit where they meet the suspenders. His expression is leering.

Unsettled, I turn back to Astrid. "Is it always this hard? The training, I mean."

She laughs. "Hard? Here in the winter quarters, this is rest. Hard is two and sometimes three shows a day on the road."

"The road?" I picture a path, long and desolate, like the one I had taken the night I fled the station with Theo.

"We leave the winter quarters at the first Thursday in April," she explains. "How's your French?"

"Passable." I had studied it a few years in school and found that I took to languages readily, but I had never quite mastered the accent.

"Good. We will go first to a town in Auvergne called Thiers." That is hundreds of kilometers from here, I recall, seeing the map on the wall of my classroom at school. Outside of occupied Germany. Until last year, I had never left the Netherlands. She continues rattling off several additional cities in France where the circus will perform. My head swims. "Not so many this time," she finishes. "We used to go farther—Copenhagen, Lake Como. But with the war it isn't possible."

I am not disappointed, though—I can hardly fathom traveling farther than Germany. "Will we perform in Paris?"

"We?" she repeats. I realize my error too late: it is one thing for Astrid to include me in the circus's future plans, but to do it myself is overstepping. "You have to prove yourself before you can join us."

"I meant, does the circus go to Paris?" I correct quickly.

She shakes her head. "Too much competition from the French circuses there. And too expensive. But when I lived in Berlin—"

"I thought you grew up in Darmstadt," I interrupt.

"I was born into my family's circus here. But I left for a time when I was married." She fiddles with the gold earring in her left ear. "Before Peter." Her voice softens.

"Peter...he was the man who was with you last night?" The somber man who sat in the corner of my room smoking had spoken little. His dark eyes burned intensely.

"Yes," she replies. Her eyes turn guarded, like a door snapping shut. "You should not ask so many questions," she adds, terse once more.

I had asked about only a few things, I want to point out in

my own defense. But sometimes one question can feel like a thousand—like the previous night, when Herr Neuhoff asked about my past. There are so many other things I still want to know about Astrid, though, like where her family had gone and why she performs with Herr Neuhoff's circus instead.

"Peter is a clown," Astrid says. I look across the practice hall at the handful of other performers who have come in, a juggler and a man with a monkey, but I do not see him. I picture his large Cossack features, the sloped mustache and drooping cheeks. He could not have been anything but a sad clown, so fitting for these dreary times.

As if on cue, Peter enters the practice hall. He does not wear the makeup I would have imagined for a clown, but baggy trousers and a floppy hat. His eyes meet Astrid's. Though there are others here, I suddenly feel like an intruder in the space between them. He does not come over, but I can feel his affection for her as he studies her face. He walks to a piano in the far corner of the hall and speaks with the man seated at it, who begins to play.

When she faces me, Astrid's expression is hard and businesslike once more. "Your brother," she says, "he looks nothing like you."

I am caught off guard by the abrupt shift of topic. "My mother," I feign. "She was very dark-skinned." I bite my tongue, trying to counter my natural instinct of offering too much information. I brace for an onslaught of additional questions, but Astrid seems content to leave it alone and continues eating in silence.

At the end of the theater, Peter is rehearsing an act, goose-stepping with legs straight out, imitating with great exaggeration the march of the German soldier. Watching him, I grow nervous. I turn to Astrid. "Surely he isn't planning to do that for the show?" She does not answer, but stares at him, her eyes narrow with fear.

Herr Neuhoff enters and crosses the hall with more speed than I would have thought he could manage, given his age and weight. He barrels toward Peter, face stormy. Had he seen Peter rehearsing through one of the windows or had someone told him about the routine? The music stops abruptly with a clatter. Herr Neuhoff confers with Peter. Though his voice is low, he gestures wildly with his hands. Peter shakes his head vehemently. Astrid's brow wrinkles with concern as she watches the two men.

A minute later Herr Neuhoff clambers toward us, red-faced. "You must talk to him," he thunders at Astrid. "This new act mocking the Germans…"

Astrid raises her palms plaintively upward. "I can't stop him. That's who he is as an artist."

Herr Neuhoff will not let the matter go. "We keep our heads low, stay out of the fray—that's how I've been able to keep this circus going—and protect everyone." From what? I want to ask. But I do not dare. "Tell him, Astrid," Herr Neuhoff urges in a low voice. "He'll listen to you. Tell him— or I'll pull him from the show."

Alarm crosses Astrid's face. "I'll try," she promises.

"Would he?" I cannot help but ask after Herr Neuhoff has walked from the building. "Pull Peter from the show, I mean."

She shakes her head. "Peter is one of the circus's biggest draws and his acts are what hold the whole thing together. Without him, there is no show," she adds. But she is still upset. Her hand shakes as she puts her sandwich away, largely uneaten. "We should keep going and rehearse the next bit."

I take a bite, swallow hurriedly. "There's more?"

"You think people will pay just to see you hang there like

a monkey?" Astrid laughs harshly. "You've only just started. It is not enough to simply swing back and forth. Anyone can do that. We need to dance in the air, do things that seem impossible. Don't worry, I will line up your trick so that when you release and fly, I'm in place to catch you."

The bread I've just eaten sticks in my throat as I remember the way she tumbled through the air. "Fly?" I manage.

"Yes. That's why it is called the flying trapeze. You are the flier and you will release and come to me. I will be the catcher." She starts for the ring.

But I remain in place, feet planted. "Why must I be the one to let go?" I dare to ask.

"Because I would never trust you to catch me." Her voice is cold. "Come."

She heads for a ladder on the other side of the room, parallel to the one we'd climbed earlier, but with a sturdier-looking swing. I follow, but she shakes her head. "You go on that side with Gerda." She gestures to another aerialist whom I hadn't seen come in and who is already climbing the ladder Astrid and I had used previously. I follow her. At the top, Astrid and I stand on opposite platforms, an ocean apart from one another. "Swing just like before. And when I say, you let go. I will do the rest."

"And Gerda?" I ask, stalling.

"She will send the bar back for you to catch on the return," Astrid replies.

I stare at her, not believing. "So I have to let go twice?"

"Unless you have wings, yes. You have to get back somehow." Astrid grabs the opposite bar and leaps, then swings around so she is hanging by her legs. "Now you," she prompts.

I jump out, kicking my toes high. "Higher, higher," she urges, her arms extended toward me. "You have to be above me when I tell you to let go." I force myself upward, driving with my feet. "Better. On my cue. Three, two, one—now!" But my hands remain stuck to the bar.

"Fool!" she cries. "Everything in the circus depends upon timing, synchronicity. You must listen to me. Otherwise you will get us both killed."

I manage my way onto the board, then climb down the ladder and meet Astrid back on the ground. "You let go in gymnastics, surely," she says, clearly frustrated.

"That was different," I reply. By about thirty-five feet, I add silently.

She folds her arms. "There's no act without the release."

"There is no way that I can do this," I insist. We stare at each other for several seconds, neither speaking.

"You want to go, so go. No one expected more." Her words shoot out at me like a slap.

"Least of all you," I retort. She wants me to fail. She does not want me here.

Astrid blinks, her expression somewhere between anger and surprise. "How dare you?" she asks, and I fear I have gone too far.

"I'm sorry," I say quickly. Her face softens somewhat. "But it's true, isn't it? You don't think I can do it."

"No, I didn't think this would work when Herr Neuhoff suggested it." Her tone is neutral, matter-of-fact. "I still don't."

She reaches out and takes my arm and I hold my breath, hoping for a reassuring word. Instead, she rips the tape off my wrist. I let out a yelp, my skin screaming at the burn. We stare at each other hard, neither blinking. I wait for her to tell me I will have to leave here, as well. Surely they will make us go.

"Come back tomorrow," she relents, "and we will try it again one last time."

"Thank you," I say. "But Astrid..." My voice sounds pleading. "There must be something else I can do."

"Tomorrow," she repeats before walking away. Watching her retreat, my stomach leadens. Though grateful for the second chance, I know it is hopeless. Tomorrow or a year from tomorrow, I will never be able to let go.

6

Noa

Theo lies across my chest, the way he likes to sleep, the warmth of his cheek pressed against me. "You should lay him down," Greta, the housemaid who watches Theo while I rehearse, has scolded more than once in the two weeks we have been here. "If he doesn't learn to soothe himself, he'll never sleep well." I don't care. During the day whenever I am not practicing, I hold Theo until my arms ache. I sleep with him close each night so I can feel the beating of his heart, like one of the dolls I had as a child come to life. Sometimes it seems as if without him I cannot breathe.

Lying now in the stillness of the women's lodge, I watch him rise and fall atop me on the narrow bed. He stirs, lifting his head as he has just learned to do. Theo's gaze follows me wherever I enter a room. A wise old soul, he seems to listen intently, missing nothing. Our eyes meet now and he smiles, a wide, toothless grin of contentment. For a few seconds, it is only us in the world. I wrap my arms more tightly around him. There is that moment each evening when Astrid frees me from practice, just before I enter the lodge, when joy and anticipation at seeing Theo rise in me. Part of me fears that he might have been a figment of my imagination, or have disappeared because I had been gone so long. Then I pick him up and he melts into my arms and I am home. Though it has been only a few weeks, I feel as if Theo has been mine forever.

There could be two boys, I remind myself—if I found my child again. Could such a thing be possible? I picture the boys together at three or four. They would be like brothers close in age, almost twins. These are dangerous thoughts, the kind I have not allowed myself to have until now.

I draw the blanket more closely around myself. I dreamed of my own family last night. My father had appeared at the edge of the winter quarters and I ran up to hug him and plead with him to bring me home. But I had awoken to the cold light of day seeping in. Going home is a dream I've held on to for all of my months in exile. When I arrived at the circus, I imagined staying a few weeks to get my strength back and then finding a normal job to earn enough money to go back to Holland. My parents were not able to accept me with a child of my own, though; they will never welcome me back with Theo. No, I cannot go home. I still need to get Theo out of Germany somehow, though. We cannot stay here.

The crashing of metal stirs me from my thoughts. The sounds of the circus come early in the morning, the laughter and arguing of the performers as they go to practice, workers fixing wagons and other equipment, animals whinnying in protest. Once, if I had given it any thought, I might have imagined joining the circus to be fun. But it is an act and behind the careful choreography is hard work. Even in the winter quarters, where circus folk supposedly come to rest, they are up before dawn to help with the chores, then hours of training, at least six per day.

Reluctantly I sit up and place Theo in his bassinet. His eyes follow me as I wash at the basin. I make the bed, running my hands along the sheets, which, though so much coarser than the fine linens in the villa, were still worlds better than anything I had slept on since leaving home. I moved to the lodge the day after I arrived. It is a long room, beds laid out dormitory-style in two rows. The lodge is nearly empty, most of the other girls already gone to practicing and chores. I dress quickly then start for the door with Theo. I do not want to appear lazy. I need to work hard to earn my place here.

I carry Theo to the front of the lodge where a handful of toddlers play on the ground. Reluctantly I hand him to Greta, who draws him close, tickling his chin until he coos. Jealousy nags at me and I fight the urge to grab him back. I still do not like sharing him.

I tear myself away and set out from the lodge toward the practice hall. Winter has begun to ease. There is a little less bite in the air and the snow has begun to melt, leaving the ground muddy and smelling of peat moss. The birds that hunt seeds call out merrily. If the weather permits, in the evenings before it gets too dark I walk Theo around the circus grounds, past the practice hall to the menagerie where the tiger and lions and other animals are penned, looking out of place against the snow-covered pine landscape like characters in the wrong storybook. It seems there are endless places at the circus to explore, from the work quarters where laundry is done by the truckload to the circus alley where some of the clowns rehearse.

I near the practice hall and pause, trying to push down my dread. Though I have trained with Astrid every day, I still have not let go and flown. Each day I wait for her to give up and tell me to leave. Come back tomorrow, she simply says. She has not kicked me out yet. But she treats me like a nuisance, makes it clear that she would rather not have me around and is only tolerating me until I go. I puzzle over again what brings out such dislike. Is it because I am new and lack talent? And yet, she is not always mean. A few days after I arrived, she had brought me a small box. Inside were folded clothes for me and Theo. Everyone had contributed something. Lifting out the faded baby caps and socks, the blouses for me that had been darned many times over, I was touched, not only by the generosity of the circus folk, who themselves had little to spare, but by Astrid, who had thought to gather the items. Perhaps she did not want us to leave after all.

The previous day as I neared the practice hall, though, I'd heard her and Herr Neuhoff speaking in low voices. "I'm doing all I can," Astrid said.

"You must do more," Herr Neuhoff countered.

"I cannot get her ready if she will not let go," Astrid pressed. "We have to find someone else before it is time to go on the road." I walked away then, not wanting to hear what would happen if the arrangement did not work out. I had originally said I would try for only two weeks. But now that time has passed, I find myself wanting to stay longer and keep trying—and not just because we have nowhere else to go.

When I enter the training hall, I am surprised to find Astrid already atop the high board where I usually stand. Am I late? I brace for her to berate me. But she grabs the bar and leaps off.

"Hup!" Gerda swings from the far board to catch her. A strange lump forms in my throat as I watch Astrid work with someone else. But I see how much she misses it, being the one to fly through the air. She must hate me for taking her place.

Gerda sends Astrid flying back, then swings to her own board. Astrid soars now like a rider taming a wild beast, bending the trapeze to her own will. She spins by her ankles, by a lone knee, barely touching the bar to which I always cling fast. Gerda watches Astrid with disinterest, almost distaste. She and the other women do not like Astrid. Within days of arriving, I heard the whispers: they resent Astrid for returning and taking her spot at the top of the aerial act while they had worked for years, and for coupling up with Peter, one of the few eligible men the war had left. The girls at the home were much the same, sniping and whispering behind each other's backs. Why are we so hard on one another? I wonder. Hadn't the world already given us challenges enough? But if Astrid notices their coldness, she doesn't seem to mind. Or perhaps she just doesn't have need for any of them. She certainly doesn't need me.

"She's magnificent, isn't she?" a deep voice asks. I had not heard Peter come up behind me. We stand silently watching as Astrid swings higher. Taking her in, his eyes seem to dance with wonder. Peter's breath catches slightly as Astrid flings herself into the air and spins not once, not twice, but three times. She circles upward, defying gravity.

But then she starts to drop downward at great speed. Peter steps forward then stops, powerless to help her. He exhales quickly when Gerda, who has swung out, grabs her by one ankle, catching her before she catapults to the ground. "The triple somersault," he says, recovering from his fright. "Only a few people in the world who can do that." Though he tries to sound nonchalant, a faint sweat has broken out on his brow and his face has gone slack with relief.

"She's amazing," I reply, my voice full with admiration. In that moment, I do not just want to be like her—I truly want to be her.

"If only she wasn't such a danger to herself," Peter says, so low under his breath I'm not sure I am meant to hear.

Astrid reaches the board and climbs down the ladder to us. Her skin is coated with sweat, but her face glows. She and Peter stare at each other with a hunger that makes me embarrassed to be in the room, though they had surely been together just a few hours earlier since Astrid's bed in the lodge had been empty all night.

"Ready?" she asks, seeming to remember that I am there, without taking her eyes off Peter.

I nod, and start up the ladder. Below a half-dozen or so other performers rehearse, twirling hoops, doing flips and walking on their hands. My schedule with Astrid is the same every day as it had been the first: training from seven until five with a brief break for a bucket lunch. I've gotten better, I think. Still, for all of the practice, I have not let go and actually flown. It is not for lack of trying. I swing endlessly to strengthen my arms. I hang upside down until the blood rushes to my head and I cannot think. But I cannot let go—and without that, Astrid has said over and over, there is no act.

We start with the moves we have already practiced, swinging by my hands, then the hock and ankle hangs. "Pay attention to your arms, even when they are behind your back," Astrid commands. "This is not merely performance. Theater is two-dimensional, like a painting. There, the audience sees only the front. But in the circus the audience is all around us, like sculpture. Think graceful, like ballet. Don't fight the air, make friends with it."

We work all morning around the moment I had been dreading. "Ready?" Astrid asks finally after a break. I can avoid it no longer. I climb the ladder and Gerda follows, taking her place beside me on the board.

"You have to release at the height of the swing," Astrid calls from the far board. "And then I will catch you just a second later on the way down." It makes perfect sense, but I leap and as with all the times before, I cannot let go.

"It's useless," I say aloud. As I swing helplessly from the bar, I catch a glimpse of the horizon through one of the high practice hall windows. Beyond the hills, there is a way out of Germany, a route to safety and freedom. If only Theo and I could swing out of here and fly away. A thought pops into my head then: *go with the circus to France.* Farther from Germany, Theo and I will have a chance to flee to somewhere safe. But that will never happen unless I can learn to let go.

"You're done, then?" Astrid asks as I swing back to the board. She tries to keep her voice neutral, as if she has been disappointed too many times to let anyone do it again. But I can hear it, that faint note of sadness buried deep. At least some part of her thought I could do it—which makes my failure even more awful.

I look out the window once more, my dream of escaping with Theo seeming to slide further from reach. The circus is our ticket out of Germany—or would be if I could manage. "No!" I blurt. "That is, I'd like to try once more."

Astrid shrugs, as if she has already given up on me. "Suit yourself."

As I jump, Astrid leaps from the opposite board and swings by her feet. *"Hup!"* she calls. I do not release on the first pass.

Astrid swings higher, drawing close to me a second time. "Do it!" she orders. I recall Astrid's conversation with Herr Neuhoff the previous day and realize that time is running out.

It is now or never. The entire world hangs in the balance.

I lock eyes with Astrid on the opposite trapeze and in that instant my trust is complete. "Now!" she commands.

I let go of the bar. Closing my eyes, I hurtle through space. Forgetting everything Astrid has taught me, I flail my arms and legs, which only makes me drop faster. I fall in her direction, but too low. She misses me and I tumble forward. There is nothing now between me and the ground, which grows closer as I fall. In that instant, I see Theo, wonder who will care for him after I am gone. I open my mouth but before I can scream, Astrid's hands lock around my ankles. She has caught me.

But it is not over yet. I hang upside down, helpless as a calf about to be slaughtered.

"Reach up," she orders, as though it is simple. "I can't help you. You have to do this part for yourself." I use all of my force to reach up against gravity, performing the world's largest sit-up, and grab on to her.

"Okay when I say 'now' I'm going to send you back with a half spin so you are facing the bar," she instructs.

I freeze. She cannot seriously expect me to fly through the air again to the bar, miles away and moving fast. "I can't possibly."

"You must. Now!" She hurls me through the air and the bar finds my fingers. Clasping it tightly, I understand then that I need to do almost nothing—she can position me as surely as a marionette on strings. But it is still terrifying.

I reach the platform with shaking feet and Gerda helps steady me before climbing down the ladder. Astrid, who has come down from her own side, waits until Gerda has gone before starting up to me. "That was close," I say when she nears me. I wait for her to praise me for finally letting go.

But she is staring at me and I wonder if she is angry and will fault me for panicking. "Your brother," she says. Anger that she has been holding back blazes in her eyes, suddenly set free.

I am caught off guard by the sudden shift in topic. "I don't

understand…" She hasn't brought up Theo since the first day
we practiced. Why is she asking now?

"The thing is, I don't believe you." She speaks through
gritted teeth, her fury unmasked. "I think you are lying.
Theo's not your brother."

"Of course he is," I stammer. What would make her suspect this now?

"He looks nothing like you. We've given you a place here
and you are taking advantage of us and lying to us."

"That's not true," I start to protest.

She continues, unconvinced. "I think you got into trouble. He's your bastard child."

I reel back, as much from the stinging slap of the word as
from her discovering the near truth. "But you just said he
looks nothing like me."

"Like the father, then," she insists.

"Theo is not my child." I say each word slowly and deliberately. How it hurts to disavow him.

She puts her hands on her hips. "How can I work with
you if I cannot trust you?" She does not wait for me to respond. "There is no way that he is your brother."

And then she pushes me hard from the platform.

Suddenly I am falling through the air, without any re-
straint or bar to cling to. I open my mouth to scream, but
find no air. It is almost like a flying dream, except my path
is straight downward. No trapeze, no training can help me
now. I brace for impact, and the pain and darkness that will
inevitably follow. Surely the net wasn't made to catch a person at such great speed.

I cascade into the net, sending it dipping within inches of
the floor, so close I can smell the hay that lines it, the stench
of manure not quite scrubbed away. Then I am flung upward, airborne once more, saved just barely from impact. It

isn't until the third time I land in the still-bouncing net and it does not rise again, but bobbles like a cradle, that I realize I am going to make it.

I lie still for several seconds, catching my breath and waiting for one of the other performers to come to my aid. But they have all disappeared, sensing or even seeing trouble and not wanting to become involved. Only Astrid and I remain in the practice hall now.

I clamber from the net then start toward Astrid, who has climbed down the ladder. "How could you?" I demand. It is my turn to be angry. "You almost killed me." I know she does not like me, but I had not actually thought she would want me dead.

She smiles smugly. "Even I would have been terrified. I won't blame you for giving up."

I square my shoulders defiantly. "I'm not quitting." After what just happened, I would never give her the satisfaction.

Herr Neuhoff rushes in, having heard the clatter as I fell from outside. "My dear, are you okay? Such a calamity!" Seeing I am fine, he steps back and folds his arms. "What happened? We can't afford an accident or the questions it might bring. You know that," he says, aiming these last words at Astrid.

I hesitate. Astrid watches me uneasily from the side. I could tell him the awful truth about what she had done. He might not believe me without solid proof, though. And what would that solve? "My hands must have slipped," I lie.

Herr Neuhoff coughs, then reaches in his pocket and takes a pill. It is the first time I have seen him do this. "Are you ill?" Astrid asks.

He waves his hand, the question irrelevant. "You must be more careful," he admonishes me. "Double the training time this week. Don't risk it by trying anything before you are ready." Then he turns to Astrid. "And don't push her before she is ready."

"Yes, sir," we say, almost in unison. Herr Neuhoff stomps from the practice hall.

Something passes between Astrid and me in that moment. I had not sold her out. I wait for Astrid to say something.

But she just walks away.

I charge after her into the dressing room, my anger rising. Who does she think she is to treat me this way? "How could you?" I demand, too mad to be polite.

"So go on and leave if things are so awful," she taunts. I consider the option: maybe I should. There is nothing keeping me here. I'm well and the weather has calmed now, so why not take Theo and make my way to the nearest town in search of ordinary work? Even being on our own with nothing would be better than staying here unwanted. I had done it once; I could do it again.

But I cannot let this go. "Why?" I demand. "What did I do to you?"

"Nothing," Astrid concedes with a sniff. "You had to see exactly what it is to fall."

So she had planned this. To do what exactly? Not kill me; she knew that the nets would hold. No, she wanted to scare me so I would give up. I wonder again why Astrid hates me so. Is it just because she thinks I am terrible at the trapeze and will never be able to manage the act? I had done what she wanted and let go. No, it is something more than that. I remember how her eyes blazed with fury moments earlier as she accused me of lying about Theo and my past. Her words echo back at me: *How can I work with you if I cannot trust you?* If I tell her the truth about my past, she might accept me. Or it could be the final straw that causes her to want me gone once and for all.

I breathe deeply. "You were right: Theo...he isn't my brother." A knowing smile plays about her lips. "But it isn't what you think," I add quickly. "He's Jewish."

Her smugness fades. "How did you come to have him?"

I have no reason to trust her. She hates me. But the story pours forth. "I was working at the train station in Bensheim as a cleaner." I leave off the part about what had brought me to the station—my own pregnancy. "And one night there was this boxcar. It was full of babies, taken from their parents." My voice cracks as I see them lying on the cold floor of the boxcar, alone in their last moments. "Theo was one of them." I continue, explaining how I had taken him and fled.

When I finish, she stares at me for several seconds, not speaking. "So the story you told Herr Neuhoff was a lie."

"Yes. You see now why I couldn't say anything." My whole body slumps with relief at having shared at least part of the story with her.

"You know, Herr Neuhoff, of all people, would understand," she says.

"I know, but having not told him from the start... I can't right now. Please don't tell him." I hear the pleading in my own voice.

"And Theo, you just grabbed him?" she asks.

"Yes." I hold my breath, waiting for her reaction.

"That was brave," she says finally. The compliment comes out grudgingly, almost an admission.

"I should have taken more," I reply. The sadness that I feel whenever I think of the infants on the train wells up and threatens to burst through. "There were so many other children." Surely they are all gone now.

"No, taking more would have attracted attention and you might not have made it as far as you did. But why didn't you just take the baby and go home?" she asks. "Surely your family would have understood what you had done and helped you."

I want to tell her the rest of the story and explain why my parents had been so outraged. But the words stick in my throat. "What I said about my father being awful before was true," I manage, resorting to that part of the lie once more. "That was why I had left, why I was at the train station in the first place."

"And your mother?"

"She is not very brave." Another part-truth. "Also, I didn't want to cause them trouble," I add. Astrid eyes me evenly and I wait for her to point out that I brought my troubles instead to her and the rest of the circus. I had told her about Theo in hopes that she might be more willing to accept me. But what if the opposite is true?

Outside the practice hall there is a sudden clattering, a car of some sort screeching to a halt, followed by unfamiliar male voices. I turn to Astrid. "What on earth?" But she has turned and raced through the rear door of the dressing room, the one that leads outside.

Before I can call after her, the front door to the dressing room flies open and two uniformed men barrel in from the practice hall, followed by Peter. "Officers, I assure you..." I freeze, my legs stone. The first I have seen since coming to Darmstadt, they are not *Schutzpolizei* as I had seen at the station, but actual Nazi SS. Have they come for me? I had hoped that my disappearance with Theo would have been long forgotten. But it is hard to see what other business they might have with the circus.

"*Fräulein...*" One of the men, older and graying at the temples beneath his hat, steps closer. Let them take just me, I pray. Theo is thankfully not here, but well across the winter quarters. If they should see him, though...

Terrified, I look over my shoulder for Astrid. She will know what to do. I start to go after her. But behind the men, Peter's eyes flare. He is trying to signal some sort of a caution to me.

As the officer nears, I brace myself for arrest. But he simply stands too close, leering down the low-cut front of my leotard.

"We've received a report," the second officer says. Younger by a good ten years, he stands back, looking uncomfortable in the close quarters of the dressing room. "Of a Jew with the circus," he adds. Terror shoots through me like a knife to the stomach. So they know about Theo after all.

The men begin to search the dressing room, opening the armoire and peering under the tables. Do they really think we've hidden the child there? I prepare myself for the questions that will surely come next. But the officers storm back out to the practice hall. I lean against the dressing room table, in a cold sweat and shaking. I have to get to Theo before they do and run. I start for the door.

There is a sudden scraping sound beneath my feet. Looking down, I glimpse Astrid. She has somehow gotten below the floorboards into the crawl space. What is she doing down there? I kneel down, assaulted by the smell of sewage and manure. "Astrid, I..."

"Shh!" She is curled up into a tight ball. Hiding.

"What are you doing...?" I stop midsentence as the older officer walks in again.

I straighten, smoothing my skirt and stepping on the crack through which I'd seen Astrid. "Excuse me!" I cry, feigning modesty. "This is the women's dressing room and I need to change."

But the officer continues to stare at the floorboards. Had he seen her? He lifts his head, eyeing me. "Papers?"

I falter. I'd fled the train station hastily the night I found Theo, leaving my identity card behind. Herr Neuhoff would get me papers, Astrid had promised, before we went on the road, assuming I managed the act. I do not have them yet, though. "I have to go get them," I bluff without thinking. Peter's look is approving: *yes, draw them away from here, stall for time.* I start for the door from the dressing room into the practice hall.

"Follow her," he instructs the younger officer, who lingers just outside the doorway.

My panic worsens: if the men follow me, they will see Theo and ask questions. "Really that isn't necessary. It will just take a minute."

"Fine," the older man says, "but before you go, I have a few questions." I freeze, skin prickling. He takes a cigarette from his pocket and lights it. "The woman on the trapeze."

"I was on the trapeze," I manage, hoping no one heard the quaver in my voice.

"Not you. A woman with dark hair." They must have seen Astrid through the gym window. "Where is she?"

Before I can answer, Herr Neuhoff rushes in. "Gentlemen," he says, as though greeting old friends. This must not be the first time they have come. *"Heil Hitler."* His salute is so authentic that I cringe.

But the officer does not smile. *"Hallo, Fritz."* He addresses Herr Neuhoff too familiarly, his voice lacking any sign of respect. "We are looking for a performer who is reportedly a Jew. Do you have anyone like that here?"

"No, of course not," Herr Neuhoff blusters, seeming to almost take offense at the suggestion. "The Circus Neuhoff is German. Jews have been banned from performing."

"So you are saying that there are no Jews with this circus? I know they're good at trickery."

"I am a German," Herr Neuhoff replies. As if that answers everything. "The circus is *Judenrein*." Cleansed of Jews. "You know that, gentlemen."

"I don't recall her," the officer says, pointing his head in my direction. The ground seems to shift beneath me. Does he think I am a Jew?

"So many new performers each year," Herr Neuhoff says airily. I hold my breath, waiting for the man to ask further. "Noa joined us this year from the Netherlands. Isn't she wonderfully Aryan? The Führer's own ideal." I admire the skilled way Herr Neuhoff makes the argument, but hate that he has to do so. "*Meine Herren*, you've come so far. Join me up at the villa for some cognac."

"We'll finish our inspection first," the officer says, undeterred. He flings open the armoire a second time, peers inside. Then he halts, standing just over the spot where Astrid is hiding. I hold my breath, dig my fingernails into my palms. If he looks down, he will surely see her.

"Come, come," Herr Neuhoff soothes. "There's nothing more here to search. Just a quick drink and then you'll want to be on the road to get back to the city before nightfall."

The officers storm from the dressing room, Herr Neuhoff and Peter in tow.

When they are gone, I sink down into a chair, shaking. Astrid remains silent below the floorboards, still not daring to come out.

Peter returns a few minutes later. "They've gone." I follow him out the back of the dressing room. Along the edge of the practice hall, hidden behind a wheelbarrow, is the narrowest of cellar doors. He pries it open and helps Astrid from her hiding place. She is pale and covered in bits of hay and manure. "Are you all right?" I see then the way he holds her, a moment's tenderness. I should leave them alone. But she turns away from him. Her pride is too hurt to let him close.

I follow them back into the practice hall. I find a cloth and wet it in one of the buckets. "Thank you," Astrid says as I hand her the cloth. It is the kindest voice I've heard her use. Her hands tremble as she wipes the brown muck from her hair and neck.

I struggle to find the words to ask my many questions. "Astrid, you hid…"

"A trick from the Great Boldini. He performed with my family years ago in Italy." She smiles. "Don't ask me how I did it. A good magician never reveals her secrets."

But I am in no mood for jokes. "Oh, Astrid!" I burst into tears. Though she hates me, I cannot help but care. "They almost found you!"

"They didn't, though," she replies, a note of satisfaction in her voice.

"But why did they want you?" I persist, even though I know my questions are too much for her right now. "Why did you hide?"

"Darling…" Peter interjects with a note of caution.

"I can trust her," Astrid says. I straighten with pride. "She will find out soon enough anyway." But she bites her lip and studies me, as if still deciding whether to confide in me. "You see, Theo is not the only Jew with the circus. I am also a Jew."

I am stunned into silence. I had not imagined that Astrid could be Jewish, though with her dark hair and eyes it made sense.

I exhale, thanking God in that moment that I had not told her everything about my past and the German soldier. Something had held me back. And it is for the best, because surely if I had she would have thrown me out.

"I was the youngest of five children in our family's circus," she adds. "Our winter quarters were adjacent to Herr Neuhoff's." I remember the dark, abandoned house over the hill that Astrid had eyed as we traveled back and forth between the women's lodge and practice hall. "I'd left it to marry Erich and live in Berlin." I glance at Peter out of the corner of my eye, wondering if it is hard for him to hear about the man Astrid loved before. "He was a senior officer at Reich headquarters." A Jew, married to a high-ranking Nazi. I try to imagine what that life had been like for her. I've been training alongside Astrid for weeks, feeling as though I had come to know her. But now a whole different person seems to appear before my eyes.

She continues, "When I came back to Darmstadt, my family had disappeared. Herr Neuhoff took me in. Ingrid is my birth name. We changed it so no one would know." It's hard to imagine anyone rejecting her. An image of my father standing at the door to my bedroom ordering me to leave appears in my mind. All of the old pain that I have worked so hard to push aside these many months wells up as fresh and awful as the day it happened.

"What about your family?" I ask, fearing the answer.

"Gone." Her eyes are hollow and sad.

"You don't know that," Peter says gently, placing his arm around her. This time, she does not turn away, but rests her head on his shoulder for comfort.

"It was winter when I came back and they should have been here," Astrid says numbly. She shakes her head. "They would not have been able to go far enough to outrun the Germans. No, it is only me. I still see their faces, though." She lifts her chin. "Don't pity me," she says. How could I possibly? She is so strong and beautiful and brave.

"Does this happen often?" I gesture in the direction in which the police had gone.

"More than enough. It's fine, really. There have been inspections from time to time. Sometimes the police come through to make sure we are in compliance with code. Mostly it has just been a shakedown and Herr Neuhoff gives them a few marks to be on their way."

Peter shakes his head grimly. "This was different. SS—and they were looking for you."

Her face grows somber. "Yes."

"We have to go," Peter says, his face stony. Though I have seen him rehearse, it is impossible to imagine the dark, brooding man bringing levity to a crowd. "Leave Germany." His words come in staccato bursts, breath urgent. He is thinking of Astrid—she needs to be out of the country, immediately, just as surely as I must get Theo to safety.

"A few more weeks," she says, soothing him.

"Then we'll be in France," I offer.

"You think France is so much better?" Peter demands.

"It won't be, really," Astrid explains, answering for me. "Once we might have found some safety in the Zone Libre. But no more." In the early years of the war, Vichy had not technically been occupied. But the Germans had all but done away with the puppet regime two years ago, taking control of the rest of the country.

"I need to go speak with Herr Neuhoff," Peter says. "Astrid, you'll be all right?" Though he speaks to Astrid, he looks at me, as if asking me to care for her.

I hesitate. I am desperate to go check on Theo and make sure the Germans had not seen him. But I cannot leave Astrid alone. "Come," I urge, reaching out my hand. "I've got some questions about what we practiced today and a sore ankle that needs taping." I make it sound as though I need her help instead.

"Here," I say, taking the now-soiled cloth from her once Peter has gone. I return the cloth to the bucket where I had found it, kneeling to rinse it and wring it out. When I straighten, Astrid is staring out the window across the valley. I wonder if she is thinking of the SS coming or her family or both. "Are you all right?" I ask.

"I'm sorry," she replies. "What I did to you was wrong."

It takes a moment before I realize she is talking about the trapeze earlier, pushing me. With all that has happened, I had nearly forgotten. "I understand now. You didn't want me to be afraid."

She shakes her head. "Only a fool is not afraid. We need fear to keep our edge. I wanted you to know the worst that would happen so you could be prepared and make sure it does not. My father did the same thing to me—when I was four." I try to grasp the idea of someone pushing a toddler off a platform forty feet in the air. Anywhere else it would be a crime. But here it was training, accepted.

"Do you have a trunk?" Astrid asks, changing subjects. I shake my head. I had left Bensheim with nothing and have only the bits of clothing she had gathered for Theo and me. "Well, we'll have to get you one… That is, if you'll stay?" There is fear in her eyes and a kind of vulnerability that had not been there before—or perhaps I had not seen it. "We can't perform on the flying trapeze without a third aerialist. And I must perform." With the Germans having come, the tables seem to have turned and she is begging me now, needing me for the act in a way I might have not imagined possible. I hesitate, considering my response.

Later that night, I lie awake. Astrid, who had not gone to Peter for the first night since my arrival, snores beside me. I think about all that she's been through. We had both been cast out by people we loved, me by my parents, her by her husband. And we both lost our families. Perhaps we are not so very different after all.

But Astrid is a Jew. I shiver, feeling the danger that is so much worse for her than it is for me. In a thousand years, I would never have imagined it. I reach for her arm, as if checking to make sure she is still here and safe. I suppose I should not have been surprised to learn the truth about her. In wartime we all have a past, don't we, even a baby like Theo? Everyone needs to hide the truth and reinvent himself in order to survive.

Unable to sleep, I slip out from beneath Theo and climb from bed. I tiptoe past Astrid and out of the lodge, crossing the field in the cold darkness. The ground beneath my feet crackles, crisp with frost. Inside the practice hall, the air is thick with rosin and dry sweat. I look up at the trapeze. But I do not dare to practice alone.

Instead, I walk into the dressing room, staring at the spot where Astrid had hidden. What had it been like for her? I slip out the back door of the dressing room into the cold night air once more, then walk to the cellar door and pull at it. The latch sticks and I marvel that Astrid had been able to put herself in the tiny space so quickly. I cannot open it. My heart pounds. Suddenly it is as if I am running for my life from the Germans, about to get caught.

The door swings open and I climb inside. Then I shut the door and I lie in the darkness. The space is long and shallow, with enough room for only one person to lie flat. And perhaps a child. Could we hide Theo here with Astrid if the police came again? He might cry out. A baby, though smaller, is not as easy to hide. I inhale the air, which is choked with the fetid smell of decay.

My mind reels back to earlier when Astrid had asked me to stay with the circus. I had not answered right away. My burden seemed heavier for knowing her secret and I could not help but wonder whether Theo and I would be safer on our own.

Then I saw it, the pleading look in her eyes, needing help but not wanting to ask. "I'll stay," I promised. I could not abandon her now.

"Good," she replied, with more relief in her voice than she surely intended. "We need you more than ever." The words seemed to stick a bit in her throat. "We'll begin again tomorrow." She turned and walked away. Remembering now, I realize she had not thanked me.

It does not matter, though. Astrid needs me, and in this moment lying in her place beneath the ground, I will do anything to save her.

7

Astrid

Out of Germany. Finally.

As the flat-roofed border station recedes in the darkness, my entire body slumps with relief. I lie back down beside Peter on the double-wide berth that takes up most of his quarters on the train. He snores lightly, mumbles something in his sleep.

It has been more than a month since the SS officers had come to the training hall in Darmstadt, asking questions about a Jew performing with the circus. We had rehearsed for it of course, the possibility that I would have to hide, plotting the possible distractions, calculating how many steps it would take me to get to the cellar from various locations, the effort it would require for me to pull up the heavy wood trapdoor. We'd even had a code word planned: if Herr Neuhoff or Peter or one of the others told me to "go fishing," I was to head for the cellar; "go camping" meant to flee the fairgrounds entirely. But we had been caught off guard when the SS came and I'd barely made it out the back door before they stormed into the training hall. It was just as well—there was nothing that could have prepared me for lying motion-less underground in that cold, dark space. Suffocated beneath the ground was the furthest thing from the freedom I felt when I flew through the air. It was death.

Remembering now, I press closer to Peter, soaking in his solidness and warmth. Who had told the police there was a Jew with the circus? I had scarcely gone beyond the winter quarters when we were not on the road, but perhaps a delivery person or other visitor had spied me and caught on. Or had it been one of our own? I eyed the other performers or workers differently after that day, wondering who might not want me around. No one could be trusted. Except Peter, of course. And Noa. She has as much to lose as I do—maybe more.

The SS had not come to the winter quarters again in the weeks before we went on the road. But I'd nevertheless been on edge ever since. The days passed slowly before our departure, each with its own threat of detection. The danger became real after that in a way it hadn't quite been before.

Erich appears improbably in my mind. What would the *obergruppenführer* think of his wife, hiding from his colleagues beneath the earth like a hunted animal? I see his face more vividly than I had in months, and wonder how he had explained my departure to our friends and neighbors. *Off to visit a sick family member,* I could hear him say in the smooth voice I'd once so loved. Or maybe no one asked at all. Had he stayed in the apartment, still smelling my scent and using the things that once were ours, or worse yet, brought another woman there? He might have moved. Erich was not one to linger on the past.

Beside me Peter stirs and I push away my thoughts of Erich guiltily. As Peter rolls toward me I feel his need for me through the fabric of our nightclothes. His hands reach for me, find the edge of my nightdress. It is often this way in the middle of the night. More than once I have awoken to find him already inside me, ready and primal. Once I might have minded; now I am grateful for the bluntness of his desire, which comes without the pretext of romance.

I climb astride Peter, naked beneath my nightdress, and press my palms against the warmth of his chest, inhaling the air mixed with liquor and tobacco and sweat. Then I rock slowly and methodically with the rhythm of the train. Peter reaches up and cups my chin, drawing my gaze down to his. Usually he keeps his eyes closed, lost as if in another world. But he is staring deeply at me now in a way he has not before. It is as if he is trying to solve a mystery or unlock some sort of door. The intensity of his eyes releases something in me. I begin to move more quickly, needing more as the heat of our connection deep inside me grows. Peter's hands are on my hips, guiding me. His eyes roll backward. As my passion crests in that silent, practiced way, I collapse forward and bite his shoulder to stifle my cries so they do not echo through the railcars.

Then I roll onto the berth beside Peter. His fingers are knotted in my hair and he murmurs softly to himself in Russian. He clings to me tightly, kissing my forehead, cheeks, chin. His passion sated now, his touch is gentle and his gaze warm.

Peter falls into an instant slumber, one arm flung over his head in a gesture replicating surrender, the other heavy across my chest. He sleeps fitfully, though, tossing and fighting a battle beneath eyelids that never quite still. I wonder what he sees, a chapter from a book I have never read. I run my hand soothingly over him until he quiets.

We became lovers the previous summer on the road. At first we would spend evenings sitting by the fire in the backyard behind the big top long after the others had gone to bed. Only later came the nights together like this one, finding warmth and company with each other. There is sadness in him, a tragedy about which I do not dare ask. Sometimes it is as if in his feverish movements he is trying to reclaim the past. I have not told him details about my years away from the circus with Erich either. Life with Peter is about the here and now. We are with each other just to be—a relationship based neither on a shared past nor future promises that we might not be able to keep. The part of me that might have wished for more from a man died the day I left Berlin.

I stare up at the ceiling beams that rock back and forth with the movement of the train. The previous morning we'd arisen before dawn. The load-in had begun hours earlier, an endless array of boxcars emblazoned with the circus logo, filled with boxes and tent poles. The workers had been up all night and their cigarette smoke and sweat seemed to encircle the train in great rings. The animals went last just before us, blanket-covered elephants urged inch by inch up ramps, big-cat cages painstakingly rolled onto the cars. "Eee!" Theo cried as he spied the last of the elephants being shoved in, four workers pushing against its massive backside. I had to smile. To us circus folk, even the children, the exotic beasts had become commonplace. When was the last time anyone here had marveled at an elephant?

Peter has a private compartment, half a railcar, cordoned off with a makeshift wall. It is nothing compared with the luxury in which my family had traveled: we'd had two carriages, our own beds, private bath and dining table, almost a miniature house on rails. Of course, that had been the heyday of the circus, the golden era.

I touch my right ear reflexively, feeling for the gold earring that had been my mother's, running my fingertip over the small, uneven ruby. There has been no sign of my family since my return to Darmstadt. My hope of hearing word of them when I went on the road with the Circus Neuhoff the previous year had failed. I could not ask anyone directly lest they make the connection between me and my true identity. And when I made casual references in the cities where we had once performed, people just said that the Klemt circus had not come that year. I'd even sent a letter to Herr Fein, the booking agent in Frankfurt who had arranged the tour for my family's circus in the larger cities, hoping that perhaps he would know where my family had gone. But it had returned with a scrawl across the front: *Unzestellbar.* Undeliverable.

Shadows race past along the wall of the carriage. We've been on the train for thirty hours, longer than we should have been but for the detours around where stretches of track have been damaged or destroyed. The train sat motionless for hours somewhere close to the border while British warplanes roared overhead and bombs fell so close that they shook our bags from the racks. But now we amble easily across the rolling countryside.

My eyes start to grow heavy, lulled by the rocking of the train and the warmth of passion Peter and I had just shared. I draw his blanket around me as cold air seeps through the cracked window. It's too cold to be on the road. The railcars are poorly heated, the cabins at the fairgrounds meant for summer.

The program had been set, though. We had started out on the first Thursday in April as we had the previous year. Once the circus would have gone where the money was plentiful, the wine-soaked valleys of the Loire and wealthy villages of Rhône-Alpes. Now we perform where we are permitted, a schedule the Germans set. That the Reich has agreed the circus may continue still all these years is no small thing. They trot us through occupied France as if to say, "See, life is still normal. How bad can it all be if such fun still exists?" But we represent everything Hitler hates: the freaks and oddities in a regime that is all about conformity. They will not permit us to go on forever.

The train slows, screeches to a halt. I sit upright, disentangling myself from Peter's arm. Though we had crossed the border into France hours earlier, checkpoints might come at any time. I jump up, fumbling for my *ausweis* and other documents. We begin to move again, the slowdown temporary. I sit on the edge of the bed, my heart still pounding. We are close to the line that once divided Vichy from Occupied France. Though both are now controlled by the Reich, there will surely still be an inspection of the train. When—not if—the guards come, I want to be one among a dozen girls in the sleeper car, not in Peter's cabin, risking more scrutiny of my identity and papers than if I simply blend in with the others.

I climb from the bed, dressing quickly in the icy air. Tiptoeing quietly so as not to wake Peter, I slip into the next car, secondhand and frayed and stale-smelling, where the girls sleep, berths stacked atop each other three high. Despite the cramped quarters, there are real linens, not bedrolls. Beneath the bunks small steamer trunks are lined up neatly, one for each of us.

Noa sleeps on one of the low bunks, clutching the baby to her chest like a stuffed animal. Her face seems even younger in slumber, unlike the night she had come to us. She is *backfisch*, my mother would have said, on the verge of womanhood. Watching her embrace Theo, something tugs inside me. We had both been abandoned, exiled in our own way from the lives we had known.

But this is no time for sentimentality. Whether she will

be able to perform as we need her to—that is the only thing that matters. As an aerialist, it is not enough to be technically good. It is personality, flair, the ability to make the audience hold its breath, as if fearing for their own lives right along with ours. Similarly, mere appearance and personality would not suffice—even the most beautiful woman would not survive a season on the circuit without the pure physical grace, agility and strength to back it up.

Noa has surprised me so far. I had thought she would give up after the first day, that she would never fly. I had not counted on her gymnastics training, though, or her tenacity. She has worked hard and she is smart and capable. And brave—her rescuing Theo from the Nazi car had more than proved that. She's as good as she can possibly be, though it will all hang on whether she can perform under the lights in front of hundreds of people two and three times per day.

Another girl has taken the berth where I was meant to have slept, so I squeeze into the narrow strip of berth beside Noa. But I cannot sleep. Instead I rehearse our opening performance that evening, marking the movements in my mind.

Beside me Noa stirs and shifts in a slow, practiced way so as not to wake Theo. "Are we there yet?"

"Soon. A few more hours." We lie beside each other, our sides bumping gently as the train sways.

"Talk to me," she says, her voice hollow with loneliness.

I hesitate, not sure what she wants to hear. "I was born in a railcar just like this one," I offer. I feel her surprise through the darkness. "My mother stepped from the stage and had me." Only my father's protest, the story went, had kept her from returning to the show immediately after.

"What was it like growing up in the circus?" With Noa, questions seem to endlessly beget more questions. She is so curious to know and learn it all.

I contemplate my answer. I hated circus life when I was younger. I longed for a normal childhood, the permanency of staying in one place and having a real home. To be able to own more things than could fit in a single steamer trunk. Even at our winter quarters during the months when I was allowed to go to school, I was different from the other girls, an outsider and an oddity.

When Erich appeared, it was the escape I'd been looking for my whole life. I tried to dress the part, mold my accent so I sounded like the other officers' wives. But long after we settled down in Berlin, something was still missing. The apartment was empty, without the sounds and smells of the winter quarters. I missed the noise and excitement of performing on the road. How could people live in one place all of the time and not get bored? I loved Erich and after a while my longing began to fade like a not-quite-healed scar. But I remained haunted by the world I had always wanted to escape. My life with Erich, I see now, had been temporary, like another act in one of our shows. When it ended, I had not shed a tear. Rather, I simply changed costumes and moved on.

I do not tell Noa any of this, though; it is not what she wants to hear. "Once when I was a girl we performed for a princess," I say instead. "In Austria-Hungary. The entire tent was filled with her court."

"Really?" Her voice is awe-filled. I nod. Empresses are gone now, replaced by parliaments and votes. Better for the people, perhaps, but somehow less magical. Would the circus fade into history, as well? Though no one speaks of it, I sometimes wonder if we are marching toward extinction with each performance, too busy dancing and flying through the air to see it.

I open the locket around my neck, revealing in the moonlight a tiny photo of my family, the only one I have. "My mother," I say. She was a great beauty—at least before Isadore had been killed and she had taken to the bottle—magnificent where I am plain, her features Romanesque. "Once, before I was born, the circus traveled to Saint Petersburg and she performed for Czar Nicholas. He was enchanted by her and they said the czarina actually wept. I'm only a fraction of what she was in the air."

"I can't imagine anyone better," Noa declares too loudly and the girl sleeping on the berth above us snorts in her sleep. Theo stirs and threatens to wake. As I pat his back to soothe him, I wonder if Noa is trying to curry favor with me, but the admiration in her voice sounds sincere.

"It's true. She was a legend." The only two women in a family of males, I would have thought my mother and I would have been closer. She loved me completely but there was a part of her that I could never reach.

"You and Erich," Noa asks, and I bristle at the familiarity with which she uses his name. "You never had children?" I am surprised, then annoyed by the unexpected change of topic. She has a way of finding the weak spot, going for the question I can least bear to answer.

I shake my head. "We couldn't." I've wondered so often whether Erich would have fought harder to keep me if there had been a baby. But our child would have been Jewish in the eyes of the Reich—would he have disowned us both? He might have children now—and a new wife, for although I had not signed the divorce papers, the Reich did not acknowledge that our marriage ever existed.

"And then when you returned to the circus, you fell in love with Peter?" Noa asks.

"No," I reply quickly. "It isn't like that at all. Peter and I are together. Don't make it more than it is."

I feel the train begin to slow. I sit up, wondering if it is my imagination. But the wheels screech as the train stops with a groan. Another checkpoint. Herr Neuhoff procured papers for everyone, even Theo. But they are still not the real thing and at each stop, I am filled with dread. Will they be good enough? Surely Herr Neuhoff had spared no expense in making sure they looked authentic. It would take only one border guard with a sharp eye, though, to notice some detail that was not right. A rock forms on my chest, making it impossible to breathe.

There is a knock outside the railcar. The door flings open and a border guard steps into the carriage, not waiting for a response. He shines a light around the car, holding it longer than is necessary on the bodies of the girls stirring from sleep. He works his way down the berths, checking each identity card in a perfunctory manner before moving on to the next. I exhale slightly. Perhaps this will be straightforward after all.

Then he reaches us. *"Kennkarte. Ausweis."* I pass him my documents, along with those that Noa hands me. I hold my breath and count, waiting for him to hand them back. One, two…

Then he takes them and walks from the train.

I bite my lip so I don't cry out in protest. "What just happened?" Noa asks, her voice panicked and confused.

I do not answer. Something, some detail of one of our identity cards, had given us away, belied the fact that they were fakes. Easy, I think, forcing myself to breathe normally so as not to panic Noa. The others are eyeing us nervously now. Noa slips her damp hand into mine, trusting as a child. I brace myself, waiting for the guard to return and drag us from the car.

"Your shoes," I whisper urgently.

"What?" Noa tenses, her nails digging into my damp palm.

"Put them on. If they should take us..." I stop, not finishing as she begins to shake. It is essential that we appear calm when the guard returns.

But he does not come. Five minutes pass, then ten, my dread worsening by the second. Had he gone for the other guards? How I need Peter here with me. Noa squeezes my fingers once, then holds fast, not letting go. The train car rocks and starts to move.

"Our papers," Noa whispers, her voice growing louder with urgency. "They're gone."

"Shh." We are still on the train. We have not been arrested. But we are continuing on without our papers, which is almost as bad.

A moment later, Herr Neuhoff appears at the door of the carriage and gestures to me. "Here," he says when I reach him. In his thick fingers he holds all of our documents. A strange look crosses his face and I wonder how much he had to bribe the guard to look the other way and not ask too many questions.

As the train picks up speed there is a collective exhale, the whole carriage seeming to relax at once. Everyone is awake now and the girls rise and dress, jostling into one another in the cramped, swaying space. Outside, the sky is lightening, pink behind the dark silhouette of a terraced vineyard, capped by a crumbling church.

Sometime later, one of the kitchen workers appears at the end of the carriage, passing out a breakfast of cold bread and cheese. The countryside begins to thin, farmhouses dotting the fields more frequently. Children peer curiously from the windows of houses and run along the tracks as our brightly painted train cars pass, hoping to catch a glimpse of the animals.

We continue on in silence, traveling over an aqueduct,

and a valley unfurls, revealing a red-roofed village beneath stone castle ruins, ringed by fields of withered brush. Mossy-roofed cottages dot the hillside. They are punctuated by the occasional chateau or church with a crumbling belfry, alabaster stone walls warmed by the sun now high in the sky.

A ripple of excitement runs through the coach. Almost there. "We have to get ready for the parade," I tell Noa.

"Parade?" Noa asks, her brow furrowing.

I sigh inwardly, reminding myself how much she still does not know. "Yes, after we arrive we will get off the train and immediately parade through town on carriages. We offer a preview to get the locals excited about the show."

I watch her face as she processes this new bit of information, looking for signs of nervousness or fear. But she simply nods, then sets Theo down so she can dress.

The girls begin to primp as well as they can in the cramped space, applying rouge and blackening their eyebrows. "Here." I pull a pink sequined dress from my trunk and pass it to Noa. She looks around, still embarrassed to change in front of the others. But there is nowhere to go, so she slips it on, nearly stumbling in her haste.

"Will they even come see us?" Noa asks. "The French, I mean? Surely to them we are still German…"

"I thought the same thing the first year after the war began," I reply. "Not to worry. The people still love the show. The circus has no borders." The audiences do not see the show as German, and they come faithfully each year.

The train wheels grind to a halt as we near the station. We do not get out right away, but continue preparing as the wagons, which had gone ahead or been leased locally, assemble out front. The animals are unloaded first, their cages placed on wheeled platforms. We shuffle toward the exit, the space becoming cramped and the midday air warm as we await our cue.

At last the door to the carriage is flung open and cool, fresh air wafts in. The station is nearly as packed as the railcar had been, dozens of spectators pressed close, waiting to welcome the circus to town. Flashbulbs pop from cameras in rapid succession. After the quiet of the train the chaos is jarring, like someone turning on the lights too quickly in the nighttime. I stop midstep, causing the girl behind me to bump into my back. I am filled with doubt, unable to move. Usually I love the open road, but suddenly I long for Darmstadt where I know every inch of the land—and where I have a place to hide. Going on the road last year as if it were not wartime was hard enough. Now I have the added burden of making sure that Noa can perform, that she and Theo are kept safe. How can I possibly carry on?

"Astrid?" Noa says in her timid voice. I turn to her. She watches me nervously, uncertain what to do.

I push past my doubts, and take her hand. "Come," I say and together we step from the train.

Scanning the crowd, I see a look in the eyes of the people, not of scorn but of admiration and hope brought by our arrival. Adults watch us with the wonder of children. The circus had always brought light to the places it visited. Now it is a lifeline. I lift my chin. If we can still give them this, then the circus is not dead. There have been circuses from the times of the Romans and Greeks, our traditions centuries old. We had survived the Middle Ages, the Napoleonic Wars, the Great War. We would survive this, too.

8

Astrid

We make our way across the station platform. The horses, which have been hitched to the beast wagons, stomp their feet impatiently, snorting steam from flared nostrils. In the cages they pull, the lions and lone tiger are on full display. There are camels, too, and a small brown bear, standing alongside the procession on a leash. Last year, we had a zebra, but it died over the winter and Herr Neuhoff had not been able to replace it.

Slowly the parade begins to move, snaking forward toward the village, a spray of faded slate rooftops cast into a hillside with a medieval cathedral at the top watching over it all. Not so very different from the dozens of villages I've seen on the road over the years. Once the circus had moved more swiftly, a town a day, setting up and performing two or three times before taking down the *chapiteau* and moving on at night. But the train lines have slowed us now and the Germans restrict where we can go. So the bookings are chosen more strategically, places where we can camp for a week and draw spectators from the surrounding villages, like spokes on a wheel. Or can we? Noa's earlier doubts echo in my mind. It has been more than four years of suffering and hardship here. It seems if the war drags on much longer, the people will simply stop coming.

The incline grows steeper and the procession slows as the horses strain against the weight of the wagons. Alongside the roadside there is a small cemetery; a tangle of headstones sits embedded in the side of the hill. At last we reach the edge of Thiers, a tangle of narrow streets lined by three- and four-story houses pressed close, seeming to lean on one another for support. At the top of the high street, the din of the awaiting crowd grows and the air crackles with excitement. A trumpet blares as the parade begins, heralding our arrival. Our open carriage, adorned with streamers and drawn by horses in jeweled headdresses, is near the front, ahead of the lions' wagon with the trainer riding atop. The grandeur and bright colors of our procession glare against the withered facades of the buildings. The streets are unchanged from the villages in past years. But for the red flags with swastikas hanging from a few buildings, it would be possible to imagine we are not at war.

We move painstakingly through town, wagons inching forward. Boys wave and catcall at us from the crowd. Beside me, Noa stiffens in response to the adulation, clutching Theo more tightly. I pat her arm reassuringly. To me this is normal, but she must feel so naked and exposed. "Smile," I say through my clenched teeth. It is a show from the very moment we step out.

On a wrought-iron second-story balcony, I notice a boy, or a man perhaps, nineteen or twenty at most. He does not join in the cheering and waving, but watches us with a mix of disinterest and amusement, arms folded. He is handsome, though, with wavy charcoal hair and a chiseled jaw. I imagine that his eyes, were I close enough to see their color, would be cobalt. Something on our wagon catches his gaze. I start to do my best show wave. It is not me he is watching, though, but Noa. For a second I consider pointing him out to her, but I do not want to make her even more nervous. A second later, he is gone.

The cobblestone street narrows so that the parade presses close to the onlookers. Hands shoot out, small children eager to touch us, the spectacle, in ways that simply would have been rude with anyone else. They cannot reach us, though, and for that I am grateful. The faces in the crowd are different this year, eyes weary from the war, skin drawn more tightly across the cheekbones. But we are changed, too. Closer one might see the cracks, the animals a bit too skinny, performers using a bit of extra rouge to cover fatigue.

The spectators follow the parade down the winding lane toward the market square, then onto another road that leads out of town once more. Though the incline is gentler than it had been on our ascent, the road is bumpy and uneven, marred with ruts and potholes. I put a hand across Noa and Theo as we are jostled so they do not fall from the bench. I might have suggested that she leave Theo with Elsie or one of the other workers; a baby has no place in a parade. But I knew that Noa would be nervous and draw comfort from having him with her. I study the child. He does not seem scared by the noise and crowd. Instead he leans comfortably against Noa with his head cocked, seeming entertained by the commotion.

A few kilometers farther, the pavement gives way to dirt. Noa takes in the crowd that runs behind. "They're still following us," she says. "I thought they might have lost interest."

"Never," I reply. The onlookers keep up tirelessly. Women jostle babies and children pedal alongside on their bikes, their

Sunday suits turning brown with dirt kicked up from the road. Even barking dogs join the melee, becoming a part of the parade themselves.

A few minutes later the road ends at a wide, flat grass field, broken only by a cluster of trees at one end. The wagon halts with an unceremonious bump. I climb down first, then reach out to help Noa. But she looks past me, eyes wide. The raising of the big top is almost as much of an attraction as the circus show itself, and not only because it is free. An army of workers with tents and metal poles and rope have fanned out over the field. The circus needs more hands than we can possibly bring with us, which is good news for the local men who are looking for work. They stand, bare-armed and perspiring, at the periphery of the flattened tarp, which covers the entire field, tied to stakes that surround it.

"I feel useless just standing here," Noa says after climbing down from the wagon. "Should we be helping or something?"

I shake my head. "Let them do their job." We can no more help raise the tent than the workers can swing from the trapeze.

All of the prep work is done but the real show has been saved for the crowd. Elephants, which had not been part of the procession but brought here directly by the train, are harnessed. On command, they start walking away from the center, heaving the *hauptmast* to its full height. Then the horses are led outward, pulling the shorter poles into place, and the whole thing seems to rise like a phoenix from the ashes, a tent the size of the massive gymnasium at Darmstadt where seconds ago there had been nothing. Though they have undoubtedly seen it year after year, the crowd lets out a stunned gasp and applauds heartily. Noa watches silently, awed by seeing the big top go up for the first time. Theo, who had been chewing on his fingers, squeals with approval.

The crowd begins to dissipate as the workers move to secure the poles. "Come," I say, starting in the direction of the big top. "We need to practice."

Noa does not move, but looks hesitantly from me to the child and back again. "We've been on the road for almost two days," she complains.

"I'm aware," I reply, growing impatient. "But we only have a few hours before we get ready for the first show. You have to rehearse at least once in the big top before then."

"Theo needs to be fed and I'm exhausted." Her voice rises to almost a whine and I am reminded yet again of just how young she is. I remember just for a second what it was like to want to do something else, to look through the window of the practice hall and see girls skipping rope in the valley and wish that I could join them.

"All right," I relent. "Take fifteen minutes. Go get him settled with Elsie. I'll meet you in the big top."

I expect her to protest again but she does not. Her face breaks into a wide smile of gratitude, as though given a great gift. "Thank you," she says, and as she carries Theo in the direction of the train, I look back over my shoulder toward the big top. Acquiescing was not entirely for Noa's benefit. The workers are still tightening the poles; the trapeze is not quite ready. And she will rehearse better if she can concentrate on flying, instead of worrying about Theo.

As Noa disappears into the train, my doubts rise anew. Since she first let go and flew last month, she has grown stronger in her training. But she is still so inexperienced. Will she hold up day after day in front of the lights and the scrutiny of the crowd?

I walk into the big top, inhaling the moist earth and damp

wood. This is one of my favorite moments each season, when everything at the circus is fresh and new. Other performers, jugglers and a few contortionists, have trickled in, working on their own acts. Peter is not here and I wonder if he is rehearsing privately, out of view, so as not to be rebuked for the political act Herr Neuhoff forbade him from performing.

Peter had mentioned it a few days earlier. "Herr Neuhoff is trying to persuade me to water down the act, bury it."

"I know," I replied. "He spoke to me about it, as well."

"What do you think?" Peter was normally so self-assured. But his face was troubled and I could see he really did not know what to do.

It was only because of me that he was considering acquiescing at all. "Don't stop yourself on my account." I did not want Peter to have to sacrifice his art for me and resent me after.

Now the workers have just finished securing the trapeze. The foreman, Kurt, has them do this before the seats and other apparatuses, knowing that I will want to practice right away. I walk to where he is conferring with two laborers about the angle at which the benches are to be set. "Has the ground been leveled?" I ask. He nods. It matters a great deal for the trapeze. The slightest unevenness in the earth could affect the speed at which we fly and destroy the precision of our routine—causing me to miss catching Noa.

I walk to one of the ladders and give it a firm tug to make sure it is secure. Then I climb up to the fly board. From below comes the murmur of some of the dancers, chatting as they stretch. I leap without hesitating. The air rushes beneath me and I stretch forth. As always in this moment I feel sixteen again, the sound of my family's laughter ringing in my ears as I fly. When I first came back to the circus, I wondered if the time away would have made me slower, if I could remember the moves. I was in my late thirties, perhaps too old for this. Others by now had retired to teaching or marriage or seedy cabarets in Dresden or Hamburg. But the air was all I had known. I was good at it still. Why shouldn't I keep going? In a few weeks my body thinned, the richness of those long dinners in Berlin melting from my midsection, and I was as good as I had ever been—better even, Herr Neuhoff remarked once. I could not tell him that I flew higher and flipped harder to reach a place in the dark eaves of the big top where I could hear my brothers' laughter, and where Erich's rejection could no longer find me.

As I swing back up to the board a few minutes later, the chatter of the performers below stops abruptly and the tent grows quiet. Noa stands at the entrance to the big top, looking young and scared. The other performers eye her warily. They have not been awful in the weeks since she joined us, but they've been distant, making clear that she does not belong. It is always hard for new performers at the circus. Indeed, they had hardly welcomed me with open arms when I returned. And it is even more difficult for someone like Noa, who is seen as not qualified, too inexperienced to succeed.

But am I any better? I wonder. I, too, had treated Noa coldly in the beginning, wished that she would go. Though I have accepted her since the police came to Darmstadt, I have viewed her as a necessity, part of the act. I have not done anything to make her truly welcome.

Suddenly guilty, I climb down the ladder to her. I ignore the others, willing her to do the same. "Are you ready?" Noa does not answer but looks around the tent. To me this is normal, almost all I have known. But I see it as she does now: the cavernous space, rows of seats being assembled endlessly after one another.

I take her hand and stare hard at the others until they look

away. "Come. The ladders are looser here than in the practice hall. And everything shakes a bit more." I keep talking as
we climb, partly to ease her nerves and partly because there
are things—important things—she needs to know about
the differences between Darmstadt and the big top. After a
lifetime I can perform anywhere—the scenery fades and it
is just me and the bar and the air. For Noa, though, every
little detail could make a difference.

"Let's start with something simple," I say, but there is terror in her eyes as she gazes downward. She is going to fold.
"Pretend they aren't there."

She takes the bar with shaking hands and jumps. At first
she is jerky, reminiscent of her first day on the trapeze. "Feel
for it," I urge, willing her to remember all I have taught her.
As she falls into the familiar forward-and-back rhythm, her
movements smooth.

"Good," I say as she returns to the board. I have been spar-
ing with my compliments, not wanting to make her com-
placent. But now I offer more than usual, hoping to bolster
her confidence. She smiles, drinking in my praise like water.
"Now let's practice your release."

Noa looks as if she wants to protest. I have no confidence
that she is ready to do it here, but we have no choice. I go
to the other ladder and climb to the catch trap, nodding at
Gerda, who has been loitering with a few of the acrobats.
She starts up the ladder behind Noa with disinterest. I study
Gerda warily. She is no more welcoming to Noa than the
other performers, but practical enough to tolerate her because we need her for the act.

As Noa nears the top of the opposite ladder, her foot slips
and she nearly falls. "Easy," I call from my board. Though I
mean it as reassuring, it comes out sounding like a rebuke.
From below come laughs from the other performers, as their

suspicions about Noa's lack of skill have been confirmed. Even from a distance, I can see her eyes begin to water.

Then her back stiffens and she nods. Noa jumps with more force than I have seen from her. "Hup!" I call.

She releases with surprising precision for her first time in the big top. Our hands lock. Once there would have been a coach on the ground to give the commands, and men to do the catching. But with so many gone to war, we have only ourselves now. My brother Jules had been my catcher. Until these past few weeks of training Noa, I had not fully appreciated his strength and skill.

As we swing back, I release her in the direction of the bar, which Gerda has sent out. With every pass, Noa's movements become stronger. She is performing in spite of—no because of—the skepticism of the other performers. Grudgingly the expressions below turn to respect. My hope rises. Noa has earned their respect and she will earn the audience's, too.

"Bravo!" a voice calls out from below. But the tone is mocking. Noa, who is on the return, nearly misses the far board. Gerda reaches out and grabs her before she falls. I look down. Emmet is holding a mop high in the air, mocking Noa.

I climb down the ladder angrily. "You fool!" I hiss.

"She's not an aerialist," Emmet replies with exaggerated patience, as though speaking to a small child. "She was a cleaner at the station in Bensheim. That's all she's qualified to do." Emmet, I know now, has been stirring up ill will among the other performers, encouraging them not to accept Noa. He has always needed to pick on others to hide his own weakness. But how had he found out she worked at the station? Surely he does not know the rest of Noa's past.

"Why now?" I demand. "The show is in an hour. We need her ready and you are undermining her confidence."

"Because I didn't actually think we would go through with this farce," he replies. Or that she would be able to do it, I add silently. A part of him, I suspect, is jealous. Noa has been able to manage mightily with just weeks of practice, whereas he has been here a lifetime with no talent to show for it. But it seems unwise to point this out to him now. "This needs to work, Emmet," I say slowly.

"For your sake," he sneers.

"For all of our sakes," I correct.

Noa, who has come down the ladder, watches from a distance. She has heard enough, I know, to be uncomfortable. There is a flash in her eyes as she expects to be rejected yet again. How is it possible after all that she has been through that she can still let people hurt her?

She stands on one side of me, the rest of the performers on the other. I am an island, caught in between.

I take a step in her direction. "We need Noa," I say firmly and loudly enough for the others to hear. It is a calculated risk; I need the good graces of the circus folk as much as she does in order to maintain my identity and hide. No one responds. But I've gone too far to back down now. "In any case, I am with her and anyone who isn't is against me." Noa's face folds with disbelief, as if it is the first time that someone has stood up for her.

The others scatter to rehearse. "Come, let's go get ready for the show," I say, taking her hand and leading her from the big top.

"You shouldn't have done that," Noa says when we are outside. Though we are well out of earshot of the others, her voice is barely a whisper. "You have to think of your own safety."

"Nonsense." I wave my hand dismissively, though in fact

she is right. "You must harden yourself to the impressions of others."

"And what do you think?" Her voice is breathy. Despite what I have just told her, I can tell she cares about my opinion more than just about anything. "Do you think I am ready?"

I hesitate. I think she needs another year of training. I think that, even then, she might not be able to do it, because the lights and a thousand eyes upon you change everything.

I think that we do not have a choice. "Yes," I lie, unable to look at the brightness of her smile. And together we go prepare to perform.

9

Noa

I follow Astrid away from the big top. Outside, spectators still mingle, buying tickets at a hastily erected kiosk and watching the workers put up the smaller tents. Crew bosses shout orders, their hoarse voices mixed with the clanging of hammers driving metal spikes into hard earth.

"Thank you," I say, referring once more to what had just happened with the other performers. Once I thought Astrid would never accept me. But she stuck up for me—and she thinks I can do this.

She waves her hand dismissively. "We can't worry about any of that now. We must prepare for the show. It starts in an hour."

"So soon?" I ask.

"It's after four." I had not realized it had gotten that late, or that the parade and tent raising had taken so long. "We begin at six. Earlier than we otherwise would have because of the curfew. We need to get ready."

"I thought we already did." I look down at the dress she

had loaned me an hour earlier on the train, so tight that my parents would have a fit if they saw me in it.

Ignoring my last remark, Astrid leads me across the crowded field to where the train has come to a rest at the end of the tracks. "The fairgrounds were built close to the tracks so we can sleep in the railway cars," Astrid explains. She gestures in the opposite direction toward some trees. "There are a few cabins and tents we could use if it was warmer. This isn't a great village for us," she adds in a low voice. "The mayor has become very close to the Germans."

"He's collaborating?" I ask.

She nods. "Of course we didn't know that last year when we booked the dates." And canceling surely would have aroused too much suspicion. Because, above all else right now, it is essential to maintain the pretense of normalcy. "We'll stay in Thiers for nearly three weeks, though, because it's centrally located and people will come from all over Auvergne for the show."

At the train, Astrid steers me to a carriage where I have not been before. The railcar is warm and crowded with women changing into costumes and patting on heavy makeup. I pause to watch one of the acrobats paint her legs a darker shade of tan. "She does that because her tights are too ripped to repair," Astrid explains, noticing my curiosity. "There simply aren't more to be had. Come." She chooses a costume from the rack against the wall of the train car and holds it up against me. Then she hands it to one of the dressing girls and disappears. I am thrust from one set of arms to the next like a bundle of laundry, embarrassed of my own stale smell from too many hours on the train without washing. Someone pulls the dress Astrid has chosen over my head, another declares it too loose and begins to pin. Am I really to wear it? It is smaller even than a swimming costume, no more than a bra and a bottom. My stomach, tighter than when I came to Darmstadt from all of the training but still far from perfect, spills over the elastic top of the briefs. The costume is ornate, scarlet silk with gold trim. It carries a faint odor of smoke and coffee that makes me wonder who had worn it previously.

Astrid reappears and I gasp. Her two-piece, scarcely a few handkerchiefs woven together, makes my costume look modest. But Astrid is born to wear it—her body is chiseled from granite, like a nude goddess statue in a museum.

"You want I should try to flip in a hoop skirt?" she asks, noticing my reaction. To her the immodesty of the outfit doesn't matter. She does not wear it to entice, but to perform well.

Astrid gestures for me to sit on an upturned crate. She takes rouge and dots my cheeks and slashes my mouth with cherry red like a clown. Other than the times I had stolen a bit of Mama's powder to look older for the German, it is the first time I have worn makeup. I stare at the stranger in the cracked mirror someone has placed on top of a steamer trunk. How have I come to be here?

Astrid, seemingly satisfied, turns away and begins applying her own makeup, which with her unblemished skin and long eyelashes hardly seems necessary. "Do I have a few minutes?" I ask. "I want to go check on Theo."

Astrid nods. "Only just. Don't be gone too long." I start down the narrow corridor in the direction of the sleeper car, hoping that the sight of me in strange makeup will not scare Theo. But as I begin to pass through the next carriage, I stop, hearing voices.

"They want a show of our allegiance as part of the performance." I crane my neck to hear better. It is Herr Neuhoff, his voice low and terse. "Perhaps a rendition of 'Maréchal, nous voilà'..."

"Impossible!" Peter snarls at the mention of the Vichy anthem. I jump back so as not to be seen. "I've never been told what to perform by the government, even during the Great War. If I didn't kowtow to the czar, I'm sure as hell not going to do it now. It is more than just politics. This is about the integrity of the show."

"Things are different now," Herr Neuhoff presses. "And a little indulgence might go a long way toward...helping things." There is no response, but the stomping of footsteps and a door slamming so hard the whole carriage shakes.

A bell rings, which Astrid had told me earlier was to summon us to the backyard, the area behind the big top where we will assemble and get ready to perform. I look longingly down the corridor of the carriage. There is no time to see Theo.

Outside, the once-barren field around the big top has been transformed with a half-dozen smaller tents that seem to have popped up like mushrooms. The midway is filled to capacity with men in straw hats, women and children in their Sunday best. At the entrance to the big top a day bill had been posted, touting the acts that one would see inside. Smaller acts, the jugglers and sword swallowers, give impromptu performances to lure the crowds. A brass band plays lively tunes to the queue at the ticket window, easing their wait. The air is perfumed with the sweet thickness of candy floss and boiled peanuts. Such treats hardly seem possible with rationing and so many struggling just to eat. For a moment I am giddy, a young girl once more. But the treats are here for those lucky few with the sous to spend—certainly not for us.

I skirt around the edge of the big top. A handful of young

boys are lying flat on the ground trying to peek beneath the tent, but one of the seasonal workers shoos them away. The periphery of the tent has been adorned with tall posters of the starring acts. Astrid in her younger years looms above me, suspended midair by satin ropes. I am transfixed by her image. She must have been about the same age I am now, and I am so curious to know her.

I pass the beer hall they'd erected at the end of the midway, a bookend to the carousel opposite. Boisterous male laughter explodes from within. It is a delicate balance, Astrid had explained: we want to lubricate the audience enough so that they will enjoy the show, but not so much that they will become unruly and disrupt it.

Peter, whom I had seen just minutes earlier with Herr Neuhoff, sneaks from the back of the beer tent with a flask in hand. How had he gotten here so quickly? He eyes me uncertainly. "Just a quick one for the road," he says, before ambling away. I am surprised—I had not imagined that performers would be allowed to drink before a show. What would Astrid say?

I reach the backyard. My eyes travel nervously toward the top of the tent. It seems impossible that the tent, nothing more than some fabric and poles, can possibly hold the hulking trapeze apparatus—and us.

Astrid, seeing my worry, walks to my side. "It's safe." But in my mind I will always see the time I had fallen toward the earth, ready to die. "How are you holding up?" she asks. Without waiting for an answer, she rechecks my wrist wraps and holds out the box of rosin for me to coat my hands once more. "We don't want you getting killed," she says. "Not after all of the work we've put in." She adds this last bit with a smile, trying to make a joke of it. But her eyes are solemn, concerned.

"You don't think I can do it?" I venture, not sure I want to hear the answer.

"Of course I do." I listen to her voice, trying to gauge whether it is forced. "You've worked hard. You've got natural ability. But this is a serious business for all of us. There is no room for mistakes." I nod, understanding. The danger is as real for Astrid as it is for me, even after so many years.

I peek inside the dark tent, which looms high like a giant cave. There is a ring in the middle, some forty feet across, set apart from the audience by a low fence. I'd heard from the other performers about the American circuses, great big ones like Barnum that had three rings. But here all eyes would be focused on the main act. The first two rows of seats are covered in a ruby velvet cloth with a satin gold star on each, designating that these are the good seats, the important ones. Behind these chairs, crude wood benches rise in concentric circles nearly to the rafters. It is the complete circus of the ring, spectators on all sides, that gets to me—there is nowhere to hide or turn away, eyes from every angle.

The crowd begins to trickle into the tent and I pull back so as not to be seen. The ushers and program sellers are in fact lesser performers who can scoot out as the auditorium fills to put on their own makeup and prepare for the show. I study the spectators as they take their seats, a mix of well-to-do townsfolk in the front and workers on the higher benches, freshly scrubbed but a bit ill at ease, as if they do not belong here. Barely a few francs for food yet they still found a way to get that ticket to the show. These are the lucky ones who can afford to forget for a few hours the hardships beyond the tent flaps.

As the sky grows gray and we near showtime, the chatter in the backyard silences and everyone grows focused, almost grim. The acrobats have one last cigarette. They are stunning in their sequined costumes and headdresses. Their flawless makeup and coiffed hair give no indication of the primitive conditions in which we'd dressed. Astrid paces in the far corner, deep in thought. Given the intensity of her expression, I do not dare to disturb her. Of course, I have no preshow ritual of my own. I stand to one side, trying to act as if I have done this my whole life.

Astrid waves me over. "Don't just stand around letting your muscles get cold," she admonishes. "You need to stretch." She bends and gestures for me to lift one leg onto her shoulder, an exercise we've done many times at the winter quarters. She straightens slowly, raising my leg, and I try not to grit my teeth but rather breathe and ease into the dull, familiar burn that travels up the underside of my thigh.

"Do you want me to stretch you?" I ask when she has helped me with my other leg. She shakes her head. I follow her gaze across the backyard to where Peter rehearses apart from the others. He's changed into an oversize jacket and trousers now and his face, stubbled minutes earlier, is an unbroken field of white greasepaint. "Astrid…" I begin.

She looks over at me, as though she had nearly forgotten I was there. "What is it?" I falter. I consider telling her about the disagreement I heard Peter having with Herr Neuhoff on the train, or seeing Peter come from the beer tent. But I do not want to worry her right before we go on.

"You're nervous," she says evenly.

"Yes," I admit. "Weren't you at your first show?"

She laughs. "I was so young I can't even remember it. But it is normal to be nervous. Good, even. The adrenaline will keep you on your toes, keep you from making mistakes." Or make my hands shake so badly that I can't hold the bar, I think.

Inside the tent, the lights are lowered and the whole house

thrown into darkness. A spotlight comes on, creating a pool of gold on the floor at the center of the ring. The orchestra strikes a stirring chord. Herr Neuhoff appears, majestic in his bow tie and top hat. *"Mesdames et Messieurs..."* Herr Neuhoff booms into a microphone.

The "Thunder and Lightning Polka" begins to play and the plumed horses prance into the ring. Their riders, among the most ornately costumed of the women, have no saddle but ride bareback, hardly sitting at all as they scissor their legs from side to side. One rider stands and tumbles from a standing position backward through the air, landing neatly on a second horse. Though I have seen the act in rehearsal, I cannot help but gasp along with the crowd.

The program of the circus, Astrid explained once, is deliberately designed—a fast act, then a slow one then fast again, lions and other dangerous animals interspersed with human pantomimes. "You want the light bits after serious," she'd said, "like cleansing the palate after each course of a meal." But there are practicalities, too, such as the time needed to bring the animal cages in and out that makes placing them close to intermission a necessity.

Watching, I realize that the design of the big top is deliberate, too. The angles of the benches are steep to face the gaze downward. The rounded seating makes the crowd play off one another's responses, and the unbroken circle is like a wire for the electricity that fills the tent. The audience sits motionless, mesmerized by the web of color, lights, music and artistry. Their eyes dance with the arc of the juggler's balls and they gasp in appreciation as one of the trainers waltzes with a lion. Astrid was right: even as war rages on, the people still have to live—they shop for their foodstuffs and tend their homes—why not laugh at the circus as they had when the world was still whole?

Next comes the high wire. A girl named Yeta stands at the top of a platform, holding aloft a long pole for balance. The act terrifies me even more than the trapeze and I have thanked God several times that Herr Neuhoff had not selected me for that instead of the trapeze. There is a slow adagio in the music, a pause for dramatic value. Then as Yeta steps out on the wire, music thunders and the whole tent seems to shiver.

Yeta's foot slips and she struggles to regain her balance. Why now, in this act she has practiced and performed dozens of times? She nearly rights herself, then wobbles again, this time too far to recover. There is a collective gasp as she falls through the air screaming, limbs flailing as if trying to swim. "No!" I cry aloud. In her descent, I see the day Astrid had pushed me all over again.

I start forward. We have to help her. But Astrid pulls me back. Yeta lands in the net, which crashes low to the ground. She lies there, not moving. The spectators seem to hold their breath, as if wondering whether to worry or if the fall is just part of the act. Workers rush forward to carry her from the ring, out of sight of the crowd. Watching Yeta's limp body, I grow terrified. That could happen to me. Yeta is rushed outside to a Peugeot that has pulled up behind the big top. I expected an ambulance, but the workers bundle her in the back of the car and it drives away.

"An accident at the first show of the season," a voice beside me says, spicy breath warm on my bare shoulder. Though we have never spoken, I recognize the woman with flowing silver hair as Drina, the Gypsy who reads fortunes on the midway before the show and at intermission. "A terrible omen."

"Nonsense," Astrid says, waving her hand dismissively. But her face is grave.

"Will Yeta be all right?" I ask, when Drina has gone.

"I don't know," Astrid says bluntly. "Even if she lives, she may not perform again." She made living without the show sound almost worse than dying.

"Do you believe the fortune-teller?" I hear myself asking too many questions. "About a bad omen, I mean."

"Bah!" Astrid waves her hand. "If she can really see the future, then what is she doing stuck here?" She has a point.

I peer into the tent where the crowd waits uncertainly. Surely the rest of the show will have to be canceled. But the performers stand close, still ready to go on. "Clowns, *schnell!*" Herr Neuhoff calls, signaling quickly for the next act. The clowns tumble in, pantomiming a city scene. Happy clowns with large shoes and tiny little hats. Musical clowns. Buffoons who mock everything.

Peter seems to fit into none of these. He steps into the ring last, his face white and red with great black lines, eyeing the audience as though they have kept him waiting. Not sad, but a serious clown, his wit acerbic, smiles hard-won. While the other clowns perform a skit in tandem, Peter dances on the periphery, creating a pantomime all his own. He holds the entire *chapiteau* captive, cajoling, teasing, sensing who is reticent to come along on the journey or perhaps weary and drawing them in. It is as if he wills the audience to please him with their response and applause, when in fact the opposite should be the case. From the darkness in the corner, Astrid watches Peter, eyes rapt.

Herr Neuhoff also watches from the edge of the ring, his face uneasy. I hold my breath, waiting for Peter to launch into the goose-stepping routine Herr Neuhoff had forbidden. Peter has not incorporated the pro-Vichy anthem Herr Neuhoff suggested earlier into his act. But he keeps his performance light, as if sensing that after Yeta's fall, anything else would be too much.

The clowns are followed by the elephants in their jeweled headpieces, the bear and monkeys in little dresses not unlike my own. The show breaks for intermission and the house lights go up. Patrons make their way back to the midway to stretch their legs and smoke. But the break is not for us. "We're next," Astrid informs me. "We must get ready."

"Astrid, wait…" A giant pit seems to open in my stomach. Until now I had just been a spectator at the show, nearly forgetting the real reason I am here. But to actually step out in front of the crowd…after what happened to Yeta, how can I possibly? "I can't do this." My mind is a blur and I've forgotten everything.

"Of course you can," she reassures, placing a hand on my shoulder. "That's just your nerves."

"No, I've forgotten everything. I'm not ready." My voice rises with panic. A few of the other performers turn in my direction. One of the acrobats curves her mouth smugly, as if everything she suspected about me has proved true.

Astrid leads me away and then stops, placing one hand on each of my shoulders. "Now, listen to me. You are good. Gifted even. And you have worked hard. Ignore the audience and imagine it is just the two of us back in Darmstadt. You can do this." She kisses me firmly on each cheek, as if pressing some of her calm and strength into me. Then she turns and starts for the ring.

A bell sounds and the audience returns to their seats. As I peer beyond the curtain at the crowd that waits expectantly, my legs grow heavy. I cannot possibly step out there. "Go," Astrid growls, pushing me out roughly as the music cues us.

As the houselights dim once more, we scamper into the ring. In the winter quarters, the ladder had been bolted to the wall. But here it dangles from above, scarcely held in place at the bottom. I struggle not to fall as it wobbles. The climb takes longer than I expected and I have only just reached the board when the spotlight rises. It licks the sides of the tent, finds me. And then I am displayed before the crowd. I shiver. Why is it that the clowns can hide behind the oily greasepaint while we stand nearly naked, nothing but a thin slip of nylon separating us from hundreds of eyes?

The music slows, signaling the start of our act. Then there is silence, followed by a drumroll that grows louder, my cue to leap. "Hup!" comes Astrid's call across the darkness. I am supposed to release right after she says it, but I do not. Astrid swings, waiting for me. In another second it will be too late and the act will be a failure.

With a deep breath, I leap from the board. Suddenly there is nothing beneath my feet but air. Though I have flown dozens of times in the winter quarters, I feel a second of sheer terror, as if it is the first time all over again. I swing higher, pushing fear away and relishing the air as it whooshes around me.

Astrid flies toward me, arms extended. I have to let go at the top of the arc for the trick to work. The catch still terrifies me, though, and more so now than ever after seeing Yeta fall. Astrid had let me fall once before, caused it. Would she do it again?

Our eyes lock. Trust me, she seems to say. I let go and soar through the air. Astrid's hands clasp mine, swinging me below her for a split second. Relief and excitement surge through me. There is no time to celebrate, though. A second later, Astrid flings me back in the direction I need to go. I force myself to concentrate once more, spinning as she taught me. Then I reach outward, hardly daring to look. Astrid has aligned me perfectly, and the bar falls into my hands and the crowd cheers. I swing up to the board, the world righting itself beneath my feet.

We've done it! My heart fills with joy and I am happier than I've been since I can remember. The act is not over, though, and Astrid is waiting for me, her face stern, intensity unbroken. We perform the second pass, this time Astrid catching me by my feet. The applause lifts me higher now. Another pass and return, then it is over. For an instant, I am almost more sad than relieved.

I straighten as the spotlight finds me on the board. The audience cheers on and on. For me. They haven't seen the work Astrid had done as catcher at all. I understand then how hard it was for her to have given up the limelight, the things she has sacrificed to bring me into the act.

The lights go down and Peter prepares to enter the ring once more, this time for a solo performance. Unlike other performers who appear once or twice during the show, he goes on repeatedly between larger acts, a thread tying the whole show together. Now he distracts the crowd with his routine, giving the workers time to finish positioning the lion and tiger cages, which had been brought in through the darkness beneath our act.

Astrid and I climb down and hurry out to the backyard in the semidarkness. "We did it!" I exclaim, throwing my arms around Astrid. I wait for her praise. Surely now she will be pleased with me. But she does not respond and a second later, I step back, dejected.

"You did well," she says finally. But her tone is understated, and her face is troubled.

"I know I was late on the first pass…" I begin.

"Shh." She shoos me away, staring into the tent. I follow her gaze to where a man sits in the front row—in an SS uniform. I am suddenly queasy. Surely I would have noticed him if he had been there during the first half of the show.

He must have come in during intermission. In my nervousness, I had not seen him.

"I'm sure he is just here to see the show," I say, wanting to reassure her. But there is no strength behind my words. What on earth is a German officer doing here? His expression is relaxed as he watches the trainer cajole the big cats into doing tricks. "Still you have to warn Peter not to do that bit in his next act..." I stop, realizing she isn't listening, but still peering rapt through the curtain.

"I know him." Astrid's voice is calm, but her skin has gone pale.

"The German?" She nods. "Are you sure?" I ask over the tightening in my throat. "They all look so similar in those awful uniforms."

"An associate of my husband's." Ex-husband, I want to correct, but in the moment it seems unwise.

"You can't go out there again," I fret. Though I am done for the show, Astrid has a second act on the Spanish web. My chest tightens. "You must tell Herr Neuhoff."

"Never!" she spits, sounding more angry than scared now. "I don't want him to worry about having me in the act. If I cannot perform, I have no value to the show." And then Herr Neuhoff's protection would be just charity. She faces me squarely. "It would be the end of me. You must swear not to tell. No one can know."

"Let me go on for you," I plead. Of course my offer is hollow—I have no training on the ropes or any other act beyond the trapeze.

I turn and look behind me desperately. Peter, if I can find him, might be able to persuade Astrid not to go on. "Astrid, please wait..." But it is too late—she strides into the ring, shoulders squared with determination. In that moment, I see just how brave she really is. I am awed—and petrified—for her.

Astrid climbs a different ladder from the one she had used earlier. This time she hangs from a single satin rope, seemingly suspended in midair. I hold my breath, studying the officer's face for some sign of recognition. But he watches her, too mesmerized to suspect. She tells a story, weaves a tapestry with her moves. It holds him—and the entire audience—captivated. I remain terrified, though, unable to breathe. Astrid's beauty and the legendary skill of her act scream like a bullhorn, threatening to betray her true identity.

"Hidden in plain sight," Astrid muses over the thundering applause as she exits the tent. There is a note of self-satisfaction to her voice, a part of her that liked deceiving the German. But her hands tremble as she undoes her wraps.

Then it is over. The entire circus steps out for a final bow, the full panoply of spectacle unfurled for the audience to admire once more. I climb the ladder as Astrid had instructed me and we take our final bow from opposing boards, not flying but simply extending one leg high out into the air like ballerinas. Children wave furiously at the sweat-glistening performers, who bow modestly in return, like actors not breaking from their roles.

Afterward some of the performers sign autographs for the crowd that has gathered at the edge of the backyard. I watch nervously as Astrid accepts praise: perhaps she should not be out here. But the German officer does not appear.

At the far end of the yard I see Peter, not signing autographs, but pacing and talking to himself as intently as he had before the beginning of the show. He is going over his performance, finding the mistakes and marking the things he will fix for next time. The circus artists are every bit as intent as a ballet dancer or concert pianist. Every tiny flaw is a gaping wound, even though it had not been noticed by anyone else at all.

When the last program has been signed, we make our way back to the train, past the workers scrubbing down and feeding the animals. "Once there might have been fireworks after the first evening show," Astrid remarks, staring up at the darkness of the sky.

"But not anymore?" I ask.

"Too expensive," she replies. "And no one seems to find explosions enjoyable these days."

Weariness engulfs me then. My bones ache and my skin is chilled with dry sweat. All I want to do is return to Theo and collapse around the sweet warmth of his body. But Astrid cajoles me back to the dressing car, where we hang our costumes and remove our makeup. She rubs warm salve into my shoulders, pine scented and tingly. "I just want to sleep," I protest, trying to shrug her off.

"Our bodies are all that we have in this business. We must take care of them. You'll be glad tomorrow," she promises, her fingers digging hard into my neck. My muscles burn like fire.

"You did beautifully," Astrid continues, her voice full and sincere, offering the praise I had longed for earlier. My heart seems to skip a beat. "Of course your legs could have been a bit straighter on the second pass," she adds, bringing me down to earth. Because Astrid will always be Astrid. "We can fix that tomorrow." Tomorrow, I think, the days of endless practices and shows stretching out before me. "I'm proud of you," she adds, and I can feel my cheeks flush.

We start from the dressing car toward the sleeper. Then I stop. I am worried still about the German officer who saw her and the possibility that he might realize who she is. Astrid will not tell anyone, but should I? I look in the direction of Peter's car. He cares for her, I can tell, and would be the best person to keep her safe. If I go to him, though, he will tell Astrid. Herr Neuhoff, I think. I have spoken little to him since arriving at the circus, but he has always been kind. It is his circus. Surely he will know what to do. I see Astrid's glowering face, hear her voice: *No one can know.* She will be furious if she finds out I have gone against her. But Herr Neuhoff runs the circus; he is my best hope of keeping Astrid safe.

I desperately want to get to Theo. He will be sleeping, though—and there is something else I must do first. "I forgot something," I say, turning back in the other direction before she can answer any questions.

I knock at the door of Herr Neuhoff's carriage, the last one before the caboose. "Come in," he calls from inside, and I open the door. I've never been here before. Inside, it is pleasantly furnished, a curtain separating the bed and sitting areas. Herr Neuhoff sits at a desk, his girth threatening to topple the rickety chair beneath. He's taken off the velvet jacket he wore in the ring and opened the collar of his ruffled linen dress shirt, which is now darkened with perspiration. A cigar stub in the ashtray gives off a scorched smell. He is going over the books, head bowed. Running a circus is a huge enterprise that goes beyond the ring or even the winter quarters. He is responsible for everyone's well-being, paying not just their wages but the rent and food. I see then his weariness and age, and the heaviness of his burden.

He looks up from the ledger in front of him, brow still furrowed. "Yes?" he says, his voice brisk but not unkind.

"Am I interrupting?" I manage.

"No," he replies, but his voice is flat, eyes more sunken

than a few hours ago. "This awful business with Yeta fall-ing. I have to file a report with the authorities."

"Will she be all right?" I ask, half-afraid of the answer.

"I don't know," he says. "I will go to the hospital at first light. But first the authorities have asked for a tax to be paid tomorrow. A sin tax, they call it." As though what we did, providing entertainment, was wrong. "I'm just figuring out where to draw the money from." He smiles faintly. "The cost of doing business. What can I do for you?"

I waver, not wanting to add to his problems. A small radio plays in the corner of Herr Neuhoff's carriage. They are con-traband now and I hadn't realized he had one. I notice, too, a neat box of writing paper and envelopes on his desk. Herr Neuhoff follows my gaze. "Do you want to write to your father and let him know you are well?" I have considered it any number of times, wondering what my parents thought had become of me, whether they worried or had written me off completely. What would I say—that I have joined a circus and I have a baby now, so very much like the one taken from me? No, there is nothing about this life that they would understand. And if they knew where I am, part of me would always hope they would come for me—and I would be heartbroken all over again when they did not.

"I could write for you," he offers. I shake my head. "Then how can I help?"

Before I can explain why I have come, Herr Neuhoff wheezes, his cough deeper and more barking than it had been in the winter quarters. He reaches for a glass of water. When the coughing subsides, he swallows a pill. "Are you all right, sir?" I hope the question is not too forward.

He waves his hand, as though swatting a fly. "A family heart condition. I've always had it. The damp spring weather doesn't help. Now, you needed something?" He pushes for my question, eager to return to the books.

"It's about Astrid," I begin hesitantly. Taking a deep breath, I tell him about the German in the front row who knew her.

His face darkens. "I feared something like this might happen sooner or later," he says. "Thank you for letting me know." I can tell from his tone I have been dismissed.

I turn back, daring to interrupt him one more time. "Sir, one last thing—Astrid would be very angry if she knew I told you."

I watch the conflict on his face, wanting to agree to keep my secret, but unable to promise without lying. "I won't say I heard it from you." The offer is little comfort. I'm the only one who knows. Worry tugs at my stomach as I walk from the train car.

When I reach our carriage, Astrid sits on the berth in the darkness, holding Theo, who is sleeping. I fight the urge to poke him so he will open his dark eyes and look at me. "He went down a few minutes ago," she says. Knowing that I just missed Theo being awake almost makes it worse. She strokes his cheek gently.

"I wanted to ask," Astrid begins. I freeze, trying to come up with a plausible excuse for where I had been. "On your way back, did you see Peter?"

"Not since we left the backyard. He was rehearsing," I say, mindful that it isn't quite the right word for fixing things after the show.

"I wish I could go to him. But he prefers to sleep alone on the road once the performances have begun." Her eyes drift longingly in the direction of Peter's train car. "After seeing Erich's colleague…" She dips her chin low to her chest.

"I just don't want to be alone." Her hands tremble against Theo's back.

She is lonely, I realize. I had gotten used to being on my own during my months working at the train station at Bensheim. Having grown up an only child, it was not so difficult. But Astrid had gone from her large circus family to Erich and then quickly found Peter. Despite her fierceness, she can't handle being alone.

"You aren't alone," I say, feeling a second-best substitute, inadequate. I wrap my arm around her. "I'm here." She stiffens and for a second I wonder if she will pull away. Since coming to the circus, it has always been me needing Astrid, depending on her. Now the opposite seems true.

Astrid stretches out on the berth with Theo in her arms. I slip in beside her, her body warm. We press our foreheads together like twins in the womb, one entity breathing together. I feel comfort in a way I hadn't since leaving home. Astrid had joked once that she was old enough to be my mother. But it is true. I see my own mother now, as clearly as I had the day she watched me leave. She should have fought for me, protected me with her life. Now, having Theo, I understand what her love should have been and was not.

"What are you thinking?" Astrid asks. It is the first time she has taken an interest.

"About the sea," I lie, too embarrassed to admit that I yearn for the family that had cast me out.

"The sea, or the people who live near it?" she asks, her tone even as she sees through my answer. "Your family— you still love them, don't you?"

"I suppose." The admission feels like a weakness.

"You cry out in the night for them," she says. Feeling myself flush, I am glad she cannot see my face through the darkness. "I still dream about Erich," she confides. "And I still have feelings for him."

I am surprised. "Even though he..."

"Turned me out? Rejected me? Yes, even then. You love the people they were before, below all the awfulness that made them do this thing, you know?"

I do. In the sadness of her voice, I can hear how very much it hurt when Erich turned his back on her. "But now you have Peter," I remind, wanting to ease her pain.

"Yes," she acknowledges, "it isn't quite the same, though."

"He cares for you a lot," I press.

Beside me I can feel her stiffen. "Peter enjoys my company. That is all."

"But Astrid... I can see how much he cares for you...and you him." She does not answer. How can Astrid not see the truth about Peter's feelings? Maybe after all she has been through, she is afraid to want more.

"Anyway, we were talking about you," Astrid says, shifting the subject. "I know you miss your family. But the past is the past. Face front, shoulder to the wind. You have Theo now. You are never going back." Her voice is firm. "You need to accept that if you are to save yourself and Theo. Unless, of course, you find his family. You want him to find his family, don't you?" she presses.

A knife of pain shoots through me. "Of course. It would be a relief," I reply, my voice hollow. Though I had thought of Theo's family, prayed for them, I cannot imagine ever letting go of him. He is mine now.

"Or if not, he could be adopted. He isn't yours. He belongs with a family. You are a young girl with your whole life before you. Someday you will have to let him go."

I *am* his family, I think. I gesture around the railcar in the darkness. "This *is* my life." I do not plan to stay with the circus forever. I need to get Theo farther away, out of Germany for good. But right now it is hard to imagine anything else.

"One day you may feel differently," she replies. "Sometimes our forever life does not last as long as we think."

Her words seem to echo through the stillness of the sleeper. I bite my lip to keep from protesting. I had given up my child once and it almost killed me. I could not survive that kind of pain again.

Of course Astrid does not know this. My past is still a hidden secret. It seems to grow now in the space between us, pushing us apart and making every bit of our friendship a lie.

"Astrid," I begin. I need to tell her right now about how I had come to be at the station the night I found Theo. About the German soldier. This secret cannot continue festering between us.

"If it is about the act, we can discuss it in the morning," she says drowsily.

"It isn't that."

"Then what?" she asks, lifting her head. I swallow, unable to speak. "Thank you," Astrid says before I can respond. There is a vulnerability to her voice I have never heard before. "That is, I don't think I've told you that I appreciate what you are doing. Without you, I couldn't possibly continue to perform." Strictly speaking, that isn't true. She could continue on the Spanish web or another solo act. But her heart is with the flying trapeze, and my being here makes that possible. "I want you to know that I am grateful," she adds, finding my hand beneath the blanket.

A lump forms in my throat, blocking the words I had meant to say. I could push through it, insist on telling the truth. But she squeezes my hand and there is a warmth between us that has never been there before. My will to tell her evaporates and blows away like dust. "What were you going to say?"

"Nothing. That is...it's about Peter." I cannot bear telling her the whole truth about my past now. But in my haste to avoid my secret, I blurt out another: "He was drinking before the show." I cringe, unsure whether I should have said this. It is not my business. But some part of me feels that she should know.

Astrid does not respond right away and I feel her stiffen with concern beside me. "Are you sure?" she asks. "He always acts strangely before a performance." Her voice is uneasy, not wanting to acknowledge a truth she already knows.

"I'm sure. I saw him coming from the beer tent."

"Oh." She does not sound surprised, only sad. "I've tried so hard to stop him."

Try harder, I want to say. How could a person as otherwise strong as Astrid not be able to stand up to him?

"I just feel so helpless," she declares, her voice cracking. I expect her to cry, but she simply shudders. I move closer and she falls into my arms, Theo sandwiched between us so tightly I fear he might wake and fuss. "So helpless," she repeats, and I know she is talking about not just Peter.

Finally, her shaking subsides and she huddles closer to me. "The show is the thing," she adds, growing drowsy. "As long as we can keep performing, everything will be fine."

My mind reels back to my conversation with Herr Neuhoff. I recall his troubled look when I told him about the German recognizing Astrid.

And I can't help but wonder if I have made a terrible mistake.

10

Noa

"I'm going into town," I say to Astrid. I hold Theo on my lap, spoon-feeding him the last of his lunch. It is a banana—a rare find by one of the kitchen workers—that I had mashed together with a bit of milk. When Theo first tasted it, his eyes widened with surprise and he gurgled at the unfamiliar richness, so different from the usual bland porridge. Good food for Theo is scarce, since I cannot register him for a ration card without raising questions. So I give him whatever I have for myself to eat that is suitable.

I set down the bowl, hoping Astrid will not protest. It is almost noon on Sunday, two days since our first show, and we have already finished four hours of rehearsing. My shoulders ache fiercely and an earthy smell rises from the dampness of my skin. "I'm going to the hotel to wash," I add. Since there is no running water at the fairgrounds, the circus keeps two rooms at a small hotel, one for the men and one for the women, where we can go to bathe each week.

Astrid reaches into her trunk and hands me a little cake of soap. "Here," she says and I take it from her gratefully. The soap that the circus had given us is little more than a scratchy pumice stone, but this bar is smooth and sweet smelling. "I made it from sap," she adds. I am continually amazed by Astrid's resourcefulness, and the things she knows how to do from growing up on the road. Then her brow wrinkles. "Be back in an hour. I want to fix your knee hang and work on the split before tomorrow's show."

"But it's Sunday," I protest. The one day we do not perform. In the backyard of the circus on Sundays, circus folk practice a bit or play cards or simply rest their weary bodies. The children run free playing tag or hoops, enjoying a day where no one corrals them back from the big top or shushes them to be quiet.

A day of rest—but not for me. Astrid has me rehearse as much as if it is any other day, with just a few hours off after lunch to feed Theo and spend time with him. Today, it seems, I am not even to have that. I know better than to argue the point. Even though I have managed my first few performances Friday and Saturday, there is still much work to be done. I have attempted only the straight pass: I swing to a great height and she catches me by my arms as I fall. But the variations we might attempt are endless: pirouettes and somersaults, the ankle-to-ankle catch. What I have learned is just a drop in the ocean of aerialist arts, miles from good enough.

"About that…" I break off. "I was thinking if I twisted at the end of the second pass, you could catch me in reverse."

It is the first time I have dared to offer a suggestion and Astrid stares at me as though I have sprouted horns. Then she shrugs and waves her hand. "That would never work."

"Why not?" I press. "I would be lined up for the return and it would look better than just the straight pass."

She purses her lips in annoyance, as though I am a child

pushing for sweets after having been told no. "You need to keep working on the fundamentals. Don't get ahead of yourself." I step back, stung. I may perform well enough for the show, but she will never consider me an equal. "Anyway, you should get started if you want to make it into town and back," Astrid says, changing subjects. "I'll watch Theo for you."

"You don't mind?" I ask, looking longingly at Theo. Though I am desperate to bathe and feel clean again, I do not want to leave him. I see so little of him on show days— by the time the last performance is over he is long since asleep. I hate to give up any of our precious Sunday afternoon together. How I'd love to bring him into town with me! He could use a proper bath, instead of the metal pail in which I pour water over him, causing him to either cry angrily or squeal with delight, depending on the temperature. But I can't bring him into town and risk the extra attention and questions.

"Not at all." Astrid walks over and takes Theo from me. There is something in the tender way she looks at him that speaks volumes about the child she never had. She has been a bit kinder to me as well in the two short days since the first show. She is still demanding of my performance. But it seems like she actually thinks I can perform and be one of them. And after we spoke the other night about Peter and the past, I almost feel that we are friends who can trust one another.

Or at least we could be, if not for the secret I am still keeping from her about my own child and the German who fathered him. I should have told Astrid weeks ago—it might have eased the damage. But I had not, and the truth remains buried between us, festering. Now it is not just the secret itself, but the deception of having kept it from her for which she would hate me.

"If you go through the woods, along the edge of the stream, it's quicker into town than the road," she offers.

I tilt my head, trying to envision the route she has described. Other than coming here by the main road the day of the arrival, I haven't left the fairgrounds.

"The path is just behind the big top," she continues, sensing my confusion. "Why don't we walk with you for a bit and I'll show you?"

I follow Astrid, who weaves through the narrow aisle between the berths with Theo. We pass a dancer tinting her hair auburn with a homemade dye. Another darns a hole in her practice leotard. By the door, a heavyset woman from one of the sideshows changes without modesty, her large breasts indistinguishable from the folds of flesh beneath them. I avert my eyes. With so many women living in one place, there is very little privacy—just one of the many things about circus life I will never get used to.

We step outside. Earlier when we'd gone to practice, the sky above the big top had been painted in pinks and blues. But now a wreath of fog sits atop the *chapiteau* like a cap drawn low across the brow. We cross the backyard of the circus, the open space where tent meets train car and the circus people spend their time, away from the prying eyes of the audience. Undergarments flap shamelessly on a clothesline. Near the cookhouse, the steamy smell of boiled potatoes wafts out, signaling the menu for dinner. I hear the clanking of dishes, a half-dozen workers washing dishes from the noon meal.

As we pass the big tent, the noises from inside are a familiar symphony, a clarinetist practicing and the grunt of the strong man mixed with the clanking of swords as two clowns engage in a mock duel. Through the gap in the curtain, the arena looks sad in the harsh light of day. The velvet seat cushions are frayed and stained. The once-clean sawdust that covered the ground is now littered with candy wrappers and cigarette butts. A pool of yellow in the corner where a horse had urinated gives the air a sour smell.

At the edge of the fairgrounds beneath a just-blossoming cherry tree sits Drina, exotic purple skirt splayed around her, large knuckles bending beneath jeweled rings as she shuffles a deck of cards. She joins the circus each year, Astrid told me, appearing at the first tour stop and staying until season's end, entertaining audiences on the midway before shows. In this strange world where almost all are accepted, Drina is still an outsider. Not just because she is Roma, a Gypsy; the circus has all kinds of races. But her act is a sort of trickery it seems, like magic. *Not circus*, Astrid said disdainfully. It is an expression I've heard often in the months since I'd joined them, used to describe performances that do not fit into the circus ideal.

Drina waves me over. I hesitate, looking to Astrid. "Can I?" I ask. "I'll only be a minute." She rolls her eyes and shrugs. I move closer, curious about the odd-looking deck of cards Drina spreads in front of her purposefully in a formation. "I don't have any money to pay you," I say.

She reaches up and grabs my hand without asking, runs her coarse fingers over the lines on my palm. "You were born under a lucky star," she says. *Lucky.* How many times had I heard that before? "But you have known deep sorrow." I shift uncomfortably. How can she possibly tell? "You will know peace," she adds. It seems rather a bold prediction for these times. "But first there will be illness—and a break."

"A break, like a bone?" I ask. "And who is going to get sick?" She shakes her head, saying no more. Suddenly uneasy, I stand. "Thank you," I say hurriedly.

I start back to Astrid, who is twirling in a circle with

Theo to amuse him. "What did she say?" Astrid asks, curious in spite of herself.

"Nothing important," I reply self-consciously.

"I don't know why you believe in such things," she scoffs.

And I don't know why you don't, I want to reply. But I fear it will sound rude. "I like the promise of the unknown, of what might be out there."

"The future will be here soon enough," she replies.

Farther from the circus grounds, we start into a forest and cut through the trees. They are denser than they had appeared from a distance, a forest of pine and chestnut. It is not so very different from the one I'd been struggling through the night I'd taken Theo. But the snow is gone and tiny shoots of grass and weed poke out of the damp earth. Light slants through the branches, which are dotted with the earliest of green buds. Something rustles in the low brush, a fox or perhaps a hedgehog. If the weather had been mild that night as now, I might not have collapsed and found my way to the circus at all.

"I thought I might also look for some extra food for Theo in town," I tell Astrid. "Some rice cereal or fresh milk."

"It's Sunday," Astrid points out. I nod. That's the catch: the one day that I can get away to town is the same day that most shops will be closed. "Of course there is always the black market…" I'd heard of such things from the time our village was occupied, as well as at the girls' home and the train station, people selling goods illegally that one couldn't get elsewhere at a higher price.

"I wouldn't know where to begin finding that." My shoulders slump. "Perhaps if I ask in town…"

"No!" she replies sharply. "You must not do anything to arouse suspicion. If you ask the wrong person, it could raise dangerous questions."

Soon the forest breaks to reveal a stream. Willow trees rise from its banks then arch, not quite dipping low enough to break the glass-like surface of murky water. "There," Astrid says, stopping and gesturing across the slight arc of a wooden footbridge that marks the edge of town.

"You aren't coming with me?" I ask, disappointed. It would have been so much easier and more pleasant to go into town together.

She shakes her head. "Best not to be seen." I wonder if she is talking about herself or Theo or both. Is she thinking still of the German who had come to the show that first night? But her eyes still look longingly toward the village. "Anyway, someone has to mind Theo," she reminds me. "You have your papers, yes?"

"Yes." I pat my pocket.

"Be careful." Her brow furrows as she studies my face. "Speak with no one unless you absolutely must."

"I'll be back in an hour," I say, kissing Theo on the head. He reaches out his tiny hand, as if to say: *take me with you.* More and more each day it is as if a veil has been lifted and he sees the world, understanding.

A tiny piece of my heart seems to break off then and there as I squeeze his fingers gently. "You should go now if you are going at all," Astrid nudges. I kiss Theo once more then start toward the base of the hill on which Thiers is situated, and begin to climb the steep path that winds through the half-timber houses with shutters the color of ash set close to the road. Partridges call out to one another from the eaves. The main street is quiet on a Sunday afternoon, with most of the shops closed. A few old women in shawls make their way toward the Romanesque church at the top of the town square. It is the oddest sort of normal—a café with well-coiffed women sipping coffee and nibbling madeleines behind round windows, men playing boules on a grassy patch by the town square. A boy of ten or eleven sells newspapers at the corner.

The hotel is no more than a large pension, two tall adjoining houses that had been combined by knocking out the wall that had once divided them. I take the key from the proprietor, who seems to know without my saying why I have come. Had he been to one of the shows, or was there something about me now that marked me as circus? I make my way through the tiny lobby, packed thick with guests sitting in chairs and smoking as they lean against the walls. The circus had been lucky to get rooms at all; the hotel is filled with refugees who had fled from Paris at the start of the war or villages farther north that had been destroyed by air raids or fighting. *L'Exode*, Astrid had called it. Whatever the reason, they had not gone back but stayed for lack of a home or place.

The second-floor room is narrow and plain, with a poorly made wrought-iron bed and drops of water from the last guest not quite wiped from the basin. I undress quickly, brushing away a bit of the ever-present sawdust from the ring that had somehow found its way beneath my skirt. I pause to study myself naked before the mirror. My body has begun to change from all of the exercise, as Astrid had predicted, hardening in some places and lengthening out in others.

But it is more than just my physical shape that has been transformed from my time on the trapeze: since we've been on the road, I find myself working harder, constantly thinking about the act. For hours after a performance, I feel the air rushing beneath my feet, like a train I cannot get off. I even dream about the trapeze. Sometimes I jerk awake, grasping for a bar that is not there. I am obsessed during my waking hours, too. I'd even crept into the arena in the darkness one

night. Though the stands were empty, eyes seemed to follow me from all directions. Only a bit of moonlight peeked
in. It was foolish to practice alone without anyone to spot
or call for help if I fell. But the hours of training during the
day simply were not enough.

I told Astrid, hoping she would applaud my determination. "You might have been killed," she spat. Whatever path
I choose it is always wrong, too much or not enough. Still,
the lure of the harder tricks calls me: if I can just add a pirouette, get a little higher to perhaps manage a somersault. I
don't have to do it. I am keeping up my end of the bargain
just by performing. But I find myself wanting more, reaching for it.

A half hour later I step from the hotel, freshly bathed. I
eye the row of shops, tempted for a minute to wander and
enjoy. Perhaps despite what Astrid said, there might be a
store or two open to find some food. Theo will be waiting
for me, though. I turn to go.

Across the street a young man of eighteen or so with coal-
black hair loiters in a doorway. He watches me in a way I'd
almost forgotten, that I had felt only one time before. My
skin prickles. Once I might have been flattered. But I cannot afford to have anyone notice me now. Does he mean to
make trouble? I lower my eyes and hurry past.

At the corner, a man sells fruit on the back of an upturned
crate. I see strawberries for the first time since the war, mottled and too green to be ripe, but strawberries nonetheless.
Desire floods my mouth. I imagine Theo's face as he tastes
the unfamiliar sweetness for the first time. I fish in my coat
pocket for a coin as I walk toward the crate. After I've paid
the seller, I put the two strawberries I could afford into my
pocket, fighting the urge to eat one now.

Behind me I hear a snicker. For a second, I wonder if it is

the dark-haired man I'd just seen. Instead I turn to find two boys, twelve or thirteen years old, pointing in my direction. I glance around to see what they might be laughing at and then realize that it's me. I look down at my sheer red skirt with patterned stockings and my low V-necked blouse. I no longer fit in with ordinary people. I raise my hands to cover my chest, my shame rising. On the trapeze I've learned how to hide behind the lights and pretend it isn't me. But here, I feel naked and exposed.

A woman walks up to the boys, their mother perhaps, and I wait for her to scold them for their rudeness. Instead, she shoos them back, putting them behind her as if to shield them from me. "Keep your distance," she warns them in French, not bothering to lower her voice. She stares at me as though I might bite. Seeing us in the ring is one thing, an encounter on the street something different entirely.

"Pardon, that's quite enough," a voice says behind me. I turn to find the man who had been watching me a minute earlier. He looks at me oddly and I wait for him to take her side. "The circus performers are our guests in the village," he says instead. I wonder how he knows I'm from the circus, and then I realize it must be how I am dressed. I take a step back.

"But look at her," the woman protests, gesturing in my direction with disgust.

I flush. Outsiders think of the circus as dark and sexual, Astrid had warned me once. In reality it is the furthest thing from the truth. If anything, life on the road is more strictly run—there is a chaperone in the girls' tent and a curfew earlier than the one the Germans had set. We are too tired to get up to trouble. Still nosy fans stick their heads in the backyard, trying to get a glimpse of something exotic or untoward. In fact our lives are boringly simple—wake, eat, dress, practice, repeat.

The woman opens her mouth to speak, but the young man interrupts before she can say a word. *"Au revoir, Madam Verrier,"* he says dismissively and she turns and walks down the street with a huff.

"Bonjour," he says to me when the woman has gone.

Remembering Astrid's admonition about not mingling with the townsfolk, I turn to go. "Wait," he calls. I look back over my shoulder. "I'm sorry that woman was so rude. I'm Lucienne," he continues, extending his hand. He does not give his last name as people did back home when introducing themselves and I wonder if that is the custom here. "They call me Luc for short." Closer now, he is taller than I realized. I barely come up to his shoulder.

I hesitate, then shake his hand lightly. *"Enchanté,"* he says. Is he mocking me? There is no guile in his face, none of the leering of the other townsfolk.

"Noa," I say haltingly.

"Like the ark," he remarks. I cock my head. "In the Bible."

"Oh yes, of course," I reply. From across the street, the boys snicker again, their mother having disappeared into one of the shops and out of earshot. Luc starts toward them, face thunderous. "Don't," I say. "You'll just make it worse. I'm leaving anyway."

"That's too bad," he says. "Can I walk you?" Without waiting for a response, he takes my arm.

I jerk away. "Excuse me," I say. Is it because I'm with the circus that he has the nerve to presume he can do that?

"I'm sorry. I only meant to help you." His tone is apologetic. "I should have asked." He holds out his hand once more. "May I?"

Why is he being so nice? He is friendly—too friendly. No

one is nice just for the sake of it these days, not unless he wants something. The German soldier appears in my mind. "I don't think it's a good idea," I say.

"A boy walking a girl, what is so wrong with that?" he asks. His eyes meet mine, a challenge.

"Fine," I relent, letting him take my arm. He starts walking once more, leading me toward the edge of town. His fingers are warm through my sleeve. He moves quickly with self-assurance, the kind of boy whom I never would have dared speak to back home.

We cross the footbridge, near the edge of the forest. I stop and pull away, more firmly this time. "I can manage myself." Letting him walk me out of town is one thing. If he comes any farther with me, though, someone from the circus might see me mingling, as Astrid said I should not. I can almost feel her eyes on me. I turn in the direction of the woods, wondering if she is watching. But I see no one. Still I am not supposed to be here. It has been well more than an hour and she will be waiting for me to practice, perhaps even worrying. "I have to go," I say firmly.

He brushes a lock of hair from his forehead, his face a mix of hurt and puzzlement. "I'm sorry to have bothered you," he says and begins to walk away.

"Wait!" I call out. "Lucienne..."

"Luc," he corrects, starting back toward me.

"Luc." I roll the name across my tongue. "I need to buy some things." In my haste to get away from those awful boys and their mother, I had nearly forgotten about finding food for Theo.

"What sort of things?" Luc asks.

I see Astrid in my mind, hear her cautioning me not to ask. "Milk, some rice cereal." I falter, not wanting to reveal the truth about Theo.

He eyes me evenly. "For yourself?"

"Yes." I meet his gaze, not wavering. He is a stranger, not to be trusted.

"Or for the baby?" he asks. I freeze, panicked. How does he know about Theo? "I saw you holding him in the parade the day the circus arrived."

Goose bumps form on my skin. I hadn't realized he had noticed me. Our lives even outside the ring suddenly seem like a fishbowl. "My little brother," I manage, praying that he will not suspect otherwise as Astrid had.

"Don't you have ration cards?" he presses, seeming to accept my explanation.

"Yes, of course," I reply, "but they're never enough."

He looks back over his shoulder toward the town center. "The shops are closed on Sunday," he says finally. "Perhaps if you come back during the week."

"It's difficult with all of the performances," I reply carefully. I consider asking him about the black market but do not dare.

"What do you do with the circus, anyway, tame tigers?" Luc's tone is chiding.

For a second I want to tell him that I have been here only a few weeks and am not really part of the circus. But they are my people now. I lift my chin. "Trapeze, actually." I am proud of how good I've become at my new craft, the work I've put in to become so. It is lost in translation to noncircus folk like Luc, who still looks simply amused. "You haven't seen the show, have you?"

He shakes his head. "Maybe I should," he says, then smiles. "But only if you'll meet me afterward. For a coffee," he adds, to make sure I hadn't thought he was suggesting something improper. "I'm sure I'll have questions about the show. What do you say?"

I falter. He seems nice enough and in another time I might have said yes more easily. "I'm sorry, I can't," I say.

Disappointment flashes across his face, then vanishes again just as quickly. "I can walk you the rest of the way," he offers. "In case you see those boys again—or their mother."

"It isn't necessary," I reply. No good would come from encouraging him. And I do not want any of the circus folk to see me with him—especially Astrid.

I start down the road before he can offer further, feeling him watch me as I go.

11

Astrid

I watch Noa cross the footbridge. A wave of protectiveness swells in me. Her first time off the fairgrounds. Will she manage it or will her nervousness cause her problems? For a minute I want to go after her and remind her again to be careful and not speak to anyone and a thousand other things. I'd like to go to town and wash properly myself, but after the German nearly recognized me the other night I do not dare risk being seen. I look around warily. The place where I am standing near the edge of the woods is not so very far from town and I don't want to run into anyone and answer questions about the child—or myself.

My mind reels back to the previous night's performance. As I peered into the tent, someone caught my eye. A man in uniform, SS pin glinting on his lapel. Roger von Albrecht. He had been a colleague of my husband's in Berlin, and had visited our apartment on Rauchstrasse a few times.

How was it, I wonder now, that of all the towns in Germany and France, Erich's colleague had come to see our circus at its very first performance, hundreds of miles from

Berlin? Such misfortune hardly seems possible. Of course he had not been such a close friend of Erich's, just an associate we encountered at holiday parties and such. Close enough, though, that he might have recognized me. We had thought by traveling to France we were moving farther from danger. But it looms here just as real.

I watch as Noa walks toward the town center, shoulders squared. She is nervous, I can tell, going into town for the first time all by herself. But she presses forward. "She really is a good girl, you know," I say aloud to Theo as I start back for the woods. I can almost feel him nod in agreement. "She loves you very much." She. What will Theo call Noa when he is old enough to speak? "Mama" seems a betrayal of the woman who gave birth to him and whose heart surely still breaks. But every child should have a chance to call some-one his mother. I shift and Theo nestles contentedly into my neck. I have never taken to children, but there is something wiser about him, an old soul. I lift him higher on my hip and begin to sing "Do You Know How Many Stars?" a merry children's tune that I have not thought of since my childhood:

Do you know how many little stars are in blue heaven's tent?
Do you know how many clouds trail all over the world?
The Lord God has counted them,
So that none of them are missing,
Among this great vast amount.

I look down at Theo. Has he heard the song before? I wonder about his parents, whether they might have sung it to him. Were they religious Jews or perhaps not observant at all? I switch to "Raisins and Almonds," a Yiddish lullaby, searching his face for some sign of recognition. He watches me with wide, unblinking eyes.

It seems so improbable, a Jewish baby finding its way to the circus and to me—another Jew. What were the odds of that happening? But we are not the only ones, I remind myself. I had been with the Circus Neuhoff about a month when I realized I was not the only Jew. I had spotted an unfamiliar man across the dining hall on the side where the workers sat, a slight, quiet laborer with a trim graying beard and a limp who kept to himself. One of the girls said he was a handyman called Metz, good at fixing small things, and so I went to him with my watch, a treasured sixteenth birthday gift from my father that no longer ran.

Metz's workshop was contained in a small shed at the edge of the winter quarters. I knocked and he bade me enter. Inside the air smelled of fresh wood and turpentine. Through a door at the rear, I could see a narrow bed and a washbasin. Small appliances and broken machine engines filled the shelves and covered the floor of the cramped space. Scattered among them were clocks of different sizes and makes, more than a dozen of them. "I was a clockmaker in Prague before the war," Metz said. I wondered how he had come to be here, but circus folk did not share much of their past. It was always best not to ask. I handed him the watch and he examined it.

As he opened a drawer to find tools I saw it: a tarnished silver mezuzah. Keeping it could have cost him his life. "Is that yours?" I asked, in spite of myself.

Metz wavered, perhaps no more knowing of my past than I his. I assumed my Jewish background was not a well-kept secret among the circus folk, but he had come during the years I was gone and perhaps had not heard. He lifted his chin slightly. "Yes."

At first I was alarmed: Did Herr Neuhoff know about this other Jew? Of course he did—he was sheltering this man just like me. I should not have been surprised. I had assumed

Herr Neuhoff had taken me in only to help the show, and perhaps as a favor to an old family friend. His kind of courage was boundless, though, and he would not have turned away a person in need, whether a star performer or a simple laborer or a child such as Theo with no skills at all. It was not about the circus or family connections, but human decency.

Herr Neuhoff had not told us of one another, though, perhaps trying to protect us in anonymity. "Beautiful." I paused. "My father had one just like it." A silent kinship passed between us.

But the mezuzah sat in plain sight at the front of the drawer, threatening his safety—and mine. "Perhaps you should be more careful with that."

The clockmaker looked at me evenly. "We cannot change who we are. Sooner or later we will all have to face ourselves."

A week later he returned the watch to me, refusing to accept money for the work. We have not spoken again since that day.

We reach the edge of the fairgrounds. I carry Theo, whose eyelids have begun to droop, across the backyard. It is a warm spring day and those who can rehearse outside. The sword swallower practices an act where he seems to cut an assistant in two and farther afield one strongman attempts to run over another with a motorized bicycle. I cringe. The acts had grown grimmer since the end of the Great War, as though people needed to see near death in order to be thrilled— mere entertainment was not enough anymore.

My heart lifts as I glimpse Peter behind the big tent, rehearsing. I have seen so little of him since our arrival in Thiers. We are too busy and too exhausted. Even on Sundays like today, our time together is not what it should be. Watching him now, my longing grows. With Erich it had always been straightforward, the way a man and a woman were supposed to be together. But Peter makes love with wild hands and lips where they have never been before and where I least expect them.

Peter is rehearsing the act I know too well, the one that mocks the Nazis' straight-legged goose-stepping—the very routine Herr Neuhoff ordered him not to perform. I had hoped after the other night's show, when he had not done the routine, that he had given up on it. He is practicing those unmistakable moves right now, though, with more determination than ever. The circus has always had to tread lightly on politics. There was a story once about an Austrian circus that had met its demise by putting a pig in a *pickelhaube*, a Prussian military helmet and uniform. But Peter seems more and more reckless these days and his skit, while subtle, is pointed enough that no one would miss the fact it was ridiculing the Germans.

Remembering, I shudder. I should have been more forceful, asked him to stop. This is not some game, poking at an animal with a stick. We have everything to lose. But watching him, my admiration grows: he is standing up to the Germans in his own way and fighting, not simply accepting what is happening and the restrictions that have been placed on us, leading to our own inevitable demise.

Or is it just the liquor that is making him bold? His raised foot wobbles midair and he sets it down hurriedly, so as not to fall. Peter has been drinking—something I can no longer ignore now that Noa had confirmed it. I am no stranger to alcohol. I had seen it among the performers in our own circus, and even with my mother when things got to be too much. Once with Peter it had been benign, a few extra glasses of wine in the evenings. I had not minded; in fact, I welcomed the way it seemed to make him more open. In front of others he spoke little. "Astrid," he would say when we were alone and I watched the drink take effect, dilating his pupils. He would really talk to me in those times, rambling tales of his boyhood in Russia before the Great War. For a moment I could see inside a bit and actually know him.

But it is different now—his drinking is getting worse. I can smell it on him in the mornings and there is an unsteadiness about him in the arena. If Noa noticed, it is only a matter of time before Herr Neuhoff does, too. Dread seeps through my skin. Drinking before practice or a show could get even the greatest performer fired. The circus cannot afford accidents and there will be no safe quarter for a performer who is sloppy or careless. And he was drinking on the first day of the tour, when things should have been fresh and new. What will it be like a month from now, when life on the road really begins to wear thin?

A commotion at the far end of the backyard pulls me from my thoughts. Herr Neuhoff storms across the grounds, face red, cigar clenched between his teeth. At first it seems he is going to berate Peter for his act again. But he is headed toward one of the Polish laborers. Milos, I think he is called, though I do not know him well. Milos is soldering a piece of tent pole, the gun shooting sparks in all directions—including toward a nearby bale of hay. Fire is a grave concern for the circus. Herr Neuhoff speaks to Milos in a low voice, trying to keep the matter quiet, but his voice rises belligerently.

Herr Neuhoff grabs the soldering gun and points in the distance. "You'll be sorry!" Milos swears. He tosses his hat to the ground, then picks it up and storms off again. Did Herr Neuhoff fire him? The circus is like a family, workers returning each year, and Herr Neuhoff is generous to them even in retirement. But carelessness cannot be tolerated.

Peter crosses the field to confer with Herr Neuhoff. I start toward them, still holding Theo. They stop talking as I near, as though they do not want me to hear. My annoyance flares. I am not some child to be sheltered. For everything I have achieved, though, I am still a woman, my status less. "What happened with the Pole?" I demand.

"I had to let him go. I had no choice. I'll find him and smooth things over, give him a good letter and a bit of severance." Herr Neuhoff's voice is uneasy.

"Letting go of an angry worker could be dangerous," Peter says. He is worried, I can tell, about protecting my identity. What if Milos tells someone, or goes to the police? As Peter watches me, I catch a flash of something deeper in his eyes. Concern, and perhaps something more. I recall what Noa had said about Peter's feelings for me. Maybe she is right. I brush the notion aside once more.

"There are all sorts of dangers," Herr Neuhoff retorts, a veiled reference to Peter's political act.

Peter does not answer but stomps away. I wonder if Herr Neuhoff will go after him. Instead, he gestures in the direction of the train, beckoning me to follow. "I need to speak with you." He stops at the door, uncomfortable in the women's carriage, even though it is empty.

Herr Neuhoff coughs, his face reddening. He pulls a handkerchief from his pocket and raises it to his mouth. When he pulls it away again, it is tinged with pink. "Are you ill?" I ask.

"My heart condition," he rasps.

I am alarmed. For all of the years I have known him, I had no idea. "Is it serious?"

"No, no," he replies, waving his hand. "But I catch every cold that comes by. The damp weather doesn't help either. As I was saying, the worker, Milos...if I offer him a severance, then word may get out and others could ask for money. But if he goes to the police...what do you think?"

I falter. There are things I can tell him that I learned from Papa. I am still a guest here, though. This is not my circus, but another time and place. I proceed cautiously. "It is a difficult decision. Everything is so different now."

"I wanted to talk to you about something else," he says, switching topics abruptly, and I realize that Milos isn't the real reason he has asked me to speak. "Astrid," he begins, using that gentle tone, the one that means he is bringing me bad news. I brace for some confirmation of what had happened to my family, the awful truth that deep down I already know. "You understand that the circus is in a very delicate position right now."

"I know," I reply. "I'm not sure what I can do to help."

"For one thing, you need to speak to Peter about the act."

This again. My worry is replaced with annoyance. "We already discussed it. I told you—we can't stop him from being who he is."

"Surely if you explained to him the jeopardy it is causing," he presses, "if he had to choose between your well-being and the show…"

"He would choose me," I say firmly, forcing more confidence into my voice than I actually feel. After what had happened with Erich, I could never be certain of that again with anyone. "But I don't want him to have to choose."

"You must," he insists. "After the show the other night, the German seeing you…"

He knows. My stomach leadens. "How did you know about that? Did Noa tell you?" Of course she had. I had confided in no one else.

"Astrid, that doesn't matter." A flash of admission crosses his face, confirming my suspicion. "What's important is that the circus has drawn more scrutiny than it can afford. I had a visit from an inspector earlier today." A rock forms in my stomach. An inspection—on a Sunday. Were they looking for me? "They are threatening to send us back," he adds.

"To Germany?" My whole body tenses.

"Possibly. Or perhaps somewhere in Alsace-Lorraine." The border region, which had gone back and forth between Germany and France for centuries, had been swiftly annexed by the Reich at the start of the war. Going to Alsace and returning to Germany were one and the same.

"Would they really do that, so soon after we've set out?" I ask, already knowing the answer.

Herr Neuhoff coughs again and rubs at his temple. "They almost didn't let us go on tour this year at all."

"Really? I had no idea." There is so much he keeps to himself.

"I know that going back is not ideal for your situation," he adds. For a second, I wonder if he is threatening me. But his voice is neutral, simply stating the facts. "You see now why I need Peter to stop."

He continues, "I've asked them for an extension, explained that the tour dates are set and that canceling would be damaging to the business. But as you know, the Reich doesn't care about business."

"No," I agree. They would not hesitate to punish us for stepping out of line.

I have been recognized and Herr Neuhoff knows it. The audacity of it all dawns on me: How could I have thought I might remain hidden in something as big and public as the circus? "I should go," I say slowly. Herr Neuhoff's eyes widen. "Leave the circus. I've brought too much danger to the show already." I have no idea where I would go. But I had left once; I could do it again.

"No, that isn't what I had in mind at all," he protests hurriedly.

"But if my presence is bringing danger, then I should leave," I persist.

"Don't be silly. The circus cannot function without you. *He* cannot function without you." Herr Neuhoff gestures with his head toward the field to the spot where Peter has returned to practicing. I wonder if what Herr Neuhoff says is true. Then I look down at Theo. He needs me, as does Noa. "You will stay. This is your home." He coughs once, then again. "If we can just ride out the season here in France."

"I understand. I will talk to Peter," I promise.

"That's a start," he says; his face remains troubled. "But I'm afraid it isn't all."

"I don't understand. What more can I do?"

"You see, the status quo is our friend and we must do whatever we can to preserve it. The circus must be kept going at all costs. So that's why I'm doing it," he says. I tilt my head, puzzled. "Since that German soldier saw you…" He takes a deep breath. "I have no choice but to remove you from the show."

12

Noa

I hurry toward the fairgrounds, not looking back toward Luc, even when I reach the cover of the trees. Halfway through the woods, I realize that I have been running. I slow to catch my breath. Meeting Luc was strange, and the way he watched me left me with a feeling of lingering discomfort. But it was exciting, too, a spark where I had not expected to feel one again. I imagine telling Astrid, confiding in her like the sister I never had.

Twenty minutes later, I reach the fairgrounds. As I near the train, I see Astrid standing by the entrance to the sleeper car, glowering. For a minute, I think she is angry that I was gone so long. Or perhaps she saw me speaking with Luc. Her eyes burn with rage as I climb onto the train. Then Herr Neuhoff's bulky silhouette appears in the doorway behind her and I realize that it is something much more serious than that.

"How could you?" she demands. "How could you do it?"

She has somehow learned my secret. About the German soldier. About the baby.

"I know the truth," Astrid snarls, coming at me. I freeze. "How could you?"

Astrid nears, arms raised, as though she intends to strike me. I step back, tripping over the edge of a steamer trunk sticking out from beneath a berth.

Astrid's face is inches from mine and I can feel her hot breath and spittle. "He's pulled me from the act." I realize she is talking about the fact that I had told Herr Neuhoff someone had recognized her at the show. She does not know my secret.

This is almost as bad, though. All of the trust I have worked to build with Astrid is gone. Her eyes glower like hot coals. "No!" I blurt. Despite his promise, Herr Neuhoff had revealed that it was me who told him after all. Now Astrid is out of the show.

"You're a liar," she says, fists clenched.

"There, there," Peter murmurs to Astrid, putting a hand on her shoulder to calm her. But he does not step between us or hold her back.

"Astrid." Herr Neuhoff steps forward, trying to intervene. "It wasn't Noa…"

But she moves around him, still coming at me. "Are you trying to replace me, you little demon?"

The idea is so far-fetched, I could almost laugh aloud—if Astrid was not so angry. "Not at all," I protest quickly. Her distrust cuts through me like a dagger. "I would never do that. I was worried about you." I had thought I was doing it for her own good, but I see now how it must look to her. A few of the other girls have gathered in the door of the carriage, and they whisper, eyeing me with unmasked hostility. Performers do not tell on one another. I had broken a cardinal rule—and risked the show. One of the girls is holding

Theo and I take him from her, clutching him close to my chest like armor.

Then I turn to Peter, who has been watching the fight. "She was in danger. You know that."

He shrugs, unwilling to side against Astrid to help me. "You shouldn't have done it. The secret was hers to tell or not." But his voice carries no force. Deep down, he knows I had done it to protect Astrid where he had not dared—and is silently thanking me for it.

"I kept your secret," Astrid growls in a low voice. I glance over my shoulder where Herr Neuhoff stands just behind me, praying he has not heard.

"This is different," I whisper. Can't she see that? I told in order to protect her. I hold my breath, waiting for her to tell the others that Theo is not my brother. But she turns away, still shaking with anger.

"We'll need to fix the damage and take precautions," Herr Neuhoff interjects, his voice more authoritative than I have heard. "Astrid will sit out the show for the remainder of our performances in Thiers."

"But Herr Neuhoff..." Astrid begins to plead her case anew. Then she stops, seeing that she has lost.

"Can she rejoin us in the next town?" I ask hopefully.

"We'll see," Herr Neuhoff replies, unwilling to promise even that much. "Meanwhile you need to prepare for the show without Astrid. Gerda will catch for you."

"But I can't," I protest. I've barely managed to fly with Astrid; there is no way I can trust anyone else. "I need Astrid." I look from Herr Neuhoff to Astrid desperately, but she simply turns away.

"Prepare them for the next show," he instructs Astrid. She has been removed from the act, but not absolved from the responsibility of having me ready. Astrid does not answer him, but turns and stares daggers at me, still not speaking.

"Come," says Gerda firmly. "We must rehearse."

I duck away and follow her from the train, grateful to escape Astrid's wrath.

The next night, I stand alone in the dressing car, apart from the other girls. Astrid is not there and, despite the warmth and noisy chatter, the carriage feels empty without her. She has not spoken to me since the previous day, even at practice. She did not sleep in our carriage, going instead, I imagine, to Peter's. When I passed her in the train corridor, I'd wanted to say something to make it better. But I couldn't find the words and she'd walked past silently, averting her eyes.

I do everything myself now, the makeup and the chalk and the tape, my hands moving where Astrid's had before. When I am fully dressed and ready, I start away from the train car in the direction of the big top. I scan the program posted at the entrance. My act has been moved to the first half of the show in order to give Gerda more time to cover both Astrid's role and her own. As I read the program with no mention of Astrid, the events of the previous day and her rage at my betrayal crash down upon me anew. She had been removed from the show—because of me. My stomach leadens, first with guilt, then dread. How can I possibly perform without her?

As I start around the big top to the backyard, I see someone lingering by the edge of the fairgrounds. A man stands separate from the rest of the gathering spectators, kicking his foot against the dirt. Luc, I realize. I stop with surprise, jumping back around the corner. What is he doing here? He had mentioned possibly coming to the show but I never expected him to actually do it. And in my worry about Astrid being removed from the act, I had nearly forgotten.

But now here he is, standing just feet away from me. My heart skips with more excitement than it should. I start toward him, then stop. He is a stranger, and one who makes me uncomfortable at that. I step into the shadow of the big top once more. Wearing a crisp dress shirt, dark hair damp and freshly combed, he looks even handsomer than when we met. He seems uncomfortable, though, keeping his head low and taking in the scene from the corner of his eye. Out of his element, not at all like the confident boy I'd met in town. I want to go to him. But there is not enough time and we cannot be seen together.

The other performers are making their way to the backyard and as they assemble, Luc slips from sight. As he disappears into the crowd, I feel a slight pang, and I fight the urge to go after him. What if he realizes that coming was a mistake and decides not to stay after all?

Looking back at the performers as they stretch and ready themselves, I notice that Astrid is not here, and though nearly the whole circus has gathered, there is a gaping hole without her. I've performed only a handful of times, guided by her strong hands. I can't possibly go on by myself.

A few minutes later, the bell rings and I hurry around the big top to take my place in the backyard. I peek through the curtain. Luc is in the first row and I wonder how he has managed such a seat on short notice. His arms are folded and he takes in the ring before him without expression. I want to run to him or at least wave. But the orchestra is nearly finished tuning and the tent goes completely dark. The opening note booms to a crescendo and the show begins. I peek out once more. Luc leans forward in his chair and a light in his eyes begins to dance as he follows the performers, scantily clad girls on horseback. My jealousy grows as he takes in their elegant, barely covered bodies.

The first half of the show, which is usually exciting and rushed, seems to take forever. To pass the time, I study the audience. In the row behind Luc sits a little girl with shiny blond curls holding a doll. She wears a pink starched dress and I can tell from the way she smooths the hem that it is her prized outfit, the one that comes out only a few times a year for special occasions. The man beside her, her father I guess, hands her a cone of freshly spun cotton candy and as she takes a bite her cheeks rise with wonder. Her eyes never leave the show.

The ring is cleared again and the clowns tumble in. Peter steps on stage and begins to perform his political routine—the very one that Herr Neuhoff forbade. He is actually doing it. Watching, I am suddenly angry: How can he choose his art, knowing the risk it brings to Astrid, and all of us? The fact that Astrid is out of the show does not mean that she is safe. The children in the audience laugh at his antics, unaware of the subtext. But the adults remain silent, some shifting uncomfortably in their seats. A couple slips out of the back of the tent.

The clowns finish to weak applause. It is our turn. Gerda and I start into the ring, finding our way in the darkness. "Gerda," I whisper as I reach the base of the ladder. "I'm going to spin just before you catch me on the second pass."

I can feel her stiffen with surprise. "Astrid never said anything about it." Astrid is in charge of all of the aerialists. She calls the shots. No one has changed her choreography before.

"It will work better," I insist. "And it changes nothing for you. The positioning will be the same. Just catch me." Before she can say anything else, I climb up the ladder. I reach

the top a second late, the spotlight already waiting for me. I
wait for Gerda's call. "Hup!"

I leap without hesitation. When I release there is a moment's panic: I have practiced only once with Gerda as my
catcher. Will she be able to manage as Astrid had? Catching
is all Gerda has ever done on the flying trapeze, though. She
grasps me easily, with forearms like thick sausages. But she
is not skilled and lacks Astrid's fire. Working with someone
other than Astrid feels like cheating, a betrayal. I look around
the ring, searching in vain for Astrid. Is she watching somewhere, hating me for going on without her?

I reach the board at the end of the first pass. Out of the
corner of my eye, I see Luc. It is one of the first rules I had
learned from Astrid upon coming to the circus: do not let
the audience—or anyone in it—serve as a distraction. I can't
help it, though. Luc is here, watching me with those same
dancing eyes as he had when I first spied him in town. He
sees only me and I am happy and suffused with fear at the
same time.

I square my shoulders. It is my act now, up to me to see
this through. I nod at Gerda. I jump exactly as I had before.
Only this time, right before I reach Gerda, I pivot midair
so I am facing away from her. But the move takes a second
longer than I planned and despite my warning, she fumbles.
I am low now, almost too low for her to reach me. There is
a slight gasp from the crowd. "Damn you," Gerda swears as
she catches me, fingers digging hard into my wrists to hold
on as we swing back, gaining height. Applause thunders as
she throws me back toward my bar.

The show breaks to intermission. I step into the backyard,
still sweaty and shaking from my near fall. From around the
side of the big top, Luc walks closer, looking for me. My
pulse quickens as he nears.

"*Bonsoir,*" Luc says with a shy smile.

"Noa!" a voice booms before I can respond. It is Astrid crossing the grounds and bearing down upon me, her eyes streaking with fury. "What the hell do you think you're doing?" she demands in German. She is even angrier than earlier when Herr Neuhoff pulled her from the show.

Luc steps forward to protect me but Astrid moves around him as though he is not there. "I told you not to add the twist," she continues to berate me.

I raise my chin. "The audience loved it." Astrid does not own the show. She does not own me.

"You were showing off for him!" She jerks her head in Luc's direction.

My cheeks flush. "That isn't true."

Before I can protest further, Herr Neuhoff walks into the backyard. I hold my breath, waiting for him to ask who Luc is, and what he is doing here. "Nice job, Noa," he says instead, smiling. It is the first time he has praised my performance and I can feel myself standing straighter, vindicated. "That variation was magnificent," he says with a smile.

I look triumphantly in Astrid's direction, wondering if she will now finally agree. But she seems to grow smaller. Guilt rises in me, replacing my joy. The ring had already been taken from Astrid. The control over the choreography was the one thing she still had—and I had stolen that, too. She turns and storms off.

"I'll be back in a minute," I tell Luc. Then I follow after Astrid, who has started away from the backyard and toward the train. I take a deep breath as she turns back to me. "You were right about the move being foolish. It was dangerous and it didn't add anything."

"That's why I told you not to do it," she sniffs, partially

mollified. "But you were showing off for him," she says again.

"Him?" Though I know she means Luc, I feign ignorance, stalling for time to respond.

She gestures toward the backyard, where Luc is waiting for me. "The mayor's son—how do you know him?"

The mayor's son? I gasp with realization. I recall then what Astrid had said about the mayor, that he is collaborating with the Nazis. Does that mean Luc is helping the Germans, too? It couldn't be.

Astrid is still watching me, waiting for an answer. "I met him when I went into town," I say finally. "I had no idea he was coming to the show."

She crosses her arms. "I thought I told you to stay away from the locals."

"You did, but some boys were being rude to me and Luc helped," I finish weakly.

"The mayor's son just happened to rush to your rescue?" Her tone is mocking. Then she lowers her voice. "Noa, we're an hour from Vichy headquarters. The mayor of this town is well connected to the Reich…" She stops abruptly as Luc walks over to us. As her words sink in, my blood chills. I had thought Luc was simply being nice. But is there a deeper reason for his interest? Astrid continues, "You claimed that you told Herr Neuhoff about Erich's colleague being at the show because you were worried about my safety. And then you do this…"

Luc, who is now close to where we stand at the edge of the backyard, interjects. "I just wanted to see the show," he offers.

Peter steps forward in front of Astrid, almost chest to chest with Luc. "You need to go back to your seat," he says in French.

"And you need to stop doing that act mocking the Germans," Luc flares with surprising force.

Peter jerks back, stunned that Luc is standing up to him in a way that so few ever have. "How dare you!"

But Luc, not intimidated, squares his shoulders. "They'll arrest you, you know."

"Who will, your father?" Though they had met only minutes earlier, hatred seethes between the two men.

Herr Neuhoff reappears. "Enough!" he orders. "We can't afford petty fights. There are officials in the audience. Gendarmes," Herr Neuhoff adds. The fact that they are not German officers is hardly reassuring. The French police are little more than puppets of the Reich these days. Peter and Astrid exchange uneasy looks. It seems too much of a coincidence just days after the German officer who knew Astrid sat in the audience.

My throat tightens. "You don't think they've come for you, do you?"

"I don't know," Astrid replies, her voice grim.

"You need to go," Peter says to Astrid. "Now." But where will she go? I wonder. When I turn to ask her, she is already gone.

The bell rings, calling the audience back to their seats from intermission. As the house lights dim, I peer into the tent. Two uniformed men stand at the back. These are not officers on leave looking for a distraction or some entertainment to relax. Their arms are folded, stance purposeful. They had not been there during the first half of the show.

I turn back to find that Peter and Astrid have disappeared from the backyard. "What should we do?" I ask Herr Neuhoff.

"Go on, just as we have. To do anything else would arouse suspicion."

From the tent comes the music of the next act, the big cats. "You should go back to your seat," I tell Luc, who is still standing beside me. "You're missing the show."

"Yes, of course." But still he lingers, brow creased. "You'll be all right? I mean, that woman, she seemed so angry at you." It is not the police, but rather Astrid who worries Luc. I take him in uncertainly. He seems so sincere. But he hadn't even told me he is the mayor's son. Could Astrid possibly be right about him?

"Can I see you after the show?" Luc presses. His voice is hopeful as he tips his head toward the grove of trees beyond the backyard. "Over there in the clearing, yes? I will wait behind the knotted oak."

"You have to go," I say, ignoring his question. I point toward his seat before slipping away.

The tiger cage is being wheeled from the stage and the next act, the high wire, prepared. Two gendarmes start forward toward the ring. I glance over my shoulder. Astrid is nowhere to be found. Could they possibly be coming for me? It seems impossible that anyone here could know about my taking Theo, but still... I look toward the back exit, desperate to go find him.

But the police reach the second row of seats and stop before the man with the little girl who had cotton candy. They crouch low as they speak to him, trying not to interfere with the show. I slink closer along the edge of the big top until I am just a few meters away from the argument, close enough to hear. One of the policemen gestures toward the exit, instructing the man to go with them. "You need to come with us." Luc twists around in his seat to see. I wait for him to say something, to intervene. He does not.

"But the show..." the father pleads, his voice rising. The orchestra halts midsong. All eyes are watching the altercation now. "Surely it can wait until the end." He places his hand on his daughter, as if protecting her.

The policemen will hear none of it, though. "Now." One reaches for the man's shoulder, prepared to drag him from the tent. What could they want with him?

"Come, darling," the father says as gently as he can to the little girl. "We will come back to the show another day." His voice breaks at the end.

"I want to see the elephants." The girl's lip quivers.

"She can stay," the policeman says coldly. "We only want you."

The man stares at the police officer in disbelief. "Monsieur, she's four. Surely you don't mean for me to leave her alone."

"Then bring her with you. Now," the officer commands.

The father takes the girl's wrist firmly, trying to leave before they are taken. But she resists, breaking into a wail and dropping to the ground, not noticing the mud that soils her dress. He is pleading with her now, desperate to cooperate before the officers intercede. There is a murmur around the ring. The townspeople have undoubtedly seen arrests before. But a father with an innocent child, taken from the show... One of the officers reaches for his truncheon.

Stop! I want to cry. I have to do something. Instinctively, I go toward the ladder at the right side of the ring and climb it. At the top, I catch the eye of the conductor and nod to him. His eyes widen with surprise. This is not in the program. Then he lifts his baton. The orchestra strikes up a lively tune and the spotlight focuses on me. Out of the corner of my eye, I see the police stop what they are doing to watch. Across the big top Astrid waves her arms, signaling me down.

It is too late. I leap from the board, swinging as high as I ever have. But now what? I have no catcher and simply swinging will not hold their attention for long. Desperately, I let go of the bar. I tuck myself into a ball and somersault once then twice through the air as I catapult downward. There is nothing to catch or stop me. Just before reaching the net I lie myself out flat, as Astrid taught me to do in case of a fall, slowing myself. I angle my rear end downward so that it, and not my limbs or neck, take the brunt.

There is a gasp as I plummet. *"Mon dieu!"* a high-pitched voice in the crowd cries. I hit the net and my head snaps forward and back. Pain shoots through me and white sparks erupt in my eyes as I slam against the floor once and then a second time, almost as hard. I lie still, too stunned and hurt to move.

I keep my eyes closed. Hands are on me, lifting me and carrying me from the net as they had Yeta the night she fell. But as we reach the ground, I shrug them off and struggle to rise on my own. Somehow despite the height and speed with which I fell, I am sore but not injured. Had it worked? I curtsy elegantly, and the applause grows. Out of the corner of my eye, I see the father carrying his daughter from the tent while the police are distracted.

"Clowns, then elephants," I hear Herr Neuhoff instruct. He has a plan, Astrid had told me once, to curtail the show without ending it abruptly. I make my way from the tent, legs shaking so much I can barely find my footing.

Astrid approaches then, having slipped out the far side of the big top and come around. "Are you all right?" she asks, and I study her unfamiliar expression, somewhere short of anger. Concern. She is worried about me—even after everything that I have done.

Tears form in my eyes. She has been so furious with me, first for telling Herr Neuhoff and then for adding the move.

"I'm sorry," I say, my voice breaking. I want so much to make everything between us whole. "I never meant to hurt you."

"I know," she says. "It's all right."

"Really?" I look up.

She nods. "Really." The forgiveness in her eyes is complete.

"I'm sorry," I repeat, needing to say it again. I burst into tears and she draws me close, letting the wetness soak the fabric of her dress without complaint.

A moment later, I straighten, drying my eyes. "But Noa, you must be careful," Astrid says once I've collected myself. Her voice is gentle but her eyes grave. "We have so much to lose now." She is talking, I realize, about Luc and the danger he could bring.

Peter approaches us from the big top and I can tell from his expression that he is angry. "Fool!" he spits at me. "Now you've caused even more trouble for the circus. What were you thinking, inviting that boy?" I am surprised—I had expected him to berate me for what I had done on the trapeze, as Astrid had. But for everything that happened, he is still furious about the mayor's son, maybe because Luc had the nerve to confront him about his act. He is worried, of course, about the danger to Astrid. I want to point out, as Luc had, that if Peter is so worried about her safety, maybe he shouldn't do acts that mock the Germans.

I do not dare. "I didn't," I protest instead. "He came on his own. He wanted to see the show."

"Of course he did," Peter retorts, his tone mocking. "The mayor's son comes and then the police? Pure coincidence. After everything we've done for you," Peter continues, gathering steam. "Taking you in and training you. And this is how you repay the kindness? We should kick you out."

Panic grows in me. What if he persuades Herr Neuhoff to do just that?

Astrid raises a hand, as if to ward him off. "Enough." Confusion clouds his eyes as she defends me. She puts her hand on his arm gently. "She did the right thing." Astrid looks at me with newfound admiration. "You could have been killed, though," she adds to me, the concern returning to her voice.

"I didn't think... I had to do something. That poor man..." My voice is trembling, though whether from the fall or Peter's wrath, I cannot tell.

"It won't matter," Peter says. "The police will go to the man's house and find him."

I hope that the man and his daughter might have had time to flee, just as I had with Theo. I want to believe against all hope that what I had done might have made a difference. But I know that they will probably not be as lucky.

"Now do you see why I had to tell Herr Neuhoff about the German?" I ask Astrid. "The arrest tonight—that could have been you."

She shakes her head stubbornly. "I would have been fine." She considers the circus a shield of armor that somehow makes her immune to the Germans. But it simply isn't true. "You can't save everyone, you know."

"I'm not trying to save everyone," I protest. "Just Theo." *And you*, I add silently. But when I had seen the police about to take that girl, something had stirred me to act, the same as it had the night I had rescued Theo from the boxcar.

"Then you must think more carefully before you act," Astrid admonishes. "Inviting the mayor's son here was foolish."

"I didn't invite him," I insist again. But I hadn't told him not to come either. "I'm sorry. I didn't mean to cause any harm."

"I know," she replies, "but our actions have consequences. Good intentions won't save us from that."

The music cues, signaling the final bow. As Astrid helps me to my feet, I feel a sharp pain across my back that I hope is nothing more than a bruise. Limping, I follow her back inside the big top and up the ladder to the perch. The gendarmes have gone. Worry mixes with my relief. Had they followed the girl and her father?

Luc has left his seat, too, I notice as I make my sweeping bows to the crowd below. I wonder if he will be waiting for me in the grove as he said. Or maybe after all that has happened, he will have given up. After everything that happened, perhaps it would be for the best.

The audience hurries from the ring after the show, not loitering as they usually do but wanting to make it home and far away from the trouble. As we make our way from the tent, Herr Neuhoff comes into the backyard. He sinks down on top of an overturned crate, breathing hard.

"An arrest at the circus," he pants. "I never would have imagined." Until recently, the circus has been a haven from the war, like being inside a snow globe while the world continues outside. But the walls are thinning. I think back to Darmstadt, recalling Astrid's reaction when I remarked that we would be safe in France. Even then she had known the truth. Nowhere is safe anymore.

Mopping at his brow with a handkerchief, he continues, "They've gone for now. But I want all of you to go back to your quarters immediately—and stay there." I wait for him to rebuke me for what I had done on the trapeze, but he does not.

I look in the direction of the grove, searching for Luc. I spy him, half-hidden behind a leaning oak. Still here. Our eyes meet. He had seen me fall and his face is racked with worry.

I start to smile, raising my hand in a low wave to signal to him that I am all right. His expression relaxes somewhat but his eyes remain locked on me, bidding me to come closer.

I take a step forward. But Herr Neuhoff is still sitting on the crate, watching. I cannot go to Luc.

I shouldn't want to anyway, I remind myself. He kept from me the fact that he is the mayor's son. Could Astrid be right about him hiding other things, as well?

Luc is still watching me, seeming to hold his breath, waiting. Several seconds pass. I take a step backward. Even if I wanted to, I would not dare defy Herr Neuhoff's order and go after the police have been here. Luc's face shifts from hopeful to confused and then disappointed as he realizes I am not coming toward him.

I take another step backward and nearly trip on something lying on the ground. By the edge of the big top, a doll lies in the dirt. I picture the girl who had been too upset at having to leave the circus to notice dropping it. Despite her father's promises, she will not be coming back. I pick up the doll and take it with me for Theo.

Then I turn back to look at Luc once more. He has started in the direction of the village, shoulders low.

"Wait!" I want to cry. But I do not and a moment later he is gone.

13

Astrid

It is not quite dawn when I climb the ladder to the trapeze in near darkness, the entire *chapiteau* lit only by a single spluttering bulb that someone had forgotten to turn off. From the benches the big top appears magnificent, but up here the fabric is faded and around the edges the tassels frayed. Old music, tinny like that of the carousel at the end of the midway, plays in my mind. I see my brothers, teasing one another as they prepared to perform. The air seems to dance with the ghosts of my family.

I take hold of the bar and jump, flying through the air. I am ignoring my own admonishment to Noa never to fly alone. I have no choice, though. I can no longer perform, but I cannot stay on the ground. "You are addicted to the adrenaline," Peter has accused me more than once. I want to argue, but it is true. There is a moment as I stare down from the board, the split second before I let go, where I am always certain I am going to die. That clarity—the focus of that moment—is what I miss most about not performing, more so than the adulation of the crowd or anything else.

The previous night when Noa had gone into the ring without me was the first time I had ever actually observed the circus in its entirety. As I watched the show, I was reminded of the time Erich had taken me to the Volksoper to see a show, *Die Jungfrau von Orleans*. Surrounded by the fashionable Berlin women and clouds of Chanel, I shifted around in my seat awkwardly, feeling as if I did not belong. But as the show began, I was able to see so much that others could not, the way the set was made to give the illusion of depth, how the act was enhanced with the little tricks all we performers had. I realized then that I could see through people, on stage or not. I had been doing it my whole life.

I fly higher, as if trying to outrun my memories. Heaving my legs upward, I swing high back to the board. Fine perspiration coats my skin and my legs ache pleasantly. That Herr Neuhoff said I might get to perform again when we reach the next town is little consolation. That is still two weeks away—a lifetime of performances. And there are no guarantees that I will be permitted to remain in the ring; now that Herr Neuhoff is aware of the peril, he will pull me from the show at the slightest of scares.

Scares like the police interrupting the show a few days earlier. Seeing the little girl's face in the audience, the full magnitude of just how bad things have become crashes down upon me. She had started that day brightly like any other— as I had that last morning in Berlin with Erich—not knowing in just hours her world would be destroyed.

I wipe my eyes, brushing away the sting. In my family one did not cry, not for illness or death or other tragedy, and even as a girl I had held my tears through it all. It could have been worse, I remind myself; it could have been me the police had come to arrest.

I leap again and hang on to the bar in midair, not trying

to swing higher, but letting the gentle rocking motion carry me back and forth. It seems for just a moment that if I do not move I can go back in time and everything will be as it once was. My body, this flight, they cannot take these from me—despite the thing Noa had done.

The *things* Noa had done, I correct myself. It was more than just telling Herr Neuhoff about the German officer. She had invited the mayor's son to the show. And she had thrown herself from the trapeze in an attempt to save that man and his daughter from the police, a stunt as foolish as it was brave. Though we are nothing alike, more and more I see a headstrongness about Noa that reminds me of myself when I was young. An impulsiveness that makes her a danger to herself—and to all of us.

Suddenly I am dizzy. Something hits my stomach then, a wave of nausea so strong I almost lose my grip on the bar. I break out in a sweat and my palms grow dangerously moist. I struggle to make my way back up to the board. Failing moments like this are why I tell Noa she should not swing alone. Looking down, I am seized with fear. Circus performers are not known to have long lives. There were those who died in their act or were injured to the point they withered away. I run through the performers I know, those in my family and beyond, to try to find a single one who had lived to his or her seventieth birthday. But I cannot.

With a last desperate swing, I soar higher and reach the platform, legs trembling. I have never fallen before, or even come close. What is wrong with me?

Another wave of nausea sweeps over me and I make it down the ladder just in time to heave into a bucket that is not my own. I carry it outside to wash at the pump before anyone notices. The stench of wet bile causes my stomach to roil anew. I press my hand against my midsection. I had practically been born in the air and have never been sick from it. I've heard other aerialists speak of such things, suddenly being unable to tolerate the height or motion, but that was when they were ill or pregnant.

Pregnant. I freeze, stunned by the idea. It simply isn't possible. But it is the only answer that makes sense. There had been a liquor-filled night right before leaving the winter quarters. I had not bled in almost three months, but that was not uncommon, and I attributed it to the toll performing and practicing took on my body. Surely if it were something more, I would have known.

I return to the big top and sit numbly on one of the benches, denial whirling through my mind. Erich and I had tried so long to have a child. Before his work became all-consuming, we would make love nearly every night and two or three times a day on the weekends. But nothing had ever come of it. I had assumed that the fault had all been mine. I'd wondered how my mother could have been fertile enough to bear five children and me none. Year after year it hadn't happened, and eventually we stopped talking about it.

The problem had lain with Erich, I realize, smugly. Not me. His perfect Aryan body was flawed. There would be no family for him with someone else either.

But my anxiety quickly eclipses any bit of satisfaction. Pregnancy had been the furthest thing from my mind, a child a long-forgotten dream. I am too old to be starting a family. Peter, with his moods and depression, hardly seems like an ideal father. We are not *that* kind of a couple. And we have no home.

I could take care of it. I have heard whispers of such things more than once during my years with the circus. Even as I think it, though, I know this is not an option.

Peter walks in and it is the one time I am not glad to see

him. I swipe a hand across my cheeks to make sure they are dry, then cover my stomach, as though he might see the difference. I do not want to tell him and add to the stress and exhaustion of performing and being on the road. He does not need to worry about this now. I wait for him to see that I am pale and shaking, or perhaps smell the stench that lingers about me.

But he is too distracted to notice. "Come, I want to show you something," he says, taking my hand and leading me from the ring to his cabin. It is close to the edge of the fairgrounds, a single, solid room not much larger than a shed. I stand in the doorway uncertainly, the smell of damp wood and earth mixing with stale smoke. I have not stayed with him since coming to Thiers because he's been rehearsing so intently I haven't wanted to intrude. Will he try to take me in his arms? I do not think I can bear to be close to him right now. Instead he beckons me past the bed. On the other side stands a new piece of furniture, a low rectangular oak chest, about five feet long, almost like an oversize steamer trunk.

"It's lovely," I say and run my hand over the wood, admiring the elaborately carved lid. "Where did you get it?" And why? Peter, with his Spartan and comfortless cabin, is not one for material possessions.

"I saw it at the local market and bartered with the woodworker. Don't worry." He smiles. "I got a good price." But it isn't that; the piece is solid and permanent, so impractical and out of place for the circus. What will he do with it when we move on?

Peter is not an illogical man and I wait for the further explanation that will make sense. He opens the lid and runs his hand along the bottom. Then he lifts it up, revealing a secret compartment, maybe a foot deep—just enough for a small person, if one laid flat. "Oh!" I exclaim.

"Just in case," he says. He means for me to hide in it, if the SS or police come again. He watches my face and I try to control my reaction to the space, suffocating and coffin-like. "We really haven't had a suitable hiding place for you here so I thought this might do," he explains, trying to sound matter-of-fact. But his face is grave. Seeing the police try to arrest the man at the show had shaken Peter, as well. He knows as I do that the Germans or the French police will come again. That we must be ready.

He is trying to protect me. But there is something in his eyes, more than concern or even just affection. I had seen that look once before when Erich and I were first married. I turn away, shaken. I recall then what Noa had said about Peter's feelings for me. I had been so quick to deny it, not wanting to see or believe. When I peer back at his hopeful eyes, though, I know that she was right. How had I not seen it before? Until now it had been easy to just mark this as a relationship of convenience. Then Noa held a mirror up to my face and I can ignore it no longer. I think back over the months, Peter constantly by my side, trying to protect me. His feelings were not sudden or new. They had been there all the time. How had Noa, so young and naive, seen everything while I had missed it?

"You hate it," he says, running his hand over the chest and sounding disappointed.

Yes, I want to say, though I had vowed after what happened in Darmstadt that I would never hide again. "Not exactly," I reply instead, not wanting to hurt his feelings when he meant well. "It's perfect," I add, too quickly. In truth, it is smaller than the hiding place in Darmstadt. I could scarcely manage it now, much less when my stomach grows larger.

"Then what is it?" he asks, cupping my chin in his hand and studying my face. "You're so pale. Are you ill? Did something happen?" His face creases with concern as he sees through my facade, sensing something wrong.

Terror seizes me then. Not at my pregnancy or the danger of being caught by the police, or even the SS. No, I am petrified of this...this thing between me and Peter. It started as two people who were lonely, drawn to each other to fill a void. And it was meant to stay that way. But at some point when I was not paying attention, it had turned into so much more—for me as well as for him.

I hesitate. Telling Peter will change everything. But I cannot worry him like this by remaining silent. And there is a part of me that desperately wants to share the news with him. *Tell him,* a voice more Noa's than mine seems to say inside my head. He loves me and that will be enough.

I take a deep breath, exhale. "Peter, I'm pregnant." I hold my breath waiting for his reaction.

He does not answer but stares at me blankly. "Peter, did you hear me?" I ask. The walls seem to draw closer and the air is suffocating. "Please, say something."

"That's impossible," he says, his voice filled with disbelief.

"It's true," I reply weakly. What did he think we had been doing all of those nights in the winter quarters?

He stands up and begins to pace, running his hand through his hair. "I mean, it's possible of course," he continues, as though I had not spoken. "Just hard to believe. And with everything that is going on right now, it complicates things."

My heart sinks. Telling him had been a mistake. "You don't sound pleased," I say, and my cheeks burn, as though I have been slapped. "I didn't plan this. I'm sorry to inconvenience you."

He sits again and takes my hands. "No, darling, it isn't that at all," he replies, his face softer now, tone gentle. "Nothing would make me happier."

"You mean, you want to be a father?" I ask, surprised.

"No," he says quickly and my heart sinks. He does not want this after all. "It's that I already am." His voice is slow and scratchy, every word hard-fought.

"I don't understand." The room around me begins to spin and bile rises in my throat once more. I will myself to take short, shallow breaths. "What are you talking about?"

"I had a child." *Had.* His face is more pained than I have ever seen it.

"Oh!" I gasp. I am stunned. I had assumed Peter had a life before me, but a child? Suddenly it seems I do not know him at all.

"I was married to a ballerina from Moscow named Anya," he says, looking away, his voice hollow. I try to picture his wife, and imagine with more than a little jealousy someone tall and willowy, with long graceful limbs. Where is she now? "We had a little girl, Katya." His voice cracks as he says her name. He tries to continue, moving his lips, but no sound comes out.

"What happened?" I ask, dreading the answer but at the same time needing to know.

He sits mutely for several seconds, unable to go on. "Spanish flu. The best doctors and hospitals couldn't help her."

"How old was she?"

"Four." He buries his head in his hands, his back shaking with silent sobs. I sit helplessly beside him, my mind reeling as I try to process it all. A few minutes later, he lifts his head, wiping his eyes. "I suppose I should have said something sooner, but it's just so hard.

"Anya died shortly after Katya," he adds. "The doctor said it was also flu. I think it was a broken heart. So it was all gone, you see." His voice catches and I wonder if he might break down once more.

"I'm sorry." I throw my arms around him and rest my head against his shoulder. But my sympathy is inadequate and it is impossible to ease a pain I did not share. I understand so much more about him then, his dark moods and his drinking.

"This brings painful memories for you," I add.

He shakes his head. "No, it is good to remember both of them. But you see why I am nervous."

"I understand." He is afraid, I realize, of having another child, loving as deeply as he once had. Then, he had all of the money and privilege in the world and it had not been enough. How could he possibly protect and care for a child now? "It will be fine," I say, forcing conviction into my voice to cover my own doubts. "We can do this." Now it is my turn to be strong.

"Yes, of course we can," Peter replies, forcing a smile. He kisses me once, then again. He brings his mouth to my eyelids, lips, cheeks, breasts. His weight pushes me back against the bed and for a second it seems he will try to take me. But he simply rests his head on my belly, not speaking.

"Before you, I had given up hope," he says finally. "I don't know what I would do without you. I love you," he adds. The feelings that he has kept pent up since we've been together seem to bubble forth. And though I once longed for them, I am overwhelmed. It is too much now, to carry him and the child.

He lifts his head and a light seems to dawn in his eyes. "We should get married," he declares, taking both of my hands in his own. *Married*. The word reverberates in my head. Once it had meant something. Now in my mind, I see the papers Erich had thrust before me, saying that none of it had mattered at all, hear the clatter of my wedding ring as it fell to the floor of our apartment.

"Oh, Peter." There was only once for me and marriage. I

cannot fathom anyone wanting me in that way—or ever letting myself get that close to a man again. "We can't."

"No, of course not," he says quickly, unable to mask his disappointment.

I cup his cheek. "In my heart, I am already married to you."

"Or we could leave," he says. I am surprised. Peter had always rejected the idea before because there was nowhere else he could perform as he does here. But now with the prospect of a child, everything has changed.

"I can't leave," I reply. "Here I can hide." At least for now. Once I might have taken the chance and fled. This is about something bigger than just my own safety now, though. I touch my stomach once more. "And Noa needs me..."

"The girl?" His expression is puzzled. "Why should she matter? I didn't think you even liked her."

"No, of course not, but still..." It's true, I admit. I disliked Noa from the first, and even more after she had gotten me pulled from the show. But she depends on me, as surely as Theo does her. "You could go if you really wanted," I offer. The words hurt to say.

He wraps his arms more tightly around me. "I will never leave you," he says, and his hand lowers to my stomach. "Or our child."

Someone who will not leave me, I think, wishing for my younger self, the one who might have believed it. "It will be all right," I say, pushing away my doubts.

"Better than all right. A family." I smile through my fears. Can such things possibly be? But my child will be Jewish. An image flashes through my mind of Noa making her way blindly through the woods in the snow with Theo before we found her. We are barely able to protect one Jewish child—how on earth would we ever protect two?

14

Noa

"No, no!" Astrid cries during practice the following Sunday, her voice ringing so shrilly through the big top that one of the jugglers practicing below drops her silver rings to the ground with a clatter. "You must go higher!"

I swing my legs harder as Gerda throws me back toward the bar, trying to heed Astrid's command. But when I make it to the board and look down, her face is still dissatisfied.

"You must get your legs above your head," she scolds as I climb down the ladder.

"But you said not to break the line of my body, so I thought…" I begin, then stop, knowing I will not win. Astrid has been ill-tempered these past few days, snapping at everything I say and berating me for the same routines that were just fine a few days earlier. Watching her lips curl with displeasure, I wonder if she is still angry about my part in having her removed from the show. She had seemed to forgive me nearly a week earlier but now I'm not so sure.

"What's wrong?" I ask.

She opens her mouth as if there is something she wants to

say. "It's nothing," she replies finally, but she does not sound as though she means it.

"Astrid, please," I press. "If there is something, maybe I can help."

She smiles but there is no happiness in her eyes. "If only that were true," she says, then walks away and starts up the ladder.

So there is something wrong, I think, knowing better than to press. "Are we going to keep rehearsing?" I ask instead, dreading the answer.

But she shakes her head. "We're done for today." She reaches the board and takes the bar, leaps without warning. Though she cannot perform in the show, this has not stopped her from flying, faster and fiercer than ever. She works without a catcher now, barely touching the bar, in a way that seems impossible even as I watch.

I walk across the practice hall to Peter, who has stopped training to watch Astrid. "We have to stop her," I say. "She's going to kill herself."

But his eyes are a mix of admiration and futility and his posture resigned. "I cannot stop her from her greatness, being who she is."

"This is not greatness—it is suicide," I retort, surprised that I dare speak so forcefully to him.

Peter stares at me oddly. "Astrid would never kill herself. She has too much to live for." There is an uneasy tone to his voice. Maybe he knows what is bothering Astrid. But before I can ask, he walks away.

Taking a last worried look up at Astrid, I pull my wrap skirt and blouse on over my practice leotard. I walk from the big top and start across the fairgrounds. It is late afternoon on Sunday, a little over a week since we arrived in Thiers, and I want to feed Theo myself and spend as much time as

I can with him before he falls asleep. Close to the tracks the water truck has pulled up and people are hurrying to fill their buckets at the back of it. There are endless buckets everywhere at the circus, for washing and drinking and other things. The first time I'd spied two with my name on them in the row waiting to be filled at Darmstadt, I'd known that I belonged with the circus just a tiny bit more.

I fill my buckets, one for washing and one for drinking, and carry them to the train, eager to change and reach Theo. I climb the stairs of the railcar, taking care not to spill. The sleeper car, where I expected to find him waking from his nap, is empty. Theo is not there.

Easy, I tell myself, starting back outside. Sometimes the girls who watch the children take them outside for fresh air. A few children are behind the train, rolling a ball, while the two girls meant to be watching them chat idly. Theo is not with them.

Where is he? My heart pounds. Has he been lost? Taken? I start across the backyard to find Astrid again. She will know what to do. Then in the distance I hear a giggle. My eyes dart toward the pens where the animals are kept. Theo is near there, in the arms of Elsie, one of the girls who minds him. I relax slightly.

But as I start across the grassy field, Elsie walks toward the lion's cage. I see her talking to Theo, pointing as they near one of the animals. The cage here is flimsy—a few metal bars, spaced too widely apart—nothing separating Theo from the fierce beast. Elsie is casual and unafraid as she walks Theo right up to the cage. His hand reaches out as if patting a dog.

"No!" I cry, my voice lost in the wind. Theo puts his hand through the cage, his fingers just inches from a lion's mouth.

"Theo!" I run toward him, feet pounding against hard earth, kicking up bits of grass and dust.

I reach Theo and grab him from the girl's arms. The lion, startled by my sudden movement, lunges at the bars with a roar, swiping the very spot where Theo had been.

I leap back, tripping and stumbling to the ground. Theo lets out a wail. A sharp rock cuts into my palm as I break my fall, but I hardly notice. I clutch Theo to my chest, shielding him. I breathe hard, not getting up, trying to comfort Theo, who is more upset than I have ever seen him. Another second and I would have been too late.

"Shh," I soothe, studying Theo. Though his face is red from bawling, he does not seem to be hurt. Then I stand, brush the dirt from my knees. "How could you?" I berate Elsie, whose face is pale.

"W-we were just playing," she explains, flustered. "I wanted to show him the lion up close. I meant no harm."

But I am still furious. "That animal—he could have killed Theo. And this outfit..." Holding him close, I notice then Theo is dressed in a sequined leotard, too large and hastily pinned to fit. "What on earth is he wearing?"

Over her shoulder, I see Astrid coming from the big top. She strides across the field, her face a mix of anger and concern. "What's the commotion?"

"She was holding Theo right up against the lion's cage," I say, my voice rising as I relive my terror. "He might have been killed!"

She takes Theo from me and he stops crying, but gulps for air as he recovers. "He seems fine. Was he hurt?"

"No," I admit, swatting at one of the flies that buzz perennially around the animal cages. I had expected her to side with me, even through her anger. How can she not be troubled by what Elsie had done? "But look at his clothes!"

"Pretty soon he'll start training," she observes mildly.

"Training?" I repeat, puzzled.

"To perform," she replies. Though we have never discussed Theo joining the act before, Astrid speaks as though it is a given.

I stare at her, caught speechless. I had not imagined Theo performing, or thought about a future for him with the circus at all. "He's just a baby," I say. Theo squawks, also seeming to protest.

"I was on the trapeze almost before I could walk," Astrid says. "Of course it was a fixed trapeze." I shudder. In Astrid's world, it is perfectly normal for children to perform. Theo will not learn the trapeze, though, or any other circus act. His life—our life—will be somewhere else.

"He's too young," I insist, not mentioning the fact that I will never let him perform at all.

Astrid does not respond. She is looking over my shoulder, squinting at something across the field that leads to town. "Someone's coming." I turn and follow her gaze.

"Luc," I say aloud, more to myself than Astrid. It has been nearly a week since the night he came to the circus. I thought after that he had given up, or was scared away. I had not expected to see him again.

That might have been for the best, I think as he nears. He is the mayor's son and, as Astrid had made clear, not to be trusted. "What is he doing here?" she asks, her voice curling with displeasure.

"I don't know," I say, suddenly defensive. It is not as if I've done anything to encourage him. My heart lifts in spite of itself as Luc comes toward us, a small bunch of daffodils clutched in one hand, his black hair lifted by the breeze. "But I'll find out." I look down at Theo, hesitating. I do not want to let him go so soon after finding him in danger, or give him back to Elsie to watch. I hate asking Astrid for anything right now, but I am too curious. "Will you mind Theo for a bit?" I muster, knowing how she will respond.

"I'm already your trainer—now I'm supposed to be your nursemaid, too?" she snaps. I do not answer. She is annoyed, but also she adores Theo and cannot deny him. "Oh, fine, if I must. Go. Don't be gone long." She takes Theo from my arms and starts back toward the train.

I hang back as Luc approaches. "You again," I say, trying to sound offhand. I am suddenly mindful of my hair, hastily pulled back, and my cheeks, too red from the strain of rehearsing. "You keep turning up."

Luc hangs back for a second, looking nervously over my shoulder at Astrid as she walks away with Theo. "I hope it is okay that I've come."

"I suppose," I say matter-of-factly.

"I didn't think you'd want me to," he says. "You didn't meet me after the show. I came as I promised and I waited to see you after for as long as I could. You never came."

"I couldn't after everything happened with the police," I say. "Besides, we had a curfew. People were watching. I couldn't get out to tell you."

"That's all right," he says, forgiving me instantly. "I brought you these." He thrusts the flowers at me awkwardly. Sweet fragrance wafts over me as I take them, fingers brushing his. I put one in my hair and a second in the top button of my blouse.

"Walk with me?" Luc starts away but I stand, feet planted. Not following. He turns back. "You're not coming?"

"Your father," I say.

A look of realization comes over his face. "What about him?"

"He's the mayor. Why didn't you tell me?" I ask.

"Because it didn't come up," he replies uneasily.

"How could it not come up?" I ask. "You're the mayor's son."

"You're right, of course," he admits, his voice contrite. "I should have said something, and I would have if I'd gotten the chance to meet up with you. I guess I was just hoping that it wouldn't matter." Or maybe because he knew it would matter a lot. "Does it?" he asks. "Matter, I mean."

I hesitate, considering. I don't care that his father is the mayor, not in the way that Astrid and the others do. If his father is a Nazi sympathizer, though, then what does that make Luc? He seems too nice to possibly be that way himself.

Luc is still watching me with worried eyes, seeming to care very much about my answer. "I suppose not," I concede finally. "But it would have been better to know." Somehow, it is the not telling that matters more. But I have my own secrets, so who am I to judge anyone on that?

"No more secrets, I promise." I hold my breath. I can hardly promise the same. But he reaches out his hand. "Now can we walk?"

I look uneasily over my shoulder. I shouldn't go with him, I think, hearing Astrid's admonition that getting to know Luc could bring danger. And I want to get back to Theo quickly. "I'm hardly dressed," I say, feeling the still-damp leotard clinging to my skin.

Luc smiles. "Then we won't go anywhere grand."

"All right," I relent. Despite my reservations, I'm curious about him—and eager to escape the chaos and intensity of the circus for just a bit.

He leads me toward the edge of the woods, the same path Astrid had shown me the day I went into town. I follow him hurriedly from the circus grounds so as not to be seen. I look back over my shoulder in the direction of the train car, imagining Astrid putting Theo to sleep. I do not want to burden her and I barely had the chance to see Theo at all. "I'm afraid I only have a few minutes."

"The others, they don't want me around, do they?" he asks.

"It isn't that." The truth, that they think he somehow brought trouble with him, seems far-fetched and too hurtful to share. "They're just a little nervous about outsiders. I suppose everyone is these days."

"I don't want to cause problems for you," he says. "Perhaps I should have stayed away."

"No," I reply sharply. "That is, I can make my own decisions."

"Then let's go," he says. We continue silently through a break in the trees that forms a small grove. Soon we reach the far side of the forest. We skirt the edge of the stream, this time headed away from the town, which looms behind us, seeming to watch with disapproving eyes. I had wanted to be alone with Luc, but now that it is just the two of us, it is awkward, almost uncomfortable.

He stops and sits on a bit of ground that juts out over the stream like a bluff, then clears some reeds and smooths a spot for me to join him. I drop to the damp ground, feeling the chill that has formed in the air now that the sun has fallen low behind the distant hills. "I brought you this." He pulls an orange from his pocket.

I have not seen miraculous fruit like this since before the war. "Thank you," I say graciously. How had he gotten it? Because of his father's position as mayor—a position that hurts others. I hand back the tainted fruit. "I can't accept it, though."

As I hand the orange to him, I notice that his index finger is bent at a crooked angle, somehow deformed. He puts the orange back in his pocket, his face crestfallen. Then he holds out something else wrapped in brown paper. "Take this, then. I bought it with my ration cards, honestly." I open it to reveal a piece of hard Cantal cheese between two slices of brown bread. I falter. Refusing food for myself is one thing, extra sustenance for Theo quite another. "Thank you," I say, moved by his generosity and selflessness for me, a stranger. I rewrap the food and stick it in my pocket.

A sound interrupts us from behind, the rumble of a truck, growing louder on the road. I stand up hurriedly, not wanting to be seen. "I have to go," I say, panicking at the questions that will arise if I am seen with Luc.

But he takes my hand, stopping me. "Come." He leads me swiftly back into the woods, following a path that shoots off in a different direction. We slow as we reach a clearing and he looks around. "All clear," he says.

Still my heart races and I am reminded of every reason I should stay away. "Those police who came to the show to arrest the man and the girl...they work for your father, don't they?"

"Yes." He lowers his head. "I'm so sorry. I had no idea that was going to happen. I'm sure it was ordered from somewhere much higher up. He must not have had a choice."

"There is always a choice."

He keeps his eyes low, not meeting my gaze. "If you don't want to see me now because of everything that happened, I understand."

"Not at all," I reply, too quickly.

"Then come." My fingers warm to his touch as he takes my hand once more and continues to walk.

Soon the forest ends, and across an open field, a barn appears darkly silhouetted against the dusky sky. Luc starts toward the barn.

"Luc, wait..." I say uneasily as we near the door of the

barn. Going for a walk together is one thing. But going inside with him seems like something more, a step too far. "I have to get back," I say. I imagine Astrid, knowing exactly where I am, watching the clock angrily.

"Just for a few minutes, so we are out of sight," he cajoles.

The wood door creaks as Luc pulls it open. He steps aside, gesturing for me to enter first. Inside, the barn is empty, the air thick with the smell of rotting wood and damp hay.

"How did you find this place?" I ask.

"This is the very edge of my family's property. Don't worry," he adds, seeing my alarmed expression. "No one ever comes out here anymore but me."

He gestures upward toward the loft. "No one will find us here."

I look up dubiously, suddenly mindful that it is just the two of us alone, far from the circus or anywhere else. "I don't know…"

"We're just talking," he says, his voice challenging. "What harm can that do?"

Luc climbs up to the loft then and helps me, fingers moist on my wrist. It is a small rectangular area, maybe two meters by three, close to the sloped A-frame roof of the barn. Rough wood boards are covered in hay that tickles my legs beneath my skirt. Luc slides back a slatted wood window panel to reveal the rolling hills that lead to the village, patchwork fields broken by mossy farmhouse roofs. Lights sparkle in some of the windows before blackout curtains fall, seeming to snuff them out like candles. It is peaceful—and so pristine, it is almost possible for a moment to forget about the war.

Luc points out at a small steeple on the horizon, silhouetted against the setting sun. "I went to *école* there," he says and I smile, picturing him as a young boy. He had lived his whole life right in this village, much as I might have back home had things been different. He goes on, "I have two older sisters, both married and living in towns not far away. My grandparents lived with us, too, when I was a child. There was always so much laughter and noise." There is a longing note to his voice that makes clear those times are far gone.

He reaches under a pile of hay and produces a darkened glass bottle, half-empty. "A bit of Chablis from my father's cellar," he says, grinning wickedly. He passes it to me and I take a sip from the bottle. Though I know nothing about wine, I can tell that it is a good vintage, the taste layered, spicy and deep.

In the corner where he had hidden the wine, I notice something still half-hidden beneath the hay. Curious, I move closer. There is a thick tablet and a set of paints. "You're an artist," I remark.

He laughs, wrapping his arms around his knees. "That's a big word for it. I sketch, when I can get paper. I paint, though not so much anymore. My mother loved art and was forever taking me to galleries wherever we went on holiday. Once I wanted to go to Paris and study at the Sorbonne." His eyes are animated as he speaks of art and his childhood.

"Is it far? Paris, I mean." I am embarrassed not to have a better sense of geography.

"About four hours by train these days with all of the stoppages. I went with my mother to see the museums. She loved art." There is a note of sadness to his voice now.

"You still live with your parents?" I ask.

"Just my father. My mother died when I was eleven."

"I'm sorry," I say. Though my own parents are still alive, his loss seems to echo my own, strengthening the ache I have worked so hard to bury. I want to touch his arm in comfort, but it seems I do not know him well enough. "Do you still plan to study art?" I ask instead.

"It doesn't seem possible anymore." He gestures to the countryside below with long tapered fingers.

"But you still want it," I press.

"Painting seems so frivolous now," he replies. "I don't know what to do—I don't want to just sit here. Papa wants me to join the LVF, but I don't want to fight for the Germans. He says it doesn't look right for the mayor's son not to go, and I can only hold him off for so long. I'd run away, but I don't want to leave Papa alone."

"There has to be another way," I offer, though I'm not sure I believe it.

"It's just this damned war," he says, his voice rattling with frustration. I am surprised to hear him swear. "It's turned everything on its head." He turns away. "What happened at the show the other day with the man and the girl, it isn't the first time. There were Jewish families in Thiers who had been here my whole life. They lived over on the east side of town, just past the market. One of the boys, Marcel, was a friend of mine at école."

"Your father, he orders the police to round them up?" I ask.

"No!" he snaps, then quickly recovers. "My father follows orders. He maintains a pretense of support in order to protect the village."

"And to protect himself," I blurt out, unable to hold back. "How can you stand it?"

"Really, he isn't like that," Luc continues, calmer now, his voice pleading. "Papa was different before my mother died. He once gave a family a house for an entire year rent-free." Luc needs to believe that his father is a good man, and he is asking me to believe it, too. I had done the same. After my own father had kicked me out, I still remembered the mornings when we'd walk into town for fresh bread, just the two of us, him whistling as we went. He had bought me an extra croissant. I was still that girl, though. What had changed?

Luc continues, "I begged my father to at least help Marcel's family. But he said there was nothing to be done." His words pour out in a tumble as though he has not until this very moment been able to share with another the things that he has seen.

"It's hard when the people we love do awful things," I offer.

We both sit silently then, the now-dark sky causing the light in the loft to dim. I notice that his jaw is square and strong, a faint late-day stubble pressing through.

"Where are you from?" he asks, changing the subject.

I shift uneasily. Until now, I have managed not to say much about myself. "The Dutch coast. Our village was so close to the sea you could walk down to the end of the road and catch your dinner." It seems so strange to be talking about the life I'd lost. I want to tell him everything, about how my parents cast me out and how I found Theo. But of course I cannot.

"Why did you leave?" Luc asks abruptly.

No matter how many times I am asked that question, I am still ill-prepared to answer it. "My father was very cruel, so when my mother died I took my brother and fled," I say, repeating the now-familiar tale. I am not ready to tell him the truth.

"It's hard not having your mother," he says, looking deeply into my eyes. I hate myself for the lies I've told. But right now, even though my mother is not dead, losing her feels more real and painful than ever. "And then you joined the circus?" he asks.

"Yes. Just a few months ago." I pray he will not ask about the time between.

"It's remarkable that you learned to do all of those tricks so quickly." His voice is full with admiration and wonder.

"Astrid trained me," I say.

"That angry older woman?" I struggle not to laugh at his perception of Astrid.

At the same time I am defensive of an outsider criticizing her. "She's amazing," I say.

"She didn't perform at the show," Luc notes, but I don't reply. I can't tell him the rest of the story, why Astrid is angry with me, without revealing to him the fact that she is a Jew. "Perhaps she's jealous that you were in the show and she wasn't," Luc ventures.

I laugh aloud. "Astrid, jealous of me? That isn't possible." Astrid is talented, famous, powerful. But then I see myself through her eyes, a younger woman with the child fate had denied her, performing when she cannot. Maybe the idea is not so ridiculous after all. "It isn't like that," I add. "Astrid is a famous aerialist. She's just very intense. Peter says she's a danger to herself," I add.

"Peter, he's the clown?" Luc asks.

I nod. "He and Astrid are together."

"He sure didn't like me," Luc says with a half smile.

"He's very protective of Astrid," I explain. "She thinks it's just for company but she can't see the depth of his feelings for her."

He watches me intensely. "I can imagine."

I look away, feeling myself blush. "The show...you never told me what you thought." I brace myself for the criticism that would surely crush me.

"You looked beautiful," he offers and I blush. "You were

amazing." He pauses for a moment, then adds, "It's just that I was sad for you."

"Sad?" My happiness fades.

"Doesn't it bother you?" he asks. "All of those people, watching, I mean?" His tone is one of concern. But there is pity, too. "You don't have to do it, you know," he adds.

I can't explain that in the spotlight I am someone else. Still, how dare he judge us? "I've found something I'm good at," I say defensively, crossing my arms. "A way to take care of myself and Theo. Not that you would understand."

Suddenly being alone with him and all of the lies between us are too much. "I have to go," I say abruptly. I stand so quickly I lose my balance, nearly tumbling from the loft.

"Wait." Luc grabs my leg to steady me, his arm warm through the fabric of my dress. I look down. Though it is not nearly as high as the trapeze, there is no net and I am paralyzed with fright. What am I doing here?

Luc draws me down to the hay once more, closer now. He places a hand against my cheek. "Noa," he says gently. Our faces are inches apart, his breath warm on my upper lip. Waves of confusion swirl around me. He likes me; I know that now. I cannot pull away.

Luc kisses me. For a second, I stiffen. I should say no for a dozen reasons: it is impertinent of him, presumptuous and too soon. Astrid would say I should not be here with him at all. But his lips are tender and sweet with wine. His warm fingers cup my cheek, seeming to lift me from the ground. Our breath mingles. For a moment I am just a carefree, young girl again. I move closer, pushing the past firmly aside as I fall into him.

When Luc pulls back, he is breathless and I wonder if it is his first real kiss. He reaches for me again, eager for more. But I put my hand on his chest, stopping him.

"Why me?" I ask bluntly.

"You're different, Noa. I've lived in this village my whole life with the same people. The same girls. You make me see the world in a new way."

"We won't be here for that long," I protest. "And then we'll move on. To the next town." No matter how much we like one another, I am leaving and there is nothing to be done. We have only now.

"I don't want to go," I blurt, embarrassed to feel my eyes burn. I've lost so much before: my parents, a child. Luc, a boy I hardly know, should not matter at all.

"You don't have to," he says, drawing me close. "We could run away together."

I tilt my head upward; surely I've heard him wrong. "That's madness. We've only just met."

He nods firmly. "You want to leave. So do I. We could help each other."

"Where would we go?"

"To the south of France," he replies. "Nice, maybe or Marseilles."

I shake my head, remembering Astrid's tale of her family and their failure to outrun the Reich. "Not good enough. We would have to go farther south, across the Pyrenees through Spain." *We.* I stop, hearing the word that has slipped from my mouth without realizing it. "Of course it's impossible." A delightful fairy tale, like one I would spin for Theo to soothe him to sleep. Children playing make-believe. I had always planned to take Theo and go. But now the idea of leaving is hard to imagine. "I have to go with the circus to the next town. I owe them that much."

"I'll find you," he promises gamely, as if the miles and borders are irrelevant.

"You don't even know where we are going," I protest.

In the distance, the cathedral bells toll. I listen, alarmed. Nine chimes. How had it gotten so late?

"I have to go," I say, pulling away reluctantly.

He follows me down the ladder and from the barn. Neither of us speaks as we make our way back through the woods. It is after curfew and in the distance the town is shuttered and still. At the edge of the circus grounds behind the train, I stop. I do not want anyone to see me with Luc so late at night. "I should go alone from here."

"When will I see you again?" he presses.

"I don't know," I say and his face falls. "I want to," I add hurriedly. "It's just so hard to get away."

"We don't have that much time. Can you meet me tomorrow night, after the show?"

"Maybe," I say, unsure how I will manage it. "I'll try. But if I can't..." If only there were a way to send word. I have no way to reach him. I scan the fairgrounds, thinking.

My eyes stop at the back of the train. Each carriage has a box underneath, I recall. The belly box. On some of the cars the workers use it for keeping tools handy. I pull out the one beneath the sleeper car. It is empty.

"Here," I say. "If I can't get away I will leave you a message." A secret mailbox that no one else knows.

"Tomorrow, then." He kisses me boldly, then steals away, glancing around carefully to make sure no one is watching.

I race back to the campsite, breathless. There is an excitement with Luc that I've never felt before. It had not been like this with the soldier. I see now how the German had taken advantage of me, and taken a piece of my youth I will never recover. With Luc, though, the past feels like a bad dream that never happened. Is that even possible?

I had not understood how Astrid could ever love again after her husband had cast her out. Now it seems that I might have a second chance, too. Suddenly everything that has happened to me seems to make sense. I used to imagine that the German had never come. But if that had been the case I would never have known Theo or come here and met Luc.

How I wish that I could talk to Astrid about it. In her rare kinder moments, she is almost like a big sister and I just know she could help me make sense of it all. She will never see past Luc's father, though, to who he really is.

As I reach the door to the train car, Elsie appears. Her face is pale and creased with worry.

"Thank goodness you're here." Still annoyed at her letting him too near the animals, I push past her into the train car. But the place where Theo usually sleeps beside me is empty once more, and Astrid nowhere to be found.

My blood runs cold. "What is it? What's wrong?"

"It's Theo. He's sick and he needs help."

15

Noa

Elsie starts down the length of the train corridor and I follow close behind. "What happened?" I ask.

She stops at the door to a carriage near the front of the train where I've never been. The sick car, they call it. It provides care to those who are ill and prevents disease from spreading to the rest of the circus, Astrid had explained once. An antiseptic smell fills the air. From inside come coughs and moans. Theo could catch worse than what he already has in there. His wail cuts sharply through the other sounds. I start forward. "He can't stay here. I'm taking him with me." Timid Elsie will not stop me.

But Berta, the woman in charge of the sick car, appears in front of us, her immense girth blocking my way. "You can't come in here," she informs me.

"Theo's sick," I protest. "He needs me."

"Herr Neuhoff's rules—no healthy performers allowed in the sick bay." Viruses make their way through camp like wildfire: dysentery, grippe. A bad case of influenza could take down the entire show.

I peer over her shoulder. Theo lies on one of the berths, tiny and alone, buttressed by a rolled blanket so he will not fall off. "Is he all right?"

Berta's brow wrinkles with concern. "A high fever," she says, not shielding me from the truth. "We're doing everything we can to bring it down, but it's so difficult with the little ones."

My stomach twists. "Please let me help."

She shakes her head firmly. "There's nothing you can do." She closes the door.

Astrid, I think, running for the sleeper car. But her berth is still neatly made and she is not there. Desperately, I race from the train across the fairgrounds in the direction of Peter's cabin, the only other place Astrid might be at this hour. It is nearly ten, late to be showing up unannounced. Too worried to care about interrupting sleep or whatever else they may be doing, I knock on the door. A minute later, Astrid appears in a dressing gown. It is the first time she has been with Peter at night since we went on the road. Taking in her tousled hair, I am furious: I had left Theo with her—how dare she hand him off to someone else?

But I cannot risk angering her now. "Help me," I beg. "It's Theo. He's sick."

Astrid stares at me with cold blank eyes, then closes the door in my face. My heart sinks. Even if she hates me, surely she won't refuse to help Theo. But then she reappears dressed and starts toward the train. I run to keep up.

"He was fine when I put him down earlier," Astrid says. "Elsie was minding him and you said you would be right back." Her tone is accusing. "How long has he been sick?"

"I don't know. They won't let me see him." I follow her onto the train.

At the entrance to the sick car, she turns back, holding up her hand. "Wait here," she instructs.

"Theo needs me," I say, grabbing her arm.

She shakes me off. "You won't be doing him any good if you get sick, too."

"What about you?" I press.

"I'm out of the show at least," she replies. "But if you get sick the act will be ruined."

It is about the show, always about the show. None of that matters to me. I just want to see Theo. "There's no time to argue," Astrid says. "I'll be right back."

Astrid closes the door and I wait outside, hearing Theo wail. Guilt surges through me. How could I have left him? An hour ago, I'd been with Luc, secretly glad to be freed for a moment from the burden of taking care of a child. I hadn't meant it, really. And even though I know it is not possible, part of me wonders if that somehow brought him danger.

From the corridor between the two railcars where Astrid has left me to wait, I gaze out the grimy train window in the direction of the village. We have no doctor and the only medicines are the home remedies that Berta keeps in her kit. I would ask Luc for help if I thought it would do any good. But we can't risk taking Theo to a town because of the questions it might raise about who he is and where he came from. Surely someone will discover the secrets we've been keeping when they see he is circumcised.

Suddenly the wailing inside the sick car stops. I am at first relieved that Theo has settled down, but I can't help thinking that something is wrong. I throw open the door, not caring about the rules. My heart stops. Theo has gone stiff and his arms and legs jerk. "What happened?" I cry.

"I don't know," Astrid says, her face more scared than I have ever seen.

Berta rushes over. "A fever fit," she says, then turns to me. "He needs a bath of cool water. Fetch it quickly." I stand paralyzed, not wanting to leave Theo again, even for a single second. "Hurry!" she barks.

I run from the train and fill the first bucket I see at the pump. The water splashes out the sides so it is only half-filled by the time I reach the sick car. Astrid takes it from me at the door and pours it into the large porcelain bowl that doubles as a baby bath. "Another!" Berta calls. When I return, I see her putting a cup of clear liquid in the tub. "Vinegar," she explains.

I start toward Theo but Astrid holds up her hand, warding me off. "You can't come in."

I try to push past her. "I have to see him. If something should happen..." I can't finish the thought. Suddenly I am back at the girls' home, my own child being ripped from my arms.

Astrid takes Theo from Berta. Seeing the concern on Astrid's face and the tender way she holds him, I know that she loves him as I do. Still I ache to have him in my arms. Astrid lowers Theo into the bath. I hold my breath, willing him to fuss as he normally would. He remains still, but his body seems to relax in the water. "I remember now," Astrid says, not taking her eyes off Theo. "They call it a fever seizure. One of the circus children had it a few years back."

"A seizure?" I repeat. "It sounds serious."

"The fit itself looks much scarier than it is," Berta interjects. "But the fever is the problem. We must get that down." Her voice is grim.

A few minutes later Astrid takes Theo from the tub and dries him, putting him back into his sleeper because we have no other clothes for him here. His eyes are open and he is calmer now. Astrid touches his brow and frowns. "He's still too hot."

Berta pulls a packet from her kit. "I bought this at the *Apotheke* before we left Darmstadt. They said it would work on a fever."

"But is it for an adult or child?" I ask. Too much could be dangerous—or even lethal.

"Adult," Berta replies. "But if we give him just a little... We don't have a choice." She pours a bit of the powder onto a spoon and mixes it with water, then spoons it into Theo's mouth. He gags in protest and spits up. Astrid wipes his face and shirt with a rag and I wish that I could do it myself.

"Should we give him more?" I ask.

Astrid shakes her head. "There's no telling how much of it he got. And we won't know for a few hours if it's working."

"The fortune-teller, Drina, said something about illness," I suddenly recall. How could she have known?

I wait for Astrid to ridicule me for listening to her. "I stopped having my fortune read," she says darkly instead.

"Because you don't think it's true?"

"Because there are some things you just don't want to know."

Berta comes over and inspects Theo. "He just needs to rest now. Let's hope the medicine works." And what, I wonder, if it does not? I don't dare to ask.

Berta walks to the berths at the far end of the railcar where two other patients lie. After she has tended to them, she dims the lights and squeezes herself into an empty bed, her thickness spilling over into the aisle.

Astrid sinks onto one of the berths, rocking Theo. Watching her from the doorway, my arms ache. "He likes to be held up."

"I know." Astrid has been with Theo almost as long as

I have. She knows what to do. Not being able to hold him is killing me, though. "I'll watch him all night, I promise. But you should go to sleep. He's going to need you when he is better."

"You think he'll be okay?" I ask with hope and relief.

"I do," she responds, her voice more certain now.

I still cannot leave him, though. Instead, I sink down to the cold, filthy floor of the train corridor. "Those are pretty flowers," Astrid remarks. I had nearly forgotten about the daffodils in my shirt button and hair. "They're from the mayor's son, right?" I do not answer. "What did he want anyway?"

"Just to talk," I reply.

"Really?" Astrid's tone is skeptical.

"Maybe he just likes me," I retort, somewhere between hurt and annoyed. "Is that so very hard to believe?"

"Mingling is forbidden, you know." You and Peter being together is, too, I want to point out. "And his father is a collaborator, for God's sake!" Her voice rises now, causing Berta to stir at the far end of the train car.

"Luc isn't like that," I protest.

"And his father?" she asks pointedly.

"Luc says he has to cooperate to protect the village." I hear the weakness in my own words. "To stop the Germans from doing even worse."

"Stop?" she spits. "There is no stopping them. Didn't what happened at the show the other night teach you anything? The mayor is saving his own skin at the expense of his people— nothing more."

Several seconds of silence pass between us. "What, do you want to date this boy?" she demands. "Marry him?"

"No, of course not," I protest quickly. I had not really thought about Luc beyond the kiss we had shared. But I wonder now, why is it so awful to want the ordinary things? Astrid herself had once done the same; now she sees it as a betrayal. "I know that you like him, Noa," she continues. "But you mustn't trust too much, or let yourself be fooled." I can tell from the way she speaks that she thinks I am innocent and naive. "Never assume that you know the mind of another. I don't."

"Even Peter?" I ask.

"Especially him," she says sharply. She clears her throat. "This nonsense with you and the boy, it will end of course when we go in a few days." Luc's promises to find me in the next village seem too silly to share. "No man is worth the whole world," she adds.

"I know," I say, memories of the German looming large in my mind. He had taken everything from me, my honor, my family. Of course Astrid doesn't know this. My guilt looms like a shadow. Astrid has given us so much. And still I am living the lie I told when I first arrived and did not know if I could trust her.

Astrid leans back against the berth, still holding Theo. Neither of us speaks further. The floor of the train grows cold and hard beneath me, but I don't want to move. The shadows grow long between us. I lean my head back and close my eyes. I dream that I'm outside in the darkness, the same bitter cold as the night I'd taken Theo and left. He is not an infant this time, though, but a toddler of almost two, older and heavier. The ground is icy beneath my feet and the biting wind fights me every step. There is a bundle on the ground, dark amid the whiteness of the earth. I stop to examine it. Another child. I pick it up but as I do, Theo falls from my arms. Desperately I dig through the snow, trying to find him. But he is lost.

I awake in a sweat, cursing myself for sleeping. Astrid sits awake, staring out the window in the distance. Behind her the sky is a lighter gray, signaling that it is almost dawn. She is still holding Theo, who is completely still. I leap to my feet and wait for Astrid to protest as I move closer, but she does not. "His fever has broken," she says instead. Theo has a faint rash on his skin, but otherwise he is fine, his skin cool. My eyes burn with relief. The blanket swaddling him is drenched in sweat. He half opens his eyes and smiles faintly at me.

"You should still be careful not to get sick," Astrid admonishes and I brace myself for her to make me leave once more. Instead, she walks to the far end of the carriage, still holding Theo. I fight the urge to follow as she confers with Berta, who has risen and is feeding one of the other patients. A moment later she returns with a baby bottle. "Let me see if I can get him to drink a bit." He sucks weakly at the bottle, then drifts back to sleep.

Astrid moves to set the bottle down. The color drains from her face suddenly and she starts to double over, seemingly sickened. "Here," she says, seeming to forget her own caution as she hands Theo to me. I draw his warmth close gratefully. Astrid sinks limply to one of the berths.

"Are you feeling sick?" I pray that she has not caught Theo's virus.

"No." Her tone is certain. But her forehead and upper lip are damp with sweat.

"Then what...?" My concern grows. She has seemed more tired than usual lately, and she has been so very terse. There is something familiar, too, about the grayness of her face. "Astrid, are you...?" I hesitate, not wanting to finish the question for fear of offending her if I am wrong. "Are you expecting?" I ask, but she does not answer. "You are, aren't you?"

Her eyes widen as she realizes I have guessed her secret. Her hand rises to her stomach instinctively, a gesture I recognize from my earlier self. "Oh!" I exclaim and suddenly it is a year ago, the realization of my own missed periods and what it all meant coming back like it happened yesterday.

Should I offer congratulations? I proceed carefully, as though approaching a snake. There was a time not so very long ago when a child had not been happy news for me—it had been pure dread. I don't know how Astrid feels. Watching her with Theo, I've long suspected how very much she wanted a child. She is older, though, and a Jew... Does she want one now? I search her face for cues as to how I should react.

It is racked with self-doubt. There is so much I want to say to comfort her. I move closer, put my arm around her. "You will be a wonderful mother. A child is a blessing."

"It's more complicated than that," she replies. "Having a child now is just so hard."

"I understand," I say too quickly.

Her brow wrinkles. "How can you possibly? I mean, I know you care for Theo, but that is hardly the same."

No, it isn't, I agree silently. I love Theo as my own, but having him can never replace that feeling of holding my child in my arms for the first time. But she doesn't know this. And she cannot really know me or understand what I am saying because of my secret. I should tell her. How can I possibly, though? The one thing that makes me who I am will surely make Astrid hate me—and want to be done with me for good.

The need to tell her wells up in me once more, too powerful to ignore. I can't hold back any longer. "Astrid, I need to tell you something. Remember when I told you about my working at the train station?"

She nods. "Yes, after you left your family."

"I didn't really explain why I had to leave."

"You said your father was unkind." Her voice is uneasy.

"It was more than that." I tell her then in my own words everything about the soldier and the baby whom I bore by him without trying to justify what I had done, the way I should have months earlier.

When I finish, I hold my breath, waiting for Astrid to tell me it is all right. But she does not. Her face is a thundercloud.

"You slept with a Nazi," she says darkly. Though it had all happened so long before I had met her, my actions still seem a betrayal. It hadn't been like that, though. To me, love had been love (or what I supposed love felt like) and I hadn't understood that there were other things. I wait for her to scream at me, ask how I could have done it. Looking back, I'm not sure myself—but it had felt so natural at the time.

"I did," I say finally. "Erich was a Nazi, too," I add. Even as the words come out, I know I have overstepped.

"That was different." Her eyes blaze. "He was my husband. And it was before." Before the war had changed everyone, and forced us to choose sides. "You got pregnant. That's why your family kicked you out."

"Yes, I had no choice but to go to the girls' home in Bensheim. I thought they would help me. Instead they took my child." My voice breaks as I say this last bit—the first time I have spoken it aloud to anyone.

Her brows draw close. "Who did?"

"The doctor and nurse at the girls' home. At first they told me that he would be placed with the Lebensborn program, but his hair and eyes were so dark..." I trail off. "I don't know where they took him. I wanted to keep him, but they wouldn't let me. Someday I will find him," I vow. I expect her to laugh or mock my dream, or at least tell me it is impossible.

But she nods grimly. "You mustn't lose hope. There could well be records."

"I wanted to tell you." Instead, I had been too cowardly.

"And the mayor's son, does he know?"

I shake my head. "No one else knows. Only you."

She stares at me. Several seconds of silence pass between us. Will she order me to leave the circus? It is the worst possible timing, of course; Theo is too sick to travel and I won't go without him. "Are you mad?" I ask finally.

"I want to be. But it isn't my place. You made a mistake, as we all do. And you paid dearly for it." My shoulders slump with relief. She has forgiven me.

My worries bubble up again. "Just one more thing," I say, and she braces, as though I'm about to reveal another secret, even worse. "You won't tell the others, will you?"

"No. They cannot know," she agrees. "Others might not be so understanding. No more secrets, though."

I nod gratefully. "Agreed."

"But Noa," Astrid says, "you need to stop seeing him. I understand the mistake you made in the past. You were young and you could not help it. This thing with the mayor's son is different, though. Surely you can see the danger you are bringing to Theo and to all of us."

I open my mouth to protest. I want to tell her again that Luc is nothing at all like his father. But outsiders spell danger for Astrid and the others at the circus. She has forgiven my awful truth about the German. Giving up Luc is the price I am to pay in exchange.

Astrid is watching me closely, waiting for my answer. "All right," I manage at last. I scarcely know Luc, but the notion of giving him up hurts more than it should.

"Promise?" she presses, still not satisfied.

"I swear it," I say solemnly, though the idea of never seeing Luc again makes my insides ache.

"Good," she says, seeming satisfied. "We should head back to the sleeper."

"What about Theo?"

She looks toward Berta, who nods. "Now that his fever has broken, he's well enough to go back." Astrid stands and starts in the direction of the sleeper car. Then she stops and turns back, her face falling. "My body..." she frets, referring once more to her pregnancy. "If I can no longer fly..." It is not vanity. Performing is her means of survival and she worries that the baby will change all that.

"My body bounced right back after I had the baby." How strange it feels to be able to say that openly, at least to her. "Yours will, too." I take her arm. "Come, you must be exhausted. How long have you known, anyway?" I ask in a low voice as we move through the dark, still corridor.

"Just a few days. I'm sorry I didn't tell you sooner," she adds. I nod, trying not to feel hurt. "It was just hard to accept myself, much less tell anyone else."

"I understand," I reply, meaning it. "Does Peter know?"

She nods. "Only him. Please, you mustn't tell anyone," she begs, trusting me now to keep her secret where before I had not. I nod. I would sooner die than tell.

"Having a child," she says, "it's terrifying."

"How far along are you?" I fear I am asking her too many questions, but I cannot help it.

"About two months."

I count on my fingers. "We will be back in the winter quarters with plenty of time." She is silent, and a puzzled look crosses her face. "You are going back, aren't you?" I ask.

"Peter doesn't want us to," she replies. I am surprised. It is hard to imagine Astrid and Peter anywhere but the circus.

Luc had spoken of leaving, too, but of course the notion of going with a boy I had just met was a fantasy. "I'll go back, though. What other choice do I have? Darmstadt has been my family's home for centuries." Other than Berlin, it was all she had known. "But you could leave, you know. Get out before we go back."

I am unsure how to respond. I had never planned to belong to this misfit group with their odd life. Leaving the circus and fleeing with Theo had always been my goal. I did not have to stay—I was not a prisoner or fugitive. I could thank Herr Neuhoff and pick up Theo and go.

But it is more than just the shelter that keeps me here. Astrid cares for us. She is more family than my own parents had ever been. And I feel part of the circus, as surely as if I had been born here. I am not ready to go—not yet.

"No," I reply. "Whatever happens now, I am with you."

At least for now.

16

Astrid

A buzz runs through the train car late Sunday afternoon as we wash our costumes and prepare for the following day. Herr Neuhoff has called a meeting in thirty minutes. The girls around me whisper nervously. What could he possibly want or have to tell us? Though I do not join in their chatter, my stomach tingles with unease. Herr Neuhoff is not one for large gatherings, preferring instead to speak with each performer or laborer individually as needed. These days, the unexpected can only mean trouble.

Noa picks up Theo from the berth and studies his face uneasily. It has been a week since the night he fell ill. The fever had not come back and he looks so healthy I sometimes wonder if the whole thing was a bad dream.

I start to walk from the train car, avoiding the sight of myself in the mirror as I pass. They say there are women who look beautiful in pregnancy and perhaps that is true. I've never seen one. The circus women grow fat like cows, sitting around, unable to perform. Their bodies do not quite come back to what they had been. My figure is only slightly changed, the faintest of bumps if one looks closely. But it is just a matter of time.

Though I do not look bad yet, I feel awful. The nausea that had started that first day on the trapeze has worsened, causing me to vomit three or four times a day. There is no extra food to spare once I have wasted mine being sick, though Noa tries to slip me bits of her own rations when I let her. But it doesn't matter—I cannot hold down a thing. My empty stomach burns like I have eaten something too spicy all day long and at night, too, keeping me awake.

"Eat something," Peter pled the previous night. "For the baby." He'd brought my dinner to the train when I did not come to the cook tent. It was a watery stew, enriched with bits of meat and turnips he'd added to it from his own rations.

But the once-appetizing aroma of onions made my stomach turn and I pushed it away, gesturing in Noa's direction. "Give it to Theo."

Ironically, as I've grown sicker, Peter has brightened. The baby has changed everything for him. I haven't seen him drink at all since I told him and the melancholy in his eyes is gone, replaced by merriment and hope.

I pull out my valise to put on some powder to conceal my paleness before the meeting. The other girls hurry from the carriage, but Noa lingers behind with Theo. I pat my hair and start out.

"Wait," Noa says. I turn back. She is biting her lip as if she wants to say something. Instead she thrusts the baby at me awkwardly. "Can you hold him while I change? He never fusses at you." I take him. It is true that while I had never cared for a baby before, Theo seems to warm to my arms.

"Ready," Noa says a few minutes later, her voice a bit pinched, as if nervous or excited. She is dressed more smartly than I would expect for a Sunday, too, her skirt and blouse crisply pressed. I carry Theo outside. The late-day sky is an eggshell blue. The air is balmy and fragrant, the first real spring evening. We pass the big top. Despite feeling ill and having no appetite, I have not stopped flying. I swing harder and higher than ever—perhaps harder than I should. I am not, of course, trying to jeopardize the pregnancy I had so dearly wanted all my life. The baby would have to understand, though, that this is our life, as well. I need to know that they can exist together.

Closer to the backyard, I can hear the murmur of the others gathered. But as we round the corner of the tent, the voices hush. The full circus is present, performers and laborers intermingled. They stand not in the main part of the backyard close to the big top. Rather, they have assembled at the far edge, where the trees meet the clearing in a kind of semicircle, forming a grove.

A canopy of leaves has been prepared, branches secured across the outstretched limbs of two oak trees. Peter waits beneath it beside Herr Neuhoff, face bright with anticipation, regal in a dark suit and top hat I've never seen. I wonder if he brought it with him from Russia. The crowd seems to part as I near into two distinct clusters, forming a sort of aisle down the middle between them. My skin prickles: What is going on?

I turn to Noa. She smiles, a faint twinkle of excitement in her eyes, and I realize she had stalled me with the baby on purpose. She hands me some wildflowers, wrapped with string. "I don't understand," I say.

Noa takes Theo from me and brushes back a lock of hair that has fallen close to my face. "Every bride needs a bouquet," she replies and her eyes dart toward Peter, as if unsure she should have spoken.

Bride. I look at Peter questioningly. But his gaze is unflinching and intent. He means to marry me here, in front of the circus. A wedding. The ground seems to wobble beneath my feet. There can't really be one, of course; our union is against the law in France, just as surely as my marriage to Erich had been in Germany. It would certainly never be recognized by any government. But still, to take my vows with Peter, and have our child born in wedlock, to a real family. In my wildest dreams, I had not imagined it.

One of the cellists from the orchestra begins to play, a song too soft and somber to be a wedding march. The circus folk stand in a semicircle, faces aglow, a little bit of life affirmation, for each so very needed. I take in the smiling expressions around me. Have they guessed my secret? No, they are happy for this moment of light in the darkness—and for us. For the first time since leaving my family in Darmstadt so many years ago, I feel as though I am finally home.

Noa leads me forward to the canopy. I reach for her, wanting her to stand up with me so I am not alone. But she puts my hand in Peter's and takes a step back.

I look into his eyes. "You planned this?"

He smiles. "I suppose I should have asked you," he says, but then he lowers to one knee. "Astrid, will you marry me?"

"It's a bit late for that, isn't it?" I chide. There is faint laughter from the others. My mind whirls: I had not planned to get married again, to Peter or anyone else. Marriages are about forever, and there is nothing certain about that anymore. I had not planned for the baby or any of this either, though. Peter is kneeling before me, his face so hopeful. He wants to make us a family.

And so do I, I realize. I see then as if watching a movie my life with Peter since I had joined the Circus Neuhoff, how he has protected me, and how close we have grown day by day. The nights without him are empty and no space complete until he is there. Noa had been right, not just about Peter's feelings, but mine. He had gotten into my heart when I wasn't even looking. Part of me curses myself for letting it happen. At the same time, though, I would not want to go forward any other way.

That doesn't change the reality of our situation—or the danger marrying me could bring to him. I lower my head to his. "Are you certain?" I whisper low, not wanting the others to hear. Though he stands in front of me, willing to risk everything, part of me still cannot believe it. How can he want to take this chance after all that he has been through?

He nods. "Never more so," he replies, voice clear and unwavering.

"Then yes, I would love to marry you," I say more loudly. I smile, batting back the tears that sting at my eyes.

Herr Neuhoff clears his throat. "Well, let's get started," he says as Peter stands. "There are few words to describe love in the least likely of places, which is also the most beautiful," he begins, his voice a softer version of the sotto baritone he uses in the ring.

He opens a worn Bible and reads, "And Ruth said, 'Entreat me not to leave thee, or to return from following after thee: for whither thou goest, I will go; and where thou lodgest, I will lodge: thy people shall be my people, and thy God my God.'"

As he reads, my eyes drift upward to the canopy. To the onlookers, it is a simple bough of branches and leaves. But I know that Peter, himself not Jewish, has designed it as a chuppa in a silent concession to my family. I wish for my father to give me away, my brothers to hoist us high on chairs after as "Hava Nagila" plays, just like when Mathias and Markus had married the Hungarian horseback riders, Jewish sisters. I have done this before without them, of course, standing before a justice of the peace with Erich in Berlin. Then

I pretended not to mind, thinking that my family would be there always. Now I feel longing and grief. I touch my stomach, thinking of the grandchild my parents will never know.

My missing family is not the only difference. Once when I had taken my vows with Erich, I had been young and unafraid. I had thought that nothing could touch us. Now I know that this union will not shield us from whatever lies ahead. Rather, it will make my burden Peter's and his mine.

Peter is not young and naive either, though. I think of the wife and daughter he lost, who surely cannot be far from his mind today. Yet he has the courage to go forward, head lifted, eyes clear. For this, I love him more than ever.

Herr Neuhoff finishes the passage. "Peter, you have something you want to say?"

Peter pulls a piece of paper from his pocket and drops it. He stumbles as he bends to pick it up, his usual composure gone. His hand shakes, nervous as a young groom. "There is so little one can be certain of these days," he begins, voice wobbly. "But finding a hand to hold while we walk this path makes even the most difficult of times better and the strangest of villages home." Around us, heads nod. Each circus performer has a past, his or her own memories of a home. Then he crumples the paper and jams it back into his pocket, so abruptly I wonder if he is having second thoughts. "Once I thought my life was over. When I came to Germany and joined the circus, I never thought I would find happiness again." His voice grows clear and strong as he abandons the words he had written and speaks from the heart. "And then I met you and it all changed. You made me believe again that good things were possible. I love you." He looks down.

"Astrid, is there anything you want to say?" Herr Neuhoff asks.

Everyone is watching me expectantly. I had no idea and

have nothing prepared. "It—it is hard to find a love you can trust," I manage. I search for the words that I have not said until now, even to myself. "I am so very lucky. You make me feel stronger, every day. I can face whatever is to come as long as I am with you."

"You are blessed indeed, Astrid and Peter, to have found one another," Herr Neuhoff agrees, saving me from having to find further words. He turns to Peter. "Do you take this woman..." In Noa's arms, Theo coos his approval and everyone chuckles.

Peter's eyes are aglow as he places an antique metal band around my finger. Was it a family heirloom or something he had purchased just for today? "I now pronounce you man and wife," Herr Neuhoff declares.

A great cheer arises from the onlookers as Peter kisses me and the musicians strike up a merry tune. Someone brings out a table and several bottles of champagne. Watching, I am touched by the details, the care with which the party has been planned. There are little trays of appetizers, simple foods made from rations that had been arranged to look grand.

"To your future together," Herr Neuhoff proposes, raising a glass, and everyone toasts in agreement. I raise the glass to my lips.

The party breaks up into smaller groups, drinking and enjoying a bit of merriment. Impromptu, some of the Romanian acrobats begin to dance, twirling in circles with their brightly patterned scarves, sequined skirts flaring like pinwheels. I try to relax and enjoy the party, but the colors and noise are overwhelming after all that has happened. I lean wearily against one of the tables. Across the crowd, Peter shoots me a knowing smile.

Behind the dancers, something moves in the trees. I straighten and glimpse someone standing at the edge of the grove. Emmet, watching the party. I do not remember seeing him at the ceremony. He is Herr Neuhoff's son, and it is only natural that he would have been invited. But his presence makes me uneasy.

The music grows livelier and the dancers form a circle, drawing me and Peter into the center of it, then whirl around us like a speeding carousel. Peter takes my hands and begins to spin me in the direction opposite those who have gathered around us. The movement and music are dizzying. As we twirl, I see Noa, standing alone on the outside of the circle, seeming to want to join in but not quite sure how.

I break away from Peter and burst through the circle. "Come," I say, taking her hand and leading her back into the center with me. Making her one of us. She clasps my fingers gratefully. I hold her hand and Peter's, too, as we begin to dance, not caring if the others think it strange. I do not want Noa to be left out. But as we spin and I grow dizzy, I find myself clinging more tightly to her, needing her as much as she needs me to keep the world upright.

The dance ends and a slower song begins. It is an older Romanian song, "The Anniversary Waltz." Noa and the others step away and I know I am meant to dance only with Peter. He draws me close. He waltzes with more skill than I might have expected, but his movements are slowed and a bit clumsy from drink. As he hums the familiar tune, his lips buzzing against my ear, I can hear my mother singing the lyrics as my brother Jules played them on his violin. "Oh how we danced on the night we were wed…" My eyes burn.

"I need to rest," I pant in Peter's ear when the song has ended.

"Do you feel all right?" he asks, touching my cheek with concern. I nod. "I'll get you some water."

"I'm fine, darling. You go enjoy the party," I say, not

wanting him to fuss over me. He starts off in the direction of the champagne. I lean against a chair, suddenly weak. A faint sweat breaks out on my brow and my stomach begins to wobble. Not now, I think. I walk around the side of one of the train cars out of sight, in search of a moment's quiet. Then I stop, hearing voices on the other side.

"The ceremony was lovely," Noa says to someone I cannot see. Her tone is uneasy.

Then I hear Emmet. "If only it was real," he says sarcastically. How dare he insult my marriage to Peter?

"It is real," Noa protests with as much courage as she can muster. "Even if the government is too foolish to recognize it."

"Best to get married here," Emmet remarks. "Before we go back, you know." His tone is conspiratorial.

There is a pause. "Back?" Noa's voice is filled with surprise. I hadn't mentioned my conversation with Herr Neuhoff, or the possibility that we would not be allowed to remain in France. "To Germany?"

"Astrid hasn't told you?"

"Of course she has," Noa lies poorly, tries to sound as though she is not surprised. But she cannot maintain the facade. "It isn't true!" she exclaims, and I wonder if she will cry.

"My father says the French tour is being curtailed."

"Your father tells you nothing." I am surprised by the strength in Noa's voice.

"Maybe you should just go home," Emmet sneers. "Oh, that's right. You can't." I stifle a gasp. How much does he know about Noa's past?

I step into the light. "That's enough."

Emmet's eyes flicker at the realization that I heard what he'd said. For a second, I wonder if he will back down. "There's a reason she was all alone with a child when we found her," Emmet says, seemingly undaunted. Over his shoulder, I see Noa's eyes widen, terrified that he has somehow learned the truth. Of course, Emmet is bluffing. He has to be. I would never tell and there's no other way he could have found out.

"The little tramp, the child has got to be hers." Emmet spits in Noa's direction. Without thinking, I reach out and slap him so hard my palm stings. He steps away, staring at me in disbelief, the imprint of my hand bright red across his cheek. "You'll pay for that," he swears.

"Get lost before I call your father," I say.

Emmet slinks away, still clutching his cheek. "Thank you," Noa says to me when he is out of earshot. "I don't understand, how could he possibly know about me?"

"I don't think he actually does," I say and Noa seems to relax with relief. "I certainly didn't tell him. Most likely he was just fishing for information." The truth is that secrets don't stay buried for long in the circus—they have a way of coming out. But telling Noa this would only worry her further.

Noa casts her eyes downward. "Is it true, what Emmet said? Are we going back?"

"It isn't certain. Herr Neuhoff mentioned that the administration was threatening it. It was just a possibility and I didn't want to upset you."

"I'm not a child," Noa says, a note of rebuke in her voice.

"I know. I should have said something. But you don't have to go back, you know."

"How could I leave the circus?" she asks earnestly, doubt clouding her eyes. "I could never go without you."

I smile, touched by her loyalty. A few months ago she was a stranger to the circus. An outsider. Now this life is all that she can imagine. "It is only a show—and no show can go on forever."

"What about you?" she asks. So young, and always with so many questions.

"As I've said before, I won't run. And I won't hide again," I vow. They would have to take me first.

"It is not so far to Switzerland," she ventures, her eyes lifting to the hills. "Perhaps if we went together..."

"No." I turn to face her squarely. "There are people who have vouched for me. People who would pay with their lives if I was gone. But not for you," I add. "You can go."

"I am with you to the end," she says, voice quavering slightly.

"Let's not talk about it anymore tonight," I say, patting her hand.

Noa nods in agreement and her eyes travel back toward the party. "The wedding was beautiful," she offers. "I dream of such things." I try not to laugh. The gathering in the woods is simple, far from elegant. "Doesn't every girl?" Noa adds. "Will you take his name?"

I had not considered the question. Then I shake my head. I had changed who I was once; I could not do it again. "What were you doing all the way out here anyway? We should get back." I start toward the party but Noa does not follow. Her eyes travel in another direction, away from the fairgrounds.

"You aren't thinking of going to that boy again are you?" I ask.

"No, of course not," she says too quickly.

"Nothing but trouble can come of that. And you promised," I remind her.

"Yes," she replies. "I'm just tired, and I want to check on Theo. I had Elsie put him down after the ceremony." I study her face, trying to decide whether to believe her.

"Astrid," I hear Peter's voice, fueled by liquor, call too loudly from the party.

"I need to get back," I say.

"I understand." Noa squeezes my hand. "And about before... thank you." Her voice is filled with gratitude.

And then she turns and walks toward the train. I want to call after her and warn her again, but I do not. Instead, I start back to the gathering.

17

Noa

Starting away from Astrid toward the train, I smile. I had known about the wedding. Peter had confided in me just a few hours earlier and I conspired with him to surprise Astrid. I'd fretted that she might mind—Astrid was not one for surprises—but now I am glad to have been part of the plan.

Peter and Astrid are together now, and about to become a family. She seems happy, really happy, for the first time since I've known her. I'm happy for her, but I can't help but wonder if things will change, whether Astrid will stay with Peter every night and become somehow less mine.

I am suddenly lonely. Luc appears in my mind. I haven't seen him since the night Theo had fallen ill a week earlier. I hadn't been able to meet him the next night after the show as he asked—Theo, though better, had still been weak and I had not wanted to risk leaving him. So I'd left Luc a note in the belly box: *Brother sick. Can't come tonight.* My note had disappeared so I had known he read it. Or so I hoped—what if someone else had found it? Even though I'd been vague on purpose, there would still be questions. For days there had been no response and I'd wondered if Luc could have lost interest so soon after our kiss, or had simply given up.

I walk to the belly box now, scarcely daring to hope. Inside is a scrap of a page from a circus program, so crumpled that I wonder if someone had mistaken the compartment for a trash bin. I smooth out the paper. A message is written on the back in blurry charcoal: *Tried to come see you. Liked watching you dance. Meet me at the town museum.*

Luc had been here tonight and had seen me dancing. I flush, excited and embarrassed at the same time. How had I not known? Worry nags at me then. The wedding was meant to be a secret. He should not have been here. But some part of me is sure that I could trust him.

I study the note once more. *Meet me at the town museum.* I know the building he means. But the old museum, which stands right in the center of town, is such an odd meeting place. And it is well past curfew. I can't possibly go there.

I had promised Astrid, too, that I would not see Luc again. I turn back now, searching for her, but she has disappeared into the gathering. Astrid will be with Peter tonight; surely she will not notice if I am gone. Still, the smart thing to do would be to stay at the wedding party until it is over and then go back to Theo. But we will be leaving soon and I might never see Luc again.

I look in the direction of the train, needing to go check on Theo before I go anywhere. Inside the sleeper carriage, Theo lies awake on the berth, as if waiting for me. I pick him up and hold him to me, inhaling his warm, sleepy smell. I've been constantly worried since he became ill, as if reminded how very fragile he is, how he might be lost in an instant.

Elsie stands from the adjacent berth, where she had been knitting. "Oh, good, you're back," she says. "Still time for me to join a bit of the party before it ends."

"I'm not back, that is…" I search for an explanation why I need her to watch Theo longer. But before I can finish, she skips from the train.

I think about calling after her, then decide against it. "Just you and me," I say to Theo, who gurgles his approval. I look from Theo to the door of the train and back again, wondering what to do. Do I dare bring him with me?

I step out into the chilled night air, then stop. It is irresponsible to take Theo out like this. But if I want to see Luc, there's no other choice. I wrap him inside my coat.

I start away from the train, ducking low and clinging to the edge of the circus grounds so as not to be seen as I hurry for the cover of the trees. Once sheltered by the forest, I start in the direction of the village, finding my way slowly through the woods so as not to trip on one of the many tree roots and rocks that jut out from the hard, uneven earth. The path is the same one that Astrid had shown me the first day I had gone into Thiers, but it is eerie now, dark shadows seeming to loom between the trees. This time it is just Theo and me, alone in the woods as we had been the night we were found by the circus. I shiver, the fear and despair of that moment falling over me once more. Dried branches crackle beneath my feet, seeming to give us away. My skin prickles, as though someone might leap out of the bushes at any moment.

I reach the edge of the forest and start for the footbridge. Then I stop, looking down at Theo, who gazes back at me with trusting eyes, counting on me to do what is best for him. This is so selfish of me, I think, my guilt rising. How can I risk his safety for this?

As I near town, the streets are deserted after curfew, lights are blackened out. I tuck Theo further beneath my coat. He squirms on my hip, no longer the newborn content to lie in my arms. I pray he will not cry out.

I do not take the main thoroughfare as I had when I came to town the day I met Luc; instead, I follow the side streets that run parallel to it, clinging to the shadows of the crumbling stone wall that runs along a climbing path.

The museum sits on the northern edge of the town center. It is a small castle that was converted to show the town's history, now shuttered for good. The road leading to the gate is exposed, bathed in moonlight.

I stop uncertainly, my skin prickling. Meeting in the middle of town like this is foolish, I think, seeing Astrid glaring at me with disapproval in my mind. A heavy chain is wrapped around the gate of the museum, locking it. I step back angrily. Is this some kind of joke?

"Noa," Luc calls through the darkness, signaling me around the side of the museum to a door. Inside, the cavernous main gallery is damp and musty. In the moonlight I can see that the once-grand hall has been pillaged. A torn painting hangs off the wall and pieces of armor lie broken on the ground. Behind shattered glass displays, exhibits are empty, their valuables taken by the Germans or looters. Something, a bird or bat perhaps, flutters in the darkness beneath the high ceiling.

"You came," Luc says, as though he had not expected me to go through with it. He puts his arms around me and I deeply inhale his scent, a mix of pine and soap, burying my nose against his neck. Though it is only the second time he held me, his embrace feels like home.

His lips near mine and I close my eyes with anticipation. But Theo squirms between us and I pull back. "Is this safe?" I ask as he leads me into a small anteroom to one side. There he lights a candle, which flickers, illuminating our long shadows on the wall. There is a scratching sound as something scurries from the corner, seeking darkness.

"No one comes here," Luc says. "It used to be the pride of the town. Not so much to be proud of anymore." He looks down. "Is this your brother?" he asks, and I nod.

"There was no one to mind him." I hear the apology in my voice. I search Luc's face for a sign of annoyance, but there is none.

"Is he better now?" Luc asks with genuine concern.

"He's fine. But it was a high fever, terribly scary. That's why I couldn't meet you last Sunday," I add.

Luc nods solemnly. "I would have tried to see you sooner, but I knew it would be impossible until he was well." He reaches into his coat. "Here, I brought this." In his smooth open palm lies a cube of sugar. Real sugar. I fight the urge to grab it and shove it in my mouth. Instead I touch it to my tongue, shivering at the taste I'd almost forgotten. Then I lower it to Theo's lips. He gurgles and smiles at the unfamiliar sweetness.

"Thank you," I say. "I haven't tasted real sugar since..." I falter, remembering how my father had squirreled some away for my birthday nearly a year earlier. "Since before the war," I finish lamely.

"I told Papa that from now on, I would only live off the ration coupons like everyone else," he says. "I don't feel right having more than others."

"Luc..." I am not sure what to say. He reaches out his hand to stroke the smoothness of Theo's palm. "Do you want to hold him?" I ask.

"Really? I've never..." I pass Theo to Luc and the baby coos, falling naturally into his large arms. Luc lowers himself to the floor slowly, still cradling Theo. Theo's eyes begin to grow heavy and then close.

Luc takes off his jacket and makes a soft bed of it for Theo, setting him down gently. Then he reaches for me, drawing me into his arms. "You found your way here with no trouble?" He kisses me, not waiting for an answer. I press closer to him, wanting more. I let his hands wander farther, and for a moment I am not broken and shamed, nor a circus freak. I am just a girl again.

But as his fingers graze my hips, I stop him. "The baby…"

"He's falling asleep."

I burrow closer in Luc's arms. "We're going," I say sadly.

"I know. I promised to come see you in the next village, remember?"

"Not there," I reply. "We're going back to Germany, or at least somewhere close to it."

His body stiffens and his frown grows deeper. "But that's so dangerous."

"I know. There isn't a choice."

"I'll find you there, too," he says earnestly.

"You could hardly come more than once."

"Every week," he counters. "More if you want."

"But it's really far," I protest.

"So?" he asks. "Don't you think I can manage it?"

"It's not that. It's just that…" I look down. "Why would you want to? I mean it's so much trouble."

"Because I can't stand the thought of not seeing you again," he blurts. When I lift my head, his cheeks are red, as though the air has suddenly grown warm. There's a look of fondness in his eyes. How can someone who has known me such a short time feel so much affection, when those who had loved me my whole life seemed to have none?

"I want to show you something." He stands and leads me to a small door at the back of the gallery. I look back to where Theo lies, still sleeping. Surely Luc does not mean for me to leave him alone.

"What is it?" I ask, my curiosity growing as Luc opens the closet. He pulls out a painting, the oils so fresh the smell tickles my nose. It is a picture of an aerialist, I realize, mid-swing on the trapeze. How had he come to have it? I study her form, the familiar arc of her body on the sweep. Her hair is light and worn in a high knot like mine. Then, taking in the familiar red costume, I gasp.

It is a portrait of me.

No, not exactly me. A more beautiful version, body grace-ful, features flawless. Luc had painted me as he sees me, the image adoring.

"Oh, Luc!" I say with amazement. I understand now the way he takes me in with an artist's eye, looking intently, studying detail. "It's stunning. You have real talent." He has captured me perfectly, from the texture of my costume to the slight look of fear in my eyes that I never quite man-age to hide.

"You think so?" His face is doubtful, but a note of pride creeps into his voice.

"Absolutely marvelous," I reply, meaning it. I try to imag-ine the hours and care it had taken him. "Why did you give up on studying art?"

His face clouds. "I wanted to be an artist. I used to paint in the loft of our barn, you know. But my father found what I was doing and he destroyed my work, forbade me from doing more. I begged him to let me become an art teacher at least, but he would hear none of it." Luc's eyes flicker as he relives the memory. He continues, "I painted in secret until he found out." Luc held up his right hand with its twisted index finger. "He made sure I could never be a real artist."

I recoil in horror, not at Luc's disfigurement, but at the

cruelty inflicted by a father on his own child. "Not enough to stop me from being useful. Just from being good at the really intricate details," he adds.

I take his hand and kiss his finger, my heart weeping. None of us, it seems, not even Luc, is free from darkness and pain. "How can you stay with him?" I demand. "He's a monster!"

Luc's eyes widen and I wonder if he will be angry with me. "He was doing what he thought was right," he replies.

We sit silently, neither speaking. Luc has trusted me with his awful secret. I should tell him, right now, about my own past. But then I hear Astrid's voice: *never assume that you know the mind of another.* Looking into Luc's clear blue eyes, I know he will not understand the choices I have made and the experiences that have brought me to make them.

Instead, I reach for him, cupping his face in my palms and turning it to me. I kiss him over and over again, not stopping, heedless of where we are and the fact that Theo is just feet away. Luc's arms are around me, hands on my waist and hips. For a second, I want to pull away. My stomach has never quite returned to what it was before childbirth. My breasts droop slightly from the milk I had carried.

But then I wrap my arms around him and let myself be swept away. Luc's hands reach under my skirt. I start to protest. We cannot possibly do this here. He lays me back gently, placing one hand under my head to protect it from the hardness of the stone floor. The German soldier, the only other man I have been with in this way, appears in my mind. I tense.

Luc cups my chin in his hand then, gently bringing my gaze to his. "I love you, Noa," he says.

"I love you, too." The words come out in a breathless rush. My passion grows, pushing the memories away.

When it is over, we lie in a heap of half-strewn clothes on

the hard stone floor, our legs tangled together. "That was wonderful!" I declare, too loudly. My voice echoes through the rafters of the museum, sending an unseen pigeon fluttering. We both laugh softly.

He gathers me up in his arms, drawing me closer. "I'm so glad we shared our first time together," he says, presuming that I am as innocent as he.

"I'm sorry," he says a minute later, taking my silence for regret. "I shouldn't have taken advantage of the situation."

"You didn't," I reassure him. "I wanted it, too."

"If we had a settled future together..." he frets.

"Or even a bed," I joke.

But his face remains somber. "Things should be different. This damn war," he swears. If not for this damn war, I think, we never would have met. "I'm sorry," he says again.

I embrace him tightly. "Don't be. I'm not." Theo wakes then, his cry cutting through the stillness. I pull away to button my blouse. Luc stands and helps me up. I smooth my skirt as we go to Theo. Luc picks him up, more confident this time. He gazes at Theo fondly. We sink to the ground once more and the three of us huddle together in the darkness, a kind of makeshift family, listening to the sounds of the night museum, the scratching of mice and blowing of the wind outside.

"Come with me," Luc says. "Away from here. I'll get a car and drive us to the border."

Us. Though Luc had spoken before about going away together, the suggestion seems more serious now, the possibility real. I try to imagine it, leaving the circus and starting a life with Luc. The idea is as terrifying as it is magnificent.

"I can't," I say, wanting desperately to run away with him but knowing the risks and the reality. Where would we go?

And what about Astrid, and the circus and a thousand other things I cannot explain to him?

"Is it about Theo? We could take him with us, raise him as ours. He would never know differently." Luc's voice is hopeful, and I am touched that he wants to take responsibility for Theo.

I shake my head firmly. "There's so much more to it than that. Astrid and the circus… I owe them my life."

"Surely she would understand. She would want you to go…" he tries again. "Noa, I want to take you and Theo away from here, to a place where you will be safe." He wants to take care of me. How I wish I was the girl I used to be. She might have let him. But I've come too far. I don't know how to do that anymore.

But I raise my finger to his lips. "Let's not talk about it anymore."

Theo begins to fuss again, tired and cold and confused by the unfamiliar surroundings.

"We have to go," I say reluctantly, not wanting to end this perfect moment but worried that someone might hear the noise and find us. Luc stands and passes Theo to me, tucking the jacket a bit closer around him.

It is late when we start back, well after curfew. The village is dark and the woods are still. Luc follows me silently as we near the fairgrounds. The music has stopped and I wonder if I have been gone so long that it has ended and everyone is asleep. But the torches still burn in the grove. In their glow, I see Astrid, standing on the edge of the clearing. I can tell from the way that she is standing, arms crossed, that she is angry.

Dread tightens my stomach to a knot. Astrid knows that I went, I think. That I broke my promise to her not to see Luc again.

"Astrid," I start forward around the corner of the train. "Let me explain."

Then I freeze.

The circus folk are still gathered in the grove where the wedding celebration had taken place. They no longer dance, though, but stand motionless, like figures in a tableau.

Taking another step forward, I understand why. In the center of the grove where the wedding ceremony had taken place just hours earlier are a half-dozen gendarmes.

And their guns are pointed at Peter.

18

Astrid

I stand frozen as the police move toward Peter, guns raised. Surely this cannot be real. A prank someone is playing on our wedding night. But no one is laughing. The faces around me are twisted with shock and terror.

A minute and an eternity earlier Peter was gazing down at me, face aglow, contemplating our future together. Then a shadow passed over his eyes and the reflection of French police filled the space behind the other circus performers.

The police had come in great numbers, foreclosing any chance of resistance or escape. Their faces are familiar from the village. Once they might have tipped their hats in greeting, or at least nodded on the street. Now they stand before him wearing ominous expressions, jackbooted feet spread wide. "Peter Moskowicz…" one of the policemen, presumably the captain, says in a low, terse voice. He looks a bit older than the others, with a graying mustache and pins adorning the front of his uniform. "You're under arrest."

I open my mouth to protest but no sound comes out. It is the nightmare I have had a dozen times, now come true.

Peter lifts his head slowly at the policeman's summons. Fury burns in his eyes. He sits motionless, but I can see his mind working, calculating what to do. The police eye him warily, but keep their distance, as though facing a strange or dangerous animal. I hold my breath. Part of me wants Peter to fight and resist, even at this most futile of moments. But that will only make things worse.

What do they want with Peter? I wonder. Why not me?

Herr Neuhoff steps forward. "Gentlemen, *s'il vous plaît,* what is the issue?" He mops his brow with a stained handkerchief. "I'm sure if we talk it over. Some of my best Bordeaux perhaps...?" He smiles invitingly. More than once he has dissuaded the police from searching the tents with good food and drink he kept for just such a purpose. But the police ignore him, drawing in closer to Peter.

"What is the charge?" Herr Neuhoff demands, discarding his cordial tone and summoning authority to his voice.

"Treason," the captain replies. "Against France and the Reich." Herr Neuhoff's eyes shoot uneasily in my direction. He had warned Peter so many times about his act and now he will pay the price.

But they haven't taken him yet. *Struggle, fight, run,* I urge him silently. I look desperately across the field in the direction of the hiding place Peter had so lovingly created for me in his cabin. He'd meant for the small space to hold me, not him. Even if he could fit, though, it is too far away and too late. There is no hiding anymore.

"Let's go," the captain says, but there is no anger in his voice. He is a gray-haired man, probably a year or two from retirement. He thinks he is just doing his job. Beside him, though, a younger officer taps a club against his leg angrily, just wanting the chance to use it.

Peter's eyes travel to the club at the same time as mine. At last he unfolds himself and stands. He will not make a scene and risk the consequences for me or the others. He walks toward the police slowly but without protest, his limbs stiff with rage. Through my horror, I feel a tiny flicker of hope. Perhaps this will prove to be not so much worse than the inspections. Herr Neuhoff can bribe the police and have him home by morning.

Peter nears the police. A sound escapes my throat as one of the policemen puts Peter's hands in cuffs, whitening his wrists as they cut into the skin and causing my own arms to ache. No one seems to hear.

Peter stands calmly, offering no resistance. But then the officer with the club reaches up and knocks the top hat off Peter's head. Surprise and rage seem to break Peter's face into a thousand pieces. He lunges for the hat. Thrown off-balance by the cuffs on his wrists, he falls sideways to the ground.

The policeman drags Peter to his feet. His wedding suit is soiled with dirt now and his limbs shake with anger. I know that he will not be held back now. "You won't have any use for that where you're going," the policeman sneers, kicking the hat. The air hangs silent as Peter seems to be thinking of a retort.

Then he spits in the policeman's face.

There is a beat of silence as the policeman stands stunned. Then he lurches forward with a roar, kneeing Peter hard in the groin. "No!" I cry as Peter doubles over in a heap. Though he does not get up, the man kicks him over and over again.

Say something, I think. Do something. But I am frozen, paralyzed by horror. The man is using his club now, raining blows on Peter's head and back. My body screams out with pain, feeling each hit as though I had been struck. Peter lies motionless in a ball. "Enough!" the captain says sharply, pulling the younger policeman away. "They want him alive." Hearing this last part, I am terrified. Who wants him? And for what? "Get him in the truck," the captain orders.

Two of the police haul Peter to his feet and start for the truck. He offers no resistance now. *I will never leave you,* he said just days earlier. He seems aged years, a beaten man.

But I will not give up. "Wait!" I cry, starting toward him. A policeman grabs the shoulder of my dress as I near, sharp nails cutting into my skin. I push him away, heedless as the fabric tears.

I reach for Peter's arm, but he shrugs me off. "Astrid, you can't come with me," he says in German, his voice low and terse. A large bump is beginning to form on his forehead where he was struck. "You need to stay here. You need to be safe."

"They'll take you to the village jail. You'll be back in a few hours," I say, desperately wanting to believe it. "They're just trying to scare us, send a warning. Soon you will be back…"

"There's no coming back," he says before I can finish. "And you can't wait for me here. You must continue on with the show. Do you understand?" His dark eyes seem to burn into me. "Promise me," he says.

But I cannot. "Enough!" the policeman who had struck Peter snarls, tearing us apart. I start to lunge at him, wanting to claw his eyes out. "Give me a reason," he threatens. I pull back. I cannot make things worse for Peter.

The police begin dragging Peter from the backyard toward an army box truck that has pulled up on the dirt road close to the edge of the big top. There is writing on the side in a Slavic language I do not recognize. A black police car sits in front of it. A driver emerges from the truck in a military uniform and opens the rear doors, revealing two long rows of benches inside. I understand then that it is all ending—he isn't coming back.

"No!" I cry, rushing toward the truck.

Arms grab me from behind, restrain me. It is Noa, though where she has come from, I do not know. She wraps both arms around me. "Think of yourself...and your baby." She is right. Still I fight against her with all the force of my body, a lion trying to break free from its handler.

"They're taking him, Noa," I say desperately. "We have to stop this."

"This isn't the way to do it," she replies, her voice firm and low. "You can't help him if you get arrested, too."

She is right, of course. But how can I stand here and do nothing while they take my whole world away? "Do something," I plead, begging Noa to help me as I have helped her. But she simply holds on to me, as powerless as I am.

Herr Neuhoff rushes forward once more, face red with anger and desperation. He holds out a small bag in his hand, heavy with coins, likely much of the remaining money the circus has. Giving it would leave us in ruin, but he would do it to save Peter's life. "Officers, wait," he begs. Please, God, I pray. Let it work. It is our last hope.

The captain turns away and I see in his eyes a flash of remorse—which scares me more than anything has. "I'm sorry," he says. "This is out of my control."

My panic redoubles and I break free from Noa's grasp, racing forward. "Peter!" But it is too late—the police are loading him into the back of the truck and he does not resist. I lunge for the door, my fingers just inches from Peter, nearly grazing him but missing. I turn to the closest policeman. "Take me instead," I say.

"Astrid, no!" I hear Noa call from behind me.

"Take me," I repeat, ignoring her. "I'm his wife—and a

Jew," I cry, heedless of the danger I am bringing, not just to myself but the entire circus.

The policeman looks uncertainly toward the captain for guidance.

"Wait here!" the captain orders. He disappears around the front of the truck to the police car and returns with some papers. "We have no record of a Jew with the circus—and you aren't listed for transport." He turns to Peter. "Is it true that she is your wife?"

"I have no wife." Peter's eyes are like stone. I step backward, ripped to the core by his denial.

"Stand back," the guard orders, closing the door and separating me and Peter for good. "No!" I cry. I reach for the truck once more. The police pry my fingers from the bumper, flinging me backward so hard I almost stumble. But I run around the truck and stand in front of it, arms folded. They will have to run me over to leave.

"Astrid, stop..." I hear Noa again call, her voice sounding so very far away.

The policeman who had beaten Peter strides toward me. "Step aside," he barks, raising the club.

"Astrid, no!" Peter cries with more anguish than I have ever heard, his voice muffled by the glass that now separates us. "For the love of God, move!"

I do not move.

The policeman swings his arm downward. I try to step back, but it is too late. The club hits my stomach with a sickening thud. Pain explodes through my midsection and I fall sideways to the ground.

"Astrid!" Noa cries, closer now, as she rushes to me. She throws her body on top of mine, trying to shield me.

"Enough!" the captain orders, moving to restrain his subordinate. The policeman does not stop. He swings back his foot and kicks me hard across my side, finding the spot Noa has not managed to cover. Something seems to break loose inside me. I scream, my pain reverberating through the trees.

Then hearing a growl, I lift my head. Herr Neuhoff marches toward the police, his face deep red with anger as he moves to place himself between us and the guard. "You dare to hit a woman?" I have never seen him so enraged. He draws himself to his full five feet three inches, seeming to grow larger and more resplendent as he faces down the German.

The police officer raises his truncheon again. Terror surges through me. Herr Neuhoff is an old man; he will never survive such a blow.

Herr Neuhoff brings his hands to his chest and a look of surprise crosses his face. He crumples to the ground, as though he has been struck. But the guard has not hit him and the truncheon remains in the air.

Noa races to Herr Neuhoff. I try to stand to go to him, as well. A knife-like pain creases my stomach and I double over once more. I drag myself across the ground to where he lies, as quickly as I can manage. There is cramping low in my stomach now, growing stronger. I feel a dampness inside my skirt, as though I had soiled myself when I was a child. Let it be just the wet ground, I pray.

I near Herr Neuhoff, whose face is ashen and covered with sweat. "Miriam," he whispers, and whether he thinks I am his long-gone wife or he is simply remembering her, I cannot say. Noa loosens his collar and he gasps for air.

A memory flashes through my mind then of playing in the valley between our winter quarters with my brothers when I was a child, sledding downhill in an unbroken sea of white. I had looked up and seen Herr Neuhoff standing on the hilltop. Set against an azure sky, he'd reminded me of the Greek god Zeus atop Mount Olympus. Noticing me, he had smiled. Even then, it seemed, he was watching out for us.

"Medic!" I cry, but no one, not the police or the guards, moves to aid us. Noa crouches by my side and we watch helplessly as Herr Neuhoff's eyes go blank and still.

Below me my skirt is not just damp but wet now, the moisture too warm to be from the ground. Blood. Am I to lose my child, too? The baby, which days ago I was not sure I wanted, is suddenly everything I have in this world. I hold my stomach, clutching it to keep the life inside me from slipping away. Then I start to pray, in a way I have not done since I was a small girl.

The truck engine revs. I raise up with my hands as it starts forward, belching exhaust down upon us. There is a banging noise, Peter pounding on the glass window, seeing what has happened but powerless to help.

I reach out as if to touch him. Sharp pain, worse than when the soldier struck me, shoots through my lower stomach. I drop and curl into a ball once more, hugging my knees to my chest.

Still lying on the ground, I turn my head to look at Peter one last time. Through the window, I see him sobbing openly now. His sorrow cuts through me, more painful than any blow. The eyes that just minutes ago gazed so lovingly at me grow smaller, the lips I kissed in our sacred vow farther away.

The truck roars and Peter disappears from sight.

19

Noa

"Astrid!" I cry, racing toward her as the rumble of the engine fades in the distance. She does not answer, but lies motionless on the ground, one arm outstretched in the direction the truck has gone.

As I near, she curls into a ball. "No, no..." Astrid calls out beside me, over and over, clutching her belly and weeping. I sit down beside her and half lift her onto my lap, cradling her like a child.

Then I turn back toward Herr Neuhoff. There is no sign of a blow. His skin is a deathly shade like ash, though, eyes cast toward the sky. I remember then his cough, his heart condition. Astrid lifts her head, her eyes widening in horror as she takes in Herr Neuhoff's still body. "We need a doctor," she says frantically, trying to sit. Then with a moan, she doubles over once more.

I put my arm around her, unsure whether she really believes we can still help him or just in denial. "He's gone, Astrid." I hold her tighter as she sobs. Then with my free hand, I close Herr Neuhoff's eyes and wipe a bit of mud from his cheek. His face is peaceful, as if he is sleeping soundly.

Astrid lies pale and weak in my arms. Her hands are clutched tightly against her stomach. The baby, I think with panic. But I do not dare say that aloud.

A crowd of performers and workers linger a good distance away, watching us. I gesture to one of the men, waving him over. "We need to return Herr Neuhoff to his carriage," I instruct, forcing some authority into my voice in hopes that he will listen. "Then contact the undertaker…" Astrid turns away, not wanting to hear the details.

"Astrid, come, let us help you." I stand and try to raise her up. But she lies on the ground beside Herr Neuhoff, refusing to move, like a dog that has lost its master. "You aren't doing Peter any good," I add.

"Peter is gone," she says, each word heavy with grief.

A hand touches my shoulder. I look up to see Luc, holding Theo. When we had reached the fairgrounds and seen the police, I had thrust Theo at Luc and raced to help Astrid. Thankfully, he had the good sense to keep Theo out of sight.

Luc starts to kneel behind Astrid, as if to help me lift her. But I wave him off; Astrid seeing him will only make things worse. "Come, Astrid," I plead, straining again to help her to her feet. I start forward with effort, nearly buckling under her weight. Luc follows at a distance, carrying Theo.

"Why?" I cannot help but ask as we limp toward the train. "Why would they arrest Peter?" When I had first seen the police, I wondered if they had learned of the wedding, which violated the laws of Vichy and the Reich. But if that had been the case, they would have taken Astrid, as well.

"The act," she replies flatly. Part of me had already known the answer. They wanted Peter because of the way in which he mocked the Germans in the show.

We reach the train and I help Astrid into the sleeper car. Though it is late, the carriage is empty, the others still clustered outside talking about everything that had happened. I help Astrid to her berth. "You should rest," I say as I take off her shoes. She does not reply, but sits stiffly, staring straight ahead. Though I have seen her here dozens of times, she looks strangely out of place. She should be with Peter, celebrating their wedding night. Now that dream is gone. It hardly seems possible.

I reach back through the door of the train to take Theo from Luc. Then I try to hand Theo to Astrid. Usually he is such a comfort to her, but now she waves him away. "Astrid, we'll have to make arrangements for Herr Neuhoff," I begin. "We'll have to cancel tonight's show, of course. But by tomorrow we should perform again. Don't you agree?" I hear a note of pleading in my voice, wanting her to take charge as she always has. She sits motionless, though, her will gone. Tears well up in my eyes and spill over. I want so much to be strong for her but I cannot help it. "Oh, Astrid, I just can't believe that Herr Neuhoff is gone." Even though I had known him for only a few months, he was in so many ways more a father than my own had been.

"He isn't the only one," she replies sharply.

"Yes, of course," I reply hastily, wiping my eyes. I have no right to cry in front of her when she has lost so much more. "We mustn't give up on Peter, though. He'll be back." She does not reply.

Suddenly her face blanches. She lies down, clutching her stomach. Then she turns away to face the wall and lets out a moan. This is not just grief, I realize, but pain. I see it then, a small pool of blood under her, seeping through her skirt onto the sheet. "Oh, Astrid, your baby!" I cry, blurting out her secret in my panic. The stain grows larger even as I watch. "I'll go into town and find a doctor."

She shakes her head with resignation. "There's nothing to be done," she replies. "It's too late."

"Someone should check you," I protest. "Let me fetch Berta at least."

"I just want to rest." How long has she known this was happening?

"I'm so sorry..." I search for the right words. "I know what it feels like to lose a child." But my child survived to be born; whether this makes it better or worse I do not know.

"It's for the best really," she says darkly. "I never would have been any good at being a mother."

"That isn't true," I protest. "I've seen you with Theo and I know that isn't true."

"You must admit, I'm hardly the mothering type." Her eyes do not meet mine.

"There are all different kinds of mothers," I say, trying to help but feeling at the same time as though I am just making things worse.

"Without a baby, I'm free to perform or do anything else I'd like," she says as if trying to convince herself. She rolls toward me. "Nothing is going to change what has happened." Then she looks past me and her eyes widen. I turn to see Luc, who stands uneasily in the doorway to the carriage, not daring to enter but not wanting to leave me either after all that had happened. "What is he doing here?" Astrid demands.

"Astrid..." I struggle to find an explanation as to why I am with Luc after I had sworn to her I would stop seeing him. But I find none.

"Convenient how he took you away from here just before the arrest," she spits in French, wanting Luc to hear. "He must have known."

"No!" I cry. Luc would never betray us. I wait for Luc to say something to deny Astrid's accusation and defend him-

self. But he does not. Astrid's distrust seeps through me. Luc
had seen Peter's act, and even warned Peter it would lead to
trouble. I recall Luc's words to Peter the night he had come
to the circus: *They'll arrest you…* Was that a prediction or
had he known what was to come?

"This is all his fault!" Astrid flares, hurling all of her
anger and sorrow at Luc. I want to tell her that Peter, not
Luc, is to blame for doing the routine after Herr Neuhoff
had forbidden it. But now is not the time. It would only
make things worse.

Luc raises his hands in surrender, unwilling to quarrel. He
steps off the train and into the shadows. I sit down beside Astrid and wrap my arms around her. Even if Luc is innocent, it
is because I was off with him that I had not been here when
Astrid needed me. She shudders violently. Then she closes
her eyes, so still I check to make sure she is still breathing.
Her losses slam down upon me then: Herr Neuhoff, her child
and Peter, all taken from her in a single night.

Or perhaps not. I look toward the door of the railcar.
"Hold him," I tell Astrid, pressing Theo firmly into her
arms.

I walk to the door of the railcar and step down, but don't
see Luc. Maybe he has gone. A moment later, he steps from
the shadows. "Is she all right?" he asks.

"I don't know," I say, fighting back tears. "She's lost everything."

"I'm so sorry," Luc says. "I feel as if this is all my fault."

"What do you mean?" A rock of dread forms in the pit
of my stomach. Had Astrid been right about him after all?

"My father was complaining about the circus a week or
so ago," Luc begins slowly. "He said the show coming here
would only cause trouble. I told him how I had warned Peter

about the routine, told him not to do it again. I thought it would help. But that only seemed to make him angrier."

"Peter chose to do the act," I reply. "That wasn't your fault."

Luc shakes his head. "There's more. Papa warned me to stay away from you or there would be consequences. I thought I'd been careful going back and forth. But if he had one of his men watching me, and he followed me here tonight and saw the wedding... I'm so sorry," he says again, grabbing my hand. His face watches mine, eyes pleading.

"You didn't mean to do anything," I say. But I pull away. Even though he hadn't meant to, Luc had brought ruin to the circus, just as Astrid had warned. I am suddenly angry, not just at Luc, but at myself.

"If you want me to go now, I understand," Luc says. "You must hate me for what I've done."

"No," I reply firmly. "I know it wasn't your fault. But we need to fix this."

"How?" he asks.

"We must do something to find Peter." Doubt clouds Luc's eyes. He has seen people taken by the police too many times and knows how impossible this is.

I square my shoulders. I had failed Astrid once before. I cannot let that happen again. "Your father," I say. "This was a police action. Surely he knows something about it."

Pain crosses Luc's face at the notion that his father was somehow involved. "I will talk to him first thing in the morning and see if he knows anything."

"Morning could be too late," I reply. "We have to go see him now."

"We?" Luc repeats with disbelief.

"I'm coming with you," I say firmly.

He puts a hand on my shoulder. "Noa, you can't."

"You don't want your father to see you with me," I say, stung.

"It's not that. But everything is so dangerous right now. Why can't you just wait here?"

"Because I have to do this for Astrid. I'm going to see your father now, with or without you." I look him squarely in the eyes. "With would be better."

He opens his mouth to argue further. "Fine," he says, seeming to think better of it.

"Just give me a minute." I look down the outside of the train where a few of the circus woman stand huddled, talking. "Elsie!" I call, gesturing her over. The girl breaks free from the group and comes to me. "I need you to watch Theo for a bit." Though I still don't like or trust her after what she had done with Theo, I have no choice. Astrid is in no shape to watch him alone.

Astrid. I look back through the doorway of the carriage at Astrid, who lies doubled over on the berth, clutching Theo. I should stay and comfort her, but I need to know what Luc learns from his father. "Watch Astrid, too," I instruct Elsie. "Both of them. I'll be back as soon as I can." I should tell Astrid myself that I am going, but I don't want her to ask questions.

"I'm ready now," I tell Luc, putting my hand in his as he starts in the direction of the trees.

Luc leads me through the forest down a path where I have not been before. A chilling breeze, colder than I have felt in weeks, causes the trees to dance wildly above us, casting ghostly shadows on the moonlit ground.

Several minutes later, the woods break to a sloping pasture that ends at a villa. I am not sure what I expected the mayor's residence to look like. Something more grand or ominous, or at least a bit larger. But it is a traditional French country house, a long sloping gray slate roof broken by three windows. There is a flagstone path ending at a rounded door, ivy climbing the wall on each side. A bicycle leans against the adjacent fence.

It is the middle of the night and I'd expected the house to be quiet. But behind the curtain the lights are still on. I stop in my tracks, suddenly losing my nerve. "Maybe this was a mistake."

"That's what I was trying to tell you before. If Papa sees you…" Luc starts to push me into the low shrubs beside the fence. The bicycle that is leaning there tumbles to the hard ground with a clatter. Before I can hide, the front door opens and a man appears in a smoking jacket.

"Luc," he calls, peering into the darkness. He is an older version of his son, wizened and stooped, but with the same blue eyes and chiseled features. He might have been handsome in his day. "Is that you?" In his voice, I hear concern, a father for all his faults still worried about his son—hardly the villain I had imagined. A rich garlicky smell comes from inside the house, coq au vin for dinner earlier perhaps, mixed with cigar smoke.

The mayor steps outside, squinting in the darkness. As his eyes adjust, they lock on me. I stiffen. "You're the circus girl," the mayor says, a note of disdain in his voice. "What do you want?"

Luc clears his throat. "One of their performers has been arrested," he says.

The mayor stiffens and for a moment I think he will deny it. But then he nods. "The Russian clown." Peter is so much more than that, I want to protest. Astrid's husband, the heart of the circus.

"Surely you can do something." Luc's voice is pleading, fighting for us.

"He was performing acts mocking the Reich," the mayor states flatly. His voice is cold. "The Germans want to try him for treason."

I picture Astrid, hear her cries as they had taken Peter. "At least let us see him, then," I venture.

The mayor raises his eyebrows, surprised I have spoken. "That's quite impossible."

He's going to be a father, I want to say, appealing to the mayor as one who has a son. But I have sworn to keep her secret and I doubt it would sway the mayor. "Our circus owner died tonight and we need Peter so much more now. Please…" I beg, searching for the right words and not finding them.

"It's out of my hands," the mayor replies. "He's been taken to the old army camp on the outskirts of town to be deported, sent east first thing in the morning."

A distressed look crosses Luc's face. "I thought they weren't using the camp anymore."

"They aren't," his father replies, a note of grimness to his voice. "Only for special cases."

"Papa, do something," Luc says, trying again, still wanting to believe. I see now the boy who had defended his father, even after the awful things he had done.

"I can't," the mayor says flatly.

"You won't even help your son?" Luc demands. There is a new forcefulness to his voice. "I suppose it isn't surprising since you sold out your own people."

"How dare you?" he thunders. "I'm your father."

"My father helped people. My father would never have stood by while our friends and neighbors were arrested. And he would have done something to help now. You are not my father," Luc spits, and I wonder if he has gone too far. "If Mama were here…"

"Enough!" the mayor barks, voice cutting through the

still night air. "You have no idea the things I've faced, or the choices I've had to make to protect you. If your mother was here, it is you she'd be ashamed of. You were never like this before." His eyes shoot daggers in my direction. "It must be her doing, circus trash with no upbringing."

Luc steps forward, putting himself between his father and me. "Don't say such things about Noa."

"Never mind," the mayor replies, dismissing me with a wave of his hand. "They'll be gone soon enough. You should come inside now, Luc."

"No," Luc says, meeting his father's eyes. "I can't stay here, not anymore." He turns to me. "Let's go."

"Luc, wait!" the mayor calls, his voice rising with surprise.

"Goodbye, Papa." Luc takes my hand and leads me away from the villa, leaving the mayor alone in the doorway.

"Are you sure you want to do this?" I ask as we pass through the gate. Luc keeps walking, eyes forward. His strides are so long I almost have to skip to keep up.

We reach the edge of the forest. "Wait," I say, stopping. "Are you sure? If you need to go back, I understand. He's your father after all."

"I'm not going back," he replies.

"You mean ever?" I ask. He nods. "But where will you go?" I ask, my concern for him rising.

Luc does not answer, but instead takes me in his arms and presses his lips against mine hard, as though trying to wipe away what had just happened. I return his kisses, willing us back to earlier that night before everything had changed.

Then he breaks away. "I'm sorry, Noa," he says.

For a moment, I think he is talking about the kiss. "About Peter?" I ask. "Don't be. You tried…"

"Not just for that. For all of it." He kisses me once more. "Goodbye, Noa." Then he starts away in the other direction through the trees, leaving me behind.

20

Noa

The funeral takes place the next day on a too-sunny morning in the local cemetery, a nest of leaning headstones along the same hilly road on the far side of Thiers we'd climbed the day of the arrival parade. Herr Neuhoff's is a lone grave behind the rest, overhung by a willow tree. Looking down at the closed oak casket, I imagine how he must look inside, lifeless body gray and waxy in his magnificent ringmaster's suit. He does not belong here. He should be back in Germany, resting beside his wife. Instead, he will lie here forever. Sadness engulfs me. He had been everything to us, protected us. And now he is gone.

In the end, it was Herr Neuhoff's health that had killed him. His heart condition had been worsening right before us, although he'd done his best to hide it so we would not worry. The stress of keeping the circus going could not have helped. We had all been too caught up in our own concerns to notice. Then the struggle with the police had simply been the final straw. Or so we thought. We would never really know.

We stand uncertainly around the coffin. Someone should

say something about the benefactor who meant so much to us. But we have no minister; Peter is gone, and Astrid is in no shape. At the front, close to the gravesite, Emmet stands alone, tears streaming down his fat cheeks. The rest of the circus folk keep their distance, and I cannot help but feel sorry for him.

As the gravediggers lower the coffin, I stifle a cry. I want to reach out and touch it one more time, as if doing so could turn back time to just a few days earlier when everything was all right. Astrid steps forward and throws a handful of dirt into the hole in the ground. I follow her example, breathing in the deep earthy smell, feeling the darkness below. Though I have never been to a funeral before, the ritual feels somehow familiar. I stare down into the dark hole. Thank you, I say silently to Herr Neuhoff. For saving Theo and me. For all of it. In my whole life, there has never been anyone who has done more. I step back and brush the dirt off my hands, then lace my fingers with Astrid's.

Swallowing back the lump that has formed in my throat, I study Astrid's face out of the corner of my eye. Her skin is pale and her eyes hollow. But she has not cried. How is that possible? A few days ago, she was beginning her life with Peter. Now all of it is gone. She shudders, and I put my arm around her, our grief pressing silently together. My eyes burn and I blink back the tears. Astrid has done so much to care for and protect me; it is my turn to be strong for her now. I wrap my arm more tightly around her shoulders.

Then the funeral is over and we start the long, slow walk back to the fairgrounds. In the distance, bells peal eleven. I take a last look over my shoulder at the gravesite.

As we skirt the edge of town, I can see wagons and lorries climbing the steep road to the market square, children walking to school more quietly than they once had. Where is Luc? I wonder. Even now, I can't help but think of him and his proposal that we run away together. For a minute, even as I said no, I could see a glimmer of hope, a life that we might have had together. Now that, like everything else, seems gone.

I have not seen him since the night of Peter's arrest, and there was no note in the belly box when I checked the past two mornings. I half expected him to turn up at the funeral and pay respects, but he hadn't. Maybe he sensed that he would not be welcome, or that Astrid might blame him yet again for all that had happened.

When we reach the fairgrounds, we do not return to the train, but mill around the backyard like parentless children. "We should rehearse for the show," Gerda says. I had nearly forgotten: it is Tuesday, with a performance tonight. Tickets have been sold and crowds will come.

"But we have no ringmaster," one of the horseback riders points out. Heads nod. Performing without Herr Neuhoff is hard to imagine. Once Peter might have filled in, but he is gone, too.

"I can do it," Emmet says. All eyes travel warily in his direction. He does not have the personality to engage the crowd. I've never even seen him set foot in the ring. But there is no other choice. "It's only for one day before we leave," he adds. "We can figure out something else after that."

"One day?" Helmut, the animal trainer, asks. "What do you mean? We aren't supposed to move on to the next village until Friday." I recall Astrid telling me we would stay in Thiers for three weeks before moving on to the next town and we are still days short of that.

"We pack after tonight's show," Emmet replies. "Tear everything down. And we aren't going to the next town." My skin prickles. "We're turning back to a site near Strasbourg, in Alsace–Lorraine." He delivers the bad news like it is some sort of trump card.

There is a collective gasp. *Tonight.* The word bounces around in my brain. Emmet had told us the circus would be sent back, but I never expected it to actually happen so soon. I turn back toward Astrid, seeking her help, but she stands numbly, as if she hasn't heard.

"Alsace," one of the acrobats murmurs. "That might as well be Germany."

I remember what Astrid had told me about Herr Neuhoff fighting to find us a way to stay in France. "Can we appeal?" I dare to ask.

Emmet shakes his head. "My father tried to get the order changed before all of this happened. Our request was rejected." With Peter's arrest and everything that happened, there would be no reprieve. And Emmet is not a fighter; he would always choose the course of least resistance. We can't count on him to ask again. "So we will perform in Alsace."

I tense, flooded with fear. I can't go back so close to Germany with Theo. It would be far too dangerous. I look southeast toward the hills and imagine what it would be like to take Theo and run. But I couldn't possibly abandon Astrid, especially now.

"What about the cities in France we've booked?" I ask. Heads turn in my direction. "If we start canceling, we won't be invited back next year. Think of the money we will lose."

"Next year?" Emmet sneers, gesturing behind him. "The circus is dying, Noa. There is no money. We've lost our ringmaster and the Germans have just taken one of our star performers." A choking noise, not quite a sob, catches in Astrid's throat. Emmet continues, "They've humored us to a point. But whether it is now or a few months from now, this is the end. How much longer did you think this could go on?"

"We have to keep going," Astrid says. It is the first time she has spoken since before the funeral, and her voice has none of its usual strength.

"To save you?" Emmet retorts.

"To save all of us," I interject, "including you. Do you know what the Germans do to those who hide people?" I step back, fearful I've said more than I should.

Emmet's eyes widen. "We will keep going where we've been ordered for the rest of the season," he relents. "At least as long as we can manage financially. Papa did not leave much."

A murmur travels among the performers. We grieve Herr Neuhoff, of course, and we will do so for a long time. The hole created by his loss is vast. But there is a practical side of things, too: How would the circus go on without him? Could it?

"Surely your father had an insurance policy?" Helmut asks.

All eyes look expectantly at Emmet, who shifts uneasily. "I believe my father had to cash it out last winter. We needed the money for expenses."

"He's telling the truth," Astrid says quietly. It is just as well, I think. The money would have gone to Emmet as his heir and he would not have used it for the greater good of the circus.

"There was a will, though," Astrid continues. Jealousy registers in Emmet's eyes—he had not known his father or his affairs as well as Astrid. "It had a provision that the circus is not to be sold." Behind me, someone exhales. No one would buy the circus in these times, but if possible, Emmet would have sold it for the profits and run.

"That's ridiculous!" Emmet flares. He had assumed that whatever was left would be his, that he would have free rein to do what he wanted. He had not expected this.

"And it stipulates that all of the performers are to be kept on, unless there is misconduct," Astrid adds.

"At least I have one less performer to pay," Emmet says coldly, crossing his arms as he delivers this final blow.

Astrid, seemingly defeated, does not reply. I motion to put my arm around her but she shrugs me off and begins to walk away. "Don't," she says as I start to follow. She raises an arm to ward me off.

"I've arranged a late breakfast for everyone," Emmet says, sounding eager to end the discussion.

We make our way wordlessly toward the cook tent. Fresh smells of sausage and rich brewing coffee tickle my nose. Inside, the few kitchen workers who had remained behind during the funeral have laid out a breakfast bigger than I have seen since we traveled to France, eggs and even a bit of real butter—a meal designed to comfort. I inventory the menu silently, cataloging as I always do the bits I might be able to take back for Theo.

"So much food," I remark to one of the servers, who is refilling the plate of fried potatoes. "It seems foolish to waste it all now, no?"

"We won't have time to pack ice if we are leaving in a few hours," the server says. "We have to eat the perishables now so they don't spoil."

I take a piece of toast and some eggs for myself, then sit down at an empty table. Emmet comes over carrying a heaping plate of food, his appetite seemingly unaffected by grief. He sits down without asking. I have not been alone with him since he confronted me at the wedding and I fight the urge to stand up and leave. Then I remember his sadness at the funeral. "Such a hard day," I remark, trying to be kind.

"Things are going to get even harder," he replies tersely. "There will be changes when we reach Alsace. We'll have to let most of the workers go." The laborers are part of the circus, and they come faithfully each year in exchange for steady work, a promise kept on both sides. How can he do this?

"I thought your father's will said everyone was to stay on," I offer.

"His will only spoke of the performers," he snaps.

"Surely your father intended..."

"My father isn't here anymore," he says, cutting me off. "We can't afford to keep everyone on. We will find help locally as we go." Just a minute earlier I felt sorry for Emmet. Now my goodwill hardens. The wheels in his mind are turning, ready to bleed the circus of its talent penny by penny in order to draw the most benefit for the least possible work. His father's body is not even cold and already Emmet is destroying things. He may be genuinely grieving his father, but he is also using it as an excuse for being as awful as he really wants. "We can make do with half as many if everyone pitches in," he adds. The suggestion belies how little he knows about what we do. Even I understand the manpower and expertise that are needed.

I look over my shoulder in the direction of the train. If only Astrid was here to reason with Emmet. Then I remember her worn face and weak voice. In her present condition, she would be in no shape to manage it. "When will you tell them?" I ask.

"Not until we reach Alsace. The workers can stay with us until then." Emmet says this benevolently, as if bestowing a great gift. But it is not for the laborers' benefit: he wants them to tear everything down—and to go back accounted for.

"What about their contracts?" I ask.

"Contracts?" Emmet repeats mockingly. "Only the performers have those."

I do not argue further. My eyes travel across the dining room toward the laborers' tables, where a thin, graying handyman is clearing his plate, shoulders hunched. I recall the story about the Jewish handyman that Astrid had told me, the man Herr Neuhoff had given refuge. With Herr Neuhoff dead and Emmet dismissing the workers, the man would have no sanctuary. Neither would Astrid or any of the rest of us.

"Some of these people have no homes to go back to," I say, staying purposefully vague.

"You mean like the old Jew?" Emmet asks harshly. I am unable to hide the surprise on my face. "I know about him," he adds.

I instantly regret having spoken—but it is too late to turn back. "If you tell him before we go, he might have the chance to escape before we leave."

"Escape? He has no papers." Emmet leans in close to me, his voice low, breath hot and sour. "I'm not telling him or the other workers now. And you better not either, if you know what is good for you." He does not bother to hide his threat. My blood chills. Emmet would not hesitate to throw a person to the wolves if it suited his purpose—including me.

Not wanting to listen any longer, I stand and pocket the napkin I used to wrap some eggs and toast for Theo. "Excuse me," I say. I walk from the cook tent back toward the train.

As I cross the fairgrounds, I pass Drina, the fortune-teller, seated beneath a different tree, closer now than the time I had seen her before. She smiles faintly and holds her tarot deck up to me, an offering. But I shake my head. I no longer want to see the future.

That night the crowds are still making their way from the fairgrounds when the crews begin tearing down the circus. Unlike the raising of the big top, its demise is anticlimactic, a sight nobody wants to see. Poles clank as they fall upon one another and the canvas begins to collapse like a parachute billowing to the earth. The enormous tent, once full of people and laughter, is gone as though it was never there at all. I step over discarded programs and crushed popcorn kernels that have been matted into the ground. What will be here once we are gone?

I scan the desolate scene, looking once more for Astrid. She had not come to the show. Earlier, as I prepared to perform, I kept searching the backyard, hoping. But she had not emerged from the train all night. It was the first time I had performed without her nearby and I felt helpless, as though the safety net had somehow been removed. With Herr Neuhoff gone, I needed her more than ever.

Gerda walks over to me. "Come," she says. "We should get changed and prepare to go." It is the most she has said to me since I joined the circus and I wonder if she senses how lost I am without Astrid.

"When do we go?" I ask as we start back to the train to change.

"Not for a few hours," Gerda replies. "They'll finish tearing down sometime after we are asleep. But Emmet has ordered everyone to remain on board."

A few more hours until we leave Thiers for good. Luc appears in my mind. I had not had the chance to tell him we were going or say goodbye. I gaze longingly over my shoulder in the direction of town, wondering if there is time to find Luc. I think about how I might sneak out unnoticed, but I wouldn't dare go to Luc's father's house after all that had happened, and I do not know where else I might find him.

In the dressing car, the girls are quiet as they remove their costumes and makeup, and there is none of the excitement of when we'd left Darmstadt. When I have finished changing, I start back to the sleeper. I expect to find Astrid, as I so often do, holding Theo. But he is with Elsie.

I take Theo from her. "Where's Astrid?"

"She hasn't come back," Elsie replies.

"Back?" I repeat. I had assumed that since she had not been at the show she had stayed here in bed, as she had much of the time since Peter was arrested.

"She hasn't been here since before the show," Elsie says. "I thought she was with you."

I peer out the window of the sleeper. Where has Astrid gone? I hadn't seen her in the big top during the show, nor anywhere on the fairgrounds as the teardown had begun after. I carry Theo from the train and scan the length of the cars toward the front of the train, but I do not see Astrid. She wouldn't have gone far just as we are about to leave. Unless she had gone in a last desperate attempt to find Peter. I look in the direction of town, my concern growing.

Easy, I think. Even Astrid in her current state would have known that was impossible. My eyes travel the length of the train in the opposite direction, toward the rear, taking in the final carriage that had been Herr Neuhoff's. Then, taking in the one in front of it, I understand. Astrid did not leave. Instead, she has gone to the place where she felt closest to Peter. I start in the direction of his railcar.

I find her lying in Peter's unmade bed, curled into a ball, facing away from me. She clutches the sheet in both hands. "Astrid…" I sit down beside her, relieved. "When I couldn't find you, I thought…" I do not finish the thought. Instead I put my hand on her shoulder and gently roll her over, expecting to see tears at last. But her face is stony, eyes blank. Though the railcar is chilly, faint perspiration coats her upper lip.

My concern rises again. "Astrid, are you feeling worse? Has your bleeding started again?"

"No, of course not."

I reach out and touch her head. "You still feel warm." I should have fought her harder when she refused to see a doctor but now there is no time.

I hand Theo to Astrid then lie down beside them, smelling Peter in the soiled sheets and trying not to think of the nights he and Astrid have spent here while on the road. I want to tell her what Emmet said about the workers, but I cannot burden her now. A moment later, her breathing evens and when I look over she is asleep.

Theo squirms restlessly beside her, not ready to settle down in the unfamiliar space. There is a loud bang and the whole carriage rocks with the force of something heavy being loaded into an adjacent railcar. "It will be all right," I say, more for myself than him. I press my palm gently against his back, moving it in small, soothing circles. His eyelids begin to flutter, staying closed longer for a second each time as they do when he is falling asleep.

When Theo has quieted, I roll over, thinking of Luc. He would find out I had left, of course, but not until it was too late. Would he learn, too, where I had gone? Once he had promised to find me, but I can't see how that's possible. We will be hundreds of miles away.

I sit up and peer out the window at the familiar site of the fairgrounds, the forest leading to town behind it. We are still here. I can get off the train and go to Luc to let him know we are going, and still make it back in time without anyone noticing. Or maybe even take Theo and leave with Luc for good, I think, remembering his proposal. But where would we go? We have no papers to cross the border, no money for food and shelter. Then I look over at Astrid. Even if it were possible, I would not dare. I close my eyes.

Sometime later there is a great heave and the train struggles forward. I sit up once more and look southeast out the window, imagining the freedom that lies just a few hundred kilometers away in Switzerland. Beside me, Astrid's body rises and falls methodically with deep sleep. My fate is tied up with hers now, whatever happens.

The train presses forward and the town of Thiers seems to shrink, growing lower and flatter into the earth as we pick up speed. And then it is gone. I touch the glass where the village had been seconds earlier, leaving Luc—and our chance at freedom—behind.

21

Astrid

The squeak of a doorknob turning, hands pressing against hard wood. Through sleep I think I am back in the winter quarters, Peter coming to tell me that he has found someone in the woods near Darmstadt. But when I open my eyes, I see that it is only Noa, hurrying into the tiny cabin we have shared in the past five days since reaching Alsace. I close my eyes once more, willing the vision of earlier times to return.

"Astrid?" Noa's voice, tight with urgency, yanks me from my memories. I roll over. She is peering out the filthy window, her body stiff and face pale. "You have to get up."

"Have they come again?" I ask, struggling to sit. Before she can answer, there is a loud clattering outside, a police inspection, officers rattling through the wagons and the tents. Once I might have run and hid. But there is no hiding place here. Let them take me, I think.

There is a hard knock on the door that startles both of us. I sit up, reach for my robe. Theo lets out a wail. Noa opens the door to reveal two SS officers. Always two, I muse. Except, of course, the night they had taken Peter.

"Wer ist da?" one of the men, taller and thin, barks. *Who is there?*

"I'm Noa Weil," she offers, managing to keep the quaver from her voice.

The officer gestures toward me. "And her?"

A moment's hesitation. "I'm Astrid Sorrell," I say, when Noa does not. "The same as when you asked two days ago," I cannot help but add. What do they think will be so different each time?

"What did you say?" he demands. Noa shoots me a withering look.

"Nothing," I mutter. No good can come from antagonizing them.

The other officer takes a step into the cabin. "Is she ill?" He nods his head in my direction.

Yes, I want to say. The Nazis are known to fear illness. Perhaps if they think I am contagious, they will leave us alone. "No," Noa replies firmly, before I can answer. Her eyes dart nervously in my direction.

"And the child?" he asks.

"My little brother," Noa says with conviction, the lie now long familiar. "His papers are here, as well."

"Are you thirsty, sirs?" Noa offers, changing the subject before he can ask further questions. She reaches behind her bed and produces half a bottle of cognac I had not known she had.

The man's eyes widen, then narrow again. It is a calculated risk: Will he take the bribe or accuse her of stealing or hoarding the liquor? He takes the bottle and starts toward the door, the shorter man in tow.

When they have gone, Noa closes the door. She picks up Theo and sinks to the bed beside me. "I didn't think they would come again so soon after the last time," she says, shaken.

"Almost every day like clockwork," I reply, turning away from her, looking out the window of the cabin where we have billeted since our arrival. In Alsace, the most worn of regions, all pretense of normalcy is gone. Across a thin strip of river lies the town of Colmar, its once-elegant skyline of Renaissance churches and timber houses crumbled after the air raids, trees that would have been blooming other years in early May snapped in half like twigs. German trucks and Kubelwagen line the roads.

"The cognac," I say. "Where did you get it?"

A guilty expression crosses Noa's face. "From Herr Neuhoff's railcar. Emmet was going through things the other day, taking what he wanted. I didn't think he would notice."

"That was smart thinking." Thank God she did not offer them food—rations have shrunk to a fraction of what they were in Thiers; we barely have enough to feed ourselves and Theo.

"But it's gone now," Noa frets. "They'll expect more next time."

"We'll think of something," I say. I lie down once more, my throat scratchy from the halo of burnt smoke and coal dust that seems to hang constantly in the air. The cabin, just big enough for Noa, Theo and myself, is scarcely a step above camping, with a roof that leaks and a floor that is mostly dirt. We cannot sleep on the train as we had in Thiers for fear the British RAF pilots might bomb the rail lines. So we have moved to the low cabins, not much more than huts without indoor plumbing, once used as work sheds by workers at the adjacent quarry. Not that they are so much safer. The fairgrounds here are close to the roadway and military vehicles rumble down it all night, making it a prime target for the air raids, as well. Last night the bombs fell so close I pulled Noa and Theo under my cot and we huddled against the cold earth until dawn.

It has been nearly a week since Peter was arrested, taken God only knows where. I see it now in my waking thoughts, like a bad dream I cannot erase. Herr Neuhoff is gone, too, left behind in a hillside grave in Auvergne. I wrap my arms around my stomach, feeling the hollowness and mourning all that will never be. After Erich and my family, I thought I had already lost everything, that nothing more could be taken from me. But this, the final blow, is too much. I had let myself hope again, against every promise I had made myself when I left Berlin. I let myself get close. And now I am paying the price.

Noa presses her hand to my forehead. "No fever," she says, the relief evident in her voice. Bless her, she tries so very hard to care for me. Her concern is a drop of water, though, unable to fill the ocean of void in my heart.

Noa reaches down and takes both of my hands in hers. "Astrid, I have good news."

For a second, my heart lifts. Perhaps she has word of Peter. Then I catch myself. Can she bring back the dead? Turn back time? I pull away. "There is no good news anymore."

"Emmet said you can perform again," she says, then pauses, watching my face for a reaction. Does she expect me to leap up with joy and change into my practice leotard? Once returning to the trapeze was all I wanted. But it does not matter anymore.

"Let's go practice," Noa urges, still trying for all her best to make things better. It doesn't help at all, but I love her for caring. "Astrid, I know how hard this is. But lying here isn't going to change things. Why not fly again?"

Because doing the normal things feels like accepting that

Peter is gone, I think. A betrayal. "What's the point?" I ask finally.

Noa hesitates. "Astrid, you must get up again."

"Why?"

She looks away, as if not wanting to tell me. "Remember Yeta?"

"Of course." Yeta had survived her fall and been sent to a hospital near Vichy to convalesce. I am suddenly uneasy. "What about her?"

"I asked Emmet about her before we left Thiers and he said she was being sent back to Darmstadt to finish healing. But then I heard the workers whispering that she had been taken from the hospital and sent east on one of the trains." Noa's voice drops to a whisper.

"Arrested?" I ask. Like Peter. Noa nods. "No one is arrested for a broken leg, Noa. That's ridiculous. She didn't do anything wrong." But even as I say this, I doubt my own words. These days a person could be arrested for just about anything—or nothing at all.

"They said if she couldn't perform, then her working papers were no longer valid," Noa continues. "You have to get better, Astrid, for all of our sakes." I realize that this was why Noa was so quick to tell the Germans I was not sick. They can smell weakness and want nothing more than to exploit it. "Please come with me to the ring. If you don't feel well enough to practice, at least watch and tell me what to fix." Noa's voice is pleading.

"Performing with a gun to the head," I say. "Where is the joy in that?" It is not about joy now, though, but survival. And Noa is right: lying here will not change things or bring Peter back. The circus, my act, they are the only things I have. "Fine," I say, standing up. She takes Theo to the cabin where Elsie is staying as I find my practice leotard and hold it up to the light, remembering the last time I had worn it, feeling Peter's touch against the fabric. My throat grows scratchy. Perhaps I cannot do this after all. But I put on the leotard. When Noa returns, I let her lead me from the cabin.

We cross the fairgrounds. The workers have done their best to assemble everything, from the beer tent to the carousel, exactly as they had been in Thiers. But the grounds here are abysmal—a dirt field at the edge of an abandoned stone quarry, uneven and pockmarked from fighting that had passed this way earlier in the war.

As we near the big top, I glimpse the trapeze through the open flap. Then I stop. How can I ever fly again, knowing that Peter will not be there to see me?

Noa takes my hand. "Astrid, please."

"I can do it," I say, shaking her off.

Inside, I can see that nothing is right. The tent has been shoddily erected with the grounds not properly prepared and with less than half the workers, most local and inexperienced. What would Herr Neuhoff have thought of his grand circus, now in tatters? The will had stipulated that the circus go on, but there are a thousand little details it could not account for, about wages and living conditions and working hours and such. It would be easy to blame Emmet. The downfall of the circus had not begun with him, though; the cracks had been months or years in coming; only now, in this godforsaken village with no one to lead us, the weaknesses have been exposed, their full depth revealed.

Enough. I steel myself. With the circus in such a state, Noa and the others need me more than ever. I start forward with new determination, pull back the flap of the big top, then lift my head to appraise the state of the trapeze apparatus. Above, a dark unfamiliar object catches my eye. For a second, I think it is one of the other aerialists rehearsing. I step back, not ready to face anyone else yet.

The person in the air does not move with any force, though, but rather hangs limply. "What on earth?" I move closer for a better look.

From the Spanish web, where I had once performed, hangs the lifeless body of Metz, the clockmaker.

"Astrid, what is it?" Noa asks as I sink to the ground. It is almost impossible to hear her over the buzzing in my ears, growing louder. "Are you feeling okay?" she asks. Her gaze is focused downward on me, not seeing the horror of what I see above. "This was a mistake. Let me help you back to bed…"

"Call for the workers," I command, but even as I say this, I know it is too late. "Go now." I want her to leave the tent to spare her from the sight. But her eyes follow my gaze upward and she lets out a bloodcurdling scream.

I grab Noa by the shoulders and force her from the big top. "The laborers," I order again, more firmly now. "Go!" Alone now, I stare up at Metz. I had seen Herr Neuhoff die just days earlier. But this is different. Metz died because he was a Jew—and because he thought all hope was gone. That could have been me. I stand silently, touching my coat where the star should have been, a moment of solidarity.

"In the big top!" I hear Noa calling outside. "Please hurry."

Two workers rush into the tent. I stand alone, watching as the laborers climb the ladder, then try to reach out with the long pole we use to pull in the trapeze bar in order to retrieve Metz.

I turn away, sickened and not wanting to see anymore. Noa hurries back in, Emmet close behind. "Damn it," he swears.

"Should we call the police?" Noa asks.

"No, of course not," Emmet snaps. "We can't afford to attract attention from the police."

"But if someone killed him, we have to report it," she protests with more force than I imagined she might show against Emmet. He does not answer, but storms from the tent.

I put my hand on her shoulder. "Noa, no one killed him. He killed himself."

"What?" I watch her expression as she grapples with the idea.

"Surely you've heard of suicide."

"Yes, of course. But how can you be sure?"

"There are no signs of a struggle," I explain. "I just wish I knew why."

Noa's face crumples. "He must have found out."

"Found out what?" I demand.

She hesitates, and I can tell she has been keeping something from me. "Emmet said he was letting the workers go."

"What?" I am stunned by the notion. Metz must have somehow learned of Emmet's plan. With his family gone and no chance of sanctuary, he had given up, taken his life instead of letting it be taken. He had not seen another way out.

"I'm sorry I didn't tell you sooner," Noa says quickly. "Emmet threatened me if I said anything. And I didn't want to worry you…" Not listening to the rest of her explanation, I walk from the tent.

Word has spread quickly through the fairgrounds and workers and performers have clustered outside the big top. I circle the gathering and find Emmet on the far side, standing uneasy and separate from the others. "How could you?" I demand. "We need these people."

His eyes widen. "You've been lying around for days, and now you want to tell me how to run the show?" he snarls. "You've got some nerve."

"It's you who's got the nerve, Emmet." Noa's voice comes from behind me. "If you had told them before we left Thiers, that man might have had a chance."

"This is none of your concern," he counters.

"Are you going to tell them or am I?" He is caught off guard by Noa's defiance.

The others draw closer now, having overheard. "Tell us what?" one of the acrobats demands.

Emmet shifts uncomfortably, then turns to the crowd that has assembled. "I'm sorry to tell you that the circus is nearly out of money. We will be letting all of the workers go."

"Except for the foremen," I interject quickly. I am over-stepping my place, but I do not care. I continue quickly before Emmet can protest, "And those who have been with the circus for more than five years." If everyone left at once there would be no one to run the show.

"Goddammit!" one of the workers swears. "You can't do this!"

"There's no other choice," Emmet replies coldly.

"You will each receive two weeks' pay and a train ticket home," I add. "Isn't that right, Emmet?"

Emmet glares at me. Clearly he had not been planning that. "Yes, yes, of course. If you go peacefully. Now, if you'll excuse me, I have business to attend to." He slinks away, keeping his eyes on us as if afraid to turn his back. When he has gone, the workers begin to dissipate, still grumbling. The performers, spared for now, go more quietly to rehearse.

At last only Noa and I remain outside the big top. Be-hind us, there is a clattering noise and I turn in time to see the two workers who had gotten Metz down carry his body from the big top. "Oh!" Noa says, covering her mouth with her hand. "Astrid, I still don't understand it. Even if things were so bad, to just give up like that..."

"Don't judge," I say, the rebuke in my voice sharper than I intended. "Sometimes the running just gets to be too much."

22

Noa

The next day, Emmet blocks my way as I start from the cook tent back to our cabin after breakfast. "Where's Astrid?" he demands, arms crossed. "She isn't back to practicing?" he presses.

"Not yet," I say. I shift the bowl of porridge I've taken for Astrid out of his view.

"Now that we are out of Thiers, there's no reason for her not to rejoin the show. So why hasn't she?"

"She doesn't feel well," I say, lying for Astrid instinctively, even though it could cost me my job if Emmet found out. In some sense it is true. "And we tried yesterday—you saw that. But then there was that business with the worker…"

He waves his hand, as though the clockmaker was of no consequence. "She needs to be back in the show by tomorrow," Emmet says. "Everyone has to pull his weight around here. No more lollygagging for that one," he adds. The notion of Astrid being lazy is so ridiculous I almost laugh aloud. I want to argue again that it is too soon for her to swing again after all that she has been through, that she needs a few more days to get back on her feet. But I know he will not be swayed. Taking my silence as agreement, he continues on.

I begin to walk again, pulling my coat over my head to avoid the thick spring drizzle that has begun to fall. I peer across the roadway where a thin strip of river separates us from the town of Colmar. I had crossed the bridge into town once since our arrival to see if there was anything to be had at market beyond our tiny rations. But my trip had been useless: the lone seller at what had once been a bustling town market had only some unidentifiable meat, which would have been too tough for Theo even without the foul smell. Indeed, the whole town seemed to be stripped bare by the years of war. The streets were nearly deserted at midday, except for a stray dog by the gutter and the SS, who seemed to watch from every corner. The shutters on the houses and shops were drawn. The faces of the few townsfolk I saw (all women, since the local men had been drafted against their will and sent in droves to fight in the east) were pinched by hunger and fear. We might as well have been back in Germany. I hurried from the town center, past the barbed wire and ditches that had been erected as a kind of haphazard fortification around the perimeter, and returned to the fairgrounds. I had not gone into town again since.

I head toward the cabin, recalling Emmet's angry red face as he insisted Astrid perform.

Since we arrived in Alsace nearly a week ago, she has lain in bed, curled up like a wounded animal. Other than her one attempt to return to the big top that ended when we found the clockmaker, she hasn't left the cabin. I've stayed close, doing what I can for her. It is not enough, though. Every last bit of her will seems gone. *Save her*, Peter's eyes had seemed to say in those final minutes before he was taken. But how? Even if I feed her, make her drink, her spirit is gone. I can barely care for Theo and myself—under the weight of all three of us, I will break.

What will Emmet do if Astrid refuses to return to the show? I shiver at the thought. I need to get her up and moving.

As I pass the train parked and empty at the end of the line, my eyes travel wistfully to the underside of our sleeper car and the belly box where Luc and I had once left word for one another. I wonder if Luc might have followed the circus after we had left Thiers, but know that it is impossible. I walk to the box and pull it open, almost hoping that something might be there. Of course it is empty. I run my hand over the rough wood, imagining Luc doing the same.

Inside the cabin, I am surprised to find Astrid sitting up on the bed in her dressing gown. "Peter..." Astrid says as I near.

I freeze. Has she gone mad from all of her grief? "No, it's me, Noa," I say, stepping closer. She is not having delusions of Peter, but rather staring at a crumpled photograph. I approach Astrid carefully and get a better look at the picture. It is one I have never seen before of the two of them sitting in the backyard under a parasol on a sunny day in street clothes, not costume.

"Where was that taken?" As she passes it to me, I notice that her once-perfect manicure is gone, the nails shredded where she has chewed on them.

"A little town just outside Salzburg. It was in summer, the first season after I returned." Before I had arrived, I think. It feels strange to imagine the circus when I was not here. "We weren't together yet, you know, just getting to know each other." She smiles, her eyes far away. "We would talk and play cards for hours. He was fierce at card games, gin rummy, poker. We would start with a drink in the afternoon and the next thing I knew the whole night had passed."

I study the photograph. Even then, Peter's eyes were somber—as though he knew what was to come. "It would have been his birthday tomorrow," she adds, and her expression saddens once more. She speaks as though he is already dead. I fight the urge to correct her, not wanting to offer false hope.

From the other cot, Theo stirs. I pick him up, kissing the top of his head. Our one blessing. Through all of the hardship, Theo has thrived. His cheeks are still round and his hair has grown thick and curly, a dark meringue. Still holding Theo, I sit down beside Astrid gently. Everything has been taken from her—a chance at a child, the man she loves. She simply has nothing left—except us. I wrap my arms around her.

But it is not my warmth she seeks. She reaches for Theo and I pass him to her, offering one of the few comforts that remain, pressing him into her arms. She clings to him like a buoy at sea, seeming to draw strength from his tiny body.

I pick up the still-warm bowl of porridge and bring it closer to her, but she shakes her head. "Astrid, you have to eat."

"I'm not hungry."

"Think of Peter."

"I *am* thinking of him."

"Every second, I know. But is this what he would want for you?" She reluctantly takes a mouthful and turns away once more.

"Emmet was asking for you," I say hesitantly.

She raises an eyebrow. "Again?" I nod. He is the boss and even Astrid will push him only so far. But what can he do to her, really?

"Please, Astrid. We need you. *I* need you." Astrid is my only friend in the world and I am losing her.

Astrid raises an eyebrow, as though the thought has never quite occurred to her. She sighs, then stands up. She takes off her dressing gown and I am surprised to find she is already wearing her leotard. Gratitude washes over me. She will not let me down. "Let's rehearse," she commands.

We step outside. It is midmorning and the backyard is busy with trainers feeding the animals, performers on their way to practice. The few laborers who remain struggle to mend equipment and put things in place with a third of their usual number.

At the door of the tent, she turns to me. "I don't want to do this."

Is it Peter or the baby or Metz? I wonder. I squeeze her hand. "I understand. But you can do it. I know you can."

At least she is here, willing to try. I start for the ladder. Then looking up where the man had hung, my stomach turns. I stop, still holding on to the ladder and staring upward.

I wonder if the memory of the clockmaker will stop Astrid. But she climbs the opposite ladder without hesitation. Then, halfway up, she stops and grows concerned. "Something is not right," she says.

Nothing is right. The fairgrounds had not been prepared when we arrived, the earth rough and strewn with debris. "I asked about leveling the ground," I say. I've performed here with Gerda a handful of times, gotten used to the rickety apparatus and the way that the slope of the earth changes my fall. But Astrid has not been here since we've come to the town. To her it is jarring, a disgrace.

"Is it the ladder?" I ask, tugging on it to show her that it is firmly secured.

But she shakes her head sadly. "It is just everything."

I watch her intently, waiting for her to climb back down

and insist on seeing the head of the grounds crew. She might refuse to perform. Then she shrugs and keeps climbing. Even this does not matter anymore. She reaches the top and grabs the bar, nearly losing her balance. It is too soon, I fret; forcing her back to the trapeze so quickly had been a mistake. But she rights herself.

I start up the ladder, wondering if she will need my help. But she holds out her hand to ward me off. "I need to do this myself." I step away from the ladder and back close to the entrance, standing in the shadow of the tent flap and giving her space to find the trapeze once more on her own. She leaps without hesitation, seeming to grow stronger and more assured as I watch.

I had wondered if the days away from the act or all her body had been through would slow Astrid or make her rusty. But it is the opposite: her moves are more intense, razor sharp. Once she had held the trapeze bar lightly with an artist's touch, but now she grasps it like a lifeline. Her moves are punishing, as if trying to break a wild mare or great steed, taking out her anger on the trapeze itself. She vaults through a series of dizzying pirouettes and somersaults. I sense a slight movement of air around me and I can almost feel Peter admiring her performance with me as he once had.

There is a noise behind me. I turn, for a second actually expecting that Peter might be standing there. But of course he is not and the space behind me is empty. The wind howls through the campground, shaking the tarp and making the sound I had just heard once more. I relax slightly.

Then suddenly an arm grabs me from behind without warning. Before I can cry out, someone pulls me from the tent. I jerk away and turn, preparing to fight my attacker.

There, in the entrance to the big top, stands Luc.

"Luc!" I blink, wondering if his tall, dark figure before

me is some sort of strange dream. But he is here. I stare at him in disbelief. How had he made it all this way to see me?

"Noa," he says, reaching out and touching my cheek. I throw myself into his arms and he wraps them tightly around me.

I pull him farther away from the big top, behind the shelter of a shed. It is best if no one sees him. "How did you find us?"

"I came to the circus looking for you," Luc says. "But you left." His face falls. "After that, I went back to my father's house. I hadn't planned to," he adds quickly. "But I needed to see if he knew where the circus had gone. I didn't want to believe that this might be partly his doing. But I had to know." I can tell from the pain in his eyes that even after everything that has happened, part of him still wanted to believe in his father. "He denied it, of course. But I found the order in his desk with his signature on it." Luc's voice is heavy with sadness. "I confronted him with it and he admitted the truth. Then I left to find you." I imagine his journey across the miles to reach me. He kisses me long and full on the lips. His face is rough from not shaving, his lips salty and unwashed.

A moment later we break apart. Though it has been only a few days, his face looks thinner, cheekbones chiseled. His eyes are ringed, as though he has not slept for days. "Have you eaten? You need rest." I search the fairgrounds for a place where I might hide him.

He waves his hand, as though the question is unimportant. "I'm fine."

I lean against him and he holds me close. "I'm so sorry I had to leave without telling you."

"I knew you wouldn't have gone like that if you had a

choice, that something must have happened." I can see the depth of his concern for me in his eyes.

"You found me," I say, nestling closer against him.

"I found you," he repeats. "The question is, what now?" He pulls away from me, straightening, and I see the conflict in his eyes. He is hundreds of miles from home—will he simply say goodbye and go back again? "I don't want to lose you again, Noa," he says and I hold my breath, waiting for him to propose a life together once more.

"But I'm going to join the Maquis." Hearing this, my hope deflates. I have heard of the resistance fighters who operate from the woods. But I have never seen them and they seem like the stuff of legend compared to the timid villagers. It sounds dangerous—and far away. "There's a unit of them east of here in the Vosges forest and if I can get there, I can help," he adds.

"But that's so dangerous," I protest, lifting my head to meet his eyes.

He smooths back my hair. "I'm not running, Noa. You've taught me not to be afraid. For once in my life I'm going to stand my ground and fight."

"So it's my fault then, that you are going to get yourself killed?" I demand, only half joking.

Luc smiles. Then as he takes my hand, his face grows serious once more. "I only meant that this thing between you and me has opened my eyes. I can't sit by and watch anymore. I have to do something. And the work that the resistance is doing, disrupting communication and the rails, is more important than ever to prepare for the Allied invasion. There's talk that it's coming soon, now that the weather has improved."

He draws me close to him once more, wrapping his arms around me and kissing the top of my head. "I don't want to leave you, though. It's time for something more—for both of us. If…if you would consider going with me."

"To the Maquis?" I ask.

"Yes. There are some women, too, who are helping with their work." I realize, proudly, that he is thinking of me, and that I am strong enough. "Would you?" he asks, eyes hopeful.

I want so much to say yes. If only it were that simple. "I can't," I say, putting my hand on his chest. "You know that."

"If it's about Theo, we can find a safe place for him until this is all over," he replies, putting his hand on top of mine and lacing our fingers together. "Then we could raise him as our own."

"I know, but it's more than that. Astrid, she's risked everything for us. I can't abandon her now." Once Astrid might have managed on her own, but she can no longer manage for herself. Everything has been taken from her except us.

"I thought you would say as much." His face grows resolute. "I have to do this, though. There is no place for me at home anymore."

"When will you go?" I ask.

"Tonight. If I set out after dark across the hills, I should be able to find the Maquis encampment before dawn." He pauses. "If only you were going with me."

"I know." But I'm not and so this is goodbye. I wrap my arms more tightly around him. We stand together, pressed close, willing the moment to last just a bit longer. I pull back slightly to peer back toward the tent. "I should go. Astrid is waiting for me." He nods. "I'm so worried about her," I confide. "First losing the baby and now Peter."

"I'm sorry I couldn't do more," he adds, his voice low with guilt.

"You mustn't blame yourself. I don't."

"Actually, that is the other reason I came."

"I don't understand," I say. What other reason could there be?

"I should have told you sooner, only I was so excited to see you again." He reaches into his pocket and pulls out an envelope. "A letter came to the village."

He holds it out and I imagine the worst, news coming from across the miles. Has something happened to my family?

But as I start to reach for it, he pulls his hand back. "It's not for you." I take it from him anyway and, seeing the Berlin postmark on the envelope, my breath catches.

The letter is for Astrid.

23

Astrid

Forty feet. That is what stands between life and death, the thinnest sliver of a divide.

I came back to the ring as I said I would and pretended to rehearse for Noa, and leaped as though nothing had changed. She has disappeared from the tent, though, leaving me alone, and so I return to the board. The movement of flying through the air had once meant everything to me. Now each swing is like a knife through my heart. The cavernous space high above the ring, which had been home, is almost unbearable.

I peer over the edge of the board as if it is a cliff, staring into the abyss of the net below. I tried to kill myself once, after Erich told me to leave. He'd walked from the apartment, ostensibly to give me time to pack and go, unable to bear watching or maybe to avoid the hysterics he considered so uncivilized. I'd run to the cupboard and grabbed a bottle of pills and vodka, impulsively downing as much as I could of both. I imagined him finding my body and crying over what he had done. But after a few minutes I realized he wasn't coming back to check. He had already cut me from his life. Instantly remorseful, I put my hands down my throat and brought up the half-digested mess. I had sworn then never to live for a man again. This loss is more, though—it is everything.

Pushing the memory away, I leap and try to fly once more. There is nothing left for me here, though. *Jump, let go of it all.* The thoughts tick rhythmically through my head with each swing. Unable to stand it any longer, I launch myself back to the board a second time. My legs tremble as I look down. Was this how it had been for the clockmaker? I see him hanging from the ropes with his neck broken, mouth agape, limbs stiff. I could jump, end it as surely as Metz had. If I die here it will be on my own terms, not at the hands of others. I stretch one foot over the edge of the board, testing...

"Astrid?" Noa calls from the entranceway below. Startled, I wobble, grabbing on to the ladder to steady myself. I had been so caught up in my thoughts I had not seen her return. Her face is a mask of worry. Had she seen what I was contemplating? Or guessed?

She does not seem to notice what I've been up to, though. Instead, she motions me toward her, watching somberly as I climb down the ladder.

"What's wrong?" I demand as my uneasiness grows. "Tell me."

She holds out an envelope to me. "A letter came for you."

I freeze. Letters can only mean bad news. I take it with trembling hands, bracing for news of Peter. The envelope bears postage markings from Darmstadt, though. I hold it at arm's length, as though its contents might be contagious. Just for a moment I want to remain suspended in time, shielded from whatever is written there.

But I have never been any good at hiding from the truth.

I tear open the seal. Inside is another envelope, addressed to me, not at the Circus Neuhoff but rather my family's former winter quarters. From Berlin. Erich's blocky script reaches out like a hand. *Ingrid Klemt*, he'd written, using my maiden name. Not his. Even after so much time, the rejection still stings. Someone, whoever had forwarded the letter, had crossed it out and added my stage name, Astrid Sorrell. I drop the envelope. Noa retrieves it quickly and hands it to me. What could Erich possibly want?

"Do you want me to open it for you?" Noa asks gently.

I shake my head. "I can do it." I rip open the envelope, which is stained and worn. A slip of paper flutters out. My eyes fill with tears as I pick it up and the familiar handwriting, not Erich's, appears.

Dearest Ingrid,
I pray that this letter has reached you, and that it finds you well and safe. I fled Monte Carlo ahead of the invasion and did not have time to write. But I have reached Florida and found work at a carnival.

"What is it?" Noa asks.

"Jules." My youngest brother, the weakest and most improbable, had somehow survived. He must have sent the letter to me in Berlin and Erich had sent it on.

"I thought they were all..."

"So did I." My heart beats faster now. Jules is alive. In America.

"But how?" Noa asks.

"I don't know," I reply, scarcely able to process my own questions, let alone Noa's. "Jules was managing the circus in the south of France when the war started. Somehow he made it out." I continue reading silently.

*I wrote to Mama and Papa for months but received no re-
sponse. I do not know if you have heard, but I am so very sorry
to tell you that they died in a camp in Poland.*

"Oh!" I cover my mouth to stop the sob that rips from my
throat. Though I have long known in my heart my parents
could not have possibly escaped, some part of me had clung
to the hope that they might still be alive. Now I am confronted with the truth and it is so much worse.

"What is it?" Noa asks. She bends to read the letter over
my shoulder. Then she wraps her arms around me from behind and rocks me back and forth gently. "Astrid, I'm so, so
sorry." I do not answer, but sit silently, letting it sink in that
the very worst I had feared is true.

"There's more to the letter," Noa says gently several seconds later. She gestures to the paper that lies crumpled in
my lap, pointing to the text a few lines down where I had
stopped reading after learning about my parents. I shake my
head. I cannot. She takes the paper and clears her throat,
then begins to read aloud:

*I have not been able to find the twins. It may well be that
it is only the two of us now. I know that you do not want
to leave your husband, but I have arranged for a visa at the
Swiss consulate in Lisbon. They say it is good for forty-five
days. Please consider coming to me, at least until the war is
over, and then you can return. We only have each other now.*

Yours, Jules

I try to process it all as Noa hands the paper back to me.
The envelope bears official markings from Berlin. Jules had
sent it to the apartment Erich and I once shared. Erich must

have read it and then sent it on by courier, trying his hardest to make sure it reached me. He had forwarded it to my family's home in Darmstadt, knowing somehow that I would go there. But there are no winter quarters for my family anymore, so the postmaster must have delivered it to the Neuhoff estate. Perhaps Helga, who remained behind each year to mind the winter quarters in our absence, had corrected my name and forwarded it onward to our first stop in Thiers.

"How did it get here?" I ask.

Noa clears her throat. "Forwarded from Thiers," she says. I nod. The circus always leaves the address of its next destination behind for bills and other mail. So many stops along the way—the letter might have never reached me at all. But it had.

"My family," I say out loud. I am not sure what that means anymore. The sob that I have held back for so many months rips from my throat. I am crying then for the brother who had lived and for the so many others who had not. My parents and brothers, all gone.

Or so I have thought these many months. But Jules is alive. I remember our goodbye at the station in Darmstadt a few years ago, made hasty by Erich's impatience to board the train. I picture Jules as he must look now, a bit older, but still exactly the same. Somewhere a tiny part of our family's circus dynasty persists, like a seed carried to a new land to be planted.

I look down at the envelope again, which is thicker than it should be if empty. "There's something else in here." Two things, actually. I pull out first a bank receipt of some sort. But it is in an unfamiliar language and the only words I recognize are my own name. "What on earth?"

Noa steps forward. "May I see it?" she asks. I hand her the paper. "I can't read it, but it looks like money for your journey, placed in your bank account in Lisbon." She hands it back.

I stare at her, dumbfounded. "I have no such account."

"It looks like it was opened about six weeks ago," she adds, pointing to the date. "Did your brother put it there?"

I study the paper. "I don't think so." There is a lone transaction, a deposit from Berlin. Ten thousand marks, enough money for me to get wherever I need to go, including America.

"Then who?"

I take a deep breath. "Erich."

Erich, having read Jules's letter, wanted to make sure I had the resources to go to my brother in America. He had given me the very last and only gift he could—a chance at escape. I shake the envelope one last time and pull out a small card. A German exit permit, also filled out in Erich's blocky script and bearing the official seal of the Reich. He had thought of everything to make sure I could get out of the occupied territories and reach safety with Jules. Had Erich done it out of guilt or love? Though it is a part of my past before Peter, so long ago it seems almost like a dream, part of me cannot help but ache for the man who cared enough to do all of this, but not enough to fight for us.

"Astrid, you can go to your brother." Noa's expression lifts with hope at the prospect of my finding safety. Then conflict crosses her face as she realizes that she will be left behind.

"I can't leave you," I say. Suddenly she looks even more young and vulnerable than the day she arrived. How can she possibly manage without me?

"You'll go. Theo and I will be fine," she replies, trying without success to force the quaver from her voice. Then, scanning the papers again, she frowns. "Your brother's letter said the visa is good for forty-five days. The letter took over a month to get here. And there's no telling how long it will take you to get to Lisbon, or to the States from there. You need to go right away. Tonight. You will go, won't you?" Noa asks, her voice somehow filled with hope and dread at the same time.

Not answering, I start for the train.

"But Astrid," Noa calls after me. "I thought we were going to practice. Of course, if you are leaving…"

It doesn't matter anymore, I finish for her silently. "You go on without me," I say. "After all the news it is really too much."

I walk back to the cabin where Elsie is minding Theo. "Darling boy," I say. His face breaks into a wide smile of recognition. As I go to take him from her, he reaches his arms for me for the very first time. Something inside me wells up then, another wave of sorrow rising and threatening to break. I push it down. Later there will be time for tears. Now I must figure out what to do.

I draw Theo close, holding him in one arm, the pass in the other, as if weighing each on a scale. How can I abandon him and Noa? With Peter gone, they are all I have left in the world—or so I thought, until Jules's letter came today. Now I must think about him, too. I am the only family he has left. And he worked so very hard to get this visa to me, my one chance at safety; letting it go to waste would be a crime.

Theo swats at my chin with his tiny hand, breaking me from my thoughts. His dark eyes look up at me searchingly. The idea of leaving Noa and Theo alone to face an uncertain fate is unfathomable. There has got to be another way.

My eyes travel to the cot. Beneath it Noa's trunk and mine are lined up neatly side by side. A plan begins to form in my mind. I set Theo down on the bed, then reach for my bag to pack.

24

Noa

Watching Astrid walk back toward the cabin, I am filled with sadness. When Luc had first handed me the envelope, I had considered not giving it to Astrid. More bad news would surely break her. I could not hide the truth from her, though. And now she is leaving. I can't blame her. I could see from the conflict in her eyes that the decision to leave us behind hadn't come easily. She has known me and Theo only a few months—we shouldn't matter at all, not when she has family—real family—that needs her. Part of me wants to run after her, though, and beg her not to leave me.

Luc pokes his head around the side of the shed where he has been hiding. "Wait here," I'd instructed him before racing to hand the letter to Astrid. I did not want her to see him, but I also wasn't ready to have him disappear and leave me so soon after we had just found each other again. Taking him in now, I feel suddenly guilty. I had lied to Astrid about how the letter had gotten here. But I could not bear to admit to her, on top of everything else, that I had broken my promise not to see Luc. "Is everything all right?" he asks.

"No," I say. "That is, yes and no. Astrid learned that her parents are dead."

"That's awful," he replies, his voice heavy with understanding. "I thought I was helping by bringing the letter."

"You *were* helping," I insist. "But how did you get it?"

"A few days ago I was in the post office when I heard a woman remark about the circus leaving suddenly. She said awful things, that the circus had taken money for shows and fled. I spoke up to tell her she was wrong. When the postmaster overheard, he said there was mail for the circus. He said he had a forwarding address, but when I saw it was a letter for Astrid, I knew I had to bring it myself. I thought maybe it was news of Peter." His voice trails off and I can see how guilty he still feels. "Now I wish I hadn't," he finishes sadly.

"No, she had to know the truth," I reply. "I'm glad you came. It wasn't all bad. Astrid's brother sent a pass from America. He wants her to come live with him." My voice breaks slightly as I say this last part.

"That's good news, isn't it?" Luc asks, sounding confused.

A lump forms in my throat, making it hard to answer. "I suppose," I manage, embarrassed by my selfishness. I want so very much to be happy for Astrid that she will be safe and free. "I just can't imagine the circus without her," I add.

There is a commotion behind us, voices as two of the acrobats walk toward the big top. Luc pulls me behind the shed so as not to be seen. "Now you can reconsider," he says. I tilt my head, puzzled. "You said before you wouldn't go with me because you couldn't leave Astrid." My mind is still reeling from everything that has happened with Astrid and I had nearly forgotten our earlier conversation. "But everything is different now." Luc's voice rises with urgency. "If she is going, surely you can, too?"

In the rush of the moment I had not thought about it. Luc is right, though: with Astrid gone, there will be nothing to keep me here. I can take Theo and go. Gazing up at the big top and the backyard behind it, though, I feel a tug of doubt. The circus is the only safety I have known since my parents kicked me out. I can't imagine being here without Astrid, but I can't imagine leaving. The circus won't be here much longer either, I remind myself. Emmet said he was closing it down at the end of the season. Then that too will be gone.

"Noa..." Luc's voice is heavy with concern. "Once the police realize Astrid has left, there will be questions." There will be more than questions—Emmet will be furious at losing one of his star performers. "It won't be safe for you here anymore. You'll go with me now, won't you?"

I gaze at him longingly, torn between the life I know with the circus and the possibility of a future with Luc. "Trust me," he pleads, his eyes round and full.

I already do, a voice deep within me says. Something clicks in my mind, snaps into place. "I'll do it. With Theo," I add quickly.

"Of course," Luc replies, as though that was never in doubt. Then conflict washes over his face. "But how? If we go to the partisans, there will be no place for a child."

"I could never go without him," I insist.

"We'll find a way," Luc replies, taking my hand. "All of us will stay together." His voice is certain; Theo is his as much as mine now. I throw my arms around his neck gratefully. "So you'll go?" His lips are on my cheek, then my neck, a thousand small kisses of persuasion.

"Yes, yes," I cry, but a second later, I force myself to pull away. We are together in broad daylight, scarcely concealed by the budding trees. The reality sinks in: I will be leaving the circus with Luc. But before we can start a life together,

I have to tell him everything. I can't go forward under the pretense of a lie. "Luc..."

"I have to go now," he says, not hearing me. "I have the name of a resistance contact about ten kilometers from here who can tell me the best way for us to reach the Maquis." He looks over his shoulder. "I will be back for you before nightfall."

"Where can I find you?" I ask.

"There's a ravine on the other side of the stone quarry," he replies, pointing. "About a kilometer east. I'll meet you there at nine o'clock."

"But the show will only be half over."

"I know, but we have to leave then to make it safely to the Vosges forest before dawn. Can you manage it?" I nod and he kisses me and starts to go.

"Luc, wait." He turns back. I am desperate to tell him the truth. But his face looks so hopeful, I cannot. "I will see you at nine."

He starts off, his step light. I want to call after him again, not ready to have him go. But soon he will be back and next time I will go with him.

As I turn back toward the big top, sadness tugs at me. It is all changing. I have only just found this place, the closest I have felt to home, and I am going—again. I can't help but wonder where it will all end and where I will be when I can finally stop running at last.

The sky is growing dusky pink as I near the dressing car to prepare for my final performance. I watch the other girls, putting on costumes and makeup as though it is any other show. I am relieved—they do not suspect anything. The difference is there, though, in the way Astrid puts on my rosin and wraps my wrists, the same as every night but with so much more care. Feeling her warm, sure touch on my fore-arms, I am filled with sadness once more. We will both be going in our separate directions. There was no reason to expect that we would stay together—it's not as if we are really family. The end has come so much sooner than I expected, though. I want to confide in her about Luc and my plan to go with him. But she will never understand. I can't just leave and not tell her, though. Perhaps a note...

The other girls have finished dressing now and are heading to the big top. But Astrid lingers. She pulls out a bag, softer than a suitcase, which I had not noticed before, tucked under one of the dressing tables. She rearranges something in the bag, which is small enough so as not to attract attention. The belongings she will take with her.

The lump in my throat reforms and grows larger. "You'll send word, of course, to let us know you are safe?" I ask, my voice no more than a whisper. She does not answer, but nods slightly as she continues pressing down the clothes, trying to make a bit more room. Of course, I will not be here to receive her message. I will be gone and she will not even know it.

Impulsively, I reach to hug her, but she stiffens and holds me back. I flush, slapped by the rejection. "What is it?" I wonder if I have done something to anger her once more.

"I'm not going."

"What do you mean? Of course you are." For a second I wonder if she is joking, but her expression is serious, eyes somber. I prepare to remake all of the earlier arguments about how she cannot stay and how foolish it would be to waste the pass. "You're going," I repeat.

She shakes her head. "You are."

I stare at her in disbelief. "I don't understand."

Astrid is holding out the envelope that Luc had brought. "You need the pass. To take Theo and go."

I do not reach for it and her hand dangles in midair. "You can't give that to me."

"You'll take my *kennkarte*," she continues. "The photo is not that good. If you dye your hair, keep your head low, no one will know you aren't me. And you will be able to take a child on the papers."

"You can't be serious." I step around her to the bag she has been packing, rummage through. Beneath a thin layer of her own clothes are Theo's cloth diapers and spare booties. She has been planning this all along.

Then she holds out the pass to me once more. "You must leave tonight, just before the show ends. There's a train station, not the one we arrived at but another, about fifteen kilometers south. You will take the train to Lisbon and get the pass at the consulate." She makes it all sound so straightforward, like going into town for bread. "Then use Erich's money to buy a ticket…" She continues on with her instructions, but I do not hear. Luc's face appears in my mind. I am supposed to be going with him, starting a life together.

Noticing the hesitation on my face, she stops midsentence. "What is it?" she demands impatiently, as if I am questioning her judgment on an aerial routine.

The pass is Astrid's one chance at survival. And she is willing to give it all up for me. "I won't take it," I say. "Staying here as a Jew is suicide."

"Exactly. Which is why you need to take Theo and go."

"The pass is yours. *You* have to use it," I persist, standing up to her more than I ever have.

"I've thought it all through," she replies, undeterred. "This is for the best. It's the only option."

"There's another way." I take a deep breath. "Just take

Theo. That way you will both be safe." The words scratch
my throat like shards of glass. I could give her Theo and then
they would both be safe. But letting go of him would kill me.

"No, Theo belongs with you," Astrid insists. "You're the
one who must go."

I am going, I think. With Luc. But of course Astrid does
not know this. She is willing to give everything for me. And
I am still lying to her.

"Astrid," I say slowly, "I *am* going."

"I don't understand," she says, her forehead knotting. "You
just said you won't take the pass. So how can you possibly
leave?"

"No, but Luc…" I start.

"Him again?" she cuts me off, eyes narrowing. "The mayor's
son. What does he have to do with anything?"

"He's here, in Alsace." Storm clouds seem to form in her
eyes. "He brought the letter here from your brother," I add,
hoping that it will help. But I can tell from the fury in her
eyes that it hasn't.

"You promised, no, swore to me, that you wouldn't see
him again," she flares. "Yet you did, even after everything
he cost me."

"I didn't… That is, I didn't mean to," I protest weakly.
Then I stop, unwilling to lie again. "I'm sorry I didn't tell
you. Luc's going to the Maquis." I wonder if this will make
her respect him more.

But her anger does not seem to soften. "Then good for
him." *Good riddance*, is what her tone really seems to say.
"And safe journey," she adds, without warmth. I feel myself
growing angry at Astrid. Luc tried to help Peter, risked his
own life to bring her the letter from Jules. And yet for everything he has done for us, she still cannot allow herself to
accept him. She hates him for who he is. She will never see

him differently. "I still don't see what that has to do with you taking the pass," she adds.

"Luc has gone to make contact with the resistance and then he is coming back. He wants me to go with him." There is silence, Astrid staring at me in stunned disbelief. "And Theo," I add. "Luc wants to care for him, as well."

"When?" she asks finally.

"Tonight."

"So you were going to leave with him without telling me? You were just going to sneak off."

"I was going to go after you had gone," I say, as if this somehow makes things better. "I'm sorry."

"You were going to take Theo, where exactly?" she demands. "You would have no shelter or a transit pass or even decent papers. There's no place for a child, no one to watch him there for you. What were you planning to do, carry him as you run around the forest with the partisans?" As she ticks off all of the failures in my plan, now laid bare, I see all of the things that Luc and I hadn't thought through in the rush of the moment.

"We'll manage," I say stubbornly.

"Well, that doesn't matter anymore," Astrid declares. "You have the pass now and you are leaving."

I try again. "Surely leaving with Luc would be safer than going alone."

Astrid shakes her head firmly. "Getting to Lisbon and out of Europe would be safest. You must be strong on your own now. You have to do what is best for Theo." She holds out the pass again, as if it is all decided.

I start to take the envelope. Then I hesitate, seeing Luc and a life together waiting for us. I hand it back. "No," I say, hearing the strength in my voice, deciding for myself now.

My future is with Luc. And if I go with him, Astrid will take the pass. That way we both have a chance.

Her eyes widen with surprise. "How dare you? I've offered you everything, and you want to give it up for some boy?"

"It isn't that simple..." I begin.

"I'm telling you one last time: Take the pass and go." She holds it out to me, her voice cold as steel. The space between us seems to grow.

I look at Astrid, wavering. Going with Luc against her wishes now will surely be the final break. Once I would have done whatever Astrid had asked, done anything for her approval. But something had changed these last days. I've been the one who has had to take care of Astrid, make decisions for her, for all of us really. I can't simply listen anymore. I have to do what I think best.

"I'm sorry," I say, stepping back.

Her eyes widen with surprise then narrow again with anger. Then she turns away.

"Astrid, wait," I say, trying again. If only I can make her understand. But she stalks off, leaving me alone.

In the distance, the bell rings, signaling the audience to their seats. And beckoning us, one last time, to the air.

25

Noa

So it is to be the last show.

Tears stream down my own cheeks now as the opening music builds to a crescendo and the house lights dim. What's wrong with me? I thought I wanted this, to leave the circus and find a path to freedom for myself and Theo and have a future with Luc. But I've just found this life and have only just learned to love it. I am not ready to go.

"Aerialists—trapeze!" someone calls. I step into the big top, looking for Astrid. I do not see her and I wonder if she is so angry that she will refuse to perform with me. But a moment later she appears from the opposite side of the tent and starts toward the ring, jaw clenched. I hesitate. How can we perform as a team when she is furious with me? The audience waits in the darkness, though, expecting and unaware. There is no other choice.

I climb the ladder opposite Astrid and grab the bar. "Hup!" she calls, voice seething. I fly through the air toward her. As I release, I see it, the rage—no, the hurt and betrayal—in her eyes. Her hands do not reach for mine. She wants to miss, to fail me as I had her. Falling here would not be as it had been when we were in the winter quarters, or even the previous village. The net has been poorly erected and the ground below is rock hard. If I fall here, I will die. I close my eyes as I start to plunge downward, away from her.

Then something grabs my ankles hard. Astrid, saving me against her own will. But she is a beat too late and has grabbed the thin part of my instep rather than my ankle, making it impossible for her to hang on. I am slipping through her fingers. Desperately Astrid flings me in the direction of the bar for the return, with none of her usual precision. She throws me so hard that I somersault through the air. The audience cheers, mistaking near miss for a daring new feat.

My arms find the bar. I swing back to the board and clamber up clumsily. As I straighten, I want to end the act there. This has already gone too far. But Astrid waits on the opposite platform, commanding me to finish what we have started. "Hup!"

Before I can answer, there is a boom, followed by rumbling and a louder thud. We exchange nervous glances, the anger between us forgotten for a moment. Air raids are nothing new; they have come since the start of the war, first by the Germans to weaken countries they wanted to occupy and more recently by the Allies on German territories. They come in crude bold strokes, not caring who might be in the way. Since our return to Alsace they have come almost daily. But this is the first time it has happened during the show. The tent has to be the biggest building outside town—might it make a good target from the air?

There comes another rumbling, closer this time. A few guests flee their seats for the exits as sawdust and plaster shake from the tent poles like snow. The big top offers no protection at all. Perhaps we should end the show and have everyone return home. My eyes lock with Astrid's. *Keep performing*, her gaze commands. We can't afford to start giving out the refunds that the crowds would surely demand if we canceled the rest of the show. My hands shake as I reach for the bar and another explosion threatens to send me falling. But I clasp on tighter. One more pass is all that stands between me and freedom. "Hup!" I fly through the air and Astrid catches me, then sends me back for a final time.

Then it is over and the audience offers a smattering of applause. Time to go—at last. I make my way from the big top and cross the backyard to the cabin where Theo and Elsie, who is supposed to be watching him, both sleep. I change into street clothes before picking up the bag that Astrid had packed. I lift Theo, who stirs and watches me with drowsy eyes, onto my other hip. "Time to go," I whisper to him before starting from the cabin.

As I cross the backyard, I spot Astrid once more. She waves me over. For a fleeting second, I hope that our performing together might have softened her anger. But as I near, her eyes still burn. She snatches Theo from me. "This I shall miss," she says, clutching him to her breast.

"Astrid..." I search for the words to make things better between us, but find none.

"Just go," she commands as she passes Theo back to me. He gives a single cry of protest. "At least I will never have to see you again." Her words are like a knife, and as she turns and walks away I know there will be no more goodbyes.

I start after her. I can't bear to go with Astrid furious at me. But there is no choice. I told Luc I would meet him at nine o'clock, just fifteen minutes from now. I have to find him.

From the tent comes the boom of the music. Emmet's voice warbles over the loudspeaker, so far short of what his father's had been. I look back with gratitude. The circus has been my haven—my safety and my home, in a way I had never expected. Even now, when it is broken and near the end, the circus is the truest family I know. Once I leave, what hope is there of ever feeling this way again?

Then I square my shoulders as I start away with Theo. What will he remember of all this? I force myself not to linger as I pass the train cars. I run low so as not to be seen, taking care not to jostle Theo too hard. *Faster*, I hear Astrid urge in my mind as I pick up speed, heading east in the direction Luc had said. I wish for the shelter of trees, but the earth here is barren and exposed. Someone might see us at any moment, ask why I am fleeing. I will myself to slow, walk normally as I struggle to catch my breath.

As I start toward the quarry and the laughter and applause of the crowd fade behind me, my doubts about leaving bubble once more. How can we possibly survive, the two of us with a child and nothing more? I push my misgivings aside. I want to go with Luc. I see the image of a life together that he promised. Despite my fears, there would be two of us, united in our struggle for our survival and Theo's. Without him, I would be alone—again.

We are well away from the circus now and the earth grows rocky, slopes sharply downward. I clutch Theo tightly, navigating the steep slope. The path I've followed ends at what appears to be a pit of roughly cut stone. Luc said he would be there at intermission, waiting for me.

But the quarry is empty.

It is early, I tell myself, pushing down my unease. I search the brush that shoots out between the rocks at the far end of the quarry, wondering if he is hiding. The branches remain motionless, though, the air still.

Five minutes pass, then ten. Luc is still not here. A list of excuses runs through my mind: he got lost, he had to double back to make sure he wasn't followed. Maybe he had become ill. Theo, tired or perhaps hungry, begins to fuss. "Shh," I soothe, fishing in my pocket for a piece of cracker I'd left there earlier. "Just a little longer."

I look over the edge of the quarry pit, across the flat, empty field. Dread forms and sinks heavy in my stomach. Luc is not coming.

How is this happening? Our plans were certain. Panic fills me. Maybe something had happened to Luc. I see his face just hours earlier. He had asked, no begged, me to go with him—and he had seemed so happy when I said yes. Had he changed his mind and decided that having me and Theo along was too much? Or maybe Astrid had been right all along. I stand still in the cold, dark quarry, tears stinging at my eyes—foolish and abandoned yet again.

Something brushes my cheek then. Theo is looking up at me, his soft fingers reaching out to me as they had in the woods the night I had taken him from the boxcar. Bits of that night come back in flashes: a small fist clenched stiffly, never to be opened again, arms reaching for a mother no longer there. Images I cannot bear to keep in the light of day. A sob tears through me. I had not cried when my father held open the door and forced me out into the cold with nothing more than my purse. Nor when I'd seen the railcar of stolen infants, dead and dying. Now the tears race forth and I am grieving for all of it. I press my hands to my eyes, willing the visions to stop. It is hopeless—I will carry that night at the train car with me forever. Saving Theo had been not just for him—it had been my chance at redemption.

Maybe it still is. I see Astrid standing before me, holding out a ticket to freedom. She is so angry that I don't know if she would give it to me now. And there is some part of me that does not want to take the pass, her only chance at survival. But I owe it to Theo to try.

I look up at the sky. *You are never going back*, Astrid said once. She is right. I can no more count on Luc than on my family for salvation. Instead, I will get us to a place where Theo will be safe, and a day at the circus would not be taken from him just because he is a Jew, where people would not stare at him oddly. It isn't Luc, or even my parents I am looking for anymore. It is a home of my own.

I peer over my shoulder in the direction of the big top. If I go back now and join the final bow, no one but Astrid will realize that I have gone. I can ask her for the pass after the show. I shift Theo to my other hip. He cries openly now, his wails cutting through the darkness as I navigate the steep slope out of the quarry.

"Shh," I soothe. I take one last hopeful look over my shoulder in the direction from which Luc should have come. Seeing no one, I turn and start back to the circus.

I near the big top once more. Then remembering the anger on Astrid's face as I left earlier, I slow. What can I possibly say to make her forgive me? As I reach the backyard, I hear the music of the final act trumpeting gaily, building to a fever pitch. The circus is assembling for the final bow. Through the tent flap I see the place where I usually stand at the top of the board, and I imagine the confused face of Gerda, who is normally beside me, wondering where I have gone. Longing fills me to go where I belong, amid the circus family one last time. And even though I am sad Luc did not come and we will be leaving again soon, part of me cannot help but feel glad to be home.

But as I draw close to the circus tent, my happiness fades. There is a strange smell in the air, like someone overcooked the caramel corn, only stronger. Something tickles at my nose then—a burning smell. There is a fire—and close. I think back to the air raid we'd heard during our act. No bombs had hit nearby, but perhaps there had been stray shrapnel or even a cigarette thrown carelessly on the midway. Is it the big top? We have always taken such great precautions against fire. Looking up, I see something flickering in the cloth by the *hauptmast*: a flame, growing larger even as I watch. Nobody, not anyone among the remaining crowds that linger in the tent nor the performers making their way to the backyard, seems to have noticed yet. No one except me.

I clutch Theo tighter and break into a dead run.

26

Astrid

I stand on the board above the circus ring. Alone, once more.

After Noa had gone, I climbed to the board. Good riddance, I wanted to say as I imagined her leaving. Instead I found myself aching with loss. Still it was not Noa whom I cursed in that moment, but me. How I hated myself for caring yet again! It was Erich abandoning me all over. I remembered the lesson I had learned the day I left Berlin, seared it into my brain now as I should have long ago: the only one I could rely on in this life was me.

It is just as well, I think now. With Noa leaving, I am free to use the pass to go to my brother. After the final bow, I will slip away before anyone notices. Pushing thoughts of Noa and Theo aside, I instead focus on Jules, who is waiting for me.

My cue comes in the music and I unfasten the ropes from their moorings. Emmet had told me at the last minute that he added the Spanish web routine back into the second act. It was only then that I noticed the new ropes, hastily installed where the clockmaker had hung just days earlier. I wanted to protest. It wasn't that I was sentimental about Metz. Rather,

I hadn't rehearsed it in weeks and the trapeze alone would be exhausting enough. But I didn't want to give Emmet cause to fight—after all, it was to be the last show before I slipped away forever.

I wrap the ropes around myself and step from the board. There is no bar to hold tight, just two thin slips of satin. I spin around them, extend my leg. If flying trapeze is like gymnastics as I once told Noa, then Spanish web is like swimming, seamless and graceful. Or at least they once were; now my arms are weak from weeks of not training and my movements are jerky. I struggle through the routine. But the audience does not seem to notice.

I make my way back to the board as applause thunders, my body bathed in sweat. I do not climb down. My act is just before the finale and I need to remain here for the final bow. As the elephants prance, interspersed with riders on horseback, there is a yell from below. "Fire!" someone calls. I see it then, a flicker of flames behind one of the bleachers, growing higher by the second. The flames are only on one side of the tent. If everyone evacuates to the far exit, it will be fine. We have done drills for fire before. Herr Neuhoff or Peter, if either was here, would have urged calm.

"Fire!" a woman screams again and everyone begins to run, crushing one another as they flee the stands, falling. Spectators in the first few rows flood into the ring, panicking the elephants and sending them charging.

I look frantically at the nightmare that is unfolding below. The entire top of the tent burns now. Once the workers would have grabbed the buckets of sand and water, always placed by each pole with such care, and fought to save the big top. But they are almost all gone now, dismissed by Emmet. A strongman tosses sand and then flings the bucket before running in the other direction. The trainers try to save the elephants, coaxing them from the tent. But the beasts fight rescue, planting their feet in panic, and the trainers flee, every creature for itself. The tiger lies motionless on its side, overcome by smoke. What would the circus be without it? Against the burning sky, I see the dark shadow of Emmet fleeing, a coward until the end.

I stand immobilized on the board, watching the scene below as if from a great distance or in a film. But the heat, growing uncomfortable against my skin, reminds me that it is real. I remember how earlier, before I received Jules's letter, I wanted to die. If I do nothing it will all be over. Would that be so awful? I feel Jules and a life in America slipping away like a dream.

No, I shake my head, clearing it. My brother is waiting for me. I have to get out. I start for the ladder. But as I begin to climb down, one of the elephants spins, knocking against the ladder and loosening it from its moorings. It sways precariously. I cling to the rungs as the ladder starts to pull out. It lists to one side, threatening to fall at any second.

I look around desperately. The bar for the catch trap is a few feet above me, almost out of reach. I lunge out, clawing at it with one hand. My fingers wrap around the bar. What now? There are too many people below, scurrying under the net, for me to drop safely. I eye the far board, then kick my feet hard to try to swing up to it. But it is too far away, no use.

I hang helplessly, smoke filling my lungs and causing my eyes to burn. My arms, already exhausted from the show, throb with pain. I must hold on. A few more minutes and there won't be anyone below me to injure when I fall. But it will be too late—the net below burns now, making a safe landing impossible.

"Astrid!" a voice calls through the smoky haze. Noa. She

stands at the entrance to the big top. Why had she come back? She starts toward me with wide, desperate eyes. "Astrid, hold on!" She looks down at Theo, who squirms in her arms, then up to me, uncertain what to do. I see her hold out Theo to one of the dancers, begging her to take him outside away from the smoke and searing heat. But the dancer panics and flees, leaving the child behind. Noa starts toward the far ladder, still holding Theo.

"Get out!" I cry. What is she thinking, risking the child and herself like that? But she continues climbing. At the top, she sets Theo down as far back as she possibly can so he will not roll off and secures the edge of his blanket to the board. Then she grabs the bar and leaps, looking out of place in her street clothes.

"Astrid, reach for me," she calls as she swings close. I do not let go. She has never caught in her life. She cannot possibly manage it. "Astrid, we have to get out." Noa saving me is the last thing I want right now. "Peter would want you to fight," she adds. "Don't give up like this."

"Peter is gone," I say numbly.

"I know. But we're here. And if you don't let go we will all die—even Theo. Astrid, you have to let go." Her words, an echo of mine to her when she first came to the show, are true. Desperately I spin and wrap my legs around the bar, stretching my arms toward her. I give a swing and reach out to her. She misses and I try again.

Our hands lock and a look of triumph forms in her eyes. "I've got you," she says, but I do not return the smile. This changes nothing.

"Just get us back," I order. But how? She cannot possibly swing me back to the perch. "There," I say, pointing to a corner of the net, close to the ladder, where there is no fire. "Throw me in that direction."

"You want me to drop you?" Her eyes are wide with disbelief.

"There's no other choice. Aim for the corner and fling hard." She looks down uncertainly. "You have to do it now." In another few minutes the rest of the net will be in flames, my one chance at escape gone. "You have to let go." She takes a deep breath and kicks her legs to gain momentum and swing us closer in that direction. I hold my breath. Noa has never been a catcher or thrown anyone in her entire life. But she releases me then and her aim is good. I sail smoothly downward, body taut and knees soft, and land in the bit of the net that is intact, just by the edge.

I look back up at the trapeze where Noa still hangs, wishing I could tell her to jump, too. But Theo is still up on the perch. "Quickly!" I cry. She swings herself back higher, desperate to reach the board. She slips, nearly falling. But her fingers grasp the edge and she pulls herself up onto it.

Noa picks up Theo and starts down the ladder. But her movements are slow and awkward as she tries to climb while holding the child who, hysterical with terror, screams and flails in her arms.

"Here!" I cry, racing to the bottom of the ladder.

"Take him," she shouts, dropping Theo to me, almost throwing him. He lands in my arms with a solid thump, bawling louder. I cover Theo's nose and mouth. I have to get him out of here. A man trying to flee the tent slams into me, sending waves of pain through my shoulder. I cling harder to Theo so as not to drop him. I look at the open door where cool fresh air beckons against the fullness in my lungs.

Overhead there is a creaking sound, which grows to a groan. "Get out!" someone screams, pushing me toward the exit. Then I turn back. Noa is still struggling to get to the ground, but she is too high for me to reach her.

The entire ladder begins to sway, listing hard in one direction. There is a thunderous crashing and the trapeze apparatus begins to come down above me. The *chapiteau* has been weakened by the flames and the whole thing is starting to collapse.

I slip through the tent flap clutching Theo. With a deafening crash, the big top falls, raining fire down. And Noa disappears from sight.

27
Noa

Theo is missing.

I reach for him frantically in the darkness. But my arms close around nothing, as they had that night I tried to reach him on the roof of the rail station. He is gone.

"Theo!" I cry over and over. There is no response.

"Here he is." Astrid. She sounds so far away. I try to open my eyes, but glass shards grind at my face and I can manage only a slit. Enough to see Theo, whom she has placed on top of me. He is here, but I cannot feel him through the searing pain, worse than a thousand bee stings.

I am lying on the ground, some fifteen feet from the big top. How had I gotten here? In the distance, what is left of the *chapiteau* smolders, reduced to a pile of charred canvas and broken poles. The fire brigade, too late, waters the wreckage so it does not spark and catch fire to the parched nearby forest.

I reach for Theo, but Astrid presses me back down gently. "No," I manage hoarsely. "I must." She moves him higher on my chest without letting go. "Is he all right?"

"Perfectly fine," she assures me. I search the child to see if the smoke had harmed his tiny lungs. He gives one cough, a protest. His coloring is good, though, his eyes bright.

Then I lie back, unable to hold my head up any longer.

"Rest," Astrid urges and as she pulls Theo back, I can see there are burn marks on her arms.

"What happened?" I ask. She hesitates, as if not wanting to tell me. "I'm not a child, remember? No more hiding the truth."

"The tent collapsed on top of you," she answers quietly.

I relive the moment in my mind, feel her pulling me from the fiery wreckage falling upon me and crushing me to the earth. "I can't feel my legs," I say, gasping for air. There is a sharp pain as I breathe inward, then a spasm of coughs shoots daggers through me.

Astrid wipes my mouth with her sleeve and when she pulls back it is stained with red. Panic crosses her face and she looks around desperately. "Medic!" she cries and I can tell from her cracked voice that it is not the first time she has tried to get me help.

But no one answers or comes to our aid. It is only us now.

"Help will be here soon," Astrid promises.

In the distance I hear the whir of a siren. The police will be here soon, too. There will be questions, an investigation. "The pass," I remember. Astrid is supposed to be leaving right now. "After tonight it will be useless. You have to go."

She waves her hand, as though swatting a fly. "I won't leave you." A few minutes earlier, she wanted me gone. But she is not angry anymore. At last, she has forgiven me. She knows all of my secrets now and has not turned away—which is the one thing I wanted all along. Relief rises over my pain.

"You have to go." I raise my hand and touch Theo. "Take him." The words hurt my throat.

"But..." Astrid begins to protest.

"Now," I add. "Or it will be too late." I lie back weakly.

"You can still go," she presses, unwilling to see the truth before her. "I'll give the pass to you like I said earlier. You can leave with Theo and the two of you can be together."

Her voice is so earnest that for a second I almost believe it. "No," I say as reality crashes down on me once more. My dream of escaping to freedom with Theo has been destroyed. I cough again, wheezing for air.

"I'm going to find help," Astrid says again, starting to rise.

"Stay with me." I use my last bit of energy to catch her hand. "I'm not going to make it."

She shakes her head, but at the same time, she is unable to deny the truth before her. "I can't leave you behind," she says, still fighting.

"What choice do we have?" The circus is gone; the fire has undone what war could not. "You have to take Theo. You're his only hope."

Theo squirms on my lap, as if recognizing his own name for the first time. I run my hand over the softness of his head and in that moment I see before me the man whom he will grow to be. He will not know me. Tears flow from my eyes, burning the raw flesh of my cheeks. Like his birth parents, I will fade from his memory forever.

Someday you'll have to let him go. Astrid's words, spoken on the night of the first show, come back to me as clearly as though she is saying them now, though her lips do not move at all. Like one of Drina's predictions come true.

"You did it," she says through her tears. "You became an aerialist." And in that moment, I have everything.

Almost everything. "Luc," I say. Though he failed me, I cannot help but think of him. Pain shoots through me as I remember Luc's betrayal. "You were right about him. I tried to go meet him like we planned. But he never came. He didn't care for me at all."

"No, no, that can't be right," Astrid protests. "He came all this way for you. It doesn't make sense. I'm sure he had a reason. If you want, I will try to find Luc for you," she offers instead. "Find out why he couldn't meet you and tell him what happened." We both know that's impossible. He has disappeared and she has no way of finding him.

But I love her for offering. "First you praise my flying and now you are being nice about Luc," I rasp. "I really must be dying." We both laugh so improbably then, my throat scratchy as an old record on a phonograph. My chest heaves with pain.

Astrid takes Theo from me, cradling him in her arms. If only they were mine. She lifts her head. There is a kind of clarity to her now and in the shine of her eyes I see the many siblings of the great circus family that had gone before her. A few hours earlier, I was not sure she could survive herself. How will she flee and care for Theo? But she seems stronger than she had been since losing Peter. And with Theo, she will not be alone. He looks at me as she rocks him gently, not understanding.

"Go now, before it is too late," I manage, using the last bit of strength I have left. Astrid does not protest, but kisses my cheek, then lowers Theo to do the same.

They need to leave now while no one is watching. I close my eyes, knowing that she will not go while I am still here. She does not leave, but lies down beside me, still holding Theo. I will my breath to slow and suddenly it is the three of us back in the railcar, sleeping together as one. I feel her shift away and the space beside me grows cold as she rises and starts for the trees.

I force my eyes to stay shut, unable to watch them leave.

When I open them again, they are gone.

But I am not alone. The sky has cleared and as I look up at the field of stars, not quite yellow, I see faces. First Peter, looking down on Astrid, watching over her. "I did it." I had saved her, though not at all in the way he had planned.

Then farther in the distance of the night sky, I see Luc. I will never know why he did not meet me. But I forgive him. *Wait for me, my love. I am coming.*

And finally I see Herr Neuhoff. In the end after the performers had taken their final bows and slipped from the stage, he stands as he had started, alone in the spotlight. He sweeps the crowd with his gaze, gives that tip of his hat, an invitation and a farewell.

And then darkness.

Epilogue

Astrid

Paris

I was never the one who was supposed to make it.

My eyes clear. I am still standing before the boxcar in the museum exhibit, staring at the empty berth. I can almost feel Noa lying beside me, cheek warm against mine as our breaths rise and fall in unison.

It was still dark when Noa's porcelain eyes closed for the last time. I had seen broken bodies before—the clockmaker and even once a trainer gored by a tiger. But Noa was beyond all of that. The heavy poles that had crashed down upon her had crushed her legs and likely broken her back. She could have just fled when the fire broke out. She had come back to save me, though—and it had cost her everything.

I brush at my eyes now, remembering. Though I'd had many brothers, she was so much closer, the sister I never had.

I'd been ready to give up my freedom for her. Of course that was out of the question with her injuries. Looking down at her piteous face and helpless, broken body, I could not bear to leave her. I was Theo's only hope for survival, though. So I waited until Noa's eyes had closed for the last time and then I set out across the barren field, Theo tucked firmly against me. I stood straighter, truly on my own for the first time.

Providence seemed to smile on Theo and me during our escape, as if saying we had already suffered enough. We'd made it to Lisbon mostly by train then on foot into the city itself. There the visa my brother had arranged was waiting at the consulate. Though the city was teeming with refugees desperate to flee, the money Erich had deposited was enough to buy us a place on board a steamer. Little breaks of luck, when before there had been so few. Perhaps it was more than I deserved.

A few weeks after our ship reached New York, we received word that the Allies had landed and were headed toward Paris. The end of the war, though not here yet, was in sight. I was flooded with doubt: maybe leaving Europe had been a mistake. We might have been safe. But there was no going back.

I never flew again after the night of the fire. We found a life outside Tampa where my brother Jules ran a carnival. I worked hard, selling tickets and concessions. Returning to the trapeze was more than Jules or I could have borne. At first, I feared life without performing would prove stifling and strange as it had with Erich. But on my own, I was free.

Only now I have come back. I clear the memories from my mind and gaze up at the circus exhibit, celebrating the acts and spectacles of that bygone era. Of course the exhibit makes no mention of the circus's greatest feat—saving lives.

There is a lone photo of Peter, resplendent in his clown

costume. Behind the white makeup are the dark, sad eyes that only I knew. A note beneath his picture reads: *Killed in Auschwitz in 1945.* That is not quite the truth. Peter, I'd discovered from the Yad Vashem archives decades earlier, had been sentenced by a Nazi tribunal at Auschwitz to die before a firing squad. The morning the guards had come for him, they had discovered that he had hung himself in his cell. I press myself against thick glass that covers the photo, cursing it for separating the image from my skin.

And what of Erich? For some time, I had not been able to learn his fate. I wondered if he had died in combat or perhaps escaped to South America like that Nazi butcher Josef Mengele and the other bastards who were never brought to justice. Then about three years after the war ended, I received a letter from a law firm in Bonn that found me through the bank account in Lisbon, informing me that Erich had left me a small inheritance. It was only then that I learned he had been killed when the apartment building on Rauchstrasse had been hit by a mortar shell. The building had been bombed on April 7, 1944, just days after he forwarded Jules's letter on to me. The air raid had come in the predawn hours when everyone who lived there was still asleep. I would have been in bed, too, and surely killed, had Erich not cast me out. I donated the money he left me to the Joint Distribution Committee.

I never married again. I had healed once after Erich, but losing Peter was simply too much. Two heartbreaks such as the ones I had known were enough for any lifetime.

Noa's face appears in my mind. There is no photo of her in the exhibit, other than a piece of her face visible behind one of the acrobats in a photo of the full circus taking its final bow. She had performed so briefly, an unnamed footnote in the centuries of circus history. But I see her, young and beautiful on the trapeze, experiencing the wonder of flying for the first time. She had known heartbreak, too, in a lifetime a fraction as long as mine. I had always wondered about Luc: Why hadn't he shown up to meet Noa that last night? Though I had disliked him, he seemed to genuinely care for her. What had stopped him from coming for her?

It is this question that in large part brought me here. That, and an idea of where I might find the answer, once I had realized the railcar pictured in the *Times* was one and the same. I stare at the carriage once more, eyes focused on the belly box below the rear of the car. Noa and Luc had left messages for one another there, thinking that no one else knew. I had seen them, though, exchanging confidences there like a childhood game of Post Office. Fools! If someone else had found out, they would have jeopardized us all. But I waited, let her have her fun, watching carefully to make sure no one else had seen. When I read the article in the paper about the circus exhibit, glimpsed the train car that was so improbably ours, I thought it was possible that the boy had left a message for Noa there, explaining.

Only now I found the belly box empty.

I lean against the side of the train car, pressing my head flat against the worn wood. Like holding up a shell to hear the sea, voices echo that are no longer there. Then I take a few steps farther along the exhibit.

There is an oil painting I have never seen before of a young woman on a trapeze. I gasp. The pale, slim figure is undoubtedly Noa, the sequined costume one of my own that I had given her. Where had it come from? If someone had painted her portrait while she was at the circus, surely I would have known.

I move closer and squint at the small plaque beneath the painting:

Oil painting found in the possession of an unidentified young man who was killed when the Germans bombed a resistance stronghold near Strasbourg in May 1944. His connection to the circus and the subject of his painting are unknown.

I freeze, my blood running cold. Noa had told me once that Luc wanted to be a painter. I had not known he was so talented. The image had been rendered with great skill, the artist having the clearest of affection for its subject. Taking in Luc's work, I am certain now that he would not have abandoned Noa.

She had told me, too, that he planned to join the Maquis, and that he had gone to a resistance location not far from the fairgrounds. I hear then the bombs that rained down the night of our last performance and know then why he had not come for her. Noa and Luc had died the same night, just miles apart, neither knowing. Tears fill my eyes and run over.

I stare at the painting of Noa, which has been encased in glass to protect it from age and wear. "He didn't leave you after all," I whisper.

In the reflection of the glass behind me, something moves. A woman stands there behind me with hair a dome of white. Noa, I think, even as I know it is impossible. I spin toward the image, fantasizing that she is here and I can ask forgiveness for all I have done.

"Mom?"

I turn. "Petra." My beautiful girl. There she stands, the child whom I was supposed to have lost all those years ago. I raise my hand to my stomach, feeling as I have so many times over the years the blow that almost took her from me. My miracle.

"Now, how did I know that I would find you here?" There

is no anger in her voice. Just a smile about those full lips and the dark eyes that I will always see as if behind a sheet of white greasepaint. Performing.

At first, my losing the pregnancy had not been a lie. There had been a sharp pain and bleeding that terrible night when the guard struck me. I had assumed after the blow that I had lost the child. But a few days later as I stood atop the trapeze, considering whether to jump, I felt that familiar nausea return. I recognized instantly what it was: my child, defiant, insisting upon life.

I had not told Noa—she would never have taken the pass if she knew I was still pregnant. It was not that I did not want freedom or to live for my child. I did, so much so I could taste it. But Noa was younger, not as strong. She needed to go, and to take Theo with her. Without the circus, Noa would have nothing. I could manage, get by, find somewhere else to perform and survive. But she could barely take care of herself and Theo with all of our help. She would not make it on her own. So I had lied.

My plan was a good one and it might have worked if not for Luc and the fire. If it had been given a chance. How had the fire started, though? Across the years I wondered if it had been set deliberately by a disgruntled circus worker or even Emmet, wanting to be free of it all. Or perhaps a stray piece of shrapnel from one of the bombs. To this day I do not know.

In the end, it hadn't mattered. The fire, not the war, had taken Noa, just as arbitrarily as Herr Neuhoff had been felled by his heart. I had no choice but to take the pass and save Theo.

And my daughter. Petra has her father's features, but she is petite like me, a four-foot-eleven surgeon for Doctors Without Borders and a force to be reckoned with. I reach over the roped stanchion and brush her bangs from her eyes instinctively as though she is six. Only her hair is almost completely white. How odd it is to see your own child age! Petra, shielded on the inside and born in America, knew nothing of the hardships we had lived. Almost nothing. My daughter had been born blind in one eye, the sole injury the guard's club had inflicted the night Peter was taken.

As Petra steps forward to embrace me, someone taller appears behind her. "Mom, come out of there." I obey and reach up to hug Theo, who stands a full head above his sister, his own hair gray and wiry. Though they are not blood siblings, their features look remarkably the same.

"You also came?" I ask chidingly. "Don't you have patients to care for?"

"We're kind of a package deal," he replies, putting an arm around his sister's shoulders. It is true—the two couldn't be closer.

They had both become doctors. Petra, who had not escaped the travel gene, circled the world in her practice, and Theo, ever content to stay, was a surgeon at a hospital in the same town where I had raised them, with his wife and my three beautiful granddaughters, themselves now grown. My two children, cut from different cloth, yet so very alike in shape. And medicine a kind of family business to them as much as the circus had been to my brothers and me.

I push the belly box shut with my backside so Petra and Theo will not see and let her lead me from the exhibit back to the other side of the ropes.

"How did you get here so quickly?" I ask Theo. "I only left New York two days ago."

"It was dumb luck that I was at a conference in Brussels when I got the call from the nursing home," he replies. "I phoned Petra and she flew in from Belgrade." Petra spent most of her time in Eastern Europe helping refugees. She had been drawn, it seems, back to this part of the world from which we had worked so hard to escape.

I look at my children adoringly. In their faces, I can see the past as surely as Drina once read the future: Peter is so readily visible in our daughter, most days it is like having him walk with me. Theo was not born to Noa, but somehow he absorbed so much of her looks, as if by osmosis, her expressions and even her manner of speech. She had loved him so in the few short months she cared for him and he could not have been more hers if she had given birth to him.

Then there is that other face always in my mind, though I never met him, never had a photograph. Noa's child, taken from her at birth. I see him next to Theo, wonder so often what he would have been like as a man.

"Mom…" Theo's voice cuts into my thoughts. "You just took off from the home. We were so worried."

"I had to see the exhibit," I offer weakly.

Theo steps back, noticing the portrait of Noa. "That's her, isn't it?" he asks, a catch in his voice. He and Petra both know about Noa. I told my children when they were old enough the truth about Noa and the way she had saved Theo. But the details of how she had come to be with the circus and the other sibling who might be out there still—well, some things are better left unsaid. I nod. "She was beautiful."

"Beautiful," I repeat. "In more ways than you will ever know, I think. It was painted by a young man she met while she was with the circus. She only knew him a short while, but they loved each other very much. I never knew what became of him—until now."

We stare at the picture for several seconds without speaking. "Are you ready to go now?" Petra asks gently.

"No," I reply firmly. "I'm not ready to leave."

"Mom," Theo says patiently, as though speaking with a child. "I know the circus was a huge part of your life. But it's all gone now. And it's time to go home."

I clear my throat. "First," I say, "there's something I must tell you."

Petra's brow wrinkles in that way so reminiscent of her father. "I don't understand."

"Come." I gesture to a bench alongside the exhibit. I sit and take their hands, pulling a child down on each side of me. "There's more to the story than either you or your brother know. Before she found Theo, Noa had a baby."

"Really?" Petra's voice is only mildly surprised. Such things are commonplace these days—hardly the scandal they were when we were young.

"Yes," I reply. It is the missing chapter of the story, the one that has never been told. I am the only one who knows it and I will not be here much longer. I need to tell them now, so the truth is not lost forever.

"She was an unwed mother and the father was a German soldier, so the Reich took her baby from her. She never knew what became of the child. Then she found you, Theo, and it was like a second chance. She loved you like her own," I add quickly, patting his hand. "But she never forgot her firstborn. I'm sorry I never told you before. The secret, it wasn't mine to tell."

"Why are you telling us now?" Petra asks.

"Because I will not be here forever. Someone needs to know the story and carry it forward." I look up at the painting of Noa once more. "I'm ready now."

Petra stands and reaches her hand toward me. "Then let's go."

I take her hand and our fingers intertwine. Theo stands on my other side. I lean toward my beautiful boy and he bows his head until our foreheads touch. "Going together once more," I say. I let them lead me slowly from the museum, feeling the unseen hands that guide us.

★ ★ ★ ★ ★

Author's Note

A few years ago while researching, I came across two remarkable stories in the archives of Yad Vashem. The first was a heartbreaking account of the "Unknown Children"—a boxcar full of babies, ripped from their families and headed for a concentration camp, too young to know their own names.

The second was a story of a German circus that had sheltered Jews during the war. The Circus Althoff had taken in a young Jewish woman, Irene Danner, who herself hailed from another circus family. Several parts of the story were fascinating to me. First, I learned that the circus had sheltered not just Irene Danner, but her sister, mother and father. Her father, Hans Danner, was in fact not Jewish and was a soldier in the German army. When the German army sent him on leave and ordered him to divorce his Jewish wife, he defied the order and instead joined his wife and children in hiding. I also discovered that Irene Danner had fallen in love with a clown who was part of the Circus Althoff, Peter Storm-Bento, and that they had children together.

Another thing that intrigued me as I researched was the rich history of Jewish circus dynasties that spanned centuries, including the Lorch family from which Irene Danner's mother had come. There were other circus families, such as the Blumenfelds, which had ten or more siblings performing and/or running the circus. Sadly they were largely annihilated by the Germans.

Reading the remarkable histories of the Unknown Children and the circuses, I knew that they somehow had to come together. And so I created the story of Noa, a young Dutch girl cast out after becoming pregnant, who despite being alone and penniless nevertheless finds the courage to rescue one of the babies from the train. I had her find an ally in Astrid, a Jewish aerialist whose heart was broken when her husband did not make the same brave choice Hans Danner had in real life, but instead disavowed their marriage.

The Orphan's Tale is not biography; and my story is not that of the remarkable circus folk I researched, but rather fiction. I have taken great liberties with the nature of the circus acts and the ways in which they lived and performed during the war. But I was so inspired by the real people I'd met in my research: the way in which Irene Danner and Peter Storm-Bento persisted in their love despite it being forbidden by the Reich, the courage with which circus owner Adolf Althoff sheltered Jews, and the ingenious ways he would hide them when the Germans came looking.

When Adolf Althoff received the honor of being named Righteous Among the Nations by Yad Vashem in 1995, he said, "We circus people see no difference between races or religions." I consider this book, while fiction, to be a tribute to the courage of these people.

Acknowledgments

I often refer to *The Orphan's Tale* as the hardest of books written at the most difficult of times. The latter was the case because I wrote this book while dealing with significant family illness, testing my mantra that "I can write through anything" to the limit. The book itself was also harder than anything I've ever written because some of the subject matter was so dark. I realized, for example, that to write the scene with the infants on the boxcar, I was going to have to figuratively put my own children on that train. While I am always grateful for those who support my writing, I am even more indebted this time because of the enormity of the task.

Learning about the circus was challenging and left me with a deep respect and admiration for the hard work and skill that go into circus acts, and especially aerial arts. My deepest gratitude goes to Suzi Winson of Circus Warehouse for her knowledge, time and patience on all things flying trapeze.

I am also very grateful to Stacy Lutkus and Aime Runyan for their help on the German and French languages respectively, and to my constant sounding board Andrea Peskind Katz. Any mistakes, however, are all mine.

I am so grateful to at long last be working with the gifted

Erika Imranyi; our collaboration is a long-awaited wish come true. My gratitude also to Natalie Hallak, Emer Flounders and the entire team at MIRA Books for their time and talent. My dream team would not be complete without wondrous agent Susan Ginsburg at Writer's House, whose constant leadership and vision are the beacons of light guiding my career.

I consider myself blessed to be part of a wonderful community of book folk, online and in person. The only thing that stops me from the temptation to list them all here is the knowledge that I would surely leave someone out. But I am eternally indebted to the book bloggers, librarians, booksellers, author friends and readers who keep me going every single day.

Every book I have written has taken a village and none more so than *The Orphan's Tale*. I thank my husband and his ability to juggle children; my mom and brother, who help us out eight days a week; my in-laws; dear friends; and my colleagues at Rutgers School of Law. Most of all, I am grateful for my three little muses, without whom none of this would be possible—or worthwhile.

THE ORPHAN'S TALE

PAM JENOFF

Reader's Guide

PARK
ROW
BOOKS

1. Noa and Astrid's rivalry changes into a close friendship despite significant differences in age and circumstances. How did this evolution happen? What do you think it was that drew them together? Have you ever found yourself in such a close but unlikely friendship?

2. Even in WWII-torn Europe, the circus was still allowed to perform. Did this surprise you? How did the setting impact your reading of the novel? What deeper meaning do you think there is behind the circus burning down in the end?

3. Who did you initially think was the narrator in the opening chapter? How did the opening chapter shape your reading experience?

4. With whom did you identify more closely, Astrid or Noa? Why? What were Noa's and Astrid's greatest strengths and their greatest flaws? Were there choices you wish Astrid and/or Noa had made differently throughout the book?

5. Noa is disowned by her family and in turn has her child ripped from her arms. Astrid leaves her family for a

husband who abandons her. How do you think Astrid and Noa were each defined by their pasts? What role does the notion of family play throughout the story? What are some of the other themes in the book?

6. What do you think drew Astrid and Peter together so powerfully? Noa and Luc? How do these two relationships differ from one another? Do you think either of these relationships could have lasted a lifetime under different circumstances?

7. What do you think of Peter's decision to continue with his mocking act toward the Reich? How do you think the story would have differed if Peter had refrained from doing the act?

8. How did you feel about the ending? Were you surprised? Satisfied?

9. What will you remember the most about *The Orphan's Tale*?

In your Author's Note, you mention being inspired by the Unknown Children, as well as a German circus that sheltered Jews during WWII. Can you go a little deeper into the personal reasons behind why you wanted to bring these stories to life?

I found both the story about the Unknown Children and the rescuers' circus in the archives of Yad Vashem. They intrigued me in different ways. First, being a mom of three small children colors my view of all things. When I read the story of the Unknown Children, babies ripped from their parents too young to know their own names, I was heartbroken. I wanted to know, what was it like for those families? The notion was unbearable, yet I couldn't look away.

The circus fascinated me in a different way. Although I have spent decades working on and researching issues surrounding World War II and the Holocaust, I had never before heard of a circus that had rescued Jews. And when I started researching, I learned an equally interesting piece of information about Jewish circus dynasties that had flourished for centuries before being extinguished by the Nazis. I knew that these two stories would somehow come together.

Told from the dual points of view of Astrid and Noa, *The Orphan's Tale* follows their poignant and timeless friendship. Was there one perspective that was easier to write? Do you have a favorite character in the story?

Trying to choose between characters is like picking a favorite among my children—I can't do it. I love them equally but in different ways. Astrid is closer to my own age and she felt like the sister I never had. I was also fascinated by the fact that her Nazi husband had divorced her after being ordered to do so by the Reich (which was inspired by real events).

Noa is more like one of my own children and I just felt so sorry for her after everything she went through at such a young age. I would describe it as almost protectiveness. But not too protective, because then you take these characters you love and start doing awful things to them. And that's where the fun begins in the twisted mind of a writer...

Your novels typically center on relationships that unfold during a specific era in history—war-torn Europe. What attracts you to this setting and period?

My interest in World War II dates back more than twenty years ago when I was sent to Kraków, Poland, as a diplomat for the US State Department. I found myself working on issues from the war and became very close to some of the Holocaust survivors. These experiences profoundly affected me and moved me to write.

I also believe the time period is fertile ground for storytelling. My goal as an author is to take my reader and put her in the shoes of my protagonist and have her ask, "What would I have done?" The war, with its dire circumstances and stark choices, is perfect for doing just that.

When you began the novel, did you have Astrid and Noa's friendship mapped out? How did their stories surprise you and evolve along the way, if at all?

With The Orphan's Tale as well as my earlier books, I know where I am starting and generally where the book will end up, but it is usually the middle that surprises me. For example, in the beginning of the book, Noa is dependent on Astrid, but there comes a point where that changes and Astrid looks to Noa for strength. There may have also been a few things about the end of the book that surprised me, but I don't want to spoil them here!

What was your toughest challenge writing *The Orphan's Tale*? Your greatest pleasure?

I refer to The Orphan's Tale as "the book that broke me." I am only half joking. I would say there were two major challenges. First, learning about the circus and aerial arts took a great deal of time. (I am biting my nails, hoping I did it justice!)

Second, writing about the train full of Unknown Children was unbearable. I knew the scene (in fact, the opening scene) needed to be written, since it was the very thing that inspired the book. At the same time, I avoided it forever. Finally, I realized that to write it deeply enough, I was going to have to figuratively put my own children on that train. It's actually too painful to think about it beyond that.

Can you describe your writing process? Do you write scenes consecutively or jump around? Do you have a schedule or routine? A lucky charm?

I start with an image or scene in my mind. I turn on the computer and throw down whatever comes out, in whatever order, for three or four months. (Someone once referred to this as vomiting on the page—sorry!) Then when I have about 60,000 words or so, the document becomes unwieldy, and I start breaking it into chapters and an outline. This is the very worst kind of writing process (the time it takes to edit is insane) and I recommend it to no one. But I don't know how to do it any other way.

The other thing I would say is that I like to write every day. I'm a short-burst writer, so if you give me forty-five minutes, I can use that, but more than three hours and I'm spent. Last year, I gave myself a hundred days of writing challenge to see if I could write for a hundred consecutive days. I did it, through bad weather and illness and the like. At the end of the hundred days, it felt so good I just kept going. I finished The Orphan's Tale on the 299th day.

Read on for a captivating excerpt from
Pam Jenoff's hit debut novel,
THE KOMMANDANT'S GIRL

Chapter 1

As we cut across the wide span of the market square, past the pigeons gathered around fetid puddles, I eye the sky warily and tighten my grip on Lukasz's hand, willing him to walk faster. But the child licks his ice-cream cone, oblivious to the darkening sky, a drop hanging from his blond curls. Thank God for his blond curls. A sharp March wind gusts across the square, and I fight the urge to let go of his hand and draw my threadbare coat closer around me.

We pass through the high center arch of the Sukennice, the massive yellow mercantile hall that bisects the square. It is still several blocks to Nowy Kleparz, the outdoor market on the far northern edge of Kraków's city center, and already I can feel Lukasz's gait slowing, his tiny, thin-soled shoes scuffing harder against the cobblestones with every step. I consider carrying him, but he is three years old and growing heavier by the day. Well fed, I might have managed it, but now I know that I would make it a few meters at most. If only he would go faster. *"Szybko, kochana,"* I plead with him under my breath. *"Chocz!"* His steps seem to lighten as we wind our way through the flower vendors peddling their wares in the shadow of the Mariacki Cathedral spires.

Moments later, we reach the far side of the square and I feel a familiar rumble under my feet. I pause. I have not been on a trolley in almost a year. I imagine lifting Lukasz onto the streetcar and sinking into a seat, watching the buildings and people walking below as we pass. We could be at the market in minutes. Then I stop, shake my head inwardly. The ink on our new papers is barely dry, and the wonder on Lukasz's face at his first trolley ride would surely arouse suspicion. I cannot trade our safety for convenience. We press onward.

Though I try to remind myself to keep my head low and avoid eye contact with the shoppers who line the streets this midweek morning, I cannot help but drink it all in. It has been more than a year since I was last in the city center. I inhale deeply. The air, damp from the last bits of melting snow, is perfumed with the smell of roasting chestnuts from the corner kiosk. Then the trumpeter in the cathedral tower begins to play the *hejnal*, the brief melody he sends across the square every hour on the hour to commemorate the Tartar invasion of Kraków centuries earlier. I resist the urge to turn back toward the sound, which greets me like an old friend.

As we approach the end of Florianska Street, Lukasz suddenly freezes, tightening his grip on my hand. I look down. He has dropped the last bit of his precious ice-cream cone on the pavement but does not seem to notice. His face, already pale from months of hiding indoors, has turned gray. "What is it?" I whisper, crouching beside him, but he does not respond. I follow his gaze to where it is riveted. Ten meters ahead, by the arched entrance to the medieval Florian Gate, stand two Nazis carrying machine guns. Lukasz shudders. "There, there, *kochana*. It's okay." I put my arms around his shoulders, but there is nothing I can do to soothe him. His eyes dart back and forth, and his mouth moves without sound. "Come." I lift him up and he buries his head in my neck. I look around for a side street to take, but there is none and turning around might attract attention. With a furtive glance to make sure no one is watching, I push the remnants of the ice-cream cone toward the gutter with my foot and proceed past the Nazis, who do not seem to notice us. A few minutes later, when I feel the child breathing calmly again, I set him down.

Soon we approach the Nowy Kleparz market. It is hard to contain my excitement at being out again, walking and shopping like a normal person. As we navigate the narrow walkways between the stalls, I hear people complaining. The cabbage is pale and wilted, the bread hard and dry; the meat, what there is of it, is from an unidentifiable source and already giving off a curious odor. To the townspeople and villagers, still accustomed to the prewar bounty of the Polish countryside, the food is an abomination. To me, it is paradise. My stomach tightens.

"Two loaves," I say to the baker, keeping my head low as I pass him my ration cards. A curious look crosses his face. It is your imagination, I tell myself. Stay calm. To a stranger, I know, I look like any other Pole. My coloring is fair, my accent flawless, my dress purposefully nondescript. Krysia chose this market in a working-class neighborhood on the northern edge of town deliberately, knowing that none of my former acquaintances from the city would shop here. It is critical that no one recognize me.

I pass from stall to stall, reciting the groceries we need in my head: flour, some eggs, a chicken, if there is one to be had. I have never made lists, a fact that serves me well now that paper is so dear. The shopkeepers are kind, but businesslike. Six months into the war, food is in short supply; there is no generous cut of cheese for a smile, no sweet biscuit for the child with the large blue eyes. Soon I have used all of our ration cards, yet the basket remains half empty. We begin the long walk home.

Still feeling the chill from the wind on the market square, I lead Lukasz through side streets on our way back across town. A few minutes later, we turn onto Grodzka Street, a wide thoroughfare lined with elegant shops and houses. I hesitate. I had not meant to come here. My chest tightens, making it hard to breathe. Easy, I tell myself, you can do this. It is just another street. I walk a few meters farther, then stop. I am standing before a pale yellow house with a white door and wooden flower boxes in the windows. My eyes travel upward to the second floor. A lump forms in my throat, making it difficult to swallow. Don't, I think, but it is too late. This was Jacob's house. Our house.

I met Jacob eighteen months ago while I was working as a clerk in the university library. It was a Friday afternoon, I remember, because I was rushing to update the book catalog and get home in time for Shabbes. "Excuse me," a deep voice said. I looked up from my work, annoyed at the interruption. The speaker was of medium height and wore a small yarmulke and closely trimmed beard and mustache. His hair was brown with flecks of red. "Can you recommend a good book?"

"A good book?" I was caught off guard as much by the swimming darkness of his eyes as by the generic nature of his request.

"Yes, I would like something light to read over the weekend to take my mind off my studies. Perhaps *The Iliad*...?"

I could not help laughing. "You consider Homer light reading?"

"Relative to physics texts, yes." The corners of his eyes crinkled. I led him to the literature section, where he settled upon a volume of Shakespeare's comedies. Our knuckles brushed as I handed him the book, sending a chill down my spine. I checked out the book to him, but still he lingered. I learned that his name was Jacob and that he was twenty, two years my senior.

After that, he came to visit me daily. I quickly learned that even though he was a science major, his real passion was politics and that he was involved with many activist groups. He wrote pieces, published in student and local newspapers, that were critical not only of the Polish government, but of what he called "Germany's unfettered dominance" over its neighbors. I worried that it was dangerous to be so outspoken. While the Jews of my neighborhood argued heatedly on their front stoops, outside the synagogues and in the stores about current affairs and everything else, I was raised to believe that it was safer to keep one's voice low when dealing with the outside world. But Jacob, the son of prominent sociologist Maximillian Bau, had no such concerns, and as I listened to him speak, watched his eyes burn and his hands fly, I forgot to be afraid.

I was amazed that a student from a wealthy, secular family would be interested in me, the daughter of a poor Orthodox baker, but if he noticed the difference in our backgrounds, it did not seem to matter. We began spending our Sunday afternoons together, talking and strolling along the Wisla River. "I should be getting home," I remarked one Sunday afternoon in April as the sky grew dusky. Jacob and I had been walking along the river path where it wound around the base of Wawel Castle, talking so intensely I had lost track of time. "My parents will be wondering where I am."

"Yes, I should meet them soon," he replied matter-of-factly. I stopped in my tracks. "That's what one does, isn't it, when one wants to ask permission to court?" I was too surprised to answer. Though Jacob and I had spent much time together these recent months and I knew he enjoyed my company, I somehow never thought that he would seek permission to see me formally. He reached down and took my chin in his gloved fingers. Softly, he pressed his lips down on mine for the first time. Our mouths lingered together, lips slightly parted. The ground seemed to slide sideways, and I felt so dizzy I was afraid that I might faint.

Thinking now of Jacob's kiss, I feel my legs grow warm. Stop it, I tell myself, but it is no use. It has been nearly six months since I have seen my husband, been touched by him. My whole body aches with longing.

A sharp clicking noise jars me from my thoughts. My vision clears and I find myself still standing in front of the yellow house, staring upward. The front door opens and an older, well-dressed woman steps out. Noticing me and Lukasz, she hesitates. I can tell she is wondering who we are, why we have stopped in front of her house. Then she turns from us dismissively, locks the door and proceeds down the steps. This is her home now. Enough, I tell myself sharply. I cannot afford to do anything that will draw attention. I shake my head, trying to clear the image of Jacob from my mind.

"Come, Lukasz," I say aloud, tugging gently on the child's hand. We continue walking and soon cross the Planty, the broad swath of parkland that rings the city center. The trees are revealing the most premature of buds, which will surely be cut down by a late frost. Lukasz tightens his grip on my hand, staring wide-eyed at the few squirrels that play among the bushes as though it is already spring. As we push onward, I feel the city skyline receding behind us. Five minutes later we reach the Aleje, the wide boulevard that, if taken to the left, leads south across the river. I stop and look toward the bridge. Just on the other side, a half kilometer south, lies the ghetto. I start to turn in that direction, thinking of my parents. Perhaps if I go to the wall, I can see them, find a way to slip them some of the food I have just purchased. Krysia would not mind. Then I stop—I cannot risk it, not in broad daylight, not with the child. I feel shame at my stomach, which no longer twists with hunger, and at my freedom, at crossing the street as though the occupation and the war do not exist.